AGE OF VAMPIRES

DEVIOUS
GODS

CAROLINE PECKHAM
SUSANNE VALENTI

New York

Belvedere
Castle

Devious Gods
Age of Vampires #7
Copyright © 2024 Caroline Peckham & Susanne Valenti

The moral right of the authors have been asserted.
Without in any way limiting the authors', Caroline Peckham and Susanne Valenti's, and the publisher's
exclusive rights under copyright, any use of this publication to "train" generative artificial intelligence
(AI) technologies to generate any works/images/text/videos is expressly prohibited.
The authors reserve all rights to license uses of this work for generative AI training and development of
machine learning language models.

Interior Formatting & Design by Wild Elegance Formatting
Map Design by Fred Kroner
Artwork by Stella Colorado

ISBN:978-1-916926-04-2

Devious Gods/Caroline Peckham & Susanne Valenti – 2nd ed.

This book is dedicated to love in all its forms. From sisters and brothers, to friends and lovers. May your heart be full and shared with the best people of all, because we're all just hurtling through space on a flying rock together. Might as well love each other hard while we're here.

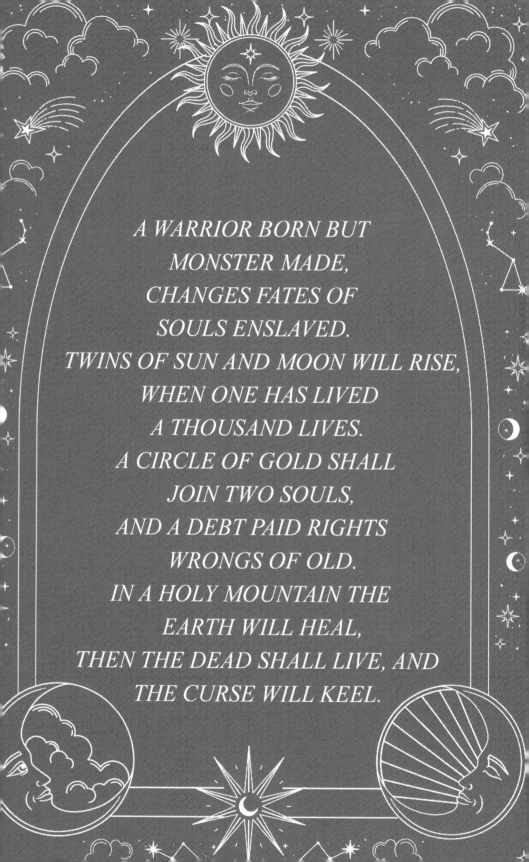

A WARRIOR BORN BUT
MONSTER MADE,
CHANGES FATES OF
SOULS ENSLAVED.
TWINS OF SUN AND MOON WILL RISE,
WHEN ONE HAS LIVED
A THOUSAND LIVES.
A CIRCLE OF GOLD SHALL
JOIN TWO SOULS,
AND A DEBT PAID RIGHTS
WRONGS OF OLD.
IN A HOLY MOUNTAIN THE
EARTH WILL HEAL,
THEN THE DEAD SHALL LIVE, AND
THE CURSE WILL KEEL.

CALLIE

CHAPTER ONE

My lips parted in horrified wonder as I stared at the transformation which had taken place in the man I loved.

I reached for him, my hand landing on his chest above his heart and my fingers trembled as I failed to feel any movement. His skin was too cold. His features too perfect.

He looked into my eyes and I could see the dawning realisation there.

"It's alright," I breathed. "It'll be alright."

"He needs blood," Erik hissed urgently.

"There's still some in the truck we took from the base," Clarice replied, and I saw her speeding away from me toward the armoured truck from the corner of my eye.

"Step away, Callie," Fabian growled.

"He won't hurt me," I replied faintly.

"Brother? Can you hear us?" Julius asked as he moved closer and Magnar's eyes wheeled towards him.

This couldn't have happened. There was no way it could be real. How could the goddess have done this to him?

It doesn't change anything. He's still the man I fell in love with.

My heart began to race in fierce denial of the truth and Magnar tilted his head as if he could hear it. With a jolt, I realised that he *could.*

I took a step closer, reducing the space between us to inches as I slid my hand further up his chest, trailing it over his neck until I cupped his jaw. I looked deep into his golden eyes and I could see the torment that raged there as he struggled to accept what had happened to him.

"It's okay," I said again. But it wasn't. I knew it. He knew it.

"Here," Clarice said and she pressed close to me, holding out a silver bottle. I eyed it with a little fear as she twisted the cap free and pushed it under Magnar's nose.

"No," he snarled. And his voice was his but not, like the rough edges of it were gone and a deeper, more seductive note had taken their place.

"It'll be worse the longer you resist," Erik said firmly.

"No!" Magnar slapped the bottle out of Clarice's grip and the blood was spilled across the ground beside us, sinking into the dirt by our feet.

I flinched back a step, withdrawing my hand and Magnar's face crumpled as he took in my reaction.

"Stay back, Callie," Fabian urged again, gripping my arm and drawing me away from him.

A feral anger grew in Magnar's eyes at the sight of Fabian's hands on my flesh. The look on his face was primal, animal and suddenly I feared what he might do to keep me away from Fabian.

"Release her," Magnar growled, his posture dipping so that he looked as if he might spring forward at any moment, the threat of violence clear in his stance. He was like a wild beast, poised to attack, his hands curling into fists as he glared at Fabian in a clear threat.

"He's only concerned for her, Brother," Julius murmured, moving to take my place before him.

Magnar's gaze stayed locked on the point of contact between me and Fabian and he bared his fangs. A tremor raced through me as I spotted them. Any feeble hope that I'd been clinging to fled me at that final bit of proof. He was a vampire. The man I loved, whose whole life had been devoted to destroying the undead was now one of them himself.

Holy shit.

Fabian hissed in response, pulling me closer possessively. Magnar shot forward so quickly that I barely had time to cry out before his fist collided with Fabian's jaw.

Fabian was thrown away from me with such force that I heard his bones breaking from the impact.

I scrambled back and Montana wrapped her arms around me protectively as my heart pounded adrenaline through my body.

Clarice cried out in panic as Fabian failed to rise from the spot twenty feet away where he'd landed.

"By the gods," Erik cursed as he moved to stand before me and Montana. "He's kept his slayer gifts like Valentina did: he was immeasurably strong before, but now..."

"He's fucking invincible," Julius murmured as he moved in front of me too.

They were all eyeing Magnar like he was a stranger who might hurt any one of us and my heart shattered at the sight. I knew in my soul that wasn't the case. He was still him. No matter what changes had been forced upon his body.

Clarice moved closer as well, trying to push Julius back too but he shrugged her off and she was forced to take up position at his side instead. The vampires were afraid that Magnar was going to hurt me and Julius and pain flooded me at the idea.

Magnar glared at Fabian until he was convinced that he wasn't going to rise again. He turned his attention back to me and Chickoa scrambled over to see if there was anything she could do to help Fabian while he was unconscious.

Magnar frowned as he noted the group of people standing between us.

"Callie?" he murmured. "Don't be afraid of me... I won't...you know I'd never hurt you-"

"I know," I agreed, pressing Montana's arms down until she released me.

"Be careful," she breathed. "He still hasn't fed yet."

I glanced at my sister and I could see how much this was scaring her but I knew Magnar. And just as I'd trusted her when she was turned, I knew I could trust him too.

I stepped around Erik and he eyed me like he wanted to make a protest but I guessed what had just happened to Fabian was making him hesitate.

My heart was pounding as I approached Magnar again and his brow furrowed as the sound of it reached him too.

"You've always made my heart race," I said, trying to make light of it. "Now you can hear how you affect me too."

Magnar frowned as he watched me drawing closer again and he stilled in that eerie way which only the undead could manage. He made no movement at all. He wasn't even breathing and the sight of it filled me with unease.

It wasn't the fact that he was a vampire that frightened me. It was the fact that this was so far from who he was. It went against the essence of his soul. He was never meant to undergo this transformation and I had no idea how he would come to terms with it. Or even *if* he would. His own father had begged for death in his position and I feared that Magnar would feel compelled to do the same.

He reached for me and I gave him my hand. His thumb shifted over my flesh as if he'd never felt it before and he moved his other hand to touch me too. His fingers trailed along my arm, raising goosebumps across my body as he stared at my skin.

I shivered beneath his gentle caress and he lifted my hand to his face.

I looked up at him as he tilted my arm in his grasp and he pressed a kiss to the inside of my wrist, right above the flickering beat of my pulse.

Erik inhaled sharply behind me as if he expected Magnar to attack me at any moment and I could feel all of their eyes pinned on us.

"Brother," Julius murmured. "Think how much it would wound you to hurt her. Be careful..."

Magnar inhaled deeply and he kissed my wrist again. I felt the brush of his teeth against my skin and my muscles tensed.

His gaze flicked up to meet mine and he released me suddenly, stepping back.

"I won't hurt you," he said firmly.

I nodded in agreement but I didn't move any closer.

"Drink, Magnar," Clarice urged. "You can't trust yourself around Callie or your brother until you do. We have bottled blood, you won't have to bite anyone-"

"The moment I give in to the bloodlust will be the moment I plunge my blade through my heart," Magnar snarled.

My pulse thundered at his words and tears pricked my eyes. I knew he wouldn't want to live like this but hearing him confirm it aloud terrified me. If we couldn't break the curse before the call of blood got too much for him then I was going to lose him.

"We'll head for the mountain," I said. "We'll break the curse before you have to feed and you'll be human again-"

"That's a long journey for a hungry vampire with two mortals in tow," Clarice murmured and I could tell she didn't think he could do it. "Especially ones who smell as good as you both do."

"I would never hurt my brother or the woman I love," Magnar snarled and Clarice recoiled a little as he turned his heated gaze her way.

"You don't have to!" Erik said in exasperation. "Just drink the bottled blood. It's only a matter of time until-"

Magnar shot towards him in a blur of motion and wrapped a hand around his throat, lifting him into the air as if it was the easiest thing in the world. Erik struggled and a faint rumbling cut through the soil at my feet.

"If you try to force my hand in this again, I'll rip your head from your body," Magnar threatened before releasing his hold on Erik just as quickly as he'd gained it. Erik stumbled back and Montana gripped his arm fearfully.

Magnar's eyes trailed to Julius's hand which had made it to the hilt of his blade and I could see the pain that act caused him. He shook his head and turned away from all of us, shooting into the trees at the top of the hill so quickly that his movement sent my hair flying around my shoulders.

"Fuck," Erik snarled and I could tell he was about to follow him.

"Don't," I said quickly. "I'll go."

Fabian groaned behind us as he regained consciousness and I turned to find Chickoa moving away from him as he began to rise.

"It's not safe," Erik protested.

"I hate to admit it but I think he might be right, Callie," Montana breathed.

A harsh sob escaped Clarice's throat and she sank to her knees in the mud as the last of the shock from the battle slid from us and the weight of everything that had just happened poured in on her. Erik's features were filled with pain too but he kept his eyes set on me as he struggled to decide what to do.

"Let me go to Magnar," I urged. "You said yourself he's kept his gifts. He's Clan of War; he was already stronger than you and now that will only be compounded tenfold. None of us are a match for him if he wants to hurt us and at least I know he will fight against the desire to harm me with everything he's got."

Erik nodded in defeat, his eyes moving to Clarice as Julius laid a hand on her shoulder.

"At least bring him some bottles of blood," he murmured and I nodded, biting my lip as I looked towards the truck where they were stored.

Fabian pushed himself to his feet and made his way back towards us. I offered him an apologetic look as I skirted him and headed to retrieve the blood.

For a moment I thought he was going to protest again but Clarice's sobs grew harsher and he dropped to the dirt beside his sister, pulling her close as their grief at losing Miles and Warren overwhelmed them.

Montana drew closer to Erik as a hollow look filled his eyes.

My heart was heavy with their deaths too but I couldn't face it yet. Magnar needed me. I wouldn't let him deal with this alone.

"I'm coming with you," Julius murmured as he fell into step beside me.

I nodded my agreement as we drew closer to the truck. Of course he was. He wouldn't let Magnar deal with this alone any more than I would.

Julius took a large bottle of blood from the back of the truck and I caught his arm before he could move away.

"He'll be alright," I breathed, my voice trembling as I tried to convince myself as much as him.

Julius avoided my eye, his thumb brushing over the top of the silver bottle.

"Callie..." He looked at me then away again as he chewed the inside of his cheek. "Magnar is his father's son. When we find him, he may ask me to-"

"No," I gasped, realising what he was saying. "We're so close to solving the prophecy. He'll be human again in a matter of days! You can't agree to it if he asks you-"

"Weren't you the one who was just convincing your sister that you'd never want to spend a single day as a vampire?" he asked me sadly. "What happened to 'I want to die a mortal death no matter what'?"

"I know," I hissed. "I'm a fucking hypocrite alright! But I don't care. This isn't the same - no one chose this for him. I never would have forced it on him and you know it. But now that it's done can't we at least agree to get to the mountain first? Before we have to make any decisions-"

"Callie, if he asks this of me-"

I slapped him and his head wheeled sideways from the force of my gifts. His jaw clenched and he looked down at me darkly.

"If you kill him Julius, I swear on everything that I am that I will-"

"He's already dead," Julius growled and he gritted his teeth as his eyes glimmered with emotion.

My rage turned to pain in a heartbeat and I threw myself at him, wrapping my arms around his neck as my tears burst free like they were breaking past a dam.

Julius wrapped his strong arms around me and being in them felt so like holding Magnar that my heart broke all over again. Julius was warm and his heart beat fiercely alongside mine. Magnar wouldn't feel like this now. He was cold and solid, his heart lying still in his chest. He *was* dead. But he was still alive too and as selfish as it was, I couldn't bear to let him leave me.

"Go to him first," Julius breathed and I felt his own tears spilling into my hair. "He needs a reason to live. And you're the best one he has."

"Thank you." I released him and stood on my tiptoes so that I could press a kiss to his cheek. His tears met with my lips and he caught my hand before I could withdraw, pressing the bottle of blood into it.

"Try to get him to drink it," he muttered and I could tell the idea repulsed him. "I can't imagine the pain it would cause him to lose control with you."

I nodded, glancing down at the silver bottle as I backed away. I needed to convince Magnar to do it for all of our sakes.

I turned and headed up into the trees, leaving Julius by the trucks and the Belvederes mourning their loss alongside my sister.

I wiped the tears from my face as I went. Magnar needed me to be strong for him. He needed to see that this didn't change anything about the way I felt for him. And he *had* to agree to stay undead until we could break the curse once and for all.

MONTANA

CHAPTER TWO

I stood beside Erik, reeling over what had just happened. Magnar was a vampire. And he clearly wasn't handling it well. I cursed Idun for everything she'd done to us, even in death she'd lingered long enough to be vindictive in her final act on Earth.

Clarice was wrapped around Fabian on the ground as she came apart, sobbing into his shoulder over the loss of her brother and his husband. I felt their pain like an arrow in my chest, their grief a tangible thing that lived in the atmosphere.

I took Erik's hand, willing my mind to sharpen as I turned to him, knowing he needed me to be strong more than anything right now. His face was stoic and his expression distant. Loss poured from his gaze and a crease had formed between his eyes that I couldn't imagine ever going away.

I slid my arms around him, wishing I could offer him more than just comfort. That I could bring Miles and Warren back. But they were gone. And there was nothing anyone in the world could do to fix it. The loss of them hurt me in a way I never could have imagined once upon a time, but I'd changed and there was no denying that anymore.

Erik slowly came back to his senses in my arms, sliding a hand onto my back, but despite being physically close, I felt so distant from him that I couldn't bear it.

"Erik," I whispered, cupping his cheek as tears built in my eyes.

I tried to make him look at me, but his gaze was fixed over my head in the direction Magnar and Callie had taken. I didn't know what to say. It was pointless asking if he was alright when I knew he wasn't. He was broken. Hurt and grieving. But his silence was something I didn't know how to bridge.

"The truck..." he murmured vaguely then pulled away from me, heading toward the vehicle up the hill. I gazed after him as the tears fell from my eyes, spilling uselessly down to the cracked earth at my feet.

I spotted Chickoa hunting through the rubble, plucking out a shattered picture frame from under a stone. She took the photo from within it and discarded the frame on the floor as she tucked the picture into her pocket, her brow heavily furrowed.

She turned her gaze to the house which was still burning, the powerful flames reaching toward the sky as it devoured her home. Smoke and blood and death carried on the wind, surrounding us all in a cocoon of despair.

"It's alright," Fabian murmured to Clarice, rubbing her back in soothing circles.

"It's not, nothing's ever going to be alright again," she croaked, and Fabian shut his eyes, his grief clear in his expression.

Julius moved to my side, gazing at the two Belvederes as their pain filled the air around us. He took my hand, squeezing. And that was enough to help my heart grow a little stronger. The slayers and the royals were my family now. I'd do anything I could to try and soothe them.

"Do you think Callie's safe with Magnar?" I breathed to Julius.

I knew my sister would never have heeded my warnings, but Magnar would be starving. What if he lost control around her? The thought made my stomach churn with worry.

"Yes," Julius said quietly. "No curse on Earth is strong enough to make him hurt her."

I nodded, a sharp lump growing in my throat as I thought about what Magnar must have been going through. His whole life had been pledged to ending the vampires. Despising them. Though he'd made his peace with Erik and his family, I doubted he could make peace with his own body being tainted in that way.

I glanced up at Julius as I forced away the last of my tears. His face was ashen and I could sense a darkness looming over him like a shadow. I laced my arms around his neck as I realised how much Magnar's curse must have been paining him too. He held me tight and his pulse thrummed in my ears as he released a shuddering breath.

"We'll break the curse," I promised and he nodded against my shoulder.

"That's all that matters now," he growled, stepping back and glancing behind him as if he hoped to see his brother approaching. But he wasn't there.

Erik drove the truck down the hill, pulling up the parking brake and remaining inside as he waited for everyone.

"You should go to him," Julius said softly and my heart splintered as I gazed toward the vehicle.

"I don't know what I can say," I admitted. "He's so hurt...I'm afraid I'll make it worse."

"You're his wife, he'll want you with him. Even if he doesn't say it," Julius said, his brow lowering.

I nodded, wiping the dampness from my cheeks, not wanting to break down. I had to be there for Erik. I just wished there was something more tangible I could do.

I parted from Julius, walking to the passenger side of the truck and tugging the door open. Erik didn't look at me as I climbed in and shut the door behind me. The thunk sounded deafeningly loud in the quiet space. My mouth grew dry as I reached across the seats and rested my hand on his arm.

He was as still as a statue, his gaze set on the hill beyond the windshield. He seemed to have withdrawn into himself even more and I couldn't be sure he was fully aware that I was sat beside him.

"I'm sorry," I whispered. He shook his head but remained silent. "I'd do anything to bring them back."

He continued to stare at nothing and my heart broke for him as the air became weighted with his anguish.

"You're in shock," I said gently, but still he didn't answer.

I settled for taking his hand and holding it firmly. After a beat, he retracted his fingers from mine.

"We should get on the road soon," he said flatly.

"Erik," I tried again, leaning forward and wishing he'd just look at me. He

21

refused to meet my gaze and it was killing me.

"There's enough blood in the trunk to last a few days at least," he continued.

"Talk to me," I urged and he turned half way toward me as if to meet my gaze, then looked away again. "Whatever you need, I'll give it to you. We'll get through this together," I promised, fighting back another wave of tears.

He finally looked at me and his eyes were as cold and as hard as steel. "I need to be alone for a while," he said, his tone hollow.

I nodded, hurt lancing through me as I retreated into my seat. I took hold of the door handle, but a wave of hesitation stayed my hand. Before I could think better of it, I lunged forward to hug him.

He didn't hold me back. His hands balled into fists and I sensed him tensing in my arms. I was desperate to help him come to terms with this, but I knew how difficult that was. I'd only recently lost my father and I was still coping with that loss every day. I knew everyone dealt with these kinds of things in their own way but leaving him alone was the hardest thing he could ask of me.

"Go," he growled and I withdrew from him sharply.

His jaw was clenched as I gazed at him, unsure how to react to this. He'd always gotten angry when trying to deal with his emotions in the past, but this felt like a wall I couldn't break through.

I bowed my head, slipping out of the truck without looking back. My soul crumbled as I shut the door and walked away. I made it three steps before I sank down to the ground and hugged my knees to my chest.

How had everything fallen apart so fast?

I set my eyes on the trees that Callie and Magnar had disappeared into, praying to see them returning. Fear trickled through me at knowing she was off alone with him in his current state.

I felt so helpless to everyone I loved. I couldn't right the terrible wrongs that had befallen us. I couldn't do anything but sit here and watch the world buckle around me.

Dark clouds hung above me in the sky, hiding the sun and threatening rain. I wished it would come and wash away last night. That we could go back in time and do things differently. We should have gone to Callie so that she could have hidden us with the ring before Idun ever showed up.

I clenched my jaw, knowing that reality would have meant Idun still lived.

But what was her death worth if it had cost us two of our friends' lives and placed Magnar under the vampire curse?

I spotted Chickoa heading across the valley to where some of her cows were huddled together under a tree; they must have been terrified after what had happened right at the edge of their fields.

I rose to my feet and headed toward her, wanting to do something useful. *Anything* to take my mind off the pain slicing through my body.

I started jogging, then running until the wind whipped through my hair and I felt some semblance of relief just from moving. I caught up with Chickoa as she clucked her tongue at the four cows and they moved toward her with tentative steps.

She spotted me approaching and nodded to one of the cows as it started to break off from the group. "Get around that side. Keep her in the herd."

I jogged forward to comply, circling the large black and white animal and waving my hands to get her back into the group.

Chickoa spoke to them in soothing words and they soon followed her, their movements more reassured. I walked at the back of the herd to keep them walking as Chickoa led the way toward the barn.

"I'm sorry about your farm," I murmured, glancing at her house and seeing the roof had caved in as the fire started to die down at last.

"It's not your fault," she said with a sigh. "I'm glad that goddess is dead." She turned to look at me over her shoulder with a deep frown. "I'm sorry about your friends."

I nodded stiffly, wanting to talk about anything other than that.

"What will you do now?" I asked gently. She couldn't stay here with the farmhouse in ruins.

"I'm still going with you to the mountain. I have a friend who will look after the farm," she said as we reached the barn and she ushered the cows inside.

I followed her and set about helping to feed and give water to the cows in a stall. When we were done, we headed back outside where a drizzle was starting to fall from the thickening clouds.

Chickoa gazed over the valley at our group huddled by the truck. She took the photo from her pocket and ran her thumb across the picture of her and her husband.

"I'll rebuild it, Terry," she said softly.

Guilt crept into my gut that we'd come here and brought this disaster down on her head. She didn't deserve to be caught up in this mess. But our fates were woven together now. And she was clearly prepared to take on the journey to end the curse for good. Honestly, we could use all the help we could get.

"Is Erik alright?" Chickoa asked me and my gut knotted at her words.

I shook my head in answer. "He's hurting so badly...and he doesn't want me near him."

She laid a hand on my arm and I glanced up at her, finding understanding in her eyes. "My husband was the same. He always retreated into himself every time something bad happened. But you just have to stick with him, Montana. He needs you more than you know right now. It is the way of some men. But if you give him time and an ear to listen every time he needs it, he'll come around."

"I hope so," I breathed, fearing what this grief might do to Erik.

"I know so," she promised. "I've seen how much he loves you. This is just a road bump. Life has a lot of those unfortunately."

I gazed at this beautiful woman who must have seen so much more of the world than I could ever wish to. She'd walked this Earth for a thousand years. Lived and loved. And it gave me hope that she could see a glimmer of light right now. Because to me, the world was a dark, dark place where the sun no longer shone.

MAGNAR

CHAPTER THREE

The trees passed me by in a blur as I shot between them. I should have collided with the trunks and yet somehow it was as easy as breathing to weave between them at this speed. Not that I *was* breathing.

I stopped suddenly and instead of stumbling as I did so, I skidded through the leaves at my feet smoothly, barely making a sound.

The ache at the base of my throat was growing more noticeable. More demanding. But I wouldn't give in to it. If I did then I truly was one of them. A vampire. My sworn enemy.

And if I accept that fact then I will have to end my life just as my father did.

I looked down at my hands, turning them over slowly as I noticed the faint scars which had always lined them were now gone. Practicing swordplay had given me countless scars on my fingers over the years and I'd always seen them as a kind of testimony to the hours I'd spent honing my craft and perfecting my skill. Now they were wiped away as if that meant nothing.

My gaze travelled down to my chest. The curve of my muscles seemed even more defined and as I pressed a thumb to my stomach I felt the hardness of my skin as it refused to give under the pressure. It was as though I'd been carved from stone.

My gods-given tattoos remained where they'd always been, the runes of the goddess's gifts marking my skin even after her death. I guessed they truly were gifts and nothing could remove them from me, even her own demise. To my disgust, the mark binding me to Valentina remained in place too and I grazed my thumb across the line of it angrily. Even my death hadn't released me from my vow to that monstrous creature.

Every other mark on my flesh was gone though. The scars I'd gotten in training and battle, the marks left on my bicep by the wolf I'd fought off in the dead of night a thousand years ago.

I turned my left arm and pain blossomed in my chest as I noticed the star I'd had inked into my skin in honour of my father was no longer there. Every tattoo I'd chosen for myself was gone and my bronze skin now glimmered with a near translucence which looked almost like sunlight.

I stilled as the soft sound of footsteps approached through the trees at my back. I didn't move an inch, but I inhaled slowly and the scent of her sailed to me on the wind. The burning in the back of my throat grew desperate but I pushed my will against it, refusing to face the reality of what my body desired from her now.

I turned, listening hard until I picked out the steady rhythm of her heartbeat.

"Magnar?" she called to me and every inch of my body responded.

I waited as she drew closer and the sight of her arriving in the small clearing was enough to make me hesitate. I didn't want to run from her; I wanted to run *to* her.

My body reacted to the sight of her beauty like I was an animal sighting my destiny. Everything about this transformation seemed to have tied my flesh more firmly in line with my instincts. I felt like a wolf in a man's body. And she was my mate.

I gave up on holding myself back and shot forward to close the distance between us. My blood heated from her proximity and the scent coming off of her skin was enough to drive me wild.

She gasped as I pulled up in front of her and I could tell that this change in me made her nervous. But I'd never hurt her. She was everything to me. The idea of causing her pain was beyond unimaginable. I would give my life for hers. I would protect her against everything this world had to throw at her and hold her tightly in my arms until the day she died.

"Are you okay?" Callie breathed as she looked up at me and I could see how unsure she felt in my presence now.

"I'm..." I didn't really know how to answer her. I couldn't totally comprehend what had happened to me but while I was looking into her eyes I felt sure of one thing. "I'm still me," I breathed. "Despite being this..." I gestured to my newly enhanced physique as I struggled to find the right word for it. "And I still love you with the fierceness of a thousand suns."

A smile captured her full lips and I ached to kiss her but I hesitated as her scent washed over me again.

My new body was a feral thing, filled with carnal desire for her which I longed to obey but I couldn't deny the hunger I felt as I listened to her heartbeat. Just beneath the perfection of her flesh lay the river of her life force which called to me like a siren in the waves.

"We can fix this, Magnar," Callie said slowly. "We can break the curse."

I stilled as I read into her words and I realised what she was saying. "You want me to stay like this?"

"Just for a little while," she pleaded and I noticed the tears which she was fighting to hold back. "We're so, so close to ending it."

I wanted to agree, to do anything at all to halt the pain I could see building within her. But I hesitated. How could I just become the thing I'd spent my life fighting to destroy? How could I abandon everything that had made me into the man I was?

I reached out to trail my fingers along her face and she closed her eyes, leaning into my touch.

The heat of her skin sent desire coursing through me and I gave in to the beast which raged in my chest as I captured her chin and pulled her closer.

She gasped as my mouth caught hers and I released a satisfied growl as she bowed to my demands, parting her lips as I pushed my tongue into her mouth.

Her skin was as soft as silk beneath my fingers and her lips moulded to mine, fuelling my desire further. I wanted more of her, all of her, every inch of her flesh and each drop of her blood.

No, not that. I forced away my desire for her blood as I focused on the indescribable feeling of her body pressed to mine. If I could keep my mind on that then the burning in my throat would pass. I knew I could force it away if I just distracted myself from it enough and Callie's touch was more than enough

29

to sustain me.

I lifted her into my arms finding she was impossibly light with my slayer gifts and vampire talents combined, as though she weighed no more than a feather resting in my palm.

I shot across the clearing, shoving her up against a huge oak tree which shuddered beneath the force of our collision.

Callie hissed in pain as I accidentally drove her against the trunk too firmly. But she didn't stop kissing me, her hands twisting into my hair as she clung on, dragging me nearer as though she needed this just as much as I did.

I growled, deep in the back of my throat as I released her lips and moved my mouth across her jaw. I caught her chin in my hand and turned her head so that I could claim her throat.

My lips moved against her skin and the thundering of her heart drove me on. Her skin was so soft and pliant, demanding more of my attention. The scent of her was driving me crazy and I was sure she could feel the thickness of my cock pressing against her.

I kissed her neck again, an ache building in my throat as I felt her pulse pounding beneath my lips.

My teeth brushed her skin and my grip on her tightened as I groaned with longing, holding her in place as I ached for more.

My fangs tingled hungrily as I brushed them against the flesh of her neck and she stilled in my arms, no longer dragging me closer.

"It's alright," she breathed and her hands released my hair as she caressed me gently instead, her fingertips trailing across my shoulders. "You can bite me if you need to."

Panic lurched through me as I suddenly realised what I was doing and I dropped her, pulling away from her in disgust.

She fell to the floor as I backed up in a flash of movement and I held a hand up between us as she scrambled upright, moving towards me again.

"I'm sorry," I breathed, revulsion flooding through me at what I'd almost done to her.

"I understand," she said, her eyes glimmering with pity. "And it's alright, I promise. You need blood and I would give you anything-"

"Not that," I begged.

She nodded, accepting what I was saying about it as her eyes moved to scan the clearing. She crossed it quickly, stooping to retrieve a bottle from the ground where she'd dropped it. I knew what was inside that vessel and I shook my head again in a firm refusal.

"I think you should consider-"

"No," I rasped, though my body shifted towards her slightly in contradiction of my words. "Please don't force this issue. I can't do that, I just...can't."

"Okay," she breathed, lowering the bottle as she accepted what I was saying. "You don't have to do anything you don't want to. But I promise you it won't change anything for me if you do. You're still the man I love, Magnar. Nothing you could do would ever alter that."

I walked towards her slowly, focusing on maintaining a normal pace instead of shooting forwards again.

"How can you love me like this?" I asked softly. "I'm not even alive anymore."

"I think you are," she replied, closing the distance between us again. I raised an eyebrow, unable to believe that she wasn't afraid of me after what I'd almost done to her.

"My heart isn't beating," I replied hollowly.

"But it still belongs to me doesn't it?"

I nodded slowly. With all the doubts that were flooding me, that was one thing I was sure of. My love for her hadn't diminished a single bit. If my heart could still beat then it would do so for her.

"So think of it like this." Callie drew close enough to touch me and she placed a burning hot hand upon my chest above my still heart. "At the second you died, you loved me and when the curse is broken, you'll love me still. This is just the fleeting moment between heartbeats, the gap between breaths. And while we're in it, our love burns as brightly as it will once it passes."

"How can I live as one of them?" I murmured though I wasn't sure how I could die and leave her behind either.

"You made me a promise; you said you'd be mine. Always. Do you still want that?" she asked, her voice seductive as the image of my life with her hovered on the edge of my imagination.

"More than anything in the world," I admitted, my voice cracking.

"Then keep your promise," she begged. "Let's break this curse and kill Valentina. And when your heart starts beating again and your bond to her is severed you can stand before the gods and claim me for your own. Not because they chose it but because *we* did. Don't let Idun take that from us. Don't let the gods destroy what we've fought so hard for."

I released a sound which was somewhere between a groan and a lament. How could I deny what she was asking of me? How could I consider breaking my word and leaving her to face this life alone? But how could I spend even a minute more as a monster?

Callie pushed up onto her toes and pressed her lips to mine. My fangs tingled as the scent of her blood overwhelmed me for a moment but I pushed it aside, focusing on this creature in my arms. It was hard to believe that the gods had had no part in her creation. She was so utterly right for me that I could easily have thought she'd been designed specifically to be mine.

I was a slave to her desires and willingly so.

My fingers slipped through her golden hair and down her back as she arched into me. A weight settled in my chest as I clung to her and I knew what my answer would be. Of course I couldn't leave her and walk away from the promise of the life I'd always desired. Even in my wildest dreams I'd never imagined I'd find a woman who was even half the match for me that she was. I would do anything for her. For us. Even allow my soul to reside in the body of a monster if that was what it took.

"Alright," I sighed against her lips, though I wasn't sure there had ever been any other answer. If it wasn't for her I never could have considered this but without her I was nothing and I wouldn't give her up. No matter the cost. Even if I was damning my soul.

Callie gasped, looking up at me with hope shining in her eyes. "You mean it?"

"I would do anything for a lifetime in your arms," I breathed. "And I wish to see this curse broken once and for all. We are overdue our happiness and if I have to wait in the moment between two heartbeats for us to take it then I will."

Callie hiccupped a laugh and closed her arms around me more tightly as she kissed me again.

I doubted there was much in this world that could have pushed me into making this decision but if the woman who ruled my heart wished to keep it even after it had fallen still then I wasn't a foolish enough man to refuse her.

MONTANA

CHAPTER FOUR

I headed through the sweeping valley to re-join the group by the truck, carrying a gallon of milk to feed Callie and Julius on our journey. It wasn't much, but most of Chickoa's food stores had been lost to the blazing fire of her home. And hopefully it would keep them nourished until we found more supplies.

As I arrived back in the yard, I spotted Callie and Magnar returning from the trees. I halted nervously, waiting for them to approach, the tension in the air building as the others stood to attention.

Magnar's eyes swivelled between us then landed on his brother. In a surge of movement, he rushed toward Julius, stopping before him abruptly. Magnar's jaw was set and an intensity blazed in his eyes that made me anxious.

"Are you..." Julius trailed off, unsure of how to finish that sentence and I could see the torment in his eyes over his brother's curse.

"I'm going to remain this way for now. We'll head to the mountain," Magnar growled, his tone even deeper than it had been as a mortal.

Julius's shoulders dropped and he lurched forward to wrap his arms around Magnar.

Magnar fell stock still and I could tell the thirst was gripping him.

I jogged toward Callie with a frown lining my features. "Is everything okay?"

"Yes," she sighed, though shadows ringed her eyes, speaking of all she was dealing with internally. "But he won't drink."

I knew Magnar was strong. He'd fight it. But it was only a matter of time before he would simply have to submit to it. It wasn't something I would have wished on anyone, but the slayers most of all. They had spent their lives fighting the vampires. To become one of them must have been torture.

Fabian turned in our direction, evidently hearing her. "I'm not letting you in that truck with him until he's had some blood."

"Then we'll be here all year," Callie snapped. "He's not going to drink. He can handle it."

"What do you know about it?" Fabian hissed and I prepared to get between them as she squared her shoulders. "You haven't the faintest clue of how demanding the thirst is. He won't have a choice in it if he waits too long. And every second he puts it off, the more likely it is that he'll lose his mind and bite you. Better to do it now before he becomes a starved animal who is unable to control himself."

"I am not like you," Magnar called, striding toward us at a fierce pace. "I wouldn't drink blood even if the thirst ripped me apart from the inside out."

"You're wrong," Clarice said gently, inching closer. "You can fight it for a while, Magnar. But you'd be a fool to put Callie at risk when we have bottles of blood at hand. Surely that's better than biting her or Julius?"

Magnar's eyes scraped over her and a tremor rolled down my spine at his fierce expression. Were they about to fight?

"I'm not drinking like a parasite," he snarled at her and I caught sight of his fangs. The others noticed too and Magnar suddenly realised it, turning sharply away from us.

"He won't do it," Callie reiterated and Fabian cursed in frustration.

Erik stepped out of the truck, his eyes endlessly dark. "Magnar, get in the front. The rest of you in the back. Now. We're leaving."

"But Magnar-" Fabian started and Erik's glare swung onto him.

"If he won't drink, he won't fucking drink," Erik snapped and a shudder ran through me at his tone. "And we can't waste any more time here. Valentina is probably on her way already."

"He's right. Let's go," Clarice said firmly and everyone moved toward the truck, filing inside.

I placed the gallon of milk in the trunk as Chickoa hurried after us. She'd gathered water from a well for the humans and she quickly put the bottles in the back of the truck with the rest of our meagre supplies. I moved to the side door, climbing inside and sitting down next to Callie, relaxing at the easy closeness of my twin. Chickoa jumped in and dropped down beside Fabian, not seeming to have noticed who she'd sat next to until it was too late to move.

Magnar shot around the front of the truck and got into the passenger seat beside Erik. He slammed the door and the whole vehicle rocked sideways.

"Fucking hell," Erik cursed under his breath.

"Sorry I..." Magnar trailed off, his shoulders hunching as he shifted away from the door.

As the truck stopped swaying, I turned to Callie beside me. "He'll get used to it," she whispered to me and I nodded, praying she was right.

Fabian's hands were curled into fists as he gazed at the back of Magnar's head in concern. After the punch Magnar had landed on him, I didn't think he'd be able to take him on even if he wanted to. It frightened me that if Magnar lost control to the bloodlust, we might not be able to subdue him.

Erik started the truck, but he didn't drive forward and I noticed his gaze was lingering on the spot where Miles and Warren had died. I leaned forward to rest a hand on his shoulder, but he shrugged me off and kicked the vehicle into gear, speeding up the road.

I sank back into my seat as I fought away the hurt at his reaction and settled for gazing out of the window as the world sailed by.

Callie glanced my way with a frown, taking hold of my hand. I gave her a taut smile, blinking back tears as I returned my gaze to the road.

The rain started hammering down from the clouds and I watched as the droplets slid across the glass in swirling patterns. My heart hurt from the loss of Miles and Warren. I pictured their faces before they'd died and the tears spilled down my cheeks. They'd loved each other so much, how was it fair that they'd been taken like that?

A tense silence fell over us all as we left the farm behind and Erik turned the vehicle south onto a long stretch of road. A road that could lead to our salvation or our demise. We had nothing left but each other and a single destination in mind. And I prayed we'd make it there soon.

The day went by at a painfully slow pace. The quiet hanging over us was rarely broken, but occasionally Callie and I would check the directions to the mountain using the ring and Erik would silently follow our instructions.

We'd already driven so many miles from the farm that the landscape around us was changing, growing more barren as we headed towards a towering mountain range on the horizon.

Evidence of the Final War was everywhere around us. Huge craters were all that remained of entire towns and we often had to weave off of the broken road and find a winding path forward through rubble and wreckage. I absorbed the sight of the world I'd always wondered about in quiet contemplation. Under any other circumstances, I would have been thrilled to explore the rolling landscapes that I'd dreamed about back in our Realm. But I couldn't capture any of the excitement I should have felt at seeing such places for the first time in my life. It was as if the world had a taint to it now, a shadow that wouldn't lift.

We finally made it back onto a stretch of road that was still intact and Erik picked up the pace again. We'd lost hours by diverting through a cluster of ruins and the sun had long since set, leaving us in total darkness.

As we rose onto a high mountain pass, I tried to get some rest, leaning back against the window and shutting my eyes. The thirst prickled at my throat and it was impossible to ignore it. I'd been trying to refrain from drinking in front of Magnar, having forgotten to do so back at the farm like the others had. But now, claws were starting to rip at my tongue as my body demanded to be fed.

I took a shuddering breath, knowing Magnar must have felt ten times worse than I did right now. And Erik hadn't drunk anything either as far as I recalled. Since I'd been turned, I'd not had to weather out the thirst for longer than a few hours, but I was determined to wait until I could do so away from Magnar. If he smelled blood, he might lose control and I wouldn't risk him hurting Callie or Julius.

The trail was long and winding through the mountains, but eventually we started descending from them once more, reaching a rocky plain of land beyond them. We continued on and on into the night and Callie fell asleep against my shoulder, rocking gently with each bump of the truck. Julius and Clarice had drifted off too, their shoulders holding each other upright as they sat side by side.

Fabian continually looked between my sister and Magnar and I had to admire his determination to keep watch despite how badly his intervention had gone last time. Occasionally, his eyes met mine through the gloom and I felt a silent understanding passing between us. If Magnar lost control, we would be ready to keep him away from Callie and Julius together.

Chickoa took the photo of her husband out of her pocket, gazing at it a while, her brow creasing with lines. "Thanks for getting me this," she whispered to Fabian, glancing up at him.

He nodded stiffly. "Memories are all we've got in the end."

She frowned at him, turning her gaze back to the picture and it suddenly pained me that I didn't have one of my father. I knew his face as well as my own, but the idea of having such a permanent reminder of him filled me with longing. Was that image in my mind going to fade one day? Would I eventually struggle to capture the way his mouth twisted at the corner when he smiled, or how those little creases formed beside his eyes?

"Why did you do it?" Chickoa asked him, her eyes narrowing as she stared at Fabian, trying to decipher his actions.

"I just...knew how much it meant to you," Fabian muttered, clearing his throat.

A clunking noise sounded beneath us and the truck juddered disconcertingly.

"No – fuck – *no*," Erik growled, slamming his palm against the wheel.

The others jerked awake as the truck stuttered to a halt and Erik thumped his fist into the dashboard.

"What's wrong?" Magnar asked him.

"We're out of charge," Erik revealed and my gut plummeted.

"How do we get...charge?" Magnar asked, clearly confused by the meaning of that word.

"We don't," Erik snapped, throwing the door open and stepping outside before slamming it behind him. He gazed up at the sky and roared his anger and my heart squeezed with anxiety.

I glanced between the others, their pale faces angled toward me.

"You better go talk to him," Fabian urged, sliding the side door open and gesturing for me to get out. "We'll work on a plan."

I gritted my jaw, rising from my seat, but Callie caught my hand.

I glanced back at her, finding her expression desperate. "We'll figure this out," she said.

I nodded, taking comfort from her words as I stepped out of the truck. Fabian promptly shut the door behind me and I threw a scowl back at him as he waved me on.

Erik had wandered further into the dusty field ahead of us, the land barren and stretching out endlessly in every direction.

He clawed his hands into his hair as he continued to stare up at the sky above, now sprinkled with stars.

I moved after him at a slow pace, trying to get my thoughts in line. What was I supposed to say? Did Fabian actually expect me to talk him down from this rage? We were stuck in the middle of nowhere and were still hundreds of miles away from the holy mountain. Hell, *I* was pissed off at our situation.

I chewed on my lower lip, moving across the field. My boots crunched on a plant which must have been dead for years and Erik turned, spotting me.

All the words in my head jumbled together until I found myself just standing there, totally void of words.

"I'm coming back," he snarled. "Just give me a minute."

I chewed harder on my lip and broke the skin with my fangs. The hunger in me was getting out of hand and even my own blood was starting to taste appetising.

I gazed at his dark expression as he warned me not to approach. I took a slow breath to ease away the stab of rejection, focusing on what he needed instead.

"Okay," I said, turning to head back to the road with a crushing tightness in my chest.

"Wait," he called and I shut my eyes, basking in the hope that hung on that word.

I didn't turn back, but I halted, waiting for him to approach. I felt him closing in behind me and his fingers brushed my back, sending electricity darting through to my core.

He circled around until he stood before me, reaching out to wipe away the blood staining my lip with his thumb.

He eyed me for a painfully long second then moved forward and wrapped me in his arms. He buried his face in my neck and I just stood there, holding him tighter and tighter, hoping it would help piece together the broken shards of his heart.

We remained there for what felt like an eternity, the scent of cypress and rain rising from him and enveloping me in its familiarity. I could almost feel the Earth turning beneath my feet and the night sky sweeping by overhead. We were the most solid place in the centre of the universe and I just hoped we could hold onto the anchor we made between us.

"Drink. No questions," Erik commanded at last, stepping away from me, a dark mask sliding into place over his features. He turned me around, pushing me back toward the truck and it took me a few more steps to realise he wasn't following.

Fabian slid the door open as I arrived and everyone else spilled out of the truck after him.

"What's the plan?" I sighed, moving to the trunk and popping it open.

"We walk," Clarice said with a broad yawn. Though she'd gotten some rest, there was still a heaviness in her eyes that said she was exhausted.

I took a bottle of blood from the stash, glancing around to check if Magnar was watching me. He'd walked into the field, approaching Erik and I stole the moment away from him to swallow the contents of the bottle. The sweet, metallic blood rolled down my throat and loosened the vice around it, making my thoughts align once more.

The other vampires moved forward eagerly, quickly drinking a bottle each, throwing wary glances over their shoulders at Magnar.

"He can cope," Callie insisted.

"Not forever," I said gently, my own worries clawing at me.

I trusted Magnar, but we didn't know for sure if he could trust himself right now. And with his added slayer strength...who knew what he was capable of?

Luckily the wind was blowing away from Magnar and he didn't look at us as we threw the empty bottles back in the trunk and closed it.

I realised it was the first time I'd drunk in front of Callie and I eyed her with a frown. She didn't seem to notice, her gaze drifting to Magnar and Erik out in the field.

"So we have to leave the truck here, I guess?" Julius said, folding his arms.

Clarice looked at the vehicle with a sullen nod. "What other choice do we have?"

"We could search for a power source?" Chickoa suggested, though as her eyes dragged across the barren landscape, no one needed to mention that there was no chance of us finding any such thing out here.

Julius stiffened, reaching for Menace at his hip and Callie's hand went to Fury. I mimicked them as I touched Nightmare and a tingle ran through my hand.

Familiar!

I stiffened, searching the skies and the vampires caught on as they turned their attention to our surroundings too.

"Shit," Julius snarled. "Hey Magnar!" he called. "Valentina's fucking watching us."

Magnar and Erik started running back to meet us, appearing at the edge of the group in seconds.

"Do you think she's close?" Clarice asked nervously.

"It's just a scout," Fabian growled, pointing out a large bird swooping through the sky far above us. "She's not near or we'd know by now."

"Can we take it out?" Callie asked, lifting Fury as if to throw it.

"It's too high," Fabian said.

"Not for me," Magnar growled, snatching Fury from Callie's hand. He leaned back, launching it into the sky with such strength that it tore through the air like a bullet.

A faint screech sounded from above then Fury pelted back toward the earth.

"Shit!" Clarice cried, lurching aside as it plummeted toward her. Magnar leapt upwards and snatched it out of the air, flipping it in his palm and handing it back to Callie as he landed. His movements were so fluid, so graceful, it somehow didn't add up with his immense size.

"Thanks," she breathed, her eyes wide.

"That was fucking insane," Julius said, his mouth going slack.

Magnar grunted then his eyes slid to the trunk of the vehicle, and he took

42

a wary step back.

"Drink," I urged but he shook his head harshly.

"You're gonna kill us all if you don't," Erik snarled at him.

"He's fine," Callie insisted. "Aren't you?" she asked him and Magnar nodded firmly.

"Come on, let's pack up and start walking," Clarice said, popping the trunk again. She zipped up the bag of bottles, placing it on her back and Julius moved to carry the water and milk.

I took Nightmare into my grip, comforted by its presence now we knew Valentina was still hunting us. A ripple of energy rolled through me as I wondered how close she was, how soon we might have to fight for our lives again.

When we'd gathered everything onto our backs, Erik took the lead, heading down the endless road ahead of us. I steeled myself for the journey before us, knowing it was going to be rough. But there was a blessed gift waiting at the end of it. We just had to make it there as fast as we could, then everything would be right again.

CALLIE

CHAPTER FIVE

We walked for hours and hours until my feet began to drag and my joints cried out for rest. I glanced about at the rest of our group and found them flagging a little too, though none of them seemed to be as exhausted as me.

The joys of being mortal.

The ruins were a barren landscape which seemed to sprawl on endlessly in every direction and I began to wonder if we'd ever find an end to them.

My stomach growled pitifully but there was nothing to be done about it. Julius and I had both drunk more milk than I could happily stomach but it didn't compare to the nourishment of real food. And despite my gifts aiding me, I could feel my body getting weaker with every passing mile.

To our left the sky was just beginning to lighten, meaning daybreak was drawing close once again. I hadn't eaten in nearly thirty six hours and though I was no stranger to starvation from my time in the Realm, I'd never pushed myself so hard physically while battling against the pangs of hunger.

Magnar had slowly been moving himself further from me as we travelled on and he prowled at the front of our group alongside Erik.

The two of them exchanged words from time to time but the rest of us were too far back to overhear them and any time we drew closer, they widened the gap again.

I chewed my lip, feeling certain that Magnar was avoiding me because of the scent of my blood. There was nothing I could do to dampen that pull he felt towards me though. And after begging him to remain in his immortal form for me, I could only support his decisions about the way he wished to deal with the consequences of remaining with us as a vampire.

Fabian moved to my side, his eyes sweeping over me as he noticed my diminishing state.

"Did you manage to get much sleep in the truck?" he murmured.

"A little," I replied with a shrug. "A few hours maybe." Probably not enough, but my mind had been too full of everything that had befallen us for me to even attempt it before then.

"We'll have to make camp at daybreak anyway," he said, glancing at the clear sky overhead. "Most of us can't travel in the sun."

I nodded, glancing towards the lighter patch of sky in the east hopefully but it looked like we still had a few hours to wait until that would be the case. After seeing that Familiar hunting us, I was afraid to slow our pace but we didn't have much choice. Julius and I needed to rest and even the vampires looked like they could do with a break. But we wouldn't be able to rest for long; Valentina was hot on our trail and all we could do was keep moving towards the mountain and hope to reach it before she caught up to us.

"Are you alright?" I asked lamely. "I mean I know you're not but... are you coping?"

Fabian shook his head, looking up towards the stars. His hair hung loose around his face, grazing his shoulders as he let out a long breath.

"Miles was my brother for over twelve hundred years. I don't know how to begin to comprehend the idea of a lifetime without him in it." His voice was so hopeless that my heart broke for him all over again. It wasn't fair. Miles and Warren had seemed so happy, so full of life and Idun had just taken that from them on a whim.

I reached between us and took Fabian's hand in mine, gripping his fingers tightly as words failed me.

He held onto me for a moment then extracted his hand, glancing at Magnar's back with a faint frown.

"It hasn't changed how you feel about him has it? Now that he's one of

46

us?" Fabian asked, clearly wanting to steer the conversation away from his grief.

"No," I replied. "I'd love him no matter what."

"And yet *my* nature always drove you away from me," he murmured.

"Not your nature," I countered. "Your past. What you were and are. I am not my sister; I could never forgive the things we suffered beneath the rule of the Belvederes enough to love one of you like that."

Fabian nodded in bitter acceptance. "Then I suppose it was always hopeless for me."

"I was never the one for you, Fabian," I murmured. "Our differences far outweigh anything we have in common." My gaze slid beyond Fabian to Chickoa as she walked to our left. She was speaking quietly with Clarice and our group had spread out enough for me to feel sure she wouldn't overhear us. "Have you apologised to her yet?"

Fabian looked towards the woman he used to love and his shoulders slumped with defeat. "I don't imagine she wishes to hear it."

"Even if she doesn't, she still deserves to. And you deserve the chance to say it too. Don't live with regrets, Fabian, or you may end up dying with them too."

Silence fell between us and Fabian's gaze was drawn to Chickoa as we walked on companionably. It was strange to remember the hatred I'd once felt for the man walking beside me. We'd been through so much together since he'd forced me to be his bride. We'd killed for each other and beside each other. And now strangely, I knew in my heart that he was my friend. And after a hundred lifetimes of solitude I hoped that when we broke the curse he might be able to regain the last of his humanity and love again.

I stumbled on a rock as I failed to pick my feet up properly and Fabian caught my arm before I could hit the ground. He pulled me upright and hoisted me into his arms before I could protest.

"You don't have to-" I began but he shook his head, ignoring me.

"Is it too much to allow me to help a damsel in distress?" he mocked and I couldn't help but laugh a little at the ridiculousness of our situation.

"So you're just going to carry me for the next few hours?" I asked incredulously.

"Give me some credit, slayer," Fabian replied with a faint smile. "I swam across the great ocean with my siblings. The journey took months of our lives while we drank nothing but salt water. I can carry a slip of a thing like you for a few hours."

I gave in, rolling my eyes at him as I hooked an arm around his neck. "Fine, but I owe you one."

"Well if you want to keep your mule fed for the journey then I won't object to it."

"I'm sure you'd sooner drink bottled blood than-"

"Unhand her!" Magnar snarled as he looked back at us and spotted me in Fabian's arms.

My heart pattered with surprise and I pushed myself out of Fabian's grip while he stilled beside me.

"She nearly fell from exhaustion," Fabian snapped. "Which you would have seen for yourself if you truly cared for her the way you claim to."

Magnar stalked closer, his eyes wild with fury as he closed the distance parting us.

"He's not lying, Magnar," I said, placing myself between them and holding a hand out to halt him. "I haven't eaten in over a day and we've been walking for thirteen hours-"

Magnar stopped before me, taking my outstretched hand in his and yanking me towards him. I stumbled against his chest and his nostrils flared as he breathed in deeply.

"Callie is *mine,"* he snarled and the way he said it wasn't like the way he said it to me when we were alone. It was commanding and possessive. Like I was an object that he could control.

I tried to pull my wrist out of his grasp but he was holding me so tightly that it was beginning to bruise.

"Stop it, Magnar," I urged as I tried to prise his fingers from my skin.

"You're hurting her," Fabian hissed, baring his fangs.

The act was like waving a red flag at a bull and Magnar launched himself forward to attack, throwing me aside as he did so in favour of his fight.

I hit the ground hard and Montana was at my side in seconds, dragging me to my feet fearfully.

Fabian leapt back as Magnar rounded on him and the two of them fell into a desperate dance as Magnar fought to get his hands on the Belvedere.

"Stop!" I shouted but Magnar either couldn't hear me or didn't care.

His foot connected with Fabian's chest as Clarice raced forward to help and he was sent crashing into her.

Erik swore as he launched himself at Magnar's back, hooking an arm around his neck as he fought to disable him.

Magnar barely reacted to the attack on him and he reached over his shoulder, snatching Erik by the back of his shirt and slamming him to the ground beneath him.

The whole hillside quaked beneath us as Erik collided with the ground and my heart leapt in panic at the ferociousness of Magnar's attacks.

"He's fucking lost it!" Fabian snarled as he scrambled off of Clarice and Julius raced forward to intercept his brother.

"Stay away from him!" Clarice shrieked in warning to the slayer.

Magnar's head turned sharply, his nostrils flaring as he looked towards his brother with hunger burning in his eyes.

He abandoned his fight with Erik as he sped towards Julius instead and I sprang to my feet, racing forward to stop him.

If he hurt his brother I knew he'd never forgive himself but he was so lost to the bloodlust that I wasn't even sure he could see who stood before him in that moment.

"Magnar!" I screamed as Julius's eyes widened in realisation and Magnar slammed into him.

They crashed to the ground and tumbled through the dust before Magnar managed to pin Julius beneath him.

He stared down at his brother, baring his fangs in animalistic desperation as his gaze slid to his throat.

"Shit," Julius breathed as Magnar lunged forwards.

"Stop!" I cried and a deep power flooded through my chest, burning along my limbs and flying out of my body before slamming into Magnar's.

He toppled forward before his fangs could breach his brother's skin and Julius released an oomph of discomfort as Magnar's weight fell on him.

Silence reigned and everyone stared at Magnar in total disbelief.

"What the hell just happened?" Clarice breathed as she moved closer.

Julius grunted with effort as he shoved Magnar off of him and he rolled onto his back unconscious.

"The Dream Weaver put him to sleep," Julius explained. "Good thinking, Callie."

"It wasn't intentional," I muttered. I hadn't even known that I could do such a thing. "I just wanted him to stop before he did something he'd regret."

"And you couldn't have managed that *before* he caved in half of my ribs?" Fabian wheezed as he drew closer too. Magnar's dusty boot print stood out on his black t-shirt and he hissed through the pain of his injuries as his body fought to heal them.

"She said she wanted to stop him doing something he'd regret," Chickoa said. "And I don't think he's going to feel too bad about hurting *you*."

Fabian scowled and Montana released a breath of laughter. I almost joined her but I felt like if I started I wouldn't stop and before I knew it I'd be sobbing.

"I told him this would happen," Erik growled, clearly not finding any humour in the situation.

"He's just over tired," I said defensively. "We all are. He'll be okay as soon as he's had some rest."

"He won't," Fabian replied tersely. "Every moment he goes without blood is another moment he draws closer to losing his mind altogether. You saw what he almost did to his own brother. If he refuses to drink then we should force him now, while he's unconscious."

"That's not a bad idea," Erik muttered.

"Don't you dare!" I moved to stand before Magnar and Julius bared his teeth as he drew his blade too.

"Look at what he nearly did to both of you," Fabian protested. He caught my hand and lifted it so that everyone could see the red fingerprints marking my wrist where Magnar had grabbed me.

I snatched my hand back. "He didn't mean to do that," I said defensively. "He just lost control for a second."

"And he'll do it again," Erik said darkly. "Until he feeds, we can't trust him. And he's too strong for us to take chances with. We should do it now while he's subdued."

"This has to be Magnar's decision," Julius growled. "And if any of you try to force it on him then you're going to have to get through us."

Fabian shared a look with his brother and my skin prickled as once again we found ourselves standing against the Belvederes. I wondered if a time would come when these lines would never have to be drawn between us.

Montana seemed torn about what decision was for the best but Chickoa drew closer to us.

"I stand with the slayers. I understand the hell of being turned against your will," she snarled, looking Fabian right in the eye. "And if he isn't ready to drink yet then that's his choice. Callie can subdue him when the bloodlust gets too much for him to bear. That's good enough for me."

"And me," Clarice agreed, glancing at Julius as her cheeks grew pale with embarrassment. "This should be Magnar's decision."

"Brilliant," Fabian growled sarcastically. "And who's going to carry him while he can't be trusted to stay awake?"

"I will," Erik muttered, stepping closer so that he could draw Magnar into his arms.

I watched him cautiously as he slung the man I loved over his shoulder and Magnar remained oblivious to all of it while he slept.

Clarice still carried the bag with all the bottled blood in it so I didn't have to worry about Erik tricking us and feeding him in secret.

We continued down the road and Montana drew closer to me, lacing her fingers through mine.

"I know it's hard to see him like this, Callie," she breathed. "But he won't be able to keep fighting the urge forever."

"It doesn't have to be forever," I murmured stubbornly, wanting to respect Magnar's wishes in this. "Just until we reach the mountain."

Monty pursed her lips like she didn't think he would last that long but I didn't say anything further. If Magnar needed to feed before we got there then I wasn't the one stopping him. But it was something he had to figure out for himself.

MONTANA

CHAPTER SIX

We finally reached a small cluster of ruined buildings that were still standing, though their exteriors were battered by the bombs that must have fallen here long ago. The light was growing brighter in the sky and though I could see a whole host of houses on the horizon, no one made any complaint about heading into the first one we reached. The roof and walls were intact but the door was lying on the floor inside. Dust coated every surface of the one-story house, but it was dry and gave us shelter from the coming dawn. So it was certainly good enough.

Callie sagged down to the floor with a groan, pulling off her boots and massaging her feet. Erik carefully placed Magnar down beside her.

"Thank you," she said and he nodded stiffly before moving away.

There was a bunch of wooden furniture about the place and Erik and Julius started breaking it up for firewood.

We'd all agreed Valentina couldn't be too hot on our trail for now and we had a view in every direction beyond the house anyway, so if she did show up we could run for it before she ever got close enough to cast a storm.

Julius and Erik set about building the fire while Callie sat across from me, stroking Magnar's cheek as he laid under her spell. I helped Clarice fix the door back into place and drew a filthy pair of curtains across the blown out window to shield us from the coming dawn.

Erik headed outside in a blur of motion, returning a second later with two flints in his hand. He knelt in front of the firewood, striking them together while Julius tried to encourage any spark that caught on the dry bark.

"I still say we force feed Magnar a bottle," Fabian grumbled as he stalked back and forth in front of the slayer. I knew he was just protective of Callie, but my sister was right. This needed to be Magnar's decision and we all had to respect that.

I dropped down opposite my sister, my mouth dry from the dusty air and the desire for more blood.

"That's not an option," Callie snarled, shifting closer to Magnar to defend him.

"He nearly killed us!" Fabian shouted, shaking his head.

"Well he's asleep for now." Clarice caught his arm, giving him a hard glare. "So drop it."

Fabian huffed, sitting down beside me and I spotted Chickoa giving him an awkward glance from the other side of the room.

Fabian rubbed his forehead with a heavy frown as he turned his gaze to the wall. I was sure his grief was as keen as the other Belvederes over Miles and Warren's death, but he buried it deep, keeping his cool exterior in place. Clarice was the only one who had truly let her emotions out. When the tears fell, she allowed them to fall until they stopped. But the men were obviously dealing with it differently.

My eyes strayed to Erik as the fire got going and he rose to his feet, backing away from it. He moved to sit beside me, dropping down without a word and I was glad of his company, even if he didn't want to talk.

Julius took a seat beside Chickoa, picking up a bottle of milk and swigging down a mouthful. He passed it to Callie but she shook her head, her gaze fixed on Magnar as he slept.

"We should get some rest while we can," Clarice suggested.

"And wake up to Valentina breathing down our necks?" Fabian said anxiously. "What if she uses this time to catch up?"

"We'll keep a lookout for Valentina, but Callie and Julius need to rest," Erik said as he scored a line in the dirt before him. "And we'll have to scout the area for supplies while they do."

"*Food*," Julius groaned longingly. "I've already drunk most of this milk. And we're not gonna survive on dust and air."

"The blood's going to run out in a few days," Fabian said in a low tone. "We have to consider that too."

I eyed Callie, my gut clenching at the thought of what he was suggesting. How were we going to get to the mountain without drinking from the slayers? But that idea was unthinkable.

"I won't drink from them even if they offer it," I whispered so low that only the vampires could hear me.

"Now you're sounding like Magnar." Fabian stood up, kicking the dusty floor as he marched off to the corner of the room.

Callie huddled closer to the fire and I spied goosebumps lining her flesh. It must have been freezing in this place and I was grateful we'd found enough wood to last the night.

Erik continued to strike lines in the dust with his hand. As I watched, the lines seemed to grow deeper under his touch and a faint tremor ran through the concrete. He lifted his head with a frown and I brushed my own fingers through the lines he'd carved in the dirt lining the floor, wondering if I'd imagined it.

"I'm going to keep watch." Clarice got to her feet, brushing the dust from her jeans.

"I'll go with you. I can use my swords to sense for Familiars before I get some sleep," Julius said, springing to his feet and they headed outside.

I wondered if the two of them had any idea of how much they were drawn to each other. It was as clear as day to me how much they cared about one another. But their pride wouldn't allow their barriers to fall, even though they always ended up following each other around anyway.

Erik took my hand and my brows raised in surprise as I glanced up at him. "Come for a walk with me." It wasn't a request and I was half tempted to roll my eyes at him for falling back on his old habits. But if that was what he needed to get through this then I had to suck it up for now.

I rose to my feet and his hand stayed firmly around mine as he guided me out of the house and across the dry ground beyond it. Clarice and Julius were heading up the road, gazing up at the sky.

We moved away in the opposite direction, walking on in silence. I wondered how far away Valentina was in this vast expanse of land. Hatred clutched me as I thought of that woman coming after us. I didn't know who I despised more: her or the gods. But I supposed it was Idun who'd hurt us the most so far.

Erik's fingers wound between mine and he tugged me to a halt as we arrived at a huge boulder jutting out of the earth. He leaned against it and I moved beside him, his hand falling away from mine.

I waited for him to talk, sure anything I said was wasted air anyway. He had to open up to me first so I could try and find a way to make this better. But until then, I remained silent.

"Blood is our main issue right now," Erik said and I frowned, having expected him to bring up Miles and Warren. "I'm not going to see you go hungry." His tone was icy and demanding.

"Well you might have to," I said with a shrug. "Until we find another way."

"You know we only have one option," he said in a low voice and I shook my head at him.

"There is no way in hell I'm asking my sister or Julius for blood," I insisted.

"They will offer eventually, because they will have to or else watch us go mad and attack them," Erik snarled and the hairs rose on the back of my neck. I'd never do that. It wasn't a choice I was going to make even if they did give it willingly.

I folded my arms. "I can't do that, Erik."

"It's not about what you want!" he shouted, sending a jolt through me.

He moved to stand before me with a glare, his upper lip curling back to reveal his fangs. "They'll offer it anyway and you'll say yes. I'm not going to watch you starve. I've already-" He pressed his fingers into his eyes, turning away from me.

A lump of emotion swelled in my throat and I moved toward him, resting my hand on his back. His muscles relaxed under my touch and I was achingly glad when he didn't step away.

"You don't have to drink from the vein, we'll siphon it into the bottles," he said heavily. "And *when* they offer, I don't want this argument. We already have to deal with Magnar. I don't want to have to force you to do anything but-"

"*Force* me?" I blurted, retracting my palm from his back as if he'd physically struck me. "You'll do no such thing. I know you're hurting right now, but you can't just push me about, Erik."

He twisted around again and the darkness in his gaze killed any more words on my lips. I backed up and his expression softened a fraction as he took in the sight of me retreating.

He clawed a hand through his hair, shutting his eyes for several long seconds. "Just...promise me you won't go hungry."

"We'll find another way," I insisted.

He shook his head, his tongue pressing into his cheek. He turned as if to head back to the house, but I caught his arm.

"Erik, please..."

"Please *what*, Montana?" he growled and it somehow hurt me more than his cruel tone that he didn't call me rebel.

"Talk to me," I said gently, desperate not to give in to this rage that was burning a path through my chest.

"What do you want me to say?" he spat. "That I fucked up? That I was sitting in that truck for long enough to drive it half way across the farm and reach the influence of that ring before Idun showed up? That I could have saved my brother if I hadn't convinced myself we were actually safe for five fucking minutes?"

My heart bled for him. I clutched his shirt, not letting him escape me as he tried to turn away again.

"How can you even think that?" I demanded. "It wasn't your fault. How could you have known Idun was going to appear?"

"Because we're always in fucking danger! That's how it is for my family. And I shouldn't have let my guard down!" His face contorted with rage and so much agony that I longed to take it away.

I clung to Erik's shirt, refusing to let him walk away.

"Listen to me," I demanded, bolstering my strength so that I might lend it to him.

I held his cheek and forced him to look at me, moving into his personal space. Because he was my husband. And he was hurt and probably felt more alone now than he ever had. But he didn't have to. Because I was right here and he needed to know that I wasn't going anywhere.

"It wasn't your fault," I repeated, slower this time as I tried to make it sink in. His jaw ticked as he surveyed me and his throat bobbed, his hard shield almost cracking. "It was Idun. And she's dead for it. I know it doesn't take back what she did, but it's *something*. Their killer is dead. And you never had a hand in their deaths."

Erik groaned and I could see him on the verge of coming apart. He ground his teeth and started shaking his head as he tugged away from me again. He turned, sprinting out into the darkness and I stumbled forward from the ferocity at which he'd left.

A tremor rocked the earth beneath my feet and energy pounced into my veins at the sudden shift of the ground. I scanned the darkness all around me, fearing the approach of some other deity that might decide to destroy our lives. But all that followed was silence. And the nothingness that spread out in every direction.

CALLiE

CHAPTER SEVEN

I sat beside the fire as the silence thickened with tension around me. I could feel Fabian's eyes on me and I ignored his gaze for as long as I could but as the minutes dragged on and his attention didn't waver, my irritation with him grew beyond the point where I could hold it in.

"Just spit it out," I growled, lifting my eyes to meet his over the flames.

Fabian pursed his lips, running a hand through his hair so that he pushed it away from his face.

"A long, long time ago, I was just a human man," he said slowly and I frowned in confusion. I'd been expecting him to start up about force feeding Magnar again and I had no idea where he was going with this. "And as a mortal being, my body was easily sated in all of my desires. But if food was scarce my stomach would growl and groan, my body would weaken and I would feel tired. If water ran low, my tongue would swell and my thoughts would grow fuzzy. Perhaps those things might have driven me to kill if I came across someone hoarding what my body needed and they were unwilling to share it, but the curse doesn't work like that. When the thirst begins, it is like a tickle in the back of your throat which niggles at you, drawing on your attention more and more. Irritating but somewhat easy to ignore. But then it becomes painful, the ache draws your attention from everything else no matter how hard you try to fight it off. You might think of anything, anyone in the hopes of forgetting about it. But it *won't* go away. You grow weak but not in the physical sense that a mortal would from a lack of food; you grow weak of mind. Things start to matter less. You begin to lose sight of what's important to you. Your emotions spiral out of control. You are quick to anger. And with that anger your basest instincts rule and aggression will win out. Every. Time. It becomes harder to see the people around us for who or what they are to us. Particularly if that person just so happens to have a heartbeat-"

"I know you think he can't handle this," I interrupted. "But that isn't your choice. Maybe he will give in to the blood lust. And maybe he won't. Magnar isn't just a vampire. He's a Blessed Crusader too. And there isn't much in this world that holds power over him."

"Blood holds power over him," Chickoa said softly and I turned to her with surprise. I'd thought she was standing with me in defending Magnar's decision on this but now it sounded like she was siding with Fabian. "I'm not saying that we should force feed him but I don't think you should kid yourself either. He needs blood now just as you need oxygen. If you fell beneath the surface of a pool, you might be able to hold your breath for several minutes. But in the end, your body would force you to take a breath. Even though you know that it would drown you. Even though you know that you would die, you'd still do it. Not because you wanted to give in but because at some point your body would take that choice from you. And that's what will happen to him sooner or later."

I shook my head in denial but her words lit a deep fear beneath my skin. If it really was just a matter of time before Magnar lost control completely then I knew what it would mean. There were only two sources of blood anywhere close to here and he loved both of them dearly. If he attacked Julius or me then I wasn't sure how he would cope with it. What if it meant he couldn't face the prospect of continuing his undead life anymore? Breaking could equal his death if he couldn't cope with what he did to one of us.

"You need to convince him to drink before the decision ceases to be his anymore," Fabian stated, his gaze skimming over Magnar as he slept on beside me. Every now and then he'd inhale deeply but it wasn't regular and the long pauses between breaths were more than a little eerie.

"Even if I accept what you're saying," I said hesitantly. "This isn't up to me. Magnar never should have been a vampire and the fact that he agreed to stay as one is a damn miracle. I don't want to push my luck by forcing him to do something which he can't come to terms with."

"I imagine he will find it easier to come to terms with drinking by choice than he would by accidentally murdering you or his brother," Fabian replied darkly.

"He would never kill one of us," I hissed.

Chickoa exchanged a glance with Fabian and I ground my teeth angrily as I realised they didn't agree with me.

I pulled my hair over my shoulder and ran my fingers through it, drinking in the heat of the flames as the aching cold finally began to leave my bones. My thoughts were tumbling over and over and I didn't know what was for the best. Even if I accepted what they were saying, I didn't see how I was supposed to convince Magnar to take a drink. It went against everything he stood for. How could I expect him to simply abandon all of that because I'd selfishly asked him to remain this way for me? And what if he refused? What if he chose death instead of blood? I didn't think I could cope with that possibility and my mind recoiled from the mere thought of it, but I knew it might happen.

A tear slid past my defences and I quickly swiped it from my cheek, not wanting the vampires to see my distress.

"It's clear how much he loves you," Chickoa murmured and I looked up at her again. "But the curse isn't him. Giving in to it or not isn't a choice. The only choice is in when and how he does it and how he feels about it afterwards. If there's anything you can do to help him come to terms with it more easily then that's all we're suggesting. Because if he hurts one of you then he may not be able to forgive himself."

I let out a heavy breath as I looked at the beautiful woman across from me. If there was one thing I knew about her then it was that she'd had more than enough years to deal with the consequences of living with regrets. And if what she was saying was true then perhaps it would be in Magnar's best interests for me to convince him to drink when he woke. He'd already lost control once and I imagined that he'd only be more desperate to satisfy his thirst when he woke from the sleep I'd forced upon him.

"I'll see what I can do," I muttered in defeat and both Chickoa and Fabian sagged in relief at my words. I guessed knowing that the member of our group who wielded the strength of the gods was about five seconds away from losing his shit at any given second was no fun. And getting him to drink would be doing the whole group a favour in the long run.

"You should get some rest," Fabian said, his brow furrowed with concern. "Who knows how long we've got before Valentina catches up to us again."

"We haven't seen any of her Familiars since that one last night," I replied with a shrug. "So hopefully we've got a bit of a reprieve."

Chickoa looked at me like I'd just said something fascinating and she shifted closer to Fabian.

"I just thought; we should be deploying our own Familiars to counter hers," she said excitedly. "We could figure out how close she is and perhaps even intercept some of her creatures on their way to spy on us?"

"Why didn't I think of that?" Fabian purred and he pushed himself to his feet, offering Chickoa a wide smile. She almost smiled back then turned away quickly, tilting her head towards the roof as she seemed to listen for something.

"I think I can hear pigeons roosting up there," she said before slipping out of the door.

"How do you make a Familiar?" I asked Fabian curiously as we waited for her to return.

"You're about to see it for yourself. Have you always been this impatient or is it a recently formed attribute?" he asked in reply.

"Always, I think," I replied with a smirk. "Though knowing that we're being hunted definitely makes me more so. If any moment could be our last then why wait around for anything?"

Chickoa returned with a triumphant smile on her face and she moved to sit beside Fabian while cupping a startled looking pigeon in her hands. She held the bird out and Fabian slit his finger open on one of his fangs before pressing the wound to the bird's beak.

"Wait a second," I interrupted suddenly, as I realised what he was about to do next. "Are you going to kill that poor bird?"

Chickoa shifted guiltily and Fabian raised an eyebrow at me with disdain. "I think the life of a pigeon is worth the sacrifice in return for the knowledge we might gain on Valentina in return."

"Don't!" I said, half rising to my feet as I took in the terror which filled the bird's eyes. "There's a better way."

"Such as?" Chickoa asked doubtfully.

"If Valentina's sleeping I can go to her. I can find out what she knows about our plans and make her tell me how far behind us she is." The idea of heading into Valentina's Dreams again stirred a deep sense of unease in my gut but I could do it. The dream world was my domain and I had no reason to fear her there. Besides, I'd happily do it in return for the freedom of that little bird in Chickoa's hands.

Fabian's mouth twitched in amusement and he plucked the bird from Chickoa's grasp. "Go on then, Pigeon Queen, let's see what you can find out," he mocked before moving towards the door and releasing the bird into the night.

A deep sense of relief settled over me as I watched it flying away and I offered him a genuine smile despite the fact that I could tell he thought I was ridiculous. But I'd spent my whole lifetime at the mercy of creatures far more powerful than myself and I'd seen my own fear in that pigeon. It had been entirely at the vampires' mercy and I knew exactly how that felt. But now it was free just as I was and I turned my mind to the task at hand instead.

I tried to ignore the fact that both Chickoa and Fabian were looking at me like I was insane and I moved to lay down with Magnar.

The floor was hard and cold but I tucked myself beneath his arm and laid my head on his chest as I closed my eyes.

Magnar shifted in his sleep and his arm wrapped around me as he drew me closer. Fabian inhaled sharply but I didn't respond; Magnar was still under the influence of my power and he wouldn't wake until I released him from it. But even when he did, I wasn't going to hide from him. I'd be right here with him and I guessed I'd have to try and talk to him about the blood situation too.

But before any of that, I had a date with a monster.

I tumbled into Valentina's dream and quickly wiped away anything she'd designed for herself. I summoned images of all of my friends, dressing us in fine black robes and placing crowns upon our heads. She hated our group because of the position she so desperately craved and

though she might have taken hold of the city I knew her pursuit of us was partly out of fear now. She knew that any one of us would gladly take her power from her and she hoped to eliminate us before we got the chance.

I advanced across a grand throne room which I recognised from my time in the Belvederes' castle. Valentina sat on a throne at the centre of a raised dais, dressed in rags as I willed her to be.

She laughed as I approached and I moved to stand before her, flanked by my friends.

"You still see yourselves as more powerful than me?" she taunted. "Even though you're running from me like a bunch of snivelling cowards?"

I shrugged dismissively. "We have more important issues than you to deal with at the moment. Besides, we killed a goddess, so why would you ever think we'd be afraid of you?"

"Idun?" she breathed, and I could tell she hadn't been sure about that.

"That bitch got too involved in our affairs," I growled. "And she learned the price of her interference, just as you will if you continue to follow us."

"We aren't following," she growled. "We're hunting. Slayer blood tastes so much better than any other and we have the right to bite in my Scarlet Empire."

I swallowed back the flicker of fear I felt at her words. "So you're chasing us across the country because you're hungry? Poor Valentina," I mocked.

"Well I quite enjoyed having Magnar as my own personal blood slave and I intend to return him to that role soon," she goaded.

I fought back a smile at that; she didn't know about Magnar's transformation yet and I wasn't going to be giving her that information either.

"And I'm sure if you try to take him again, he will enjoy ripping your black heart from your body," I replied darkly and the false Magnar I'd conjured stepped towards her, drawing his blades. She shrank back and he laughed at her as he drew closer.

"Show me where you are," I said softly but my words were laced with the power of my kind.

Valentina gritted her teeth but she couldn't resist the weight of my gifts. The scene around us shifted and I found myself standing in a darkened room where a sleeping Valentina lay unawares.

"Nice try," I murmured as she attempted to hide the details of her whereabouts.

With another nudge from my gifts, Valentina revealed the rest. I recognised the ruins not far from the farmhouse we'd fled hours ago. She was with a large group of biters and they had sent Familiars out to hunt for us in every direction but so far they hadn't figured out which way we'd gone. It looked as though the eagle Magnar had destroyed hadn't managed to send the information of our whereabouts back to her either and a deep sense of satisfaction filled me. She didn't even know which direction to take yet. A helicopter sat waiting to transport them when they found us though and that was more than a little concerning. No matter how far ahead we got, she'd be able to catch up quickly with that thing. But for now she didn't know which way to go so I could take comfort from that.

"Thanks for that," I murmured as Valentina scowled at me. "Sweet dreams."

I conjured nightmares into existence to haunt her and I smiled darkly as I withdrew from her consciousness and the sound of her screams followed me.

I wrapped her in the clutches of my power and I was sure that she would be stuck inside that nightmare for several hours before she'd be able to break free.

MONTANA

CHAPTER EIGHT

I headed back to the house with a pressing weight in my chest. I couldn't find Erik and I suspected he didn't want me to look for him. Dawn was drawing in and he'd soon have to return to the house anyway. I hated knowing he was out there alone with only his despairing thoughts for company but the more I pushed him to open up to me, the more space he put between us.

I reached the house, finding Julius and Clarice returning from their scout.

"Find anything?" I asked nervously, but their expressions didn't give me much cause for concern.

"No Familiars," Julius yawned. "I'm gonna get some sleep."

Clarice and I followed him inside and the scent of smoke filled my nostrils from the fire. It filtered out of the broken window, but the strong smell made my nose wrinkle. As my eyes fell on Callie and Magnar curled up together beside the flames, a smile captured my lips. My discomfort at the smell was worth the peaceful look on my sister's face a million times over.

Julius dropped down onto a moth-eaten sofa, propping his head up on his hands.

Fabian was staring at Callie intently and I sensed something was going on. "What?" I questioned and his gaze moved to me as if he hadn't noticed I'd arrived.

"Callie's going to Valentina's dream to find out where she is," he said, and my heart lifted with hope.

"Oh," I said in surprise. "That's a great idea."

"So long as Valentina's asleep and not about to storm down our front door," Clarice said anxiously.

"Don't worry, baby, I can sense if her and her biters get too close." Julius patted the hilt of Menace while Clarice frowned at the casual nickname he'd used without even the trace of a joke. He noticed our attention on him and promptly shut his eyes, hugging Menace to his chest.

I threw Clarice a grin and her cheeks paled with embarrassment before she moved back to the door, resting her back to the wall beside it.

"So she can just walk into people's dreams?" Chickoa questioned and a smile spread across my face.

"It's her slayer gift," I explained and Chickoa nodded slowly, her brows lifting.

Callie stirred and I rushed to kneel before her, squeezing her shoulder. Her eyes fluttered open and a wicked smile gripped her features.

"Well?" I asked hopefully.

"She doesn't know where we are." She sat upright, turning to check on Magnar's still form before eyeing the room again. "And now she's having one hell of a nightmare."

Julius gazed at her through hooded eyes and I could sense how close he was to falling asleep. "That's good," he mumbled. "Sleep time. Snooze… dreaming about food. Fresh potatoes…" His eyes shut again and Callie snorted a laugh.

"How far away is she?" Fabian asked, his shoulders tense.

"She's a few days behind us," Callie said, her brows drawing together. "But she has a helicopter ready to go as soon as her Familiars locate us."

"We shouldn't waste any more time here than necessary," Clarice said. "Get some more rest, Callie."

My sister nodded, giving me a comforting smile before dropping back down beside Magnar. She placed her head on his chest and his arm hooked around her automatically, drawing her closer.

I moved across the room, laying down and hoping to get some rest myself. But with Erik outside somewhere, I knew I wouldn't be able to sleep until he returned safe and sound.

"Dawn's close," Chickoa whispered so she didn't disturb anyone, peeking through a gap in the curtains.

The door opened and Erik strode in, bringing a weighted presence with him. His expression was empty and his eyes shadowed.

Clarice explained about Valentina and he nodded stiffly before moving to lay down beside me without a word.

I tried to catch his attention, but he shut his eyes, leaning his arm back to cup his head with his hand and feigning sleep.

I released a shuddering breath, trying to will my body to get some rest. My fingers brushed Erik's and his hand flexed then curled around mine. My limbs relaxed from his touch and I willed sleep to come for me.

"If the clouds are out, I'll wake you guys in a few hours," Fabian said. "We need to get supplies and move out of here."

I mumbled a response in agreement, curling up beside Erik and aching for the fullness of his embrace. But I had to settle for his hand holding mine tightly; a promise that there was still a chance to make everything right again. And for now, that was enough.

Someone nudged me in the side with their boot and I groaned, dragging myself from sleep. Erik wasn't beside me and I found Julius standing over me sheathing his swords.

"Clouds are out. Time to go," he breathed and I nodded, the drowsiness ebbing away fast and my vampire strength flooding my veins.

He pulled me up by the hand and I looked to Callie and Magnar beside the dying fire with a pang of concern.

"We're leaving them alone?" I asked, spotting Chickoa and Clarice heading out of the door.

Fabian remained, looking anxious as he stared down at the two of them. "I can stay here and keep watch."

"We need you out there," Julius said firmly. "The quicker we gather supplies, the sooner we can leave."

Callie rolled over and mumbled, "I'll keep him asleep, just go."

"Swear it," Fabian insisted and I moved to draw him away, wanting my sister to get as much rest as possible.

"Yeah, yeah," she murmured, burrowing closer to Magnar again as her face fell still as if she'd just passed out.

"That's good enough, come on," Julius demanded, heading across the room and through the door.

Fabian hesitated but I gave him an encouraging look and he followed me outside.

The clouds were out, hanging low in the sky, stretching boundlessly into the distance. They were eerily still, the wind dead around us and the world achingly quiet. I wondered if Odin was still watching us now or if he'd turned his gaze away from our group. How much did our predicament really affect a divine being like him?

The others were gathered on the road and I remained at Fabian's side as they started moving along it at a fierce pace. No one wanted to stay in this place longer than necessary, but we wouldn't get far without supplies. I just hoped we could find some food and water for Callie and Julius in these barren ruins first.

"I'm starving," Fabian muttered, rubbing his throat as we jogged after the group.

My own tongue was prickling with need and I eyed the bag on Clarice's back hopefully. "We can drink soon."

"Yeah..." Fabian cleared his throat and I looked to him questioningly. "But I'm used to three bottles a day."

"That much?" I asked in horror.

He nodded stiffly. "I spent a lot of time hungry back before we built the empire. And I swore I'd never go hungry again after we made the Realms."

"Right," I clipped in anger. "But the humans could go hungry while you kept yourself well-fed?"

Fabian threw me an apologetic frown. "It wasn't always like that. We made too many vampires, too many mouths to feed. And vast areas of the land were ruined for farming after the Final War. A lot of the bombs dropped were chemical based. They left many of the fields unable to bear crops for the humans..."

I pursed my lips, dissatisfied with his answer. "But all that food was left untouched in the ruins. What about that?"

"The empire is still new, I know our system was flawed, but I started trying to improve things before Valentina took over," he growled.

"Only because you wanted to impress Callie," I muttered.

Fabian's eyes slid to Chickoa up ahead then back to me. "Well, it's not about that now. If we break this curse I fully intend to build a better empire."

"What changed?" I asked.

"Callie reminded me of what I'd been lacking in life. I'd been obsessed with making the empire great, but I'd forgotten about the individuals." His brow furrowed and he reached out to rest a hand on my shoulder. "I'm sorry you suffered in your Realm, Montana."

"Thank you," I whispered, his words meaning a lot to me after everything my family and I had endured. Though they would never be enough to undo what had been done.

I glanced over my shoulder, eyeing the endless plain that stretched toward the snow-capped mountain range in the distance.

"I want to be on the road by midday," Erik barked back at the group. "Pick up the pace."

We did as he said and I brushed my fingers over Nightmare's hilt, hoping it would let me know if Valentina's Familiars were close. It hummed angrily but it was often set off by the presence of the Belvederes. It was hard to decipher anything beyond that.

A creeping feeling ran up my spine that had nothing to do with my blade and everything to do with my instincts. But I had to have faith in my sister's dream; Valentina wasn't close. So why did I get the feeling that something else was?

MAGNAR

CHAPTER NINE

I moved towards consciousness with a heaviness in my soul which I couldn't quite understand. I took a deep breath that I didn't really need and my eyes snapped open as the most alluring scent swept towards me.

I was lying on my back on a hard concrete floor and I frowned up at the ceiling above me in confusion, trying to remember how I'd gotten here. The space was empty and echoing, the wind moving between several holes in the brickwork. I was aware of the warmth of a fire which burned beyond my feet but I didn't need the heat on my cool flesh. It didn't matter much to me but I guessed it had been built for the sake of Julius and Callie.

I breathed in deeply again and Callie's hair fluttered against my lips. She was curled up next to me, her arms wrapped around me lovingly and she rested her head on my chest as she slept.

The rawness in my throat pulled at me but I ground my teeth against it until I forced it aside in favour of appreciating the moment in her arms.

Memories of the night before came to me and I frowned as I realised what she must have done. My mother had sometimes wielded her gifts in a similar way and she'd used them against me more than once if she decided I'd had enough ale before I was in agreement with her on the subject.

I remembered bearing down on my brother, aching to satisfy the devil inside me with the taste of his blood on my lips. This girl in my arms had saved me from that. I owed her the world once again.

The thought of his blood made my mouth grow dry and I inhaled slowly as the scent of Callie's called to me. It was like the movement of the tide, reaching out to me and then drawing away again but with each pulsing movement it called to me more forcefully.

My fangs ached with the desperate desire to pierce her flesh and my grip on her tightened a little as I battled against it.

I won't hurt her. I'd never hurt her. I want her for everything other than blood and this curse will not force me to see her differently.

I gritted my teeth and held my breath so that her scent wouldn't call to me so.

I twisted my fingers through her hair, marvelling at the way it caressed my skin like a waterfall of soft feathers. I'd never felt anything so sharply as I did now that I was in this form and even the simplest things drew my attention.

Callie took a deep a breath and pushed herself up suddenly, peering down at me in confusion.

"You're not supposed to be awake," she murmured, propping her forearm on my chest as she looked down at me.

"I guess I wasn't tired anymore. Are you going to trust me to *stay* awake?" I twisted a lock of her hair around my index finger, watching in fascination as it caught in the daylight which spilled into the room from a hole in the wall to our left. Her hair really was like liquid gold; there were more tones to it than I'd ever been able to see before and I was enraptured by it as I continued to twist it around my finger.

"Are you going to behave?" she countered.

My eyes fell on her lips as I considered what she deemed to be misbehaviour. My mind felt sharper after my sleep, more like my own again but the rawness in my throat was more present than ever.

"I'll try," I promised half-heartedly. "Where is everyone else?"

"Scouting for supplies. This town was destroyed in the Final War and it's almost all rubble so I'm not holding my breath. But we're almost out of water and we have no food..."

"When was the last time you ate?" I asked harshly, realising I'd forgotten all about food on our journey yesterday. That wasn't what my body craved for nourishment anymore and the thought hadn't crossed my mind amongst the battle I'd been waging against the clawing thirst.

"When was the last time you drank?" Callie countered.

I swallowed thickly at her words and she eyed me cautiously as she pushed herself up a little more. She slipped a hand through her hair, pulling it over her shoulder so that her neck was exposed to me on her left side and I couldn't help but stare at the smooth skin which flickered beneath the pressure of her pulse.

"You can bite me," she breathed and she shifted a little closer, baring herself to me. "I don't like watching you suffer."

I opened my mouth to respond but I couldn't find the words as the sound of her heartbeat filled my senses instead.

"Don't tempt me," I groaned, fighting with everything I had to keep myself still.

"I mean it," she said, inching closer to me. "I don't want to force you to do anything you're uncomfortable with but after yesterday...maybe you should reconsider?"

My throat tightened painfully as I bucked against the idea but the scent of her skin was calling to me and the sight of her neck bared to me like that was the sweetest form of torture.

"Please, Callie," I begged. "I don't want to crave you for your blood. I want to crave everything of yours but that. The idea of feeding from you, using you like that..."

"If I was starving and you gave me some food would you think I was using you?" she asked, shifting closer to me so that she could look me in the eye. She was still baring her throat to me and I was filled with more love for this woman than she could possibly know. I lay before her made into a monster and she loved me still, trusted me so much that she was willing to be alone with me. To feed me from her own body. But I didn't know what partaking in such a thing would do to me. To my soul. To hurt the one I loved so much...

I leaned forward slowly and she tilted her chin as I touched my lips to her neck. I groaned as my mouth met with her silky skin and she released a breath as I kissed the spot she was offering to my teeth.

"I want you like this," I growled, my mouth trailing higher. I devoured every inch of her flesh, caressing her with my lips, my tongue, even my teeth, but never biting down.

The ache in my throat grew more desperate but I fought against it, concentrating on the desires of the rest of my body instead.

I made it to the corner of her mouth and she pulled back slightly, smiling at me.

"You're trying to distract me from the point of this conversation," she murmured.

"Were you put up to this?" I asked, frowning as the idea occurred to me. Had one of the parasites encouraged her to try and tempt me into feeding? My frown deepened as I realised I couldn't really call them that anymore without insulting myself too.

"No." She bit her lip like she was hiding something and I reached out to tug it free, my desire for her growing as I focused on her mouth.

"But?" I prompted, sliding my fingers down her neck and eyeing her throat again.

"I may have promised to keep you asleep while they were gone." Her eyes flashed guiltily but I could tell she didn't really feel bad about lying to them. They all thought I would hurt her but she knew better and her faith in me stirred feelings in my chest which were almost enough to prompt my heart into beating again.

I chuckled, shifting upright and bringing her with me so that we sat looking at each other.

"You never could do as you were told," I said.

"And you never could stop bossing me around anyway."

"Mmm," I caught her waist and dragged her onto my lap. It was ridiculously easy with my immense strength and I was careful as I moved her, not wanting to hurt her by accident again.

"The offer stands," she murmured, tipping her chin again.

"Noted." I dragged my gaze from the hammering of her pulse and captured her mouth with mine instead.

I kissed her gently, losing myself in the feeling of her soft lips against mine. She trailed her fingers down my chest, resting them on my belt and I felt her smiling beneath the pressure of my lips.

"How long until the others come back?" I asked.

"Long enough," she replied and I couldn't help but groan as she pushed herself into my lap more firmly, rocking her hips over the hardening length of my cock and moaning softly in appreciation of what she found there.

I kissed her again, slowly, losing myself in the feeling of her mouth on mine. I slid my hands beneath her sweater, tracing the curve of her spine as she arched her back into my touch.

The heat of her blood beneath her flesh whispered promises of ecstasy to me but I refused to listen to the dark desire which was growing alongside my lust. I refused to bow to it. I couldn't. I *wouldn't*.

Our kiss deepened and she moaned as her need for this drew me on.

I didn't want to rush with her. I wanted hours to memorise each and every detail of her body and explore all the things I hadn't been able to feel with my mortal senses.

I pushed her sweater over her head and her hair tumbled free of it, falling around her with the faint light from the window glinting off of it.

"I could just look at you all day," I murmured, taking in the glimmer in her eyes and the flush of her cheeks.

"I hope not," she teased, leaning closer to kiss me again. She ground herself into my lap, moaning with pleasure as she rocked over my cock where it was bulging against the confines of my jeans.

I hooked my fingers into her bra and she caught my hands quickly, leaning back with amusement in her eyes.

"I don't want you destroying my underwear," she warned as she pushed my hands away and unclasped it herself. "Who knows where I'll find another bra out here."

I chuckled darkly as she pushed the lacy garment off of her, freeing her breasts for me, her nipples peaked and drawing my focus.

"Women never wore such things in my day," I reminded her, dipping my head to suck her nipple between my lips.

"Well it's not my fault you're so old," she teased, tugging my chin up so that she could kiss me again.

She pushed her body flush to mine and the feeling of her warm flesh against my cold skin was exquisite. Her hardened nipples grazed against my skin, the difference in our temperatures keener as she pressed them against my chest and I skimmed my hands up her sides. Goosebumps rose along her flesh wherever it met with mine and she moaned hungrily as she pressed her tongue into my mouth.

I lifted her gently, holding her up with one arm while I tugged her leggings and underwear off. She shifted back to kick the last of her clothes aside then crawled over me, pulling at mine.

I watched the desire lighting her eyes as she tugged my jeans free and she took in the hard length of my cock, biting down on her bottom lip.

I caught her wrist, drawing her closer again as I kissed her. I didn't want to waste time toying with her, I wanted to show her how much more I desired her body than her blood. Though as that thought occurred to me, the burning in my throat drew all of my attention and I stilled as I tried to fight it off again.

The scent of it was intoxicating, overwhelming, blinding-

I gasped as she drove herself down onto me, gasping as my cock pushed into her body and my attention was driven back to her flesh as she rolled her hips to take me deeper inside of her, moaning louder as I filled her.

I kissed her again, pushing my hands into her golden hair as she ground her hips against mine and I was lost to her flesh, moving in a slow and heady rhythm, her pussy tight and wet around my shaft.

I claimed her breast with my mouth, grazing my teeth along her nipple just enough to elicit another moan from her.

I took hold of her hips as I thrust upwards, fucking her harder, making her moans of pleasure rise higher. A groan rolled up the back of my throat at the slickness of her cunt enveloping my flesh.

We began to move faster, fucking harder, her fingers biting into my shoulders and mine gripping her ass hard enough to leave marks on her flesh. Sweat gilded her skin, her tits bouncing, moans echoing off of the walls.

I could feel her body tightening around mine as she continued to move up and down in my lap, sighing my name in a way that set my blood alight.

I loved that I could make her feel like that. That I could draw that much pleasure from her body and make her ache with longing for me just as I did for her.

I gripped her hips, guiding her movements on me and she gasped as I shifted my thumb to her clit and pushed her body harder, my cock striking deep inside her.

I drove her closer and closer to her climax, kissing her deeply before moving my mouth down the curve of her neck.

My fangs brushed her skin and the thirst pulled at me, begging me to take even more satisfaction from her body. I growled as I fought against it, driving my thumb down more firmly, slamming my cock in deeper so that she cried my name.

"Do it," she urged, pulling her hair aside again as my mouth moved against her throat.

"I don't want to hurt you," I protested though the scent of her blood was calling to me in a way that rivalled the pleasure she was drawing from my body. I ached for it as I ached for her and the idea of taking both at once was more than a little tempting.

I shook my head against that thought as it occurred to me. I couldn't do it to her. I refused to let the curse control me like that. But despite the arguments thrumming through my skull, my fangs grazed her flesh and I could feel a well of pleasure awaiting me if I would only give in...

"I can handle it," she argued, catching the back of my neck in her hand and driving me down against her throat as if she wanted it too.

Her hips moved faster, and I growled as I fucked her harder, my teeth grazing her flesh, almost drawing blood.

I fought it for another second before my resistance buckled and I groaned as I thrust into her firmly at the same moment my teeth pierced her flesh.

Callie cried out in utter bliss, fisting my hair and pulling me closer as she came around my cock and the delicious sweetness of her blood rolled over my tongue.

Her hand tightened into my hair as she held me against her neck and I drank deeply as she came apart in my arms. She kept moving on me, forcing me closer to my own climax as I swallowed mouthfuls of her blood and my fingers dug into her ass so hard I had to be bruising her.

My body rocked with the combination of the two sensations overwhelming me and my arms tightened around her as I tumbled into an explosion of ecstasy, coming hard inside her, filling her with my seed and marking her as my own.

The burning in my throat receded and I forced my fangs from her neck even though the desire to drink more still tugged at me. I pulled back, looking up at this beautiful creature who had claimed me as hers while she panted in my arms, contentment lining her features.

She kissed me again, not caring that my lips were coated with her blood as she pushed me backwards and I gave in to her command, falling onto my back and bringing her down with me.

"Are you okay?" she breathed, trailing her fingers along my jaw as I looked up at her.

"Me? Shouldn't I be asking you that?" I raised an eyebrow at her as my body tried to recover from the dual pleasure she'd just delivered to me, my entire being buzzing with the rush of it, of her.

In the back of my mind I knew that I should be feeling worse about what I'd just done to her but the feeling of her blood in my system was more than anything I ever could have expected. I was alive with it, every inch of my skin tingling with energy and satisfaction. I wanted more of it and I was tempted to push her down beside me and bite her again. I shook my head to clear it of the idea as the bloodlust pulled at me and it slowly started to recede.

"So it wasn't as bad as you thought it would be?" Callie teased.

I couldn't help but laugh a little at the thought of what she'd just done to me. She'd seduced me into drinking from her. I wasn't sure if I should be pleased or angry but I couldn't bring myself to be the latter.

Her blood had cleared my mind, energised my body and sent endless pleasure racing through my limbs.

"Does it hurt?" I asked, my pleasure dimming a little as I brushed my fingers against the puncture marks on her neck.

"It doesn't actually," she said with a frown.

"You don't have to lie to me," I said. If I was going to do this to her then I wanted her to be honest about the way it felt. "I don't want to do something to you which causes you pain-"

"It didn't," she said earnestly and I hesitated as I looked into her eyes, sensing she was telling the truth. "I actually kinda...liked it." She bit her lip as her cheeks coloured and I smiled widely as I thought of the way she'd come right as my teeth drove into her flesh.

"You liked it?" I asked, wondering how such a thing could be the case but the blush in her cheeks told me she meant it and the memory of her pussy locking tight around my dick confirmed it.

"It doesn't burn. There's no venom." She shrugged and I tilted her chin up so that I could inspect the wound and I frowned in confusion as I realised she was right. No silver venom marked the puncture wounds I'd delivered to her.

82

Callie leaned down to kiss me again and I ran my hand along her naked flesh with a smile.

"You could definitely do that again," she breathed and a deep warmth spread through my chest. Perhaps being a vampire for a while wouldn't have to be all bad after all. And as she'd assured me, we still had plenty of time until the others returned, I didn't see why we shouldn't have another round of that now.

I flipped Callie onto her back in a jolt of movement so sudden that she gasped in surprise. My fingers trailed between her thighs, smearing through my cum which marked her there before sinking into her sweet cunt.

I took her leg and draped it over my shoulder, looking down at her as she moaned softly beneath the ministrations of my fingers inside her. My cock was rock hard already and she bit her lip as her eyes fell to it - a single word falling from her lips which was absolutely impossible to deny.

"More," she demanded. And with a dark grin, I took my fingers out of her and drove my cock into their place, the sound of her cry of pleasure only making me want more too.

MONTANA

CHAPTER TEN

Clarice passed out bottles of blood as we hurried along the road and I gulped mine down, relishing the way it soothed the burn in my throat. A morning's rest was nothing in comparison to drinking this life-giving nectar. My body came alive as the blood swam into my veins and sent a thrill tumbling down my spine. It was the most twisted kind of pleasure, and one I was growing far too accustomed to. The guilt didn't usually kick in until after I'd sated my needs and it was all too easy to push it out of my mind when the hunger sharpened.

Clarice wordlessly took the empty bottles back and returned them to her bag. The only reason we'd need to keep them was if we could refill them and no one made any comment on how that might happen. As far as I was concerned, the slayers were off limits. No matter what Erik had decided for me.

He walked at the head of the group, his mood sullen again. I didn't think he'd gotten much sleep this morning. I imagined he had so much on his mind right now that rest wouldn't have come easy. After our argument, we'd barely said two words to each other and I was beginning to feel like I wasn't doing enough to make this right. He might have been acting like a bossy asshole again, but I knew why. And I desperately wanted to do something about it.

As we closed in on the line of ruins at the far end of the long road, I jogged to his side, throwing him a small smile.

His mouth twitched and he took my hand, lifting it to his lips and placing a kiss on the back of it. After my drink, my skin was coursing with electricity and he charged even more into my blood from his touch. I released a soft breath, brushing my shoulder against his as we walked on, glad we weren't going to continue arguing.

That thought was short-lived as he said, "I meant what I said last night."

I rolled my eyes, biting down on my tongue as I tried to keep it from spewing a harsh retort.

He's grieving, give him time. Let him be an asshole if he has to be.

"I'm aware," I said airily, not mentioning the fact that I still had no intention of following his demands and drinking from the slayers.

"I'm not sure you are," he said tersely, releasing my hand.

I took a breath, setting my eye on the first row of houses as we approached them. A rat darted across the street ahead of us and everyone fell still.

"It's just a rat," Julius called. "I'll tell you if Menace senses any Familiars."

We continued moving but the tension in the group had definitely increased. We hurried into the ruins down crumbled streets and past silent doorways, searching for anything that resembled a supermarket.

"We better split up," Fabian said, shooting to the front of the line. "It'll be quicker."

"Fine, meet back at the house in two hours," Erik agreed, then glanced around the group. "We'll stay in pairs. Watch each other's backs."

"There's nothing here but dirt and rats," Julius said, lazily swinging Menace in his hand.

"Well if a dirty rat monster comes after you, I can watch your back," Clarice said sweetly, clapping him on the shoulder.

Fabian looked to Chickoa with a tentative smile. "Do you want to pair with me?"

I expected her to refuse but she shrugged and headed after him down a side street.

"See you later," Clarice called, moving after Julius down another road.

I was suddenly left alone with my husband and that seemed like a much more terrifying prospect now that his anger was back in place.

86

He stared at me for several long seconds and I walked away from him before he could start lecturing me about the slayers' blood again. I took the lead, turning right down a narrow alleyway, hearing the near-silent footfalls of Erik following.

I took another right turn and spotted a row of stores that looked promising. I hurried toward them down the cracked road, passing buildings which had been ravaged by bombs, knowing whatever had laid inside was long since gone.

I reached the end of the row, pushing my hand against the glass pane of a door that was miraculously still intact. It opened and I was even more surprised as I stepped into the small store. Erik entered behind me, sweeping his eyes over the road as he lingered in the doorway before moving further inside.

I frowned as I gazed around at the place. The rows of shelves were empty as if the contents had been taken. Erik swept his finger across one of them and it came away clean. "Whatever was here has been recently moved."

My gut spiralled as I turned to him, his tone sending a flicker of fear through me. "Who would take human food in this place?"

"My guess would be humans," he said dryly and I frowned. His eyes lit up as an idea struck him. "And if there's humans here, there's blood." He turned toward the door, yanking it open and I darted after him, frustration filling me.

"Wait." I grabbed his arm, but he didn't stop moving. "There can't be humans out here, how's that possible?"

"Because even I am not one hundred percent efficient at everything I do," he said and I gave him a prompting look to make him go on. "We didn't catch every human who remained in the entirety of America after the Final War. Some of them live on the verges in places like this, away from our kind."

My mouth fell open and I stopped walking. He turned back to me, his brows lowering as he took in my expression. Humans lived out here? Free. Without the vampires to ever tell them what to do...how to live...when to die.

My gut twisted as I thought of all the years I'd wished for such a life. And it was somehow thrilling to know there'd been rebel humans out here all along who'd escaped their rule.

The vision came crashing down around me as my vampire husband strolled toward me.

"We'll take what we need, nothing more. It's how we used to live. No one has to die," he said and my thoughts scattered as I realised what he was suggesting.

"Erik we can't," I gasped. I couldn't do that to humans. People who were just like I'd been. I shook my head in refusal. "I won't become one of the vampires I feared my whole life."

His brows stitched together and his eyes scraped down me. "Like me you mean?" he asked coolly.

"I- that's not what I meant," I spluttered.

He nodded stiffly, his eyes dark.

I gazed at him, unable to believe we'd gotten back here. To the place we'd been when I was just a girl locked up in his beautiful castle. I pushed the thought away, determined not to let what had happened break us. But he was making it so hard. And I didn't know what he needed.

I opened my mouth to say something – *anything* that could make this better. But as words met my lips, a scream caught my ear. I froze as adrenaline surged through my veins.

"That wasn't Clarice or Chickoa," I breathed and Erik nodded, his pupils dilating.

The scream sounded again and I threw caution to the wind, sprinting in the direction it had come from.

We sped down streets left and right, moving deeper into the ruined town. I rounded a corner into a wide square and at the heart of it, I spotted a human girl on her knees before a tall male vampire with bright grey eyes. He had his hand on her shoulder and I ran forward in alarm, desperate to stop this beast's attack. Had the biters found us? Had they come across humans here in this wrecked town?

"Not so fast," the male called to me in a southern drawl, raising a hand. I eyed the girl before him, slowing to a halt in fear of him killing her. "One more step and you'll be ash."

Erik flew into view beside me, snarling as he gazed at the man.

The vampire raised his hand higher and I spotted guns pointed at us from the surrounding buildings. Every window, every alley. They'd penned us in. But who the hell were they?

I took Nightmare from my hip and tried to feel out how many vampires surrounded us.

Eight of the weaker, four of the strong, Nightmare whispered in my mind.

"We don't want any trouble," Erik growled. "We're just passing through."

"Passin' through?" the man echoed. "No you ain't just passin' through, is he boys?"

A holler of agreement sounded from beyond the darkened windows and doorways, and I tensed with discomfort.

"Who are you?" I demanded, taking a step closer to Erik.

"Name's Memphis," he said with a smile that sent a chill through me. "And you're tresspassin' on my territory."

Seven of the weaker, three of the strong, Nightmare said and I frowned in confusion as it changed its mind.

"You don't own any land in this country," Erik said in a deadly voice. "But I'll make an exception if you let us go. We're not here for you."

"What are you here for then, huh? Blood?" he asked, drawing the human to her feet and she writhed in his arms. "I hear your kind don't drink from the vein," Memphis growled and my muscles tensed as he brushed the hair from the girl's neck.

"You're working for Valentina," I snarled, lifting Nightmare.

Memphis nodded slowly. "Valentina Torbrook has a mighty high bounty on your heads."

Five of the weaker, two of the strong, Nightmare hissed excitedly.

Erik stiffened, his hands curling into fists. "Whatever she's offering, I'll double it."

"See now, I don't think you're in any position to negotiate, Prince Erik," Memphis drawled. "I don't hear any gold jingling around in those pockets o' yours." Laughter rang out again and Memphis grinned hungrily. "Besides, perhaps this ain't just about the money. Perhaps this is also about the revenge I so dearly want on you for callin' yourself my ruler without so much as a presidential election." His expression turned to a deadly grimace and he pointed directly at Erik with a knife in his grip. "We prey off free humans out here in the way it should be, ain't that right?" he spoke to the human and she trembled in his arms.

My gut knotted and I clenched my fists, panic rising in me as I tried to see a way out of this.

"We're not travelling alone," I blurted. "We have a whole host of warriors with us. The Belvederes never travel without an entourage of guards. If you kill us, you'll have a hundred Elite to deal with."

Memphis considered my lie and I hoped he'd buy it.

"Is that so?" he mused. "'Cause the new queen sent word that you're travelling all on your lonesome." He smirked and my shoulders stiffened.

"Erik still has many loyal followers," I tried to bluff.

Memphis gestured to the empty square around us. "And where are these so-called followers, girl? Do my eyes deceive me? Am I blind to an army who stands at your backs?" He started laughing again and his laughter was echoed from the concealed vampires.

Watch out! Nightmare screamed and I grabbed Erik, pulling him down with me as I ducked as a blur of gold whipped over our heads.

Memphis lurched sideways and Vicious tore past his ear, cutting it open. He hissed in agony as the sword flew through a doorway behind him and a scream sounded from within it.

My heart soared as I turned to find Julius but I couldn't spot him.

The human girl fled, darting off into the streets, using the distraction to her advantage.

One of the weaker, one of the strong, Nightmare corrected again and I finally realised what was happening. Our friends were here, picking them off.

Memphis's face twisted into a snarl. "Kill them!" he roared.

Erik threw me to the floor with force and I cursed as he fell on top of me. "No!" I screamed, trying to force my way up, but the bullets never came.

I stilled and Erik shifted off of me so I could see Memphis who was gazing around in shock.

"Die motherfucker!" Julius burst from the shadows with Menace raised, charging down Memphis like a harbinger of death.

Erik flew to his feet, sprinting toward Memphis as he sped away across the square.

Erik and Julius took chase, disappearing down an alley out of sight. But I wasn't worried. One Elite was easy enough for them to dispatch.

I moved to pick up Vicious from the ground, weighing the heavy blade in my hand as it reluctantly accepted me. Chickoa, Fabian and Clarice jumped down from a window above, splattered with blood and looking fierce.

"Thank the gods you're okay," Clarice said as she jogged toward me and pulled me into a hug.

"Thank *you* assholes, you mean," I said with a smile. "You saved us."

"Fucking revolutionaries," Fabian said with a scowl. "They live beyond our borders and thwart our rule when given the chance. If Valentina's paying them off, she must be offering them a place in the city. It's the only thing they'd want."

"Fuck!" Julius roared as he and Erik sped back out of the alley, tearing toward us with dread in their eyes.

Twenty five of the weaker and eight of the strong! Nightmare screamed inside my mind and my gut dropped.

"There's a horde!" Erik bellowed. "Run!"

CALLiE

CHAPTER ELEVEN

I pulled my clothes on and smirked at Magnar as I noticed him watching me.

"Are you going to get dressed?" I asked, raising an eyebrow as he lay still on the cold, hard floor looking just as comfortable as if he were in a four poster bed.

"If I have to," he agreed. He stood fluidly and retrieved his jeans from the ground before tugging them back on. I couldn't help but stare a little at the strange new way he moved. It was as if the rugged edges had been shorn off of him and everything he did now seemed almost rehearsed to perfection.

I ran my fingers through my hair, trying to straighten out the tangles that he'd pushed into it. I wished we'd been able to pack for this trip; the further south we got the less signs of old civilisation there seemed to be around us and I was beginning to worry that we wouldn't end up finding many supplies along the way.

I trailed my fingertips over the bite on my neck, my heart leaping a little at the memory of Magnar giving it to me. I'd been more than willing to feed him from my body but until he'd done it I'd looked on it like a sacrifice I was willing to make for him. I'd never imagined feeding a vampire could feel like *that* and I couldn't deny just how much I'd liked it. I wasn't sure if I should feel guilty about the fact. For as long as I could remember, the idea of a vampire biting me had haunted my nightmares. I couldn't have thought up anything worse, let alone imagined doing it quite like we just had.

Magnar being turned was confronting in so many ways. He was undoubtedly different now in some respects. But he was also entirely the same. Just like Montana. And the truth of that fact had to equal my own opinions shifting too. There was no more us and them. There couldn't be. We were all just people who had ended up on different paths. There were good vampires and bad humans and a mix of everything else in between.

"So have I proved myself trustworthy to stay awake now?" Magnar asked as he drew closer to me, wrapping his arms around my waist and pulling my back to his chest.

"You certainly seem more like yourself again now that you've fed," I replied. "So presuming you keep behaving then I don't see why not."

Magnar brushed his fingertips across the puncture wounds on my neck and I tilted my head to look around at him as his brow furrowed with concern.

"I wish I hadn't done this," he murmured.

"You seemed to enjoy it enough at the time," I teased, biting my lip at the memory.

A smile almost claimed his mouth but he fought it off. "I've become the monster I always hated. And now I've used the woman I loved for-"

I raised my fingers to his lips and pressed them shut as I twisted in his grip to face him fully. "You didn't use me," I said firmly. "I offered. And I liked it." I pushed myself onto my tiptoes and took my fingers from his mouth so that I could kiss him instead.

He groaned in defeat as his hands trailed through my hair.

"I don't deserve you," he breathed.

"I'm just glad you're back to yourself again. Now that you've fed you can stop feeling so on edge and we can concentrate on avoiding Valentina and getting to the mountain."

"And then I won't ever have to bite you again," he added firmly.

"Well it's a long journey so no doubt we'll get to do that a few more times yet," I replied, brushing my thumb across his lips and feeling his fangs against my skin with a thrill of excitement.

Magnar gave me a filthy look. "In all the ways I might have imagined our lives together I never could have predicted this."

"Me either. But we might as well make the most of it while we can. And everyone will be pleased that we don't have to worry about you losing it anymore too. But you owe Fabian an apology."

Magnar stilled and it suddenly felt like I was in the arms of a statue instead of a man.

"I'm not apologising to that parasite; he had his hands all over you," he growled.

I looked up at him with a frown. "You know, you were never possessive like this before and I don't think I like it much."

Magnar pursed his lips but he didn't respond.

"I'm not your property," I added, raising a brow.

"I know," he sighed. "I just...this body feels more animal than man sometimes. And it's hard to contain my impulses."

"Well you fought against the impulse to bite me for long enough," I said. "So I think you can work a little harder to control your asshole impulses too."

Magnar released a breath of laughter. "Fine. But the idea of another man touching you drives me insane-"

"You never used to be this jealous. I was tired and he was carrying me, it wasn't like we were fucking."

Magnar sighed. "Next time you're tired, I can carry you."

"That's not the point."

"I know."

"So you'll apologise?" I pressed.

Magnar's mouth fell into a flat line but I refused to release him from my gaze until he nodded.

"Good. Everyone will be relieved that you've fed now anyway. It's not much fun expecting the guy with super strength to lose the plot at any given second."

"Super strength?" he teased. "Is that what you call it?"

"For want of a better-"

"Silence," Magnar interrupted me and I fell quiet as I waited to see what he'd heard.

Magnar released me and stalked across the room, gathering his swords as he moved towards the doorway.

"You know, when you say silence like that, it makes me want to punch you," I muttered as I followed him, grabbing Fury on the way.

Magnar chuckled softly but pressed his finger to his lips. I strained my ears but couldn't hear anything as he slipped outside.

Magnar moved swiftly between the shadows in the ruins and I cursed beneath my breath as I struggled to match his pace.

Fury began to grow warmer in my palm and I swallowed against a lump in my throat, hoping that our friends hadn't come across anything bad out here.

Magnar waited for me with his back pressed to a crumbling wall and I moved towards him as quickly as I could while staying quiet.

I strained to listen again and I stilled as I heard what sounded like a crowd of people shouting with excitement in the distance but that didn't make sense.

"We need to move quickly," Magnar breathed.

"Okay," I agreed.

"I mean quicker than you," he added, his eyes burning with excitement at the idea.

"Oh," I replied, remembering what it had felt like when Fabian ran with me before and not entirely sure that I wanted to repeat the process. It had left me feeling more than a little dizzy when he'd returned my feet to the ground. "I'm not sure if I-"

Magnar laughed as he snatched me into his arms and I had to resist the urge to curse him out as he shot forward into the ruins.

The wind whipped through my hair as I clung to his chest and the world moved past me in a startling blur. I couldn't make sense of it and my brain spun as I tried to comprehend what we were passing.

I closed my eyes and pressed my face to Magnar's chest as he chuckled and the rumbling tone of it travelled right through my body where it was pressed to his.

My stomach swooped as he leapt skyward and I couldn't help but peek between my lashes as he bounded between various footholds until finally coming to a halt on the third floor of a crumbling building.

My heart was pounding as he set me back on my feet and a wave of dizziness passed through me, causing me to grip his arm firmly while the world righted itself around me. The sound of the baying crowd was much closer now and fear washed through me as I tried to get my bearings.

I glanced back over the ruins in the direction we'd come from and frowned as I realised how far we'd travelled.

I stumbled as the floor trembled beneath my feet, the ground rumbling as an earthquake shook the foundations of the building.

Magnar crossed through the exposed concrete shell of the apartment block and I hurried after him as I regained my balance, placing a hand on Fury once more.

The blade was near scalding to the touch and I gasped as it screamed warnings to me about more vampires than it could easily count.

I moved to the arch of a window, drawing close to Magnar as we looked out.

The ruins beyond our hiding place were more intact and rows of buildings still stood, lining streets amongst the rubble.

My heart leapt as I spotted Montana racing towards us along the road with Fabian, Chickoa and Clarice at her side. Erik and Julius shot behind them a second later and fear seized me as horde of vampires chased after my sister and the others.

Magnar released a growl of rage and leapt out of the window before I could even react. He slammed down onto the roof of the building beside ours then started running for the edge of that roof, racing towards the road my sister and the others were fleeing along.

I shook my head in denial of the fear I felt as I jumped out after him, drawing on my gifts as I fell.

My stomach swooped as I plummeted down two floors and I rolled as I hit the hard tiles of the roof below.

I regained my feet quickly and raced after Magnar just as he dropped down into the road.

I skidded to a halt as I reached the edge of the building and looked down at the street.

The ground was shaking more violently and my heart raced in response to it.

Montana and the others had made it beyond the building I stood upon and they shot around a corner as I watched them. My sister and the rest of the group disappeared out of sight and I looked back towards Magnar with my heart in my mouth. A portion of the horde who had been chasing them were fast closing in on him as he moved towards a rusted truck which was abandoned at the side of the road.

My heart slammed into my ribs as fear flooded me and the man I loved stood alone in the face of that crowd.

With a snarl of rage, Magnar hoisted the truck into his arms and launched it down the street. I gasped as the large vehicle rolled end over end, the sound of metal slamming into concrete filling the air. It tumbled towards them, flattening the vampires who were too slow to get out of the way and blood mixed with ash to stain the ground.

"Come on then!" Magnar bellowed as the surviving feral vampires scrambled to recover from what he'd just done. "Let's see how you fare against the gods' latest creation!"

ERIK

CHAPTER TWELVE

I raced between Fabian and Montana, keeping my hand around my wife's wrist as we ran. Clarice was towing Julius along behind us, giving him an extra boost of speed. The rebel vampires were gaining on us fast and I cursed the world at the injustice of it. We were not going to fucking die here at the hands of a bunch of revolutionaries after we'd been chased from our city, faced a horde of biters and killed that bitch of a goddess.

Memphis was crying out, leading the front line of his bastard insurgents as they chased after us. Bullets ripped through the walls and tore up the ground around us, but we darted left and right down alleys, avoiding the onslaught as much as we could. I'd already taken two bullet wounds, but Montana had avoided injury as of yet, and I damn well intended for it to stay that way.

As I spied the road that led out of town, I dragged Montana on, snarling my abject rage at our situation.

The ground trembled beneath my feet, shifting and rumbling.

Just what we need. A fucking earthquake.

The crumbled houses around us shook violently and I spotted one up ahead which was already in disrepair, looking ready to fall apart. We charged past it and I glanced over my shoulder, spotting the group of rebels speeding up behind us. I wished that ruined building would crush them with all my heart. As I thought it, the earth shook so ferociously that I actually got my wish. Half of the group were cut down by tumbling stones and the rest held back, helping their comrades from the rubble.

Julius whooped, but I felt no such relief. They weren't going to be taken out so easily. And I needed to get everyone the fuck away from here as soon as possible. I wasn't ever going to take our safety for granted again.

We sped down the road in the direction of the house we'd taken shelter in. Bullets tore through the air as some of the rebels broke away from their group. Montana cried out and her hand left mine as she crashed to the ground. Fury reared in my chest as I spotted the blood staining her back, awakening a feral beast in me.

The others sped past me as Clarice cried, "Get her up!"

I stood in front of my wife, gazing at the five lessers led by Memphis as they charged up the road toward us. My upper lip peeled back as anger consumed me. Something pounded in my blood, a strange kind of energy that sent a wave of heat into my veins.

The ground quaked more aggressively as I stepped toward them, ready to rip them apart. Bullets tore past me, so close I knew I was seconds away from death.

The ground shuddered and a fierce cracking noise exploded through the world as the earth moved before me. The road shattered as a huge tower of rock shot upwards from the ground between us and them.

I couldn't understand what was going on, but somehow I knew in the depths of my soul I was making it happen.

I blinked away my confusion, bellowing my anger at any who would seek to hurt us. Valentina had her claws in these freaks and I'd make them pay the price for ever assisting her.

A great boom filled the air as the pillar of earth split apart and dirt and rocks tumbled everywhere. In place of the huge mound, a chasm opened up, swallowing everything around it. Houses, rusted cars, vampires.

The rebels' screams raked against my eardrums and a sick satisfaction filled me as they tumbled into the dark, the ground eating them up.

Someone caught my hand and I trembled as I turned to face Montana beside me, her wounds almost healed.

"What happened?" she gasped, turning her gaze to the devastation before me. Half of the ruins had fallen and dust swirled into the sky in a never ending spiral.

A shout caught my ears and I spotted Memphis dragging himself out from beneath a mountain of debris.

His eyes fixed on me and more of his people crawled out of the devastation like ants.

Montana tugged my hand, but if I could destroy them with this savage power, I had to. I called on the heat in my blood again but instead a fierce pain gripped my throat. I was drained, suddenly so desperate for blood that it beat into my body like a war drum.

Montana forced me to move and I staggered as I followed her, rasping as the need in my throat grew unbearable.

I clung to her hand. The only thing keeping my thoughts aligned was her and if I let go, I feared I'd fall into the dark pit of the thirst.

Gunshots rang out again and my head pounded as the noise drilled into my skull.

Blood hit my nostrils and I lost my grip on Montana's hand. The others had taken shelter in a building up ahead and Clarice was standing in the doorway, gesturing for us to hurry.

I followed Montana up to the door, but that wasn't why I was going there. Blood was in the air, calling to me, the need thumping through my body until I started to forget why I was here.

My thoughts swam as I stumbled into the house and my eyes locked on a single target. His heartbeat thrummed in my ears like the rush of wings. I lunged at him with all my strength, throwing him back against the wall and the whole structure shuddered.

"What the fuck!" Julius cried as I pinned him in place, my fangs bared as I eyed the thumping pulse at the base of his throat.

I leant forward to take what I needed but strong hands pulled me back. Julius started hitting me and my thoughts clunked back together.

"Stop it!" Montana leapt on Julius to stop the onslaught of his fists, but I didn't care, I relished the pain, hitting the floor beneath him as blood leaked from my split lip.

Clarice stepped over me, reaching into her bag and holding out a bottle. I gasped, snatching it from her, my nails tearing her hand open in my desperation to reach the contents. I poured the liquid into my mouth and fell into ecstasy, a fire igniting in my chest and building, building, building.

I released a groan, dropping the bottle beside me and thumping my head back against the floor.

Fabian and Chickoa were barricading the door in my periphery, a wooden dresser pulled into place in front of it.

I shut my eyes to block out the world, furious with myself. I'd been trying to save us and had ended up nearly killing one of us instead.

"That thirst thing is fucked up," Julius growled and a deep part of me wanted to apologise but I couldn't bring myself to do anything but lay there.

Someone brushed their fingers over my face and I opened my eyes to find Montana leaning over me, her face constricted with concern.

"We need to get to Magnar and Callie," Julius growled. "Let me out there."

"Don't be a fool," Fabian snarled at him. "There's too many of them."

"There's less now after that earthquake," Clarice said with hope in her tone. "Do you think Odin's helping us?"

I grumbled something incoherent, unable to voice the insane possibility rolling through my mind. That I'd done that. That I was somehow capable of seizing power over the earth. As if I was a...

My mind spun to Idun. I'd drunk from her. Her golden blood had washed down my throat, mouthful after mouthful.

I caught rebel's hand, sitting upright and she gazed at me intently.

"What is it?" she asked, clutching my shoulder.

"I took powers from Idun," I announced, looking around at the others, knowing how crazy I sounded.

"What the hell do you mean?" Fabian growled as gunfire pelted the wall outside. He thrust his shoulder against the dresser covering the exit to keep it in place.

"I drank from her," I said. "The ground...I think I can move it."

Everyone stared at me in disbelief and irritation prickled my skin. I pushed myself to my feet and moved to a window across the room, gazing through a crack in the shutters.

"I can do it again but I needed blood after the last time. It drained the fuck out of me," I said.

"Oh you think?" Julius balked, touching his neck as if I'd actually bitten him.

"If what Erik says is true, he can't be blamed," Fabian said in a dark tone.

I shook my head, grunting my frustration. "I didn't say that." I glanced at Julius, the apology hovering on my lips but my pride not letting it out. I was so knotted up inside, like every emotion I held was more forceful, more potent. I could barely look at rebel since we'd left the farm. Guilt swallowed me up every time I got near her. Even now, as my gaze slid to her beautiful, adoring eyes, the pain grew bigger. I was supposed to protect her. I'd made a vow to do so. But she'd come closer to death in my company more times than she ever had in her life.

She could have died at Idun's hands because you got careless.

A wave of pain crashed against my chest as my brother's face came to mind. Just before he'd died. I was teetering on the edge of losing it again. My rage was blazing inside me with nowhere to go.

"Let me out," I demanded, moving toward the barricade.

"Are you insane?" Clarice bit at me, grabbing hold of my arm.

"I'm fed, I can handle myself," I insisted, shoving Fabian out of the way.

"Erik, it's suicide!" Montana shouted, her eyes shimmering with fear as she moved forward to stop me.

A torrent of bullets ripped the window shutters apart and everyone hit the floor. I started running, diving toward the open space and landing in the yard on the other side of the window. Memphis stood there with a rifle in his arms, his face set in a sneer. I avoided the bullets with a burst of speed, weaving left and right to close the distance between us.

Everything that had happened swelled up inside me. Miles, Warren – *that bitch Idun!*

I ground my teeth, desperate to let this anger out. I needed to. I had to try and shake it from my bones.

The soil shuddered and cracked beneath my feet. The dead grass on the ancient lawn sprang to life, growing green and long, spreading out and forming vines that tangled around Memphis's legs.

He turned his gaze to them in horror, trying to shake them off. I brought him to the ground with a ferocious punch and fell onto him as the earth sank beneath us.

I threw my fists into his face, over and over. Seeing Valentina beneath me, Idun, Andvari, every Biter who'd tried to kill us. Bone crunched and blood spewed beneath my knuckles.

The ground sank so deeply around us that we were in an eight foot pit, the earth pressing in on all sides. The mud started piling on top of us and I willed it to choke him, to drive into his mouth and flood his lungs, his gut. He flailed wildly, coughing and spluttering as I held him down and the dirt filled his body.

When all I could see was pain in his eyes and the bitter regret of ever crossing me, I finished him by ripping into his chest and squeezing his heart until he turned to ash.

I knelt in the dirt, coated in muck and blood, the rage in my heart not even remotely lessened.

My shoulders shuddered and I buckled forward as the grief found me, ripping a hole into my chest so wide I was certain it was the only thing I'd ever feel again.

MAGNAR

CHAPTER THIRTEEN

My muscles swelled and tensed as the writhing power of my gifts combined with my new abilities as a vampire. Callie's blood fuelled me like nothing I'd ever experienced before. It flooded my body, charging my limbs with a euphoric feeling that was raw and brutal in its design.

I smiled as I chased after the truck I'd launched at the feral vampires and I slammed into them like a charging bull.

Bodies flew in every direction at the collision and I laughed as I tore through those who were unlucky enough to be left standing nearby.

I didn't bother drawing my blades, opting to carve into them with my bare hands instead.

I bellowed a challenge as I ripped open chests and smashed hearts within my fists.

The rotters started screaming in panic. They were no longer running towards me but had turned away. They tried to escape but I was too fast. I was faster than the wind and swifter than death itself.

I broke bones, crushed skulls and bathed in blood so bright it was blinding.

Heat rose in my veins as the joy of the battle took over. This was what I'd been born to do. I was Clan of War and now I was a monster as well. The bloodlust rose in my veins like wildfire, taking root in every corner of my soul and driving me on to kill and kill and kill.

The screams of horror were like a song of joy to my un-beating heart and I waded forward endlessly as Callie's blood powered me beyond all reasonable understanding.

As my mind caught on the girl I loved, I swung around, looking for her in the devastation I'd created.

She stood in the street behind me, staring on with her lips parted as she looked at what I'd done.

I shot towards her and she gasped as I slammed into her, lifting her into my arms before chasing after the rotters who had escaped us.

We flew down abandoned streets and the sound of gunfire called me on. Our allies were close and my brother's scent trailed to me on the wind. He smelled delicious but nothing could compare to the intoxicating scent of the woman in my arms.

I raced down a long street before rounding a corner and skidding to a halt as I spotted a group of rotters trying to force entry into a large building at the end of it.

Dirt spewed into the air on the far side of the house and I stared at it in confusion for a moment before I set Callie on her feet again.

She gripped my arm before I could race into battle and I glanced down at her, my muscles coiling in anticipation of the fight to come.

"They have guns," she warned. "Don't forget you aren't invincible."

"I've survived death once already. I like my chances of doing it again."

I pulled my arm out of her grip and charged to take on the opponents who were trying to gain entry into the house.

I pulled my swords from my back this time, wanting to see how my skill with the blades was escalated by my added strength and speed.

To death and back again, Venom purred in anticipation as I headed straight for the cluster of enemies.

A few of them turned and spotted me as I closed in and they shouted warnings to the rest.

They raised their weapons and gunfire rang out but I dove beneath the line of fire.

I twisted towards them with impossible speed and bullets slammed through my right side.

Pain flared in my stomach and I gritted my teeth as I swung Tempest in a wide arc, carving into the first of my opponents. I healed almost instantly and grinned in fierce satisfaction at the near invincibility of my flesh.

The vampires dove aside but ash trailed in the wake of my blade as two of them met their end.

More bullets were fired and I twisted Venom before my chest, shielding my heart with the sword while taking the gunfire in the rest of my body.

The pain from my wounds only spurred me on and I carved a line straight into the shrieking crowd, fighting to free my brother from the building behind them.

The wind changed and I looked up as Callie's scent washed over me and she dove into battle at my side, Fury poised above her head.

A vampire raised his gun, aiming it at her and I leapt between them as he pulled the trigger. The bullet slammed into my chest, knocking me off of my feet and the pain of the wound blinded me momentarily.

Callie cried out furiously as she vaulted over me, driving Fury into his chest before he could fire again and finish me off.

The door to the building burst open as our allies spilled back out to join the fight and finish the rotters once and for all.

Julius ran forward as he spotted me on the ground but the pain was already receding and I regained my feet in a fluid motion.

A group of rotters had banded together and they charged towards us, raising their guns as our allies fought the few closest to us.

I turned towards the building beside us, dropping my blades as I ripped the heavy metal door from its hinges with a grunt of effort.

I raced forward as the rotters took aim and swung the door at them, knocking them all to the ground with the savage blow.

Callie and Montana ran on beside each other, the two twins working together to destroy our enemies with their blades.

Silence finally fell and I retrieved Tempest from the ground, listening to its assessment and grinning as it confirmed that we were alone once more.

"That's all of them?" Clarice asked, looking to me for confirmation.

"It is," I agreed, reclaiming Venom too.

Erik walked towards us from the back of the house, his gaze distant and his body caked in mud. He looked around at the blood and ash which lined the streets but it was hard to say if he took any pleasure in our victory. His gaze shifted across his family and Montana and a little of the tension left his limbs but that was it.

"Well, I suppose something good has come from your transformation, Savage," Fabian commented as he took note of the devastation I'd caused.

"You're welcome," I snarled. His statement was hardly filled with gratitude considering the fact that I'd likely just saved his life.

"I take it you finally fed then?" Fabian asked, his gaze sliding over me. "Was it the bottle or the vein that corrupted your morals in the end?"

I snarled at him as his face fell into a smug smile and Callie shifted closer to me.

"You were demanding he feed last night and now you're taunting him for it?" she asked Fabian angrily. "Make up your mind. The two of you need to stop this stupid bickering."

I fought against the desire to cave Fabian's head in and turned my gaze to her instead. Callie raised an eyebrow at me and I scowled as I realised she still expected me to apologise to him for last night.

The air was thick with tension and I rolled my shoulders, slamming my blades back into their sheathes as I tried to calm the swirling anger in my chest.

"Callie thinks I owe you an apology," I growled, my eyes on Fabian though I could feel everyone else's attention on me too as I spoke.

Fabian snorted in disbelief and folded his arms. "Let's hear it then."

"I'm sorry," I growled and I noticed Julius staring at me like he thought I'd gone mad. Fabian's brows rose and I could see the pleasure he was taking in seeing me forced to grovel to him but I wasn't done. "I'm sorry that your puny body is no match for my strength. And I'm sorry that you felt you needed to go crying to Callie because I'd hurt your feelings. But mostly I'm sorry that I'm stuck looking at your fucking face for days on end while you sniff around her like a mutt begging for scraps."

Fabian hissed at me and I snarled right back. Julius laughed loudly and clapped me on the back while the others stared on, unsure what to do about our exchange. I was happy enough to take the Belvedere on if he thought he was a match for me now but Fabian made no move to engage me.

Callie released a breath of frustration and turned her back on me, taking her sister's arm before they strode away down the street.

My gut twisted, knowing I'd disappointed her. But I wasn't going to be whipped into submission and I certainly wasn't going to start grovelling to Fabian Belvedere for forgiveness.

"Well, now that we're all friends again, maybe it's time we got back on the road?" Clarice suggested, breaking the tension by stepping between us.

"Fine by me," Erik muttered and he headed after Callie and Montana, the haunted look in his eyes unchanged by anything that had taken place.

I offered Fabian a taunting smile and fell into step with my brother while he scowled at me. I might have been a vampire for now but I would never see myself as one of them. We simply needed to get to the mountain and end this damn curse. After that I'd never have to see Fabian again.

MONTANA

CHAPTER FOURTEEN

We started walking south, heading past the devastation Erik had caused with his incredible powers. Between him and Magnar, they were an unstoppable force. But it did little to ease my anxiety as Erik walked at my side, caked in filth and his shoulders shaking. Since he'd killed Memphis, he'd been stoic, barely saying two words to any of our group.

Julius and Clarice had found a few supplies before the attack. There was enough water and food to last the humans a while longer, but our biggest issue now was blood. And I was starting to see why Erik had been so anxious to convince me to drink from the slayers if it came to it. Which it surely had to now. We were down to our last few bottles and though Magnar had drunk from Callie, that didn't make me feel any better about the idea of doing the same. Clarice had watered down the last of our supply, splitting it into the extra bottles she carried. But there was still only enough for a week at the most...

I walked at Erik's side; it was pointless to ask him if he was alright. But I just wanted him to know I was there. Whenever he was ready to talk, I'd listen. And I sensed that time was drawing closer. The anger had left his posture but the defeat in him was somehow worse. He walked on as if he wasn't aware of the world around him, his eyes glazed with dark thoughts that held him in their grip.

The road was endless ahead of us and my skin started to tingle as the clouds grew thinner above. We were far beyond shelter now and I feared what would happen when the clouds broke. If the sun beat down on the other vampires, they'd be depleted fast. And all the blood in the world couldn't help them from that.

"Plan B, hm?" Julius muttered to Clarice, drawing to a halt at the front of the line.

Clarice looked a little guilty as she dropped the pack from her shoulders and unzipped it.

Everyone closed around her in a circle as she took four large backpacks from her bag. She gave her siblings an anxious frown, but didn't explain what was going on.

"We found these back in the ruins," Julius said, scooping one up and looking at Fabian.

"And your point is?" Fabian asked, eyeing the bag suspiciously.

"The clouds aren't going to be here much longer," Clarice said with a sigh. "Julius and I thought...well if you guys don't mind..." She looked from me to the slayers and Magnar. "I think you'll have to carry us in these."

"I'm not getting in a backpack," Fabian balked, looking horrified and a smile tugged at my lips.

Callie met my eye and my amusement grew as laughter bubbled from her throat.

The sun was making a good effort to break through the clouds and I spotted dark veins spreading out from Clarice, Fabian and Chickoa's eyes. I turned to Erik, frowning as I didn't find the same happening to him.

He looked up at the sun, his steely eyes reflecting the golden hues back at me. "What..."

The sun broke free entirely and Clarice gasped, steadying herself against Julius's shoulder.

"Brother, holy shit," Fabian breathed at Erik, his voice dry as the sun beat down on him. "You're alright."

Erik gazed down at his mud-stained hands, his brows pinching together sharply.

"Idun's blood," Callie said in awe. "It must have given you this gift too."

"Well thank fuck for that," Erik said, very almost breaking a smile.

"There's no way I was going to get in one of those." He pointed at the bags and Magnar released a dark laugh.

"In you go then, Fabian." Magnar picked one up and tossed it at him.

Fabian glowered, but the darkness around his eyes was growing thicker and I could see the decision in his gaze as he made it. "*You* are not carrying me," he growled, pointing at Magnar.

"I wouldn't carry you if you begged me to," Magnar said in a low voice.

Clarice stepped into a bag, her lips pursed as she sat down in it. Julius knelt before her, releasing a chuckle.

"It's not funny," Clarice said as he drew the bag over her head.

"Not funny at all," Julius said seriously, then turned to us with a bellow of laughter as he lifted the pack onto his shoulders.

Chickoa and Fabian climbed into theirs and Erik moved to carry his brother.

"I hate you right now," Fabian called to him as Callie crouched down to close the top of the bag.

"Yeah, yeah. I'm sure you wish you'd had some of Idun's blood when you had the chance," Erik said as he lifted Fabian onto his back.

Chickoa sighed as Magnar moved to carry her, zipping the top over and shrugging her onto his shoulders as if she weighed nothing.

Erik angled his face to the sky, drinking in the light of the sun. I smiled at him, sensing a wave of peace flooding him at last.

"*Fuck* that feels good," he sighed, his eyes opening and falling on me. His mouth hooked up at the corner and my heart danced with joy to see the glimmer of happiness on his face.

The cry of an eagle caught my ear and my gut clenched. I reached for Nightmare and sensed it was a Familiar as I spotted it high above.

"Looks like Valentina found us again," Callie growled then lifted her middle finger at the bird.

Julius turned, bending over and pulling his pants down to bare his ass. "Oh look the moon's out," he said, shaking his butt as the eagle released another cry.

Laughter burst from my throat and Erik gave me a bemused look.

"I hope she saw what happened back there. She might be more cautious about attacking us in the future," Callie said.

"Yes, we can hope," Magnar chuckled, aiming a kick at Julius so he stumbled and hit the ground on his backside.

"Ow!" Clarice cried from the bag on his back. "What's going on out there?"

"Julius is getting naked," Erik said, releasing a breath of laughter that made my heart squeeze with joy.

"Oh, what a surprise," Clarice replied as Julius rose to his feet and tugged his pants up.

"Should we kill it?" I eyed the bird cautiously but even as I said it the eagle soared away across the land, heading back in the direction we'd come from.

I eyed the horizon with a scowl. Valentina was somewhere out there, hunting us alongside her cruel followers. But maybe Callie was right; if she'd seen what Erik and Magnar were capable of now, she might call off her hunt.

"Let's get off the road," Erik said, his mirth falling away. "We need to lose her."

"She has a helicopter," Callie said anxiously. "How are we going to outpace that?"

"Run," Erik answered, eyeing the two slayers. "Keep up. We'll head off the road."

He took off at a fierce speed and I sprinted after him as we veered into the expansive land to our left. There was a renewed strength in Erik's stride as he led the way forward and Magnar powered along at his side.

Callie and Julius soon fell behind, but their slayer strength allowed them to run at a decent pace. I just feared how long we could keep this up.

We'd eventually moved so far away from the ruined town that if Valentina was on her helicopter she'd have trouble locating us again now. When the slayers tired, we slowed to a quick walk, but I kept my ear trained towards the sky, worried that the engine of the approaching helicopter would reach me.

When another hour passed and I started to relax a little, I fell into step with Callie, sharing a small smile with her as we headed on together. I eyed the bite mark on her neck and my brow lowered.

"Did it hurt?" I gestured to it as Julius went ahead of us to join the others.

"No..." She bit her lip guiltily. "I think I liked it," she breathed and my eyes widened.

"You what?" I gasped.

Her cheeks flamed and she tucked a lock of hair behind her ear as she turned her eyes towards Magnar. "We were kind of...in the middle of something when he did it."

"Oh!" I laughed, shaking my head in astonishment. "Well...I like it too under those circumstances."

She eyed me with relief spilling into her expression. "Erik bites you?"

I bit my lip, nodding and she released a musical laugh.

"Well now I feel slightly less embarrassed about it," she said, linking her arm through mine. The scent of her blood called to me from her veins and I abruptly released her arm, stepping firmly away. After hours of running, my hunger had sharply increased.

She eyed me curiously, but I didn't elaborate. I hated the idea of my sister knowing how much my fangs hungered to meet with her veins.

I cleared my throat, wanting to change the subject. My eyes fell on Erik up ahead and a heavy pressure built in my chest. "Callie...Erik won't talk to me. I don't know what to do. He's grieving and I know he needs time but this silence...it's killing me. Is it selfish of me to want him to open up if he doesn't want to?"

Callie frowned heavily, turning her gaze to Erik too. "You're not selfish, Monty. I'd struggle too if Magnar shut me out."

A lump grew in my throat at her words and I found myself unable to reply.

She brushed her hand over my back with an apologetic look. "When Dad died, I got angry too. I took my slayer's vow even though Magnar didn't want me to. But he stood by me despite the fact I took that decision away from him. I'm so grateful to him for that." She took a slow breath. "What I'm saying is, Erik needs you so much, like I needed Magnar then. Sometimes just being there is enough."

"That's what Chickoa said," I murmured, knotting my fingers together. "But it makes me feel so useless...like I should be doing more."

"Then do more," she breathed. "Keep trying until he lets you in again. I know he will, Monty. Just hang in there."

I sighed, feeling slightly better. We walked on and I set my mind on every footfall. One after the other, on and on and on.

After a while, Callie toyed with the ring on her finger then held it up to me. "Fancy seeing if it shows us anything new?"

I nodded, reaching out to brush my fingers over it and the moment I did, I felt my soul being ripped from my body and joining with hers.

We flew high up into the sky and I caught a glimpse of our group on the endless plain below before the world became a blur. We were rushing across the land, passing over the wasted desert which stretched for miles and miles then across a line of mountains. Eventually, a huge body of water became clear on the horizon and my gut fluttered with the glimpse of the sea. It sparkled under the sun, its colour so azure it outshone the sky.

We wheeled away from it over dense forest, swamps, then the holy mountain loomed high above the ground. A mass of clouds swirled at its peak, its presence washing over me as the power of that place dripped through to the core of my being.

The vision faded and I sucked in air as I was returned to my body beside Callie.

"Did you see the ocean?" I breathed and her eyes glittered with light as she nodded.

"It was so...big," she laughed and I grinned, nodding eagerly.

"I hope we get to see it up close," I said as energy flooded my body and guided my feet to a quicker pace.

Callie smiled serenely as we bathed in the afterglow of all we'd witnessed. "I hope so too."

CALLIE

CHAPTER FIFTEEN

My feet dragged along the soaking wet road as we neared the end of our sixth night traipsing south. Freezing rain slammed down on us endlessly and my saturated clothes were clinging to my body in a way that made me feel colder instead of warmer. I ached for fresh food and drink. Anything more nutritious than the packets of junk food we were surviving on.

Sometimes the vampires had run and carried me and Julius to cross the distance faster but they hadn't felt up to that for the last few days. I knew their blood supplies were dwindling and I guessed they wanted to conserve their energy so that they didn't have to consume more than necessary.

"Let's stop for a few minutes," Montana sighed, stretching her arms above her head. "We can check the ring, see if we can spot anywhere further ahead that might be good for shelter?"

Sometimes when the ring showed us the journey ahead of us we'd been able to see how close we were to the next town and make plans on when to stop for a rest which had proved helpful several times already.

The last two nights we hadn't been close enough to anything habitable though and Erik had conjured a shelter out of the soil at the side of the road. I'd never seen powers like the ones Idun had bestowed on him but using them drained him quickly and he didn't seem keen to wield them more than necessary.

I sank down at the side of the road and Magnar moved to stand over me, shielding me from the worst of the rain.

Julius dropped down beside me and he rubbed his hand over his face to wipe some of the water from his skin.

Everyone apart from Fabian sat down opposite us and Clarice took the pack from her back, tossing a bottle of water to Julius. He caught it neatly, draining half the contents before passing it to me.

The warm liquid flowed down my throat and I fought a grimace as I dreamed of something more refreshing.

"At least two of us don't have to go thirsty," Fabian muttered irritably as he kept his distance from us. He hadn't come close to me all day and it was clear he was feeling the thirst more strongly today.

Julius scowled as he pulled a small blade from his belt. "You want my blood?" He pressed the tip of his middle finger to the blade until blood welled. "There you go, you can suck on that." He smirked at the vampires, enjoying his joke and daring them to object.

All of them stilled at the scent of his blood and I couldn't help but wonder when exactly they'd last had a drink.

Clarice moved forward and dropped to her knees before him, taking his hand in her grasp and holding his eye as she pushed his finger into her mouth.

Julius released a noise in the back of his throat which was somewhere between a groan and a growl. He hissed in pain as she drove her fangs down too and tried to withdraw his hand but she held him firmly. He shifted uncomfortably as she watched him with an amused smile pulling at her lips for another few seconds, then she released him.

"Thanks," she said lightly and I couldn't help but laugh at the look on his face as he inspected his finger and wiped the venom from the wound she'd given him.

"Well that'll teach me not to offer again," he muttered, his eyes following Clarice as she walked away from him.

She sat opposite us again, her eyes sparking with light from her drink as she smirked at the slayer.

Fabian released a snarl and stalked away into the night, heading on down the road.

Montana shifted closer to me, holding her hand out and I leaned forward so that she could brush her fingers against the ring.

I fell still, my soul flying from my body as we were transported high above the road. We stopped short of passing through the thick clouds overhead but the persistent drizzle made the view beneath us seem fuzzy, like it was out of focus. Before we could shoot towards the mountain, the landscape sprawled out ahead of us and I kept my attention on what lay closest to us.

On the edge of the horizon, a town was just visible by the light of the moon between the rain clouds and my heart leapt at the thought of resting within four walls again.

We shot forward but instead of focusing on the rest of our journey I pushed my attention onto the town and the vision slowed a little as we glided over it.

I felt Montana's excitement beside me as we spotted clusters of buildings which hadn't been destroyed by the bombs in the Final War, perfect to create a camp for the night.

The rest of the vision resumed, ending in the mountain but I didn't pay it much attention.

As I slid back into my body, a smile captured my lips.

"There's a town," I said excitedly.

"A few more miles along the road," Montana added, taking Erik's hand as she shifted away from me again.

He nodded, leaving his hand in her grasp but he didn't entwine his fingers with hers.

I chewed my lip as I noticed Montana's face falling, wishing there was something I could do to help her situation with Erik but no one could control how someone else grieved. I just had to hope that he'd find his way back to her sooner rather than later. For both of their sakes.

"Let's go then," Julius said, getting to his feet again. "With a bit of luck we can find some more food there too."

Magnar offered me his hand and I smiled at him as he hoisted me to my feet.

"If it's only a few miles, maybe we should run?" Clarice suggested. "It would be nice to get out of this rain."

"I'll meet you there," Julius replied, shaking his head. "I don't much care for the speed at which you travel."

"Are you afraid you can't handle the pace?" Clarice teased.

"I'm not afraid of any-"

Clarice shot towards him, sweeping him over her shoulder before he could stop her. Her laughter carried to us on the wind as she shot away down the road and I couldn't help but laugh too while Julius swore loudly.

"I hope we can find some clean clothes there," Chickoa groaned before speeding away too.

Magnar gave me a slanted smile as he lifted me into his arms and I didn't even object despite the fact that this wasn't my favourite method of transport. I was dog tired, filthy dirty and aching for something substantial to eat. Not to mention how desperate I was to get out of this damn rain. If there was even the slightest chance that we could find a solution to any of those issues in that town then I wanted to get there as quickly as possible.

I closed my eyes and leaned into Magnar's embrace as he started running and the cold wind and freezing sleet whipped against me mercilessly as he increased his speed.

I could hear the others keeping pace initially but Magnar's strength made him faster than them and he soon left them behind despite the fact that he was carrying me too.

He finally skidded to a halt on the rain-drenched tarmac of the town and he gave me a little squeeze as I kept my face pressed to his chest in a vain attempt to shield myself from the elements.

"Looks like the gods are finally smiling on us," Magnar murmured and I opened my eyes to see what he'd found.

My lips parted as I spotted the huge building and I frowned at the letters which hung above the wide entrance.

"P... rrr... Skeee-"

"It says 'Pure Skies Mall'," Fabian said impatiently as he pulled up beside us and the look on his face gave away the fact that he thought I was an idiot. "That means *stores*, if you don't know that either."

I turned to scowl at him as Magnar set me on my feet but inside, my stomach plummeted with embarrassment.

"Did that feel good?" I asked as I tried to fight off my shame at not being able to read the sign for myself.

Fabian's eyes softened and he opened his mouth to respond but I stalked away from him, dragging Magnar behind me as I went. Heat crawled along the back of my neck and I blinked a few times, fighting not to let them see how humiliated that had made me feel. If Magnar realised I was upset about it then he'd only get angry with Fabian himself and that wouldn't help any of us. But it wasn't *my* fucking fault that I couldn't read and if anyone should be made to feel bad about it then it should have been the Belvederes.

I released my grip on Magnar as I pushed my way through an old rotating door and I sighed in relief as I stepped into a dry space.

The others moved inside behind us and I turned to find my sister amongst them.

Montana smiled as she noticed me looking for her and I hurried to her side as I tried to wring some of the water from my hair.

"Shall we see if we can find some clean clothes?" I asked her.

It felt like I'd barely spent any time with her over the last few days and though I knew she was trying to help Erik deal with his grief I was starting to miss her. I couldn't even remember the last time we'd done anything alone together and I felt like I could really do with a few hours to just be us.

"That sounds like heaven," Monty replied, taking a step towards me but she stopped again suddenly, biting her lip as she glanced back at Erik.

He was frowning at her like he didn't approve of her leaving with me and she nodded slowly before looking back to me again.

"But... I should probably stay with Erik for now," Montana said, her eyes dropping to my shoes as she spoke.

"What?" I asked with a frown, reaching out for her but she stepped back, clearing her throat.

"He needs me," she said vaguely, her eyes sliding to my neck as she drew further away from me.

"I need you too," I replied in a small voice.

She opened her mouth to respond and it was like a war was taking place behind her eyes. "I'll see you later, Callie," she breathed before turning away and hurrying into the mall with Erik.

I stared after her as she left me there, not quite believing that she'd just shut me down like that. The others started heading further into the darkened space to explore too and I had to fight against the tears which pricked the backs of my eyes. I knew that Montana loved Erik and that he needed her right now but I never would have expected her to do that to me.

Magnar moved towards me and he pulled me under his arm as he noticed my dark mood.

"What's wrong?" he asked softly but I shook my head, not wanting to voice it while the others were still close enough to hear me.

"Let's go and see if we can find some new clothes," I murmured, leading him towards a staircase on our left instead of following the others.

When we made it to the top of the stairs, I headed for the first shop that I could see and moved into the sprawling collection of clothes which hung throughout the space.

I yanked off my sodden sweater before I'd even found anything to replace it but Magnar caught my wrist in his grasp before I could continue to undress.

"Tell me what's wrong," he urged roughly and I released a breath as I moved closer to him, leaning my head against his chest.

"I don't know," I replied honestly. "It's just, this journey is pretty awful and I haven't eaten properly in days and I'm filthy dirty and..."

"And?" he prompted, knowing that none of that was really the problem.

"*And* Montana is hardly speaking to me. Aside from checking the ring she's barely come near me for two days and I just asked her to spend some time with me and she said no. Just like that. I know that Erik needs her now but I don't understand why she's pushing me away-"

"It's not you, Callie," he said gently, raising an eyebrow at me as if I was missing something really obvious. "Their blood supplies ran out three days ago and you smell..." he lifted my wrist to his lips, a faint smile tugging at his mouth. "Delicious."

My heart lifted at his words and a wide smile tugged at my lips. "Really? That's it? If she needs to feed she can just bite me. I'll go and-"

"No," he said, catching me before I could go in search of my sister. "If you go while she's with the others then they'll all want to feed from you and you don't have enough blood to go around."

"But if Julius agrees as well then maybe-"

"There are six vampires to the two of you. If we're all feeding from you it'll weaken you too much. I'm not going to stand by and watch that happen."

I wanted to protest but I was worried that he was right. Magnar hadn't bitten me for three days himself and I knew he'd be needing to again soon. But if I was feeding three of them then even if we kept to the same rate I'd have to give blood every day. I wasn't sure if I could handle doing that for any length of time.

"We'll talk to Montana together," he said as he saw my resolve wavering. "As soon as we can get her alone."

"Okay," I agreed. I wasn't sure if it was the right way to go about it or not but Magnar was right; I couldn't just become an all hours buffet for every vampire who kept our company.

One way or another we were going to have to figure out how to deal with this situation but my priority was always going to be my sister. I'd help her first and then figure out what to do from there.

MONTANA

CHAPTER SIXTEEN

It felt so good to get into new clothes, but my relief was short-lived as the persistent pounding grew in my skull and the ache in my throat grew unbearable.

I headed out of the clothes store and lowered myself onto a bench at the heart of the mall, having parted with Erik when I'd headed into the women's store. I groaned, digging my fangs into my tongue as the thirst clawed and raked at my insides. The thought of blood made me so desperate I wanted to scream.

"Hey." Erik appeared, speeding forward and dropping to his knees in front of me. He pushed the hair away from my face and gave me an anxious look. He'd changed into a black sweater and jeans, his hair still damp from the rain.

"I'm fine," I said, but my voice was croaky and dry.

He shook his head, guiding me to my feet. I staggered forward, nearly hitting the floor, but he lifted me into his arms and shot through the mall in a blur.

I was so dizzy when he planted me down that I sank to the floor and clutched my knees to my chest. I kept hold of his hand, needing him so badly in that moment.

We were in what I presumed was a food hall with counters ringing the space. A white stone fountain sat at the heart of it which had long since stopped running. Julius was sitting at a table with Clarice, spooning beans into his mouth from a tin.

"It's alright," Erik promised, squeezing my fingers before stepping away toward Julius.

Fabian and Chickoa were investigating the store fronts around the edge of the circular space, but as they spotted us, they headed over.

"She needs blood," Erik said to Julius.

"We all do," Fabian rasped, his skin looking near transparent up close. His hunger was clear and worry pooled in my gut at the sight.

"It's a miracle none of us have lost our minds yet," Clarice agreed, looking to Julius hesitantly. The small drink she'd taken from him clearly hadn't been enough to sate her thirst.

Julius eyed us all, swallowing the beans in his mouth. The scent of his blood invaded my nostrils and I found myself unable to voice my arguments against this idea. I was snared in the clutches of the curse so profoundly, I'd lost the will to do anything but drown in the pain inside me.

"Back the fuck up." Julius pointed around at the vampires, but reached out and caught my arm, tugging me closer.

Tears prickled my eyes and I shook my head, but I still couldn't get the words out.

No, I won't hurt you. I don't want to drink from my friend.

Julius yanked me into his lap and I pressed my hands to his chest, releasing a pained whimper as the smell of his blood took me hostage. My fangs ached, my throat burned. It took everything I had not to rip into his flesh and sate this need.

"Chill, damsel," he said gently, lifting his wrist beneath my nose. "I'm not gonna sit here seeing you suffer."

"But you're happy for all of us to?" Fabian growled. "We're dying here. And if you and Callie don't start offering out blood freely, you're not going to get a choice in it."

"Stop it," Clarice begged of Fabian. "We can last a little longer. We're Belvederes."

My throat swelled and my tongue thickened in my mouth. I brushed my shaking fingers over Julius's raised wrist with a moan of longing.

"Feed," Erik commanded me, but I wouldn't do it.

"Oh for fuck's sake," Julius muttered then grabbed Nightmare from my hip and slashed his wrist open.

I lost it. The scent was too much. The deep red of his blood filled my eyes and I couldn't see anything else. I fell on him with a primal need, hating myself but too desperate to do anything else but drink. The rich taste of his life force rolled along my tongue and down my throat, his heart pumping more and more into my mouth. It was the best thing I'd ever tasted. More so than any blood I'd ever drunk. It was pure ecstasy, flowing through me and making my mouth water with how intensely sweet it was. Julius placed his free hand on my back as I fed and electricity coursed along my spine as I desired more of him.

I clutched his shirt in my fist and felt the chair falling backwards so we crashed to the ground. I straddled him, drinking deeply, my mind in a haze. I couldn't stop. I wouldn't. It was too good. And I couldn't remember why I'd ever refused it.

A deep groan rolled from my throat and I shut my eyes, taking more, more, more.

Hands seized me and I kicked wildly like a caged beast as Erik folded his arms around me and held me to his chest, pulling me off of Julius. The urge built in me to fight, to get back to that blood and finish every last drop.

Erik ran his hands through my hair in soothing strokes. "Shh, take a breath."

I did as he said and the clouds in my mind fizzled away. Shame took their place and I pressed my forehead to his chest as the weight of what I'd done settled over me.

I pulled out of his arms, but he kept close as I turned to face Julius on the ground. He was frowning as he pushed himself to his knees and pulled his sleeve over his bloody wrist.

Chickoa and Fabian were circling closer and Clarice shook her head at them, begging them to back off.

"I'm sorry," I breathed to Julius as he righted himself.

"Don't be," he said. "Though I don't think I can call you damsel anymore. You're more of a wolverine."

I shook my head, not having the words to express how grateful I was to him. I settled on a thank you and he nodded stiffly, backing up again as Fabian hounded closer.

"We need blood," Fabian snarled and the tension in his voice set the hairs rising on the back of my neck.

"You can't have mine. Back off," Julius growled, reaching for Menace at his hip.

"Everyone just relax." Clarice got between them, raising her hands.

"Relax? How can we relax?" Chickoa said, holding her throat. "I'm going to lose it." She backed away, moving to the fountain and clinging to the edge of it as she kept herself away. After a beat, she turned and sped from the area in a blur of motion.

"Why are you so calm, Clarice?" Fabian asked her coolly. "Has the slayer been feeding you on the sly?"

Clarice's mouth parted in horror. "Of course not!"

"Yeah? Then why are you not baying for his blood like I am," Fabian growled.

"Enough," Erik snarled, stepping forward to intercept them. He eyed Julius with a deep frown creasing his face. "Julius, go. Get out of here."

Julius's eyes swept over us and he took a step back as if considering doing just that. Then his gaze fell on Clarice and his expression changed to a dark acceptance. "I'll fill a bottle. Find something to siphon the blood. No more biting."

"You're sure?" I gasped, my heart aching with what he was offering.

"Yeah..." Julius straightened. "The way you're all looking at me is giving me the creeps. And I'd rather you were fed than have three Belvederes get too hungry to stop resisting their urges."

"I'll get a funnel," Fabian said, sprinting from the room with obvious excitement.

Clarice hung her head, moving toward Julius and he didn't retreat like he had from the others.

"Are you sure about this?" she asked.

He nodded, reaching out as if to take her hand, then thinking better of it as he dropped it to his side. "It's fine. What other choice do we have?" he said bleakly.

No one had an answer, because there wasn't one.

Fabian returned to the room with a plastic funnel and Clarice took an empty bottle from her backpack, placing it on the table. Julius snatched the funnel from Fabian, planting it in the bottle before rolling back his sleeve and squeezing more blood from the wound.

Clarice licked her lips and Fabian kept inching closer. Erik held back, his posture rigid as Julius picked up Nightmare again and cut into his other arm. The blood spilled into the bottle and he soon had it full enough. He plucked the funnel out and pushed the bottle toward Clarice.

Fabian shot forward but Julius lifted Nightmare to point at him. "Ladies first," he snarled and Clarice tentatively took the bottle, then moaned as she placed it to her lips and started drinking.

When she'd had a few mouthfuls, she held it out to Fabian with a sigh of longing as if it pained her to hand it over.

Julius plucked it from her grip, passing it to Erik instead.

"You asshole," Fabian growled, his hands curling into fists.

Erik took the bottle, drinking a few gulps then held it out to Fabian. His brother finished it in one go, then he launched the bottle across the room.

"That's not nearly enough!" Fabian roared and Erik caught his arms, yanking him away from Julius. My gut clenched in fear as I watched, moving forward in case I needed to help him.

"It will have to be," Erik snarled in his ear. "Calm down, Brother."

Fabian went slack in his arms, bowing his head. "I'm sorry," he breathed, looking to Julius. "I'm used to drinking more. I don't handle the thirst well."

Julius nodded stiffly but didn't reply.

"There's none for Chickoa," Fabian sighed.

"This blood store is closed," Julius muttered. "For now anyway."

Clarice moved toward him with a faint smile. "Thank you. Come on...let's find some bandages."

"It's fine," Julius muttered, but followed her anyway. As she guided him away from us, he passed Nightmare back to me and I held onto it with a weight in my soul at what he'd offered us.

"One slayer isn't enough for us," Fabian said as Erik released him at last. "Callie has to give blood too. Magnar is keeping every drop for himself."

"It's not like that and you know it," I said, folding my arms. "And she doesn't have to do anything. It's her choice."

"Well it's time she made that choice." Fabian headed away and I gazed after him anxiously, moving to follow.

There was no way I was going to see my sister forced into this. Fabian had no right to demand it of her even if he was desperate.

I turned to Erik as we jogged after him. "We can't let him force her."

"She's got a guard dog with the strength of a dinosaur," he said with a smirk. "I'm more concerned about my brother."

CALLIE

CHAPTER SEVENTEEN

I sighed with a deep satisfaction as I pulled on warm, clean, *dry* clothes and the chill which had built in my bones over the last few days finally subsided.

Magnar had changed too, though I could tell that the freezing rain had been more of an irritation to him than an actual issue and for once I could see one good reason to envy those who were held captive by the vampire curse.

I grinned as I yanked on the fluffiest pair of socks I'd ever seen and scrunched my toes up inside them happily.

"I've never known someone to get so excited about clothes," Magnar murmured as he watched me.

"Never in my life have I had my pick of what I'd like to wear like this," I replied. "And I don't think I'll ever get over the thrill of it now."

"Well it's nice to see you smiling," he said as I got to my feet. "Even if I wish you'd keep your clothes off instead of piling them on."

I snorted a laugh and made to walk past him but he caught my waist and dragged me against him instead.

"Can't I keep you to myself for a few more moments?" he begged and butterflies writhed in my belly at his words. The last four days had been spent on the road and with no real shelter we hadn't actually been away from the others in all that time.

"So long as you promise not to remove my new clothes," I countered.

Magnar sighed as his hands shifted across my lower back and he pulled me against him more firmly.

"I can't promise that." He caught my mouth with his and I melted in his arms, twisting my fingers into the material of the black t-shirt he'd pulled on as I drew him closer.

He pushed me until my back collided with the glass storefront and I laughed as his cool fingers shifted beneath the hem of my sweater, sending shivers across my skin.

One of his hands moved to cup my jaw, tilting me towards him as his tongue invaded my mouth and a groan of longing escaped him.

His mouth moved lower, his fangs brushing against my throat as I arched into him, urging him on. He released a dark laugh at my impatience and I tightened my grip on him.

"Didn't I say so!" Fabian's voice rang out and Magnar twisted away from me, snarling like a feral animal as he dropped into a defensive stance before me.

"Just wait a second, Fabian!" Montana called as she hurried after him and I reached for Magnar's hand to keep him beside me.

"We don't have time to wait," he snapped. "I'm thirsty *now.*"

My heart pounded as I realised what this was about and Magnar growled at Fabian in a clear challenge.

"Can we have a word?" Erik asked from the back of the group, planting a hand on Fabian's shoulder to halt his advance.

I tugged on Magnar's arm, forcing him to stay beside me as I stepped closer to them.

"Okay," I said hesitantly, eyeing my sister. I expected to see the same hunger burning in her eyes as I did in the Belvederes' but strangely all I found there was concern.

"We have a bit of an issue," Erik muttered and I could tell he felt a little uncomfortable about voicing this request.

"It's more than a *bit* of an issue," Fabian hissed, his eyes lingering on my throat.

I swallowed nervously as I recognised the desire I saw there. I'd given in

140

to that hunger in him once and I'd sworn I'd never do it again.

"You can't expect to feed six vampires from two mortals," Magnar said firmly.

"Easy enough to say when you're well fed," Fabian replied. "We don't all travel with our own personal blood slave."

"Don't call her that." Magnar's voice dropped menacingly and Fabian shifted into a fighting position.

"We came here to *ask,*" Erik said quickly. "Before the situation gets any more desperate and we have to demand it."

"I *am* demanding it," Fabian countered.

"You can demand it again and I'll gladly rip your head off and stuff you in one of those bags for the rest of the journey," Magnar replied and I could tell he meant it.

"It's alright, Magnar," I said with a sigh, realising I didn't really have a choice about this. "It'll be fine."

Fabian took a step forward and Erik's eyes glimmered with what I could have sworn was excitement for a moment but Magnar shifted to block their path.

"Look at the size of her," Magnar snarled. "How do you expect her to sustain three vampires for the next few weeks?"

"Well she's managing well enough to keep *you* going," Fabian replied darkly.

"Maybe we can just get everyone fed tonight and then tomorrow we can think about how to deal with this going forward?" Montana suggested and I could tell this whole conversation was making her really uncomfortable.

"Okay," I breathed and I pushed my sleeve up as I prepared to face my nightmare once again.

Magnar's hand curled around my exposed wrist as he stopped me from advancing. "If one of them places their mouth upon your flesh I'll rip their fangs from their gums and force them down their throats," he snarled.

"We have a funnel and a bottle if you're willing to cut yourself?" Erik suggested, eyeing Magnar cautiously.

I glanced up at Magnar and he nodded reluctantly.

"Let's get this over with then," I sighed as I followed them from the store.

"I'll go and find Chickoa," Fabian murmured before speeding away from us.

Erik led the way back downstairs and through the mall and Montana moved to walk beside me.

"I'm sorry about before," she murmured.

"It's okay, Magnar realised what was bothering you so I understand. You'll be back to normal again once you've fed."

She cleared her throat awkwardly. "Well actually, Julius already..."

"Oh," I replied, surprised that the slayer had been willing to help her and feeling immensely grateful to him for it. "That's good then."

Montana nodded but I wasn't entirely sure she agreed.

"I hate that you have to do this," she breathed.

"The stronger we are the sooner we can get to the mountain and end this curse once and for all," I replied. "We've all made sacrifices to get this far, I can make this one too."

She nodded again silently, taking my hand in hers. "But if it's too much then you have to tell us."

"Okay," I agreed.

We arrived at an old food court and Fabian appeared, towing Chickoa along with him. Her cheeks were stained with the evidence of tears and I tried to hide my surprise as I noted her hand in Fabian's. Her gaze locked on me desperately and I gave her a brief smile as I dropped into a chair.

Fabian shoved a bottle and funnel across the table at me and I took Fury from my hip.

I pressed the blade to my skin and sucked a breath in between my teeth as I struck it across the flesh of my forearm.

I held the cut over the funnel and stared as my blood ran into it.

Chickoa drew forward, moaning in desperation as she watched my blood drip from my skin. Her fingers tightened on Fabian's as if they were the only thing stopping her from leaping at me.

As the bottle came close to filling, Magnar tore a strip from his shirt and drew me away, pressing it down over the wound.

"Thank you, Callie," Montana breathed and I nodded awkwardly.

The other vampires eyed what I'd given them as if they didn't think it was enough but Magnar glared at them and they didn't voice any objections.

Fabian passed the bottle to Chickoa first and she groaned as she lunged towards it.

I took Magnar's hand as I turned away from them, not wanting to watch as they devoured my blood.

There were some tins of food gathered on one of the tables and I dropped down before them hungrily. The cut on my forearm burned with pain and I sighed as I pulled a can of corn towards me. I just hoped that we would make it to the mountain soon because I wasn't sure I enjoyed being on the menu.

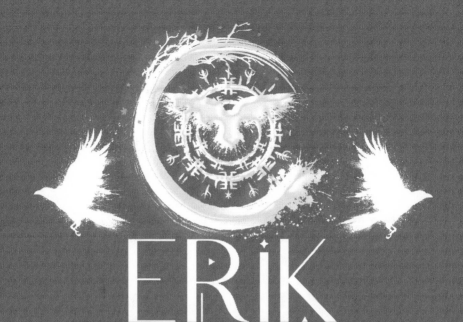

ERIK

CHAPTER EIGHTEEN

I'd had enough blood to sate my thirst at last. My body was antsy and flushed with adrenaline.

Fabian finally looked more like himself as he sank down on a chair with a relieved sigh. I moved to join him, dropping into a seat opposite as Montana moved to sit with Callie and Magnar.

"Better?" I asked and he nodded, his eyes bright.

The light in his eyes dimmed a little and I sensed there was something playing on his mind. "I'm glad to be back to myself again, but I feel like I'm weaker than everyone else. Magnar *just* turned and he's able to go without blood for longer than me. And now I've drunk Callie's blood, I feel like I've betrayed her trust. I promised to protect her, but I was on the verge of biting her earlier, Erik."

I frowned deeply, seeing the regret in him. "I think Callie is starting to understand how the bloodlust works now. She knows we're all struggling."

"But you don't lose your head, you manage to hold back," he hissed.

"You're doing fine, Fabian. You haven't bitten anyone," I said firmly and some of the tension eased from his posture.

"How are you holding up?" he asked and I could tell we weren't talking about the blood anymore.

I dropped my eyes, a knot growing in my chest at the memory of Miles and Warren's deaths. "Alright," I grunted, but I knew Fabian didn't buy it.

He shook his head, reaching out to lay a hand on my arm. "I know it sucks. It really fucking sucks, Erik, but you'll get through this. You've got so much to live for and Miles wouldn't want you to ruin it over this."

Guilt swelled inside me as his eyes drifted to Montana. I guessed my brother had noticed my cool front around her and I hated myself for it. Hated that I reacted this way when my emotions got too much.

"You're an idiot," he said on a breath. "Sort it out. Don't screw up the only good thing that's ever happened to you. Don't be like me."

He patted my arm, rising to his feet and beckoning Chickoa over. I frowned as I realised what he meant. He'd broken things between him and the woman he'd once loved. The woman he'd been going to marry. And losing Chickoa had devastated him. If I kept pushing Montana away, I was going to lose her too. And that thought didn't bear thinking about.

"I'm going to scout outside for Familiars, wanna join?" Fabian asked her and she nodded keenly. A flame of hope sparked inside me that maybe he could fix things with her...given time.

I rose to my feet with a sense of urgency rising in my veins. We didn't know how much time on Earth was left to us now. And I couldn't waste another second of it holding back from Montana.

I stole her away from Callie and Magnar and my heart clenched with what I wanted to do. I'd barely touched her since we'd left the farm. We'd hardly kissed. And when we had, a dark weight had hung between us.

I could see in her eyes how much she pitied me and I despised it. Every look was a reminder of what we'd lost. But I was done feeling out of control. I needed to regain some power and I wanted my wife to look at me like I wasn't broken again.

I guided her into a store under the guise of exploring, but the curious look in her gaze told me she had her suspicions. Maybe she sensed it. She was so tuned in to me, I wondered if she'd felt every inch of the pain I'd endured the past week. She'd stood by me through all of this bullshit. Every demand I'd made of her, every harsh word and every time I'd turned away from her. It had cut into her piece by piece. And I hated myself for the reaction I'd had to Miles's death.

But the words wouldn't come when I tried to make myself tell her why I acted like this. How it was the only way I'd ever dealt with my feelings. And if I couldn't tell her then maybe I could at least remind her that I still loved her. More dearly than anything in this world. And maybe it was making me act like a prick, but if being a prick kept her safe, then it was the easiest thing in the world to fall back on.

I eyed the hardware store we'd strolled into with a flicker of amusement. She took an aisle to the left and I took the one to the right, the shelving low enough that I could keep my gaze on her. I watched as rebel trailed her fingers over some of the tools, her hand brushing a saw, a hammer then an axe. Her movements captivated me and I remained quiet as I observed her, her eyes floating over the various objects she'd probably never seen in her life. *My fault.*

We reached the end of the aisle and she lifted her beautiful eyes to meet mine. Dark, endless, and filled with so much love that I could feel it pouring from her in waves.

She picked up a bow-saw with a slanted smile. "Did you bring me here to kill me, Erik?" she teased.

I chuckled darkly, taking the saw from her hand. "If I wanted to kill you, I wouldn't use this."

"What would you use?" she mused, turning her back on me as she wandered further into the store.

My gaze dropped to the curve of her ass and I padded after her as my jeans grew tighter in anticipation of all I wanted to do to her.

I picked up a nail gun from a shelf. "Maybe one of these. Quick and painless."

She spun around to eye the tool, her lips twisting with amusement. "How romantic."

"You know me, rebel." I shrugged and her eyes danced with light at the sound of her nickname on my lips. A weight fell over me as I focused on all of the shit I'd been putting her through recently. She deserved an apology. More than an apology. She deserved a better husband.

I placed the nail gun back on the shelf, stuffing my hands into my pockets. "I've fucked up," I said with a frown.

She fell still, waiting for me to continue.

"I know I've been...difficult lately."

She eyed me hopefully, folding her arms. "Go on."

I took a step toward her. "I've been an asshole."

"And?" she asked, looking desperate to hear what I had to say.

"And...I've let you down."

She dipped her head, inspecting her boots as if preparing what to say. My gut twisted as I waited, my heart not ready for what she was going to voice. Part of me wished she'd scream at me, hit me even. But she wasn't like that. She'd try to understand why I behaved the way I did. But I didn't want her to figure it out, because then maybe she'd realise this was a side of me that was never going away.

"You haven't let me down," she said firmly and my brows drew together as I waited for the ball to drop. "You've been through a lot. I get it."

"That doesn't excuse the way I've acted," I said harshly, then bit my tongue as the demon inside me reared up again. I ground my teeth, stepping forward to close the distance between us. The angry part of me thumped and wailed to be let out. I was tumbling out of control again and I needed to seize back an ounce of it or I'd go mad.

I pushed her back against the wall behind her, capturing her chin in my grip. She inhaled slowly, her pupils dilating as she waited for me to kiss her. Her lips were full and red and so tempting. She wasn't going to demand it of me. Not after all the times I'd brushed her off.

I skated my hand to her neck and held her firmly. Her throat bobbed beneath my palm and I felt myself hardening for her, demanding to take her.

I eyed a rack beside her, snatching a length of rope from it as I released her.

She shifted against the wall, her lips parted as she watched me. I beckoned her closer and she obeyed, drifting toward me with curiosity in her gaze.

"Hands up," I commanded and her eyes narrowed.

"Why?" she asked, surveying the rope in my hand.

My mouth pulled up at the corner. "Please," I added and she lifted her hands.

I tied her wrists, binding her to the metal rack above her head.

She quivered before me and I brushed my thumb against her bottom lip with a wanton groan. Her hips swayed with need and a thrill hit me at how much she was enjoying this.

I moved into her personal space and she tilted her chin toward me to try and tempt me into a kiss. I almost gave it to her, but a dark piece of me wanted to keep her like this. Needy and wanting. Completely at my mercy.

She bit into her lower lip and shifted closer again, pressing her body flush to mine. She aimed for a kiss once more and I smirked, leaning out of reach.

Her brows drew together sharply, but still she didn't beg me for it. I wanted that kiss as badly as her, but not as much as I wanted to withhold it.

She tugged at her hands and the rack trembled above her.

"Break free and I won't touch you," I growled and she stilled, eyeing me with a flicker of vulnerability.

I grazed my thumb down her cheek and she shivered from my touch, arching her back so her breasts brushed my chest. I cupped one in my hand, toying with her as I tugged her shirt down to release her from it. My mouth captured her nipple and she moaned loudly, her hips bucking as she tried to get nearer. My hand slid down her stomach until it was between her thighs and I rubbed against the thin yoga pants until she moaned. Still, she didn't beg me and a wave of frustration filled me.

"What do you want?" I demanded against her flesh.

"You...please," she gasped and the words were like music to my ears. I bit and sucked her skin until my fangs left reddened marks on her breasts. Her begging grew more frantic and her hips jerked hungrily to meet the strokes of my palm.

I removed my hand from between her thighs, lifting it to grip her throat instead. I dipped my head, the scent of her everywhere, invading my senses and almost making me want to forget about this damned game. But I was in control again. I'd seized back a single inch of power in my life and I didn't want to ever let it go.

Her lips parted and her eyes widened. She wanted that kiss. But I was going to make her work for it.

I teased the corner of her mouth, moving to her ear and nipping her sensitive flesh. Her hips thrust into mine more violently and a low laugh left my throat.

"Erik," she begged, but not breathily this time. More demanding. More angry.

That's how I feel, rebel.

I continued my torment, sucking and kissing her neck, keeping her in place with my other hand. She lifted her knee in an attempt to caress me, but I lurched backwards, releasing her throat.

"Asshole," she snapped, yanking against the rope. "Untie me."

"Behave and I'll give you what you want," I told her.

Her jaw ticked and that rebellious nature in her rose to the surface. She didn't want to play my game, but for some reason the war in her eyes lessened and she nodded stiffly, falling still.

I moved closer again, sliding my hand into her pants, my fingers trailing over her clit and circling in the wetness between her legs. She moaned, her head falling back as I drove two fingers inside her and pumped them slowly, watching her expression as she gave in to me. I had her right where I wanted her, pushing her towards bliss, then drawing her back again, not letting her have her climax. I slid my fingers in and out of her, then slicked them over her clit, circling and caressing until she was on the verge of ecstasy again. She cried out, bucking against her restraints and a twisted part of me got off on it as I pulled my hand away again.

Her eyes daggered onto me, accusing and full of ire. "Erik," she snarled. "Stop it."

I cocked my head, watching her fight her binds then sliding my hand out of her pants and lowering to my knees as I pulled them off of her. She kicked me as I ripped them from her along with her shoes, socks and panties and I released a dark laugh as I rose to my feet.

I met the gaze of my fiery little creature as she spewed a line of curses at me, but I only hooked one of her silken legs over my hip and shoved my pants down enough to free my throbbing cock.

"Don't stop this time," she growled as I lined myself up with her soaked pussy, the smile dropped from my face.

"I'm in charge," I warned her. "Surrender to me, rebel."

I drove my hips forward, filling her tight pussy with every inch of my cock and she cried out, her arms dragging at her restraints as my fingers gripped her hips, angling her just how I wanted her. I fucked her fast, making her take me just how I wanted it and she reared forward enough to drive her fangs into my shoulder in a vicious attempt to hurt me, but I relished the pain, fucking her even harder.

Her pussy started to clench around my cock, my girl clearly enjoying the rough way I took her, but before she could find release, I finished with a growl of delight, stilling inside her and fisting my hand in her hair as I stole a kiss from her lips. Then I pulled out of her, leaving her whimpering, desperate for more while I tucked myself away and readjusted my pants.

The evidence of my claiming of her coated her inner leg and she glared at me in utter fury while I savoured the high of my control over her.

"Untie me," she snarled.

"If you want to come, you need to behave," I warned.

"Fuck your game, Erik. I don't want your hands on me again. Let me go."

Those words cut through the bullshit game I was playing in an instant and I lunged forward, breaking the rope with my bare hands.

She shoved me away and grabbed her pants, pulling them on and storming across the store, leaving her shoes behind. Guilt crashed through my chest and I darted after her, beating her to the door and barring her way.

"Wait," I begged.

"Get out of my way," she hissed, trying to push me aside.

I caught her wrists and she ripped them free of my grip. "Don't touch me."

"Montana," I tried.

"I know you're going through some awful shit right now, Erik. But I won't be your fucking outlet."

Shame washed through me. I knew she was right. I was supposed to have been trying to make things up to her, but I'd fucked up again. I'd succumbed to this burning need inside me to regain power over the world and hurt her in the process.

She tried to move around me once more but I couldn't let her go. If she walked away now, I didn't know if she'd ever come back. "Please, just wait. I'm sorry, rebel. Let me make it right."

I reached for her and she slapped my hand away. "No, I've had enough. You want to wallow in this on your own? You want to punish the people who love you? Then fine, but I'm not going to be a part of it."

I stepped forward, needing to make this right.

Fuck! What have I done?

I'd screwed things up so royally, I didn't even know how to begin fixing it.

"Move," she demanded, but I shook my head, my heart fracturing, my soul coming apart.

I fell to my knees and wrapped my arms around her, pressing my forehead to her stomach. "I'm sorry – please— just wait a second."

Montana stiffened, gazing down at me in alarm. "Erik, stop," she demanded, trying to draw me to my feet.

I pulled her down before me and dragged her into my arms in a fierce embrace. "I don't know how to put this into words, but let me try. Please let me try." The irony didn't pass me by that I was now begging Montana for a moment in her company after I'd forced her to do the same to me.

She blinked away tears as she stared at me, shaking her head. "I'm trying to be here for you, but I can't. Not like this."

"I know, I *know*," I groaned, gripping her hand as I sat back on my heels.

She fell quiet, folding her legs beneath her, her expression taut as she waited for me to speak. She was giving me a chance. And I suspected it was my final one. So I had to give her everything I had. The darkest parts of me, the pain, the grief, the loss. And my response to it all.

"I just feel so..." I took a deep breath, trying to hold her gaze as I opened my heart to her. "Powerless."

She nodded slowly and I squeezed her hand, praying she'd hear me out on this. Though it was the last thing I deserved right now.

I dropped my eyes to my knees, emotion welling and welling until I knew it was going to spill over. There was nothing I could do to stop it. She was my rebel, my wife, my soulmate. And I owed her an explanation.

"When I was given this curse by Andvari...I lost who I was. I became a monster, I killed people I loved. And it happened over and over and over." Pain stung my heart as I relived what I'd done to my family when the thirst had gripped my body for the very first time. Montana remained quiet and I kept my eyes downcast. "When we claimed the New Empire, I swore to myself I'd never lose control again. That my family would never be hurt, never be hunted. And everything I've done since was in an effort to protect that vow." My brows pinched together as I readied to voice the rest of this. Every fucked up inch of me laid bare. "When I met you, I silently swore that you would fall under the protection I could offer. At first, I just wanted you because I was selfish. I wanted you because you gave me something to live for beyond the empire my family had built, even beyond breaking the curse. But then it was more than that and every day since it's been more still. Every day I've tried to keep you with me, keep you safe. And not just you, my family. The gods want this prophecy solved, though they're trying their damned hardest to make it the most difficult task on Earth. But I was happy to take it on, knowing everyone I loved was still safe. I'd actually let go for once. Relinquished control. I didn't need to hold everything together anymore. But when Miles died-" my voice cracked and Montana gripped my fingers reassuringly. "When the goddess destroyed him and his husband so easily, I realised how stupid I was for ever thinking we didn't need to be constantly prepared. That one split second couldn't crush everything I'd worked to protect." I shut my eyes, willing my soul to let out this anguish, because what was the point in holding it all in? It wasn't just hurting me, it was hurting *her*.

Montana crawled into my lap, wrapping herself around me in a loving embrace. I held her tightly, my heart finally finding some peace in this wretched situation.

"You're not in control," she said softly, running her hands down my back in soothing circles. "We don't get to control everything. That's life, Erik. Bad stuff happens. Awful people do awful things. And sometimes we can't do anything to stop it. We're not gods. And we can't see the future. I know you'll always protect me, and I'll protect you too. But we can't do more than that. We're just not able to."

I nodded against her shoulder, knowing she was right. That I had to accept that I couldn't always control my fate or anyone else's.

She linked her fingers around the back of my neck, pressing her forehead to mine. "I can't stand to see you killing yourself over something you never had any say in. We all could have made different decisions that night. But we didn't. We're here and half of us are still alive because of the sacrifices we made for each other. Any one of us could have died that night. And I'm so sorry it was your brother and his husband."

I let her words settle over me, giving in to her, every part of me unravelling like twine. I tilted my chin up to kiss her and she kissed me back with no judgment, no fear. Only love flowed between us. Pure and sweet and wholly innocent. Something a forsaken creature like me never should have known the taste of.

When she leant away, I felt reborn. My heart stitched back together in perhaps not quite the same way, but something stronger. Something that could face whatever fate would find us on this path. Good or bad. Together.

MAGNAR

CHAPTER NINETEEN

I lay in a large bed within the furniture store beside Callie, breathing in and out despite the fact that I didn't have to. But the scent of her skin washed over me with every inhalation and it was intoxicating. She was sleeping on me again and I was pretty sure I'd never grow tired of her doing so. I'd gotten some sleep the previous night and this new body of mine didn't need any more yet so I simply lay with her and enjoyed the peace between us while she rested.

It was a strange thing to lie there for hours and not feel the pull towards sleep. But it had given me plenty of time to turn over my thoughts on several things.

I was beginning to analyse some of the changes in my behaviour since my transformation. And Callie was right, I *was* more jealous, easier to anger and bordering on overly possessive of her. It was as though I was a slave to my instincts now, especially when the thirst was upon me. And a lot of those instincts revolved around Callie. I felt drawn to her, tied to her, I was at once protective of her and fiercely in awe of her.

But I needed to work harder to hold back on my impulses to shield her from the other members of our group. She was more than capable of speaking her own mind and I could see that my behaviour was bordering on overbearing already. I found it harder to resist those impulses than the call of her blood somehow. It was like I was hardwired to protect her and I saw countless threats against her at all times. Perhaps it was because of my newfound immortality. It wasn't something I'd asked for or ever wanted to keep. But it did highlight the fragility of her mortal flesh. And I couldn't bear for anything to happen to her.

The burning in my throat had been growing more desperate throughout the night. After the blood she'd sacrificed for the other vampires, I hadn't been able to bring myself to bite her before she'd fallen asleep even though she'd offered it. I needed it, ached for it, craved it like it was sunlight and I was lost in the dark.

But I hadn't succumbed.

She deserved to rest, at least one night before I had to drink from her again.

Callie flexed her arms, her fingers brushing against my cool flesh lightly and sending electricity racing across my skin. She rolled off of me with a yawn, turning her back on me and stealing the warmth of her skin as she went.

"Are you awake?" I asked hopefully, turning towards her and drawing a pattern along her side with my middle finger.

"No." She arched her back, pressing her body against mine and I released a dark laugh as my blood heated.

"Hmm, how about now?" I slid my hand under the oversized t-shirt she'd stolen from me to sleep in and brushed my fingers up her stomach and along the curve of her breast. A deep satisfaction filled my chest as I felt her nipple hardening beneath my touch and I continued my slow exploration of the curves of her body.

"Still sleeping," she breathed but she pushed her ass against me in defiance of her words and I smiled as I started kissing her neck.

The thirst rose in me like a tide and my vision darkened as I moved my lips against the silky skin beneath her ear. I fought it back as hard as I could, inhaling deeply as the scent of her filled me with a desperate longing.

I tugged on her nipple just a little and a soft gasp left her lips. She ground her ass against me again as my cock pressed firmly against her.

"I'll have to work harder to wake you up then," I murmured.

I explored the swell of her tits for a few more moments as her breathing grew ragged then slid my hand lower. I reached the top of her underwear and pushed my fingers beneath it as she took a sharp breath. I groaned longingly as I felt how wet she was for me, and she moved her ass against the hard length of my dick in demand. I grazed her earlobe with my teeth and she moaned as I started to move my hand against her clit.

"If you're sleeping then you should be quiet," I teased and she ground her body back against mine with a soft laugh.

"I'm awake now," she breathed, trying to turn in my arms but I held her in place as I continued to torment her. I could feel her body moving closer to the edge and I wasn't going to let her go until she toppled over it.

She pushed herself back into me more demandingly, sighing my name as I kept moving my hand.

I ran my tongue along the length of her neck and she groaned again, her hand fisting in the sheets. I could hear her pulse pounding beneath her flesh and my fangs brushed her neck as the temptation to bite her grew and grew. I needed it like she needed air to breathe but I refused to give in to it yet.

My body ached for hers with the same level of desperation as my bloodlust and I was overwhelmed by the two desires she woke in me. Callie ground herself against me again and I growled hungrily for everything this woman in my arms could offer me.

"Just take me," she begged and I laughed darkly, refusing to give in to her demand while revelling in the fact that she was as eager for me as I was for her.

"You'll make too much noise," I protested in a whisper.

"I won't," she said. I drove my fingers down more firmly and a breathy moan escaped her lips as I proved her wrong.

I could feel her body tensing as she kept writhing in my arms. I was pushing her closer and closer to her climax and her breaths came faster as her body begged me to continue. My own arousal grew in time with hers and I had to fight hard against the urge to take this further just yet. I wanted to wring every inch of pleasure from her body and I intended to take my time in doing it.

Her heartbeat pounded so intensely that I could feel it where my chest was pressed against her back. It was almost like I could feel my own heart moving in response, driven on by the urge to be with hers. The heat of her body filled me with life and I was clinging to her like she was a raft in a sea of all that was wrong with this world.

Callie ground herself against me even more forcefully and I drove my fingers down harder, groaning as her body finally fell apart beneath my touch. She turned her head into the pillow and cried out in bliss as I finished her.

I smiled as I withdrew my hand from her underwear and turned her in my arms so that I could kiss her.

She reached up, twisting her arms around my neck as I pushed her down into the soft mattress and kissed her fiercely.

I could feel her heart pounding as I pressed my weight down onto her warm body and she kissed me harder, clearly not done with me yet.

Her hands moved over my shoulders and skimmed along my back, leaving a line of fire in their wake. She reached the waistband of my boxers and tried to push them off.

I stopped kissing her for a moment and looked down at the beauty of her face. Her blue eyes were alight with desire and I was achingly tempted to give her what she wanted.

"I love you," I breathed as I took in the heated look in her gaze.

Callie bit her bottom lip, holding back a smile and removed her hands from my back so that she could trail them down my chest. My body tensed beneath her touch and a mischievous grin lit her face.

"I think you're getting too used to having me at your mercy," she breathed, her eyes glimmering with promise as her fingertips carved a burning trail across my cool flesh.

She caught my arm and used her gifts to push me away suddenly so that I fell onto my back beside her. I laughed in surprise as she took control and climbed on top of me, smiling wickedly as she leaned down to kiss me. I pushed my hands into her golden hair and held her close, devouring the way her mouth moved against mine.

My fingers brushed along her neck and I could feel her pulse hammering beneath her skin, calling to me like a promise on the wind. I ached to take her blood but this moment of longing before I succumbed to it was the sweetest kind of pain.

She shifted her head and ran her lips along my jaw and down my neck, advancing slowly as my desire for her grew. She dragged her teeth across my throat, nipping at my flesh in an imitation of what I wanted to do to her. My muscles tensed in anticipation of each kiss that she placed on my skin as she dropped lower, her lips carving a line down the centre of my body.

I couldn't believe that this girl was mine. She was everything I'd ever dreamed of having in all the darkest days of my past. She was light and laughter and the promise of a better life. It was like she'd found all the fractured pieces of my battered soul and had wound herself between them, fusing them together again and making me into a better man. Perhaps even a man who was deserving of a love like hers. And if I wasn't, then I was going to be. I wanted to be worthy of her more than anything. And I'd spend every day of the rest of my life trying to prove that I could be just as soon as we'd broken this curse.

Callie shifted lower, her kisses lighting a fire of desire which flooded through me as her lips moved across my stomach and she hooked her fingers into the waistband of my underwear.

"Callie," I breathed in protest and her name was like a prayer on my lips as I half warned her to stop and half begged her to continue.

"Shh," she breathed with a laugh as she grazed my flesh with her teeth. "You're supposed to be the quiet one."

She didn't stop and any protests I might have voiced died on their way to my lips as she pulled my underwear off of me and moved beneath the covers.

She took my cock into her mouth and my hands fisted in the sheets as every muscle in my body tensed in anticipation of the pleasure she was driving me toward.

"Holy shit," I breathed as she took possession of my body and I had to battle against the urge to cry out as she hummed darkly, vibrations rolling through my cock.

I gave in to her, releasing all control as she drove me closer to the edge, taking my dick to the back of her throat then wrapping her tongue around it as she withdrew. I wanted so badly to come in her pretty mouth, to watch her devour me and bring me to ruin but I needed more from her and the fire in my throat was desperate to be sated too.

I caught her wrist with a growl of desire and dragged her back up to kiss me again. I flipped her beneath me, ripping the black t-shirt off of her so that I could see every inch of her flesh.

She reached for me and the heat of her skin almost burned against mine.

I leaned forward to kiss her, pulling her underwear off as I moved between her thighs.

Her lips were soft and compelling against mine and I lost myself to her kisses, holding back on taking that final pleasure from her flesh for just a few more moments.

Her hands trailed over my shoulders, running down my arms before gripping me tightly and urging me on.

My throat burned for her but the rest of my body did too and I wanted all of it. All of her.

I caught her wrists and pinned them above her head as I drove myself inside her.

She cried out as I pushed the full length of my cock into her body with a savage thrust which stole her breath and she arched off of the bed, pressing her chest to my skin.

Her hips moved in time with mine, begging me to keep going as her muscles tightened around me.

I kissed her again, devouring her desire as I drove myself into her again and again and my own release simmered on the horizon, drawing me against her more and more firmly.

She drew her lips away from mine, tilting her chin and giving me access to the pounding pulse in her neck.

I groaned as I ran my mouth across the flesh she was offering, inhaling deeply as her blood called to me and the thirst rose like an angry beast demanding to be satisfied.

She shuddered beneath me as I grazed my fangs along her skin and it was hard to believe she wanted this as much as I did.

"Magnar," she moaned while I fucked her harder and the last of my resistance crumbled to ash as I drove my fangs into her neck.

Her blood swept into me on a tide of pleasure and I tightened my grip on her wrists as I drove my cock into her harder, faster, stealing everything from her body at once.

She cried out as I drew every inch of pleasure from her body, forcing an orgasm from her and I kept going as she shuddered beneath me, arching into me as I drew closer to the edge myself.

She was everywhere, everything, her blood flooding my veins like it was my own and her scent overwhelming me as I drank more and more. I would never get enough, I could drink every last drop and I wasn't sure if it would satisfy me.

I growled as I fell into my own climax and I forced my fangs from her flesh as my love for her drove aside the desire to take more than I needed.

I moved my mouth back to hers, releasing my grip on her wrists and running my fingers down the soft skin of her arms.

She sighed in satisfaction as she kissed me, her lips soft and hungry as she reached up to brush her fingers across the stubble lining my jaw.

I looked down at her, my heart filled with love for this woman who was mine. There was no better place in the world than lying here in her arms.

"We should go," she breathed though she made no move to leave. "The others will be looking for us soon."

"Perhaps our luck will hold and they won't find us," I murmured and she laughed softly.

We'd agreed to get going as soon as possible this morning and I knew I was holding onto this brief window of peace before we had to press on and increase the gap between us and Valentina again. But I treasured every moment in her arms and relinquishing even one of them pained me.

She looked up at me with a knowing smile and I started toying with her golden hair.

"Maybe I should offer to feed the others again before we head off," she said hesitantly and I stilled, releasing my hold on her hair.

"No. You've given them enough for now," I growled.

"Well either way, we need to move," she replied, pushing on my chest in an attempt to force me back.

She wasn't strong enough to make me move even with her gifts and she frowned at me as I resisted. I sighed dramatically and rolled aside so that she could get out of the bed.

I watched her dressing in the new clothes she'd found for herself and reluctantly pulled my own clothes on too. The grey t-shirt strained a little across my muscles but it was a better fit than a lot of what I'd worn since waking in this time.

I buckled my belt and retrieved my swords from the floor, following Callie out into the dim mall.

She led the way back to the food court where we found the others waiting for us.

They were sorting through a huge mound of things that they'd gathered from the various stores while Callie and Julius got some sleep. I moved towards my brother as he spooned food into his mouth from a packet. He had two neat cuts on his wrists which had almost healed over thanks to his gifts. I sighed as I took a seat beside him, wondering how the two greatest vampire hunters in history could have ended up in this situation. One of us feeding from the woman he loved and the other handing out blood to the monsters he'd pledged his life to destroying.

"We found a store filled with camping equipment," Clarice explained as Callie drew closer to her, eyeing the stash they'd collected with interest. "There are sleeping bags and enough packets of dehydrated food for you and Julius to survive on for weeks."

"That's great," Callie replied with a smile.

"Yes, it's perfect that two members of our group are so well fed," Fabian replied irritably. "Or should I say three?" he asked as his gaze travelled to me and I stilled under his scrutiny. I knew Callie had given me far more blood than she'd offered them last night but I couldn't do much about that and I didn't exactly feel bad about it either.

"Do you need more?" Callie asked, thumbing the bandage on her arm. "Already?"

Erik shifted uncomfortably and Clarice exchanged a glance with Chickoa. Montana was the only vampire who didn't seem desperate to say yes.

Fabian eyed the bloody bandage on her arm, seeming to reconsider his request. She didn't even have the gifts of my clan to help her heal from the injury and I ground my teeth at the idea of her doing that again.

"I don't wish to harm you," he murmured, looking at Callie in a way which made me want to rip his eyes from his face. "If you cut yourself every time you offer us your blood then you're going to be covered in injuries before long."

Callie's gaze shifted to me uncomfortably. "The bites hurt too," she said with a shrug. "Except when Magnar does it."

Fabian rolled his eyes and Clarice smiled knowingly as Erik cleared his throat.

"Well if you want me to bite you like *that* then I won't hurt you either,"

Fabian said suggestively.

"What do you mean?" Montana asked with a frown.

Erik gave me an amused look before he replied. "We don't release any venom when we bite if we're in the middle of taking other kinds of pleasure at the time," he explained.

Julius released a bark of laughter, thumping me on the arm and I couldn't quite keep the smirk from my face either. Callie's cheeks flushed as she realised what she'd just admitted to and Montana started laughing as well.

"Oh well...I'll just cut myself again then," Callie said, refusing to acknowledge what she'd just learned.

"Not today," I said firmly and the vampires' eyes all turned to me.

"My brother is right," Julius agreed. "Our blood is meant to sustain our own bodies, if you expect it to sustain yours too then fine. But it will be on our terms. You can have more tomorrow when we stop to make camp. If that's not good enough for you then you can try to take it from us."

"And I'll be standing beside them," I growled in case that wasn't clear.

The vampires nodded in agreement and some of the tension left my body as I moved to help them pack up the supplies they'd found. It wasn't a perfect solution but it would have to do. I just hoped we'd make it to the mountain before their hunger became too intense.

"We still need to grab the tents," Erik said, looking over at me as he started to move away.

I rose from my chair to join him, my gaze lingering on Fabian as Callie started to help him pack supplies into a bag.

I almost wanted to tell him to move away from her but I ground my teeth against the impulse and followed Erik into the dark corridors instead.

We walked along in silence for a while until the sound of the others talking was lost to us.

"You and Callie seem to have found a way to handle your transformation well," Erik said.

"I owe her everything," I replied. "If it wasn't for her I would have taken my life when this curse was placed upon me but she makes it somehow... bearable."

"Bearable? Is that what you call the way she feeds you?" he taunted and I couldn't help but laugh.

"She seduced me into it," I protested weakly but it was obvious that I didn't feel as much guilt over our situation as I should have.

"The things we do for love," he murmured and I nodded in agreement. I wouldn't have dealt with any of this well if it wasn't for Callie and the effect she had on me was undeniable. It was hard for me to imagine the selfish way I'd lived my life before she'd come along.

"She has some objections to some of my behaviour since I was turned," I said, voicing the issues that I'd been mulling over while she slept.

Erik raised an eyebrow at me, encouraging me to go on and I frowned as I realised I was opening up to the man who had been my enemy for most of my life. But I didn't see him like that now; the time we'd spent together under Valentina's spell had bonded us in a way I couldn't quite describe and ever since then I'd found it impossible to summon any hatred towards him.

"I was never a particularly jealous man before this. But now I find myself bordering on violence every time another man looks at her for too long and if they touch her-"

"Many of my people have taken mates over my lifetime and I saw that kind of behaviour time and again. Until recently I didn't understand it; I didn't think I could feel love like that in this form, but since I found Montana that changed. I would do anything to protect her, I'd die for her... When she left me to go with you after our wedding I felt like she'd ripped my heart out and taken it with her. And the idea of her spending nights with your brother and you out in the ruins-"

"You had nothing to fear there," I replied. "Her heart was always yours and there was never any doubt in it."

Erik looked up at me and I felt like he wanted to say something else but he released a heavy breath and led the way into the camping store instead.

"Just as you have nothing to fear from Fabian," he said as he began to pass the tents to me, piling them into my arms. I frowned at the rolls of synthetic material which were nothing like the tents I'd slept in with my clan but kept my mind on the conversation at hand.

"I know that Callie has no interest in him," I said. "But I was there at the wedding, I saw what that mark forced her to do. I know how the thoughts of him were sewn into her mind so that she was left struggling to understand her own feelings and I didn't exactly react to that in the best way at the time. I

166

made mistakes. I treated her badly and I regret it more than I can say but *he* didn't even try to fight that mark. He made it harder for her, he pursued her and-" I could feel my anger building again as I thought back on it and I forced myself to take a deep breath before I let it take control of me.

"Fabian spent a thousand years as one of the most powerful creatures on Earth," Erik replied. "He had his pick of any woman he wanted and he never really cared about any of them aside from Chickoa. I think he'd forgotten what love felt like and when Idun offered it to him, he wanted to take it. But now that Chickoa is here I think he's realised that what he felt for Callie wasn't real. Just as the things Valentina made us feel for her pale into insignificance next to the twins."

My jaw ticked at that and I couldn't help but admit that he was right. Callie didn't hold me accountable for what that bitch had made me do with that necklace and I guessed I should have tried to be more understanding about Fabian's situation too.

"It's easier to think clearly when I'm well fed," I admitted.

"The thirst makes everything harder," Erik sighed, rubbing at his throat. "It makes us act more like beasts than men."

I ran my tongue over my fangs as I was forced to admit that the evil I'd always seen in the vampires had never really been in them at all. It was the curse and the gods who had created it who were deserving of my hatred; not the people caught in its grasp.

"I have killed countless numbers of your kind," I murmured. "I thought of you all as evil, undeserving of any form of life after death..."

Erik gripped my arm as he looked at me. "And I have done the same to your people. We demonised you as you demonised us but now we stand united against our true enemies and we will end this curse together."

"The most powerful creatures in existence united at last," I replied with a dark smile. "May the gods have mercy on anyone who dares stand against us now."

MONTANA

CHAPTER TWENTY

We travelled on as quickly as we could for another few days until we reached the mountain range Andvari's ring had shown us. We'd finally left the ruins behind and the world was greener here, having escaped the onslaught of bombs in the Final War. In the past weeks, I'd seen more of the world than I ever had in my life. But nothing compared to seeing the expanse of nature before me now, lush and green and rolling on forever.

We still had a long way to go before we reached the holy mountain and we were constantly looking over our shoulders, expecting Valentina to catch up at any moment. But from what we could piece together from the ring and what the vampires knew of our destination, we were still a week or more away from it.

We headed off of the road, taking a direct path across rocky hills as we moved higher and higher into the mountains. Soon, we were forced to walk single file along a narrow track that weaved between tall rock faces either side of us. The clouds were thickening and rain speckled my cheeks as we walked ever on.

I'd not had nearly enough blood in the last few days to fully diminish the ache in my throat and I was sure the other vampires felt the same. We maintained a steady pace, never pushing ourselves too hard, but with the difficult road across these mountains, it was likely we'd be depleted by the time we reached the other side. The only comfort we had was that Valentina wouldn't be able to land her helicopter up here if she located us.

The track widened a little as we scaled a steep hill and someone bumped shoulders with me as they moved forward. I glanced up to find Julius beside me, the sound of his thumping pulse making me nearly groan with hunger. His breathing was growing heavier. We'd laboured on all day into these mountains without a moment's rest.

"Break?" I murmured, but he shook his head firmly.

"No need," he mumbled.

I glanced over my shoulder at Callie, panting as she hurried to catch up, and the strain in her expression was all I needed to see to make my decision.

"Let's take a break!" I called out to the group.

Julius didn't refuse again as he dropped down onto a boulder and took a bottle of water from his pack, passing another one to Callie. They gulped them down as the vampires moved to perch on the rocks in the area, statuesque in a way that highlighted our inhuman nature.

Julius took out a couple of dehydrated bars of food for him and Callie, and my sister fell on one ravenously. I frowned, hating how much this journey was putting on the slayers. They not only had to support themselves, but they had to feed us too. I still refused to drink Callie's blood, taking as little as possible of the blood Julius drained for us into bottles. I found it easier not to lose my mind when I drank by keeping him and Callie pictured in my head.

Besides, the less I took the more there was for Fabian who always seemed on the edge of going psycho and biting one of them. The hungrier he got, the more he fell back on his asshole ways. But Magnar kept a constant eye on him to make sure he never acted on his impulses. I knew it wasn't really Fabian's fault, but his swinging moods set all of us on edge.

The rain turned to sleet and everyone groaned their misery. Callie pulled her coat tighter around her but it was clear she was shivering beneath it. I might not have been able to feel the cold, but there was nothing enjoyable about this, and now our visibility would be reduced along the next trail.

"I hate this mountain." Fabian kicked a rock and it slammed into a cliff face, breaking a huge chunk off of it. His posture was stiff as he started stalking back and forth in front of Chickoa. She reached for his hand to stop him and he stilled, eyeing their fingers as he gripped her palm. She quickly pulled away again, looking down the path.

Thunder cracked overhead and I shuddered, thinking of Valentina. But I didn't think there was much chance of her trekking all the way up into this mountain range.

The sleet grew more persistent and Julius and Callie rose to their feet.

"Better get moving," Callie said, bobbing up and down on her heels to try and coax some warmth into her body.

I dropped my pack, unzipping it and taking out a scarf I'd taken from a store back at the mall. It was thick and made of cream wool. I'd only really taken it out of sentiment, knowing I would have longed for something like it in the Realm. I moved toward my sister and wound it around her neck. Her eyes lit up as she beamed, brushing her fingers over the soft, dry material.

"Thanks, Monty," she said, tucking the bottom of it into her coat.

I nodded, giving her an encouraging smile as we all started walking again. Magnar and Erik took the lead as usual, the two of them often spending the days together at the front of the group, their newfound bond obvious even if they never put a voice to it.

The path wound higher and higher and as we rose onto an exposed track with a sheer drop to our left, the wind started to batter us. I squinted against the fog of sleet and rain as we trekked ever on. Each footfall had to be carefully placed as the path grew narrower and I eyed the drop below us with my gut churning. Vampire or not, I did *not* want to fall down there and hit those sharp rocks.

We finally made it away from the frightening drop where two paths lay before us. One that continued up and another that led down to the east.

We moved closer as a group and Julius placed an arm across Callie's shoulders as we huddled together. The fog was thickening and it would be too easy to lose each other in it if we strayed away from one another.

The battering sleet had soaked Callie's hair and the scarf I'd given her was already drenched. We looked like the strangest group ever with Julius and Callie bundled up and the rest of us just in sweaters and jeans which were now thoroughly wet.

"They can't take much more of this," Erik said, nodding to Callie and Julius.

"I'm fine," Callie said through chattering teeth.

"You're not," Magnar growled, protectiveness flaring in his gaze.

"You'll get hypothermia before we ever get off this mountain," Fabian agreed, his brow creased with concern.

My stomach knotted as I looked between the two of them, fearing what would happen if we didn't find somewhere dry where we could build a fire and pitch the tents soon.

"I say we get down from here," Erik said, eyeing the path that descended away to our left. "We can head east for a while and pass these mountains via the coast."

"It's quicker to go straight over," Callie said firmly, but Magnar shook his head.

"What point is speed if you're dead before we reach the other side?" he insisted and Callie nodded in defeat.

"East then," Clarice said, pointing to the path we needed to take and we hurried on in that direction.

After a mile of travelling down the steep decline, the fog lifted a fraction and the sleet turned to a drizzle of rain. I eyed Callie and she looked decidedly better already. I relaxed a little, glad of the choice we'd made. It was hard to judge the level at which the slayers could cope. My skin didn't feel the bite of the cold and though I'd not been a vampire long, it was becoming more difficult to recall exactly what that kind of discomfort felt like.

The track brought us down to a cliff that rose high up above us. Water cascaded off of it and Julius hurried forward to fill the water bottles from the falling streams.

Trees gathered at the edge of the wide clearing, giving us shelter from the wind. The sky was growing darker and I wondered if the sun was close to setting, but it was hard to tell what time of day it was through the thick clouds.

I moved to join Erik as he dropped to the ground, sitting down beside him. He pushed a damp lock of hair away from my face with a comforting smile and his fingers left a tingle of electricity in their wake. I took his hand, placing a kiss on each of his knuckles in turn and he watched me closely.

"How hungry are you?" he asked in a low whisper so only I could hear.

"I'm alright," I promised, rubbing my throat. "It's not terrible."

"Not terrible isn't alright," he said with an edge to his voice.

I turned to look at Callie across the clearing as she took shelter under a tree, pulling off her coat and swapping the damp sweater beneath it for a new one from her pack. I spotted the bandages on her arms from where she'd cut herself to feed everyone and my heart went out to her.

We have to break this damn curse.

"I'm fine, Erik," I pressed, leaning against his shoulder and drinking in the small moment of peace.

He placed a kiss on my head and I sighed, happy that we'd worked through our issues at last. His demeanour had vastly improved since we'd talked about his feelings and I felt closer to him than I ever had.

Julius returned from collecting water, dropping down in front of us and Clarice moved to join him. His eyes slid over her and a burning intensity filled his gaze. I shot a glance at Magnar as he headed over to Callie then gave Julius and Clarice a bemused look.

"So Magnar still doesn't know about the two of you kissing, right?" I teased, wanting to focus on something good for a change. Both of their expressions in response to my words told me they didn't think there was anything good about it.

"No," Julius hissed. "And he's not going to find out."

"You're admitting it now at least," Erik said with a smirk.

Clarice rolled her eyes. "It was just a kiss, not a fucking marriage proposal. We were drunk."

Julius nodded his agreement, the two of them working hard not to look at each other.

"Magnar couldn't exactly blame you now, considering he's one of us," Erik said with a shrug. "I don't see why you're so uptight about it. Anyone can see you're obsessed with each other."

Julius's mouth fell open and Clarice folded her arms, shaking her head.

"*Obsessed?*" Julius balked. "I don't get obsessed with any girl. Especially not a parasite."

Clarice shifted away from him, a flicker of hurt passing through her eyes then vanishing as quickly as it had arrived.

Julius pressed his lips together and I sensed he felt guilty over the remark but he was too proud to apologise.

"Slayers are repulsive," Clarice said blandly and Julius's frown deepened.

"We could die out here," I said, looking between the two of them. "I just don't see the point in having regrets."

"There's nothing to regret, Montana," Julius said with a scowl. "And I'll ask you to stay out of my business."

"Oh but you had plenty to say on the matter when you first learned I was with Erik. You even told my sister about it before I was ready," I said, trying not to let too much anger into my voice. I didn't want an argument; I'd only meant to let them know they shouldn't have to hide it if they cared about one another. What was the point in it? Magnar was a vampire now anyway, he could hardly object if Julius declared his feelings for Clarice.

Julius's brow furrowed heavily. "I didn't mean to do that."

Silence fell and Clarice got up and walked away, joining Fabian and Chickoa who stood at the edge of the trees.

Julius fiddled with a pebble on the ground, looking sullen.

"Love doesn't come around very often in life," Erik said and I turned to him, my heart softening at his words. "If you think there's even a chance of having that with my sister, take it, Julius. You'll only hate yourself if you don't."

Julius glanced up, a vulnerability glowing in his gaze. "I'm a slayer," he said, his voice broken.

"We're all just people," I said gently. "You must have realised that by now."

Julius glanced past us towards Clarice, a decision growing in his eyes. "You really think she might...that she..." He gave us an intense look, not finding the words.

"Yes," Erik and I answered together.

Julius rose to his feet, patting down his jeans, clearly deciding what to do.

"Do you think we should pitch the tents here for the night?" I asked Erik.

A howl sliced through the air and Erik sprang upright so fast that a wind gusted around me. I jumped up after him, my gut constricting as I turned my eyes to the shadows between the trees.

"Familiars!" Callie called, racing toward our group with Fury in her hand.

"Into the trees!" Magnar bellowed. "Don't let them catch us in this clearing!"

174

CALLIE

CHAPTER TWENTY ONE

I ran to my sister's side as we dove into the cover of the forest and Fury screamed warnings in my mind. I'd never known the blade to get so worked up about Familiars before and a deep dread pooled in my gut as I sensed that something was really wrong.

Erik and Magnar moved together, waiting for the rest of us to go on ahead before following at the rear of the group to protect us.

Montana caught my hand and we started running. I couldn't match her pace but she pulled on my arm, urging me to move faster as we ran down the steep hill.

I glanced over my shoulder, trying to spot the others but I'd lost sight of everyone within the trees.

My heart hammered in panic as we ran on and I stumbled as the ground sloped away at an impossible angle.

I gasped as I tripped over my frozen feet, colliding with my sister and knocking the two of us to the forest floor. She cried out as we started rolling and I wrapped my arms around my head.

My limbs tangled with Montana's as the rocks beneath us battered my bones and the world was reduced to a spinning whirlwind around me.

We slammed to a halt and pain raced through my body as I crashed into

Montana.

She screamed in agony as she took the brunt of our collision and I rolled away from her in panic as I looked up at the huge tree we'd crashed into.

Montana hissed as her body fought to heal the devastating wound to her spine where she lay twisted against the towering trunk.

"It's okay, Monty!" I breathed, fighting off the pain of my own injuries as I hurried to help her.

I dragged her away from the tree as her legs failed to move and her face scrunched in pain at the horrific injury.

I rearranged her legs so that they lay straight and tears glimmered across my vision as she cried out, squeezing her eyes shut.

I leaned over her, gripping her hand as the pain of my own injuries clamoured for my attention.

Something wet stained my cheek and I raised a trembling hand to my face as a drop of my blood fell between us, landing on her chin.

Montana gasped, her nostrils flaring as her eyes snapped open and a savage hunger filled her expression.

"Get back!" she warned, slamming a palm into my chest and knocking me off of her as she scrambled away on her elbows. I fell back on my ass into a heap of brown leaves from the force of her shove but I pushed myself back to my knees quickly.

"It's okay, Monty," I insisted as she groaned in pain, her body healing slower than it should have.

She needed blood and my veins were full of it. I wasn't going to see her suffer when I held the answer just beneath my skin.

"It's not," she wailed desperately, her gaze flicking from my eyes to the wound on my cheek to my eyes again as she fought against the hunger which battled to claim her.

A chorus of animal howls started up through the trees and I looked about desperately, realising I'd lost Fury in my fall.

"This isn't a negotiation," I snarled as I scrambled towards her.

Montana shook her head desperately as I moved to kneel before her. "Please don't make me, Callie, I can't bear it if I-"

"We shared a womb, Monty," I snapped. "My blood is yours anyway."

She reached out to warn me back but I batted her arm aside with the aid of my gifts before pressing my wrist to her mouth.

Montana clenched her teeth, tears squeezing from her eyes as she fought off the desire to bite me with all of her might.

The howling came again. Closer this time.

"*Now,* Monty," I urged.

A sob escaped her lips before her fangs burrowed into my flesh.

I gritted my teeth, refusing to so much as flinch as her venom washed into my veins and fire flamed under my skin.

The next sound to escape her was a moan of longing as she grabbed my arm with both hands, holding me against her as she drank with the desperation of a starving soul.

Another tear slipped from her eye and I reached forward to brush it aside, her skin cool against the pad of my thumb.

"It's okay, Monty," I breathed as she drew more and more of my blood from my body into hers. "I'd do anything for you."

A guttural snarl sounded far too close to us for my liking and I twisted my head around as I tried to search for the source of it.

Montana didn't seem to have noticed as she continued to feed, lost to the bloodlust of her kind. But I didn't pull my arm away. I trusted her just like I trusted Magnar. She'd stop when she'd had enough. She wouldn't take too much.

A huge crash sounded between the trees and branches broke as heavy footsteps pounded towards us. Something big was heading right for us and my heart leapt as I scoured the hillside for my blade.

Montana released me suddenly, springing to her feet with lithe fluidity just as a lumbering black shape burst between the trees.

My lips parted in horror as the huge bear bellowed aggressively and I scrambled upright, fighting against a wave of dizziness as I stood too quickly.

Montana hissed like a cat, dropping into a fighting stance as she snatched Nightmare from her hip.

The bear's eyes were two black pits of hell where a vampire had taken root in the place that used to house its soul. I had no doubt that Valentina was the one responsible for creating this monster and fear trickled down my spine while it swung its gaze between me and my sister as it tried to decide on which of us to attack first.

The howls of the other Familiars carried between the trees again and adrenaline trickled through my limbs.

Montana didn't give the bear the option of picking between us as she sprang forward in a blur of motion with Nightmare aimed straight for its throat.

The bear roared, spittle flying as it stood on its hind legs, swinging a thick paw at my sister's head.

Montana managed to avoid the blow, swiping her blade across the bear's shoulder as she twisted aside.

I ran to help, ducking beneath the bear's paws and aiming a kick at its chest, hoping to break its ribs with my enhanced muscles.

The bear roared, rounding on me and lunging for me with its jaws wide.

Montana leapt onto its back, wrapping an arm around its thick neck as she drove her blade between its shoulders.

The bear bellowed, swinging around to try and dislodge her and it slammed into me, knocking me aside.

I tumbled through broken branches and fallen leaves and something hot brushed against my fingers.

I smiled savagely as I grabbed Fury and leapt to my feet again, shaking my head to clear it as darkness momentarily curtained my vision.

Montana was still clinging on, stabbing the bear again and again as the possessed creature bellowed in rage and fought to throw her off.

It reared back onto its hind legs and I darted towards it, releasing a battle cry as I slammed Fury upward with all of my might.

The blade sang with joy as it found the animal's heart and Montana fell on top of me as the creature exploded into ash.

I released a laugh of surprise as Monty wrapped her arms around me and I hugged her fiercely in return.

"I'm so sorry I had to bite you," she breathed.

"I'm not if it means I can hug you again," I replied as I crushed her in my arms. "Besides, I was the one who broke your back in that fall."

"You're definitely heavier than you used to be," she agreed with a chuckle.

More howling picked up between the trees and I released her as our moment of victory paled into terror again.

"We need to get off of this mountain," Montana breathed. "Everyone else will have continued down the trail."

I nodded my agreement as I concentrated on Fury's sense of the world around us. It was still casting warnings about Familiars but none seemed to be too close to us in that moment.

"Come on then."

We ran through the trees until we found the trail which led through the mountain pass and started down it as quickly as we could manage without risking another fall.

The sound of coyotes howling was echoing off of the steep rock faces all around us and it was impossible to tell how close they might be.

We rounded a sharp corner and I stumbled to a halt as Montana grabbed my hand.

A pack of twelve huge coyotes stood barring the pass. Their teeth were on display as they snarled and saliva dripped from their jaws. Their eyes lit with the excitement of the vampires who were controlling them as they spotted us and my heart plummeted in fear.

I took a step back then another as the earth started trembling beneath my feet.

Montana gasped as she almost fell and the coyotes sprang forward. But before they could close the distance to us, the rumbling grew louder and the ground split apart beneath them.

The pack howled as they plummeted into the huge crater that had opened up in the ground and my mouth dropped open as Erik ran out of the trees and sagged to his knees on the far side of it, drained by the use of his powers.

The wind trailed through my hair, pulling it downhill towards him and his gaze snapped up, filled with a desperate hunger as my scent washed over him.

"Erik," Montana begged, moving before me as he leapt to his feet, the thirst clawing against his self-control.

Magnar sprinted out of the trees, his shirt half shredded from his encounter with the Familiars. He snarled a warning at Erik as he slammed into him, immobilising him before he could approach me.

More howling echoed along the pass behind us and I looked around in fear as the Familiars came for us again.

"We have to jump," I breathed, eyeing the chasm before us.

Montana nodded fearfully, taking my hand as we raced towards the edge.

My boot hit the lip of the newly formed gouge in the ground and I propelled myself into the air with my sister at my side.

My stomach swooped as I looked down at the unending drop beneath us and we soared across the chasm.

We crashed to the ground before Magnar and Erik and I released her hand as I rolled to absorb the impact of my landing.

Magnar held Erik against the rock face as the hunger burned in his eyes and I scrambled forward, holding my wrist out for him.

Magnar snarled angrily but he didn't stop me from presenting my flesh to the man my sister loved. Erik's eyes met mine for half a second before his fangs pierced my skin and I could sense the regret he felt at what he was doing to me.

He swallowed deeply as the seconds dragged on, gripping my arm and holding it so tightly it hurt. I could feel the blood being pulled from my body in a way that made my head spin.

A soft whimper escaped my lips and Magnar ripped him off of me instantly, throwing him back with a growl of rage.

Erik hissed, dropping into an aggressive stance as he regained his feet and Montana shot towards him, holding a hand out in an attempt to subdue him.

My breath caught in my throat as Erik and Magnar faced off as if they were enemies again for a moment and I felt like I was transported back in time.

The urge to feed slowly slipped from Erik's gaze and he shook his head to fight off the last of the bloodlust.

"Thank you," he breathed, his eyes on me.

Magnar's posture relaxed slightly and he pulled me under his arm.

"It's fine," I replied though the burning in my wrist was now almost unbearable.

I rubbed at the two bite marks on my skin as I tried to remove the venom and Erik quickly pulled a bottle of water from his pack, tossing it to me so that I could wash the wounds. I fumbled as I tried to catch it and Magnar snatched it from the air a moment before it could hit the ground.

He released a heavy breath and twisted the cap off before cleaning the bites for me gently. Relief found me as the pain subsided and I took a quick drink from the remaining water.

"The others are ahead of us," Erik said as he eyed me with concern. "We need to go."

I took a step forward but I stumbled as I did so. Magnar released a low growl and swept me into his arms as dizziness swamped me.

"Let's get off of this fucking mountain," he snarled, not giving the others the option to voice an opinion before he shot away down the trail, carrying me with him.

MONTANA

CHAPTER TWENTY TWO

We powered on, putting as much distance between us and the mountain range as we could. Valentina was hot on our trail; I could sense it in my bones. We were pushing ourselves to our limits to lose her, but we had no choice. It was a race to escape. If she found us in this state, we were dead.

We were running on fumes and with each passing day, the other vampires and I only drank a third of a bottle of blood each. I'd lasted well after my drink from Callie, but now the hunger was back and it was starting to drive me to madness. She'd refused to let anyone drink from her for a couple of days after Erik and I had taken so much, and I couldn't blame her. But now Julius was having to provide for us all and it wasn't nearly enough.

We sloshed through wetlands for miles and the beating sun meant we had to carry Chickoa, Fabian and Clarice again. The heat was unrelenting and Callie and Julius were struggling more than ever as they waded through the knee-high mud and battled under the sun's intense rays. It might have been winter, but it sure as hell didn't seem like it in this place.

Sweat beaded on Callie's brow and I shifted towards her, taking her hand. "Let me carry you," I urged.

Magnar had offered more than once but he already had Chickoa on his back and despite his strength, it didn't make sense to burden him with more than necessary. My hands were free as Julius had insisted on carrying Clarice and I so desperately wanted to help my twin.

"I can manage," she said breathlessly. "I don't wanna be a-" She stumbled, falling toward the mud with a cry, and I lunged to catch her.

I pulled her upright, turning around and offering her my back.

"Get on," I insisted and she sighed, lacing her hands around my neck and jumping up to wrap her legs around my waist.

I supported her thighs then started wading through the bog, able to move fairly easily if I kept my pace up. My feet didn't sink in quick enough if I kept going, placing foot after foot as I followed the group.

Hours passed and we finally left the wetlands behind, meeting a forest instead and heading into the shadows.

Callie jumped down from my back at last, thanking me.

We paused in the clearing as everyone dropped their packs and let the others out.

Clarice stood up from the bag beside Julius, wrapping her arms around him. He drooped with exhaustion and his ass suddenly hit the ground. He'd powered on for so many miles with Clarice on his back while hauling himself through the bog. It was a miracle he hadn't succumbed to exhaustion sooner. Clarice dropped down beside him and Callie took a bag from her shoulders, hurrying forward to give him water.

"Fuck that fucking mud," Julius panted heavily, snatching the water and drinking deeply.

As Erik opened the bag for Fabian, his brother sprang out of it in a blur of motion. His fangs were bared and he suddenly sprinted toward Callie and Julius with a cry of desperation.

"Stop him!" Erik shot after him and I ran forward to grab him, fear lancing through me.

Magnar got there just as Fabian's fingers caught Callie's hair. He threw him with all his might into the forest. Chickoa screamed, clapping a hand to her mouth. Trunk after trunk snapped as Fabian crashed through the trees, launched so far away that a distant crash finally sounded as he hit the ground.

"Fucking hell. Rein it in, Magnar!" Erik snapped at him, tearing into the woodland after Fabian.

I stared around at the group in horror, unsure what to do.

Chickoa glared at Magnar, shaking her head. "You need to control yourself. What if he's dead?" her voice cracked and emotion welled in her eyes.

Magnar turned sharply toward Callie to check she was alright, ignoring everyone's frustration with him. He ran his hand along the side of her face and his gaze was filled with so much love that I couldn't find it in me to be annoyed with him. He hadn't drunk in days and I knew he was approaching breaking point too.

A second later, Erik returned with Fabian in his arms and relief fell through me at the fact he was alive. Almost anyway. His head had been torn off and his chest had caved in.

Erik grumbled his irritation as he laid Fabian on the ground. He looked over at Callie and Julius. "He's going to be even worse now after I wake him up."

"How about we don't wake him up then?" Magnar suggested, folding his arms.

"We can't leave him like that." Clarice ran toward her brother, kneeling down to stroke his lifeless face.

"I'm not giving any more blood until I've caught my breath," Julius said stiffly.

"I'll do it." Callie moved forward, but Magnar caught her arm.

"No," he said in a gruff tone.

An argument broke out and I shut my eyes, the pounding in my skull driving me toward a cliff I didn't think I'd come back from. The bloodlust rose and I took a wary step away from the group, pressing my spine against a tree. The curse was driving deeper, demanding I feed and the chaos in my mind was getting harder and harder to shut out.

"I'm putting him in a bag," Magnar insisted.

"Stop it," Clarice snapped, and I heard a scuffle then a pained *oomph*.

I opened my eyes and found Clarice on the ground at Magnar's feet. Julius shot in front of him, throwing a punch at his face. Magnar didn't react physically but his face contorted in confusion.

"What the fuck?" Magnar bit at him.

"You shoved her," Julius growled, snatching Clarice's hand and pulling her to her feet.

"She got in my way," Magnar defended himself. "I only pushed her aside."

"You have the strength of an ox!" Julius berated him and my lips parted as I watched the brothers fight for the first time ever. And over a vampire no less.

"I'm fine," Clarice said sharply, stalking away from them and tossing her blonde hair over her shoulder as she went.

Erik had moved in front of Fabian defensively and his eyes locked with mine across the group as if he was desperate for me to find a solution to this situation.

I stepped forward, forcing down the jagged lump in my throat that signalled my ever-rising hunger, and headed around the slayers to Fabian on the ground.

"It's up to Callie," I said, looking to my sister.

She stepped past Magnar and his shoulders stiffened but he let her approach as she knelt down before him.

"Help me hold him down, rebel," Erik muttered, angling Fabian's head against his neck and pressing down on his shoulder with his free hand. I held his other arm and Magnar's shadow fell over us.

"I'll restrain him," he offered.

"We can manage together," Erik said curtly. "And I don't think he'd appreciate you touching him right now."

Magnar released a huff and backed off. I increased my weight on Fabian as his head reconnected with his body, the jagged skin of his neck stitching back together.

Callie cut her wrist and held the wound over Fabian's mouth. The smell trapped me in a cage I couldn't get out of. I shut my eyes, but that somehow made it worse so I opened them again and forced myself to look at my sister's face instead of the blood. Erik's eyes were on me with the same intensity and I swear I could hear my sister's pulse louder than any sound in the world.

Fabian reared up beneath us, digging his fangs into her arm and holding her wrist in place.

Callie winced, but didn't pull away. We all knew she had to give him enough, though it practically killed me not to take any for myself.

I will not hurt her again.

I am strong.

I can control this hunger.

Erik grabbed Fabian's hair, yanking his head back when he was sure he'd had his fill. Fabian started thrashing and roaring, desperate for more and both me and Erik fell onto him to hold him down as Callie backed away.

Slowly, he stilled beneath us, dragging in a slow breath as his wounds healed.

I heard a crash and turned, spotting Magnar uprooting a tree and cursing his anger.

"What's wrong with him?" I whispered and Erik gave me a frown.

"It's a mate thing," Erik said in a low tone. "He's possessive over Callie. Allowing a vampire to feed from her goes against every instinct in his body. Would you like it if a female vampire bit me?"

At his words, a fierce wave of jealousy seized my body and I shook my head ferociously, making Erik smirk.

Fabian groaned heavily, thumping his head back on the ground. His eyes travelled across all of us and landed on Magnar. "I'm sorry. I can't handle the thirst like my family can. I just..." He shook his head and pain flared in his eyes.

Magnar nodded stiffly, the tension easing in his posture.

I relaxed my hold on Fabian and fell down to hug him gently. He'd lost a fight to the curse. It wasn't really him. I knew that as well as every vampire in our group did. And maybe Magnar was starting to understand that too.

When I released him, he rose to his feet.

"Here, fill a bottle," Callie said, holding out her wrist and Clarice grabbed the funnel and a bottle from her bag, placing it beneath the flow of blood.

The bottle slowly filled then Clarice took a few sips, breathing a sigh of relief. She passed it to me and I threw an apologetic look at Callie before taking a mouthful. Bliss raced through my skin as it rolled down my throat, a moan rising in my throat at the feeling of sating the curse.

Holy fuck, I'll never get enough of this.

When everyone but Magnar had had a drink, we prepared to leave again, the vampires looking slightly more resilient than before. But it wouldn't be long before the thirst got its claws in us again. The meagre mouthful we'd each taken wouldn't sustain us for long.

"Callie, stay behind me," Magnar said, directing the rest of us to go ahead. "I'll protect you if anyone loses their mind again."

Callie sighed, but no one complained as we started walking under the shelter of the thick canopy above. I fell into step beside Erik and his fingers brushed mine, sending a rush of energy into my veins. After my drink, my skin felt overly sensitised and I revelled in his touch.

We'd barely had a moment alone since we'd left the mall. But the love between us had somehow grown fiercer. We'd overcome an obstacle in our way and I knew we could handle anything the world threw at us. Every graze of our hands, every lingering look was a promise I was desperate to fulfil.

"Not far now," he said, eyeing our surroundings. "We'll be crossing into Florida soon."

I smiled, the idea of truly ending this curse such a tantalising thing that it almost didn't seem possible. "What's the first thing you'll do as a human?"

He threw me a grin and I nudged him playfully.

"Well after *that*, I want to take you home, lay in the sun and eat every new food I've seen produced in this world over all these years and never had the opportunity to try. What's pasta like?" he asked and I smiled, thinking back on how many pasta meals I'd had in my life. It was about the most exciting thing we'd been given in our rations in the Realm. It was kind of sad that Erik had never tried it, then again, he had caged my kind, so I wasn't going to go feeling that bad about it.

"It's um, chewy and soft. It goes well with tomatoes. My dad used to make this great sauce. He found some wild basil growing on the edge of the Realm once and planted it in a pot in our kitchen. It gave the food this kind of...tang."

Erik gave me a curious look. "What else did you eat?"

I shrugged. "Bread...beans...rice. We had to make everything last so we often made stews and soups with whatever we had left. We had to bulk out our rations with water so they never had much taste, but the basil always improved it."

He frowned as he realised how starving we'd really been. The regret in his eyes told me he'd never forgive himself for that. But I didn't want to dwell on the past now, not when we were so close to changing our future.

"A beach!" Clarice cried excitedly. "And the clouds are back out!" she cried her joy and we raced after her through the trees.

The crash of waves and the briny scent of sea salt had filled the air for the past hour, and I was beyond excited to see my first glimpse of a sandy beach and the open ocean.

Erik tore along at my side as the eight of us crashed through the undergrowth. Sand hit my boots as we broke out onto the white expanse. The sun was low behind the clouds, painting them in pastel tones that set the sky on fire.

I stumbled to a halt, my mouth parting in awe as I gazed across the incredible sight. The sand stretched away from us in both directions and at the edge of it was a sea as blue as sapphires.

I knelt down, pushing my fingers into the soft sand, delighting in the strange feel of it.

Callie dropped down beside me, grinning from ear to ear as she dug her fingers in too.

"I love it," she cooed and I laughed, flicking some at her.

"Come on!" Julius whooped and I turned, spotting him stripping down butt naked and sprinting away into the sea.

I raised a brow at Erik as he dragged his sweater off and started unbuckling his pants, my gaze falling down his muscular body as he got undressed. Callie was staring at Magnar stripping off too and I caught her eye, the two of us laughing as our men sped away into the sea together, their gleaming muscles and bare skin quickly drawing our gazes back to each of our partners.

Chickoa sat against a palm tree, shaking her head. "Boys," she muttered.

Clarice ripped her own clothes off and my mouth fell open as she turned to us in all her curvaceous glory, her tits looking me right in the eye. "Race you to the ocean."

She bounded off into the sea and Julius stared at her from the water, frozen in place as waves crashed against his broad shoulders.

We rose to our feet, but Callie's eyes drifted to Fabian who was wading into the sea as naked as the others.

"There's a lot of dick in that sea," she said with a frown.

"And tits," I added with a snort as Clarice leapt above the surface, whooping her joy as a wave slapped her in the chest.

"Well if you can't beat them…" I got to my feet.

Callie whipped her shirt off and discarded it in the sand, and I dragged

191

mine over my head too then tugged off my yoga pants.

"Take another item off, rebel, and you'll regret it!" Erik bellowed at me, and I planted my hands on my hips, pouting at his hypocritical bullshit.

Magnar pointed at Callie and shouted, "You too, drakaina hjarta!"

I tugged my bra off, tossing it aside.

"Montana Belvedere!" Erik roared, wading back toward the beach in fury.

Belvedere? Since when had I taken his name? That asshole was going to get slapped when I got out there.

I gave him a taunting smile and dropped my panties just as Callie finished stripping too. Together, we rushed across the beach and ran out into the water. As my feet hit the sea, energy flooded me. I forgot about blood, about Valentina, the holy mountain and the gods. The waves crashed against my skin and I delighted in the swirling mass of water as it pushed me back then drew me out into it as the waves receded. Callie dove under the water, resurfacing in front of Magnar and he snared her in the cage of his arms.

"I hope you didn't open your eyes underwater," he growled, glancing over at Fabian who was swimming past them.

"I did wonder what that dangly sausage was as it sailed past my head," Callie said in response, winding her arms around Magnar's neck as he lifted her against him and boomed a laugh.

I waded toward Erik and he hounded forward to meet me, cutting me off from the group.

"Stay beneath the water," he commanded in his oh-so-royal tone, and I rolled my eyes.

He caught my waist, dragging me into his arms and I folded my legs around him as our lips met. Salt mixed with the sweetness of his skin and I sought more of that delicious taste, pressing my tongue into his mouth.

I inhaled as his cock thickened between my thighs and I leaned back from his kiss with a wild grin. "Now how are you going to walk out of the sea without everyone seeing how much you want me?"

"You may have to make sure I'm finished wanting you before we leave," he murmured, and I slapped his chest.

Water splashed over us in a torrent and I fell under the waves with Erik, wheeling my arms and pressing my feet to the sand to get up.

When we resurfaced, Magnar stood there with a wide grin on his face, clearly responsible for that giant splash that had knocked us under.

"That should sort out your problem, Erik," he smirked and Erik grinned at him in a challenge, pushing his hands through the water and sending a huge wave at Magnar. It crashed over Magnar and Callie and my sister laughed before splashing us back.

Clarice swam toward us, standing upright and revealing her full breasts, taking in the open water that stretched away toward the horizon.

"Do you have to be naked?" Erik cursed, shielding his eyes from his sister's tits. "Julius is trying really hard not to stare." He pointed to the slayer who was swimming a few feet away, his eyes fixed on his brother, then slipping to Clarice for half a second before returning to Magnar.

Magnar laughed and my mouth parted in surprise at his casual reaction to the idea of Julius being interested in Clarice. He waved his brother over but Julius shook his head and dove under the surface.

Clarice swam into a deeper part of the sea, rolling over to let her hair trail around her in the water, looking like some mythical creature.

Fabian breached the surface beside us, his eyes so much brighter after his drink. I smiled serenely, ignoring the dull ache in my throat. I didn't want the curse to spoil this moment. It was too perfect. And after everything we'd been through, a night in this beautiful place was just what we needed.

CALLIE

CHAPTER TWENTY THREE

I lay in the last of the sun as it dipped towards the sea, soaking in the feeling of it against my skin as I trailed my hands through the soft sand.

We hadn't seen a Familiar in days and there were hundreds of routes we could have taken since we left the mountain pass. We'd all agreed we were safe enough from Valentina for now to afford one night in this place and with our slayer's weapons, we'd be able to detect her if she got close again.

Montana was beside me and we were drinking in the warmth of the sunlight together while our skin dried.

Magnar and Erik were setting up camp a little way along the beach while Clarice, Fabian and Chickoa hid from the sun within the tents. I'd felt a little sorry for them when the sun broke free of the clouds and they were forced into hiding once again. The sun on my skin was one of the best feelings in the world and happiness was building in my soul just because of the light it cast down on me. I couldn't imagine having to hide from it for a thousand years. It was a cruel twist to their curse which seemed to serve no purpose other than to punish them.

Julius had taken charge of building a fire and though I'd initially offered to help him and the others with their tasks I didn't feel particularly bad about it when they'd refused. I watched as Julius tracked up and down the beach collecting driftwood to build the huge bonfire and I was looking forward to sitting around it once the sun dropped and the warmth was stolen from the world once again.

My stomach was feeling a little empty but I was fighting off the urge to find food; Magnar had promised to cook for me and Julius tonight and I wanted to keep as much space in my stomach as possible for whatever he made for us. Every meal he'd cooked when I was travelling alone with him had set my tastebuds alight with joy and I wanted to truly appreciate my dinner tonight.

Erik had suggested that Montana and I enjoy some time on the beach like our dad would have wanted and I got the feeling that he was feeling incredibly guilty about our lives in the Realm. And despite the fact that I'd gotten past my hatred for him and his siblings over that, a part of me still agreed. They *should* feel bad about us never seeing a beach before: We should have come here with our parents and played in the sand as children. So if I got to lay in the sun now as payment for his guilt then I wasn't going to refuse. But I guessed I had to forgive him for it now too.

"I can't believe we're really here," I sighed, keeping my eyes closed as I listened to the crashing waves against the shore.

"Dad would be so happy if he could see us now," Montana agreed.

I twisted the chain our father had given me around my finger, tugging it close to my throat. It felt empty now that it didn't hold our mother's ring anymore but I hadn't taken it off. It was the last thing I had left of his.

"Maybe he can," I sighed. I'd never been religious but I had to admit that now we knew the gods existed it made sense for there to be some kind of afterlife too. "Maybe him and Mom are watching us now and thinking 'I wish they didn't have to go through so much shit to get there but I'm so damn pleased they're at the beach'."

Montana laughed and I smirked as I turned my head towards her.

"I imagine he'd be more concerned about the men we've chosen for ourselves than about us finally having the opportunity to build sandcastles," she teased.

"Monty - is that a *vampire* you're stepping out with?" I demanded in my best -which admittedly was pretty shocking - impression of our dad.

"And Callie, does that man have a sword in his pocket or is he just pleased to see you?" Montana responded and I laughed.

"Do you remember when he caught you sneaking out to meet that boy... what was his name?" I asked.

"I have no idea what you're talking about," Montana replied airily.

"Yes you do. It was Peter. Or Terrance or something like that. The one with the dodgy eyebrow-"

"He did *not* have a dodgy eyebrow!" she replied indignantly. "And Dad made sure I never did meet him anyway."

I sniggered and she flicked sand at me.

The silence stretched as I bathed in the sunlight with a smile tugging at my lips.

"Do you think..." Montana began but she stopped before finishing her thought.

"What?" I asked, opening my eyes again.

"I'm worried he might be ashamed of me...of who I am now, *what* I am. Who I love..."

I reached out to take her hand, forcing her to look back into my eyes.

"*Never,* Monty," I growled. "Don't ever think that, even for a second."

She looked like she was on the verge of tears as she went on. "But he hated the vampires so much. He taught *us* to hate them. To fear them. He dreamed of getting us as far away from them as possible and yet I ended up falling in love with one of the men responsible for all of our suffering. And becoming a vampire myself-"

"He would be *so* proud of you, Monty," I said firmly. "I never could have seen Erik the way you did; as the man he was before the curse. I never would have realised that it wasn't their fault. That the gods were the ones to blame in all of this. Your heart is so big and you're so forgiving. Without you none of us would be here now. We'd have no hope of undoing this curse and stopping Valentina. Dad hated us living in a prison but he never questioned why the vampires felt they had to put us in one. And I know that Fabian was an ass and that mistakes were made but I can understand the idea of the Realms. Especially now we're in this situation..." I pulled my hand from hers, turning my arm over and eyeing the cuts and bite marks on it. Montana frowned uncomfortably as she looked at my damaged skin.

"Being drained for the sake of a bunch of vampires helps you to sympathise with them?" she asked disbelievingly.

I snorted in amusement. "Yes. Because I can see how the bloodlust works. That they can't control it and how *it* controls *them.* And if they'd left the humans free after the Final War and allowed their kind to hunt us then I think there's a good chance that the humans would have been wiped out in the end. There weren't enough survivors after the bombs fell to feed all of them and the Belvederes did their best to protect our lives by taking our blood in a way that wasn't fatal. It makes sense. Even if I hate it."

"And none of it will ever stop unless we end the curse," she murmured.

"Which we will," I said firmly. "And then Fabian can give me that damn divorce, Valentina can die in the most horrible way imaginable and we can live out our lives in a house with a view of the sea surrounded by a bucket load of kids."

"A bucket load?" she laughed. "And can you really see Erik and Magnar living in the same house as each other?"

I glanced over at the two of them as they built the camp, setting up tents and hanging out our wet things to dry in the sun. They were working together pretty seamlessly and as I watched, Magnar laughed in response to something Erik said.

"Actually, on second thoughts, maybe we should get houses side by side," I said. "Because otherwise I'm worried that the two of them might get so friendly that they'll cut us out of the equation all together."

Montana bit her lip against her own laughter as she watched them, catching my fingers between hers again.

"*This* is why Dad wanted us to come to the beach," she murmured as our amusement died away. "To have fun. Just sit in the sunshine and laugh for once."

"Not a care in the world," I teased.

"How about we make a deal," she offered. "For one night only, nothing else exists. No Valentina, no Biters, no Andvari or Odin. No ring and no fucking mountain. Just us," she said firmly. "The people we care about. No walls around us, no tomorrow."

"With only the sea and the sand." I grinned, liking the idea.

The sun was just touching the horizon and I pushed myself up to watch as it shimmered above the waves. Montana rose too, holding her hand out for mine and we sat together in silence as the sky turned orange and the blue water glimmered on eternally.

My heart felt lighter from our time together. Just being in her presence made my soul hum with satisfaction. We were two halves of the same whole and no matter our choices or curses, our vows or our loves, in the end we still completed each other.

In all my life I never could have imagined a moment as perfect as this. Simply sitting with my hand in my sister's as the waves rolled in and the sun disappeared.

I knew it couldn't last. We had so much to do to free the world from the curse that the gods had laid on us. But for one night only we let that all go.

And I allowed myself to bathe in that peace.

Hand in hand with the truest love in my life.

MONTANA

CHAPTER TWENTY FOUR

I was bathing in bliss an hour after the sun had set, lying back in the sand beyond the fire beside my husband. Julius had given us more blood and I finally felt whole again. My priorities had changed entirely now I was fed, and I didn't give a damn about blood right now.

I rolled toward Erik, sliding a hand up his bare chest. He'd replaced his pants but nothing else and I delighted in the hard planes of his stomach beneath my roaming fingers.

"Move an inch lower and I'm going to lose it, rebel," he muttered, pushing a hand into my hair with a roguish grin.

The others were chatting, not paying us any attention but a cool blush still crawled into my cheeks.

His hand skated across my bare shoulder. I'd put a vest and shorts on after our dip in the sea and Erik caressed my exposed flesh hungrily.

"Let's go for a walk," he said suggestively, and my mouth hooked up at the corner.

"We've done a lot of walking today," I teased, circling my finger through the hair that led beneath his waistband.

He released a low growl. "I like walking," he said, his eyes sparkling with mischief. He placed two fingers on my side, marching them up to my shoulder.

I smiled, leaning forward and bracing my hands in the sand on the other side of him.

I brushed my lips over his and he caught the back of my neck, groaning as his tongue invaded my mouth.

"Get a room!" Clarice called and someone threw something at us. I laughed as Erik picked up the empty bottle and tossed it back at the group.

"There's no rooms out here," I said, burying my face in Erik's chest.

"Come on." Erik pushed me up, hauling me to my feet as he stood. "Worth a look," he said against my ear, sending a shiver down my spine.

"Go a mile at least," Fabian begged. "I don't want to hear it."

"You're just jealous you haven't got anyone to play with." Julius aimed a kick at Fabian's shin.

"Neither do you, slayer," Fabian said with a smirk, but Julius only shrugged.

Erik snared my hand, dragging me away from the fire and we headed across the sand, running shamelessly into the night.

Anticipation built in my chest and my body hummed with how much I wanted Erik. It had been too long, and he finally seemed himself again. I was aching with how much I needed my body to reunite with his.

When we'd run far enough, he released my hand. I could barely even see the fire in the distance, the orange glow of it vaguely flickering on the horizon. Erik moved in front of me and the light of the moon peeking through the clouds illuminated his dark expression.

"I'm owed a private strip show," he said thoughtfully.

I gave him a playful look. "I'm pretty sure you became a very angry prince when I stripped earlier."

"That's because you did it in front of the others," he gritted out, his fury over that still evident. "But now they're not here and I've been thinking about that little stunt all day."

"What about it specifically?" I teased, taking a step forward but he backed up. We always played cat and mouse like this and I fucking loved it. Despite the wrath in his eyes, I could see the want in him, the light too, and I was sure no darkness would find us tonight.

"I've been thinking about bending you over and spanking your ass for disobeying me," he said, his eyes dragging down at me as if mentally peeling off my clothes.

I stepped closer again, biting into my lip as I reached for him, but he retreated once more.

"Strip," he commanded.

"Make me," I dared.

"Mouthy as always," he murmured, lifting a hand to grip my chin as his iron eyes scored across my features.

"Just how you like it," I answered, a little breathy from the power that emanated from him. I was reminded of those days in his castle, fighting with him, fearing him. How had we gotten here? With this beast looking at me like I held the world between my hands?

"Ever the rebel," he agreed. "But when you bow, you do so only for me."

"And only in private," I said, a grin twisting my lips.

"But I will kneel for you anywhere, my love," he swore. "You are the only goddess I will devote myself to now."

I shivered as his hand trailed to my throat, caressing before fisting in my shirt and tugging me one step closer. "Strip for me and I will worship you with pain and pleasure. Submit to me tonight and let me show you the power you can reap from me in that submission."

My throat thickened and I nodded, peeling his hand from my shirt and stepping back, our eyes remaining fixed.

I pushed my hair back from my face then caught the hem of my top and dragged it over my head. His eyes lit with excitement as he took in the lacy bra I'd gotten from the mall. I'd found it in a store full of nothing but lingerie and this one had sparked excitement in me. It was a garment I only wanted him to see. The way it pushed up my breasts and the thin material gave him a glimpse of what lay beneath.

I tugged my shorts off, kicking them away from my feet and he took in the matching panties with equal desire. He released a low growl in his throat and the noise sent heat coursing through my veins. He was the key to all my desires and his gaze alone unlocked me.

"More," he demanded and I took pleasure in the control this gave me, reaching behind my back and unhooking my bra.

I shrugged my shoulders and let it fall to the sand at my feet, twirling to let him see more of me.

"Enough?" I asked sweetly and he shook his head, his eyes wanton.

I hooked my fingers in my panties, tilting my head as I held him in suspense.

"Off," he ordered and I rolled them slowly down my legs, slipping them over my feet and dangling them on one finger as I stood upright before him.

His gaze scraped hungrily down me, so penetrating it was like his hands were on me already.

"You have no idea what you do to me," he said in a rumbling tone that made my skin skitter with pleasure.

I stepped forward, approaching slowly and pressing myself against him. His cool body was flush to mine and the feel of his muscles tensing made me inhale a breath.

"What is it I do to you Erik Belvedere?" I asked lightly, slipping my hand between us and running it down his chest to his waistband.

I spread my fingers and dragged them lower over his pants, brushing my tongue over my fangs as I felt his large cock swelling beneath my palm.

He moaned hungrily then pushed me back a step. I pouted and he released a dark chuckle. In a surge of movement, he swept me off my feet and I dropped onto the sand with him holding my waist. He pushed my legs apart and I released a desperate whimper as his mouth immediately dropped to my breasts. My nipples hardened under his torment as he moved between each of them, nipping and sucking before blowing cool air onto them. I rolled my head against the sand, digging my nails into his shoulders as he continued to pleasure me.

He ran his tongue between the valley of my cleavage, licking all the way down to my belly button. I inhaled deeply, my hips rising to meet the wetness of his lips.

He lifted one of my legs, slinging it over his shoulder as he crawled backwards and placed a line of kisses along my pubic bone.

My back arched and I clawed at the sand as he continued his sweet torment. "Erik - fuck - *please*."

He laughed and the deep tone vibrated through to my core. He moved backwards, bypassing the spot where I so desperately wanted his mouth and kissing my inner thigh instead. He caressed the back of my knee as he held my leg over his shoulder and the combination was pure fire. I moaned and writhed, longing for more.

His mouth moved ever higher and I teetered on the edge of insanity then he spoke against my skin. "Tonight, pleasure will be answered with pain." He dug his fangs into the spot he had just been kissing and I cried out, my flesh sparking at the sudden change in sensations.

His bite deepened and I cursed as he finally slid his fangs free and licked away the blood he'd drawn from me. His kisses returned, soft and gliding higher, grazing over my clit and making me writhe in the sand. He grabbed my hips, using the strength contained in his body to flip me onto my knees. I gasped, catching myself before I face-planted the sand just as his palm clapped against my ass and sent another spike of delicious pain through me.

My back arched as he did it again and I felt myself get even wetter for him, this roughness so fucking good. He spanked the back of my thigh then my ass again, palming the skin and squeezing hard until I was sure his hand print was marked on me. He gripped my hips, tilting them up and burying his face between my legs, lapping at my wet pussy and groaning into it, the vibration making me moan like a heathen. He fucked me with his tongue, working me up into a complete frenzy before reaching around to pinch my clit. Hard.

I yelped as his tongue continued its divine torment while his fingers pulled and tugged on my clit, hurting and pleasuring me at once. The combined sensation had me coming apart and suddenly I was falling into ecstasy, my hips pushing back to take more of his wicked mouth, and he laughed into my pussy as he claimed his first orgasm from me. But knowing him, that was never enough.

He flipped me over onto my back before I'd finished coming and dropped his face between my thighs, his tongue dragging over my sore clit and soothing the pain he'd caused.

My orgasm fell quickly into another one and I screamed as electricity darted through my body so powerfully it was like the stars were falling from the sky and crashing into my flesh.

My back arched and my hips bucked as I wrapped my thighs around his neck, but he never stopped, his tongue soft and circling, pushing me further and further into realms of pleasure I had never experienced.

His fingers drove into me next and my eyes rolled back into my head as he wrung more pleasure from me, the third orgasm seizing every inch of my body in its grip. He drew his fingers in and out in a tortuously slow rhythm while his tongue matched the same pace and my head swum as I finally came down from the wave of bliss.

"Faster," I urged, needing more already.

He bowed to my command and I cried out as my body throbbed under the intensity of his tongue.

I wrapped my other leg around his neck, drawing him closer, carving great gouges in the sand with my hands.

A fourth climax ripped through me and I made so much noise, I feared it would reach the ears of our group. But I didn't care. The world was lost to me as I rode out the waves of pleasure spreading through my body in an endless ripple.

Erik lifted his head as I released my thighs from his neck. He licked his lips and the sight was so erotic that I almost came undone again. He caught my waist with a feral look in his eyes, flipping me over again in one swift movement. He drew my hips back at the same moment I heard him push his pants down and I braced myself against the sand as he drove his thick cock inside me.

He gasped his delight, his hips slamming against me as he claimed me in this way that felt wholly animal. He reared over me, pushing my hair aside and digging his fangs into my neck, biting deep.

"*Yes*," I sighed, relishing the pain as ecstasy met with it in the middle. The sound drove him on and he pushed deeper inside me, filling me until I garbled his name, every inch of his cock so far inside me that I was stretched to accommodate his size. He caught my chin, turning my face sharply so my mouth met his at the awkward angle. I tasted myself on his tongue and an icy blush invaded my cheeks.

His hips moved more aggressively, one of his hands digging into my waist while the other held me firmly against his mouth. As he slammed into me again, I buckled forward into the sand, receiving a mouthful of it. I laughed and Erik snorted his amusement, pulling out of me and pushing me onto my back,. I was covered in sand and I couldn't stop laughing until he dropped over me again and shoved himself inside me.

The sand rubbed between our skin, causing a friction that was somehow incredible, every nerve in my body alive with it. I snared my legs around his waist, clinging to his shoulders as he buried himself in me with another fervent thrust that blew my mind.

I gasped, my body tightening sweetly around every inch of him. He was fire and I was ice, my body pooling into something entirely fluid beneath him.

I gazed into his eyes and the intensity that passed between us rocked another rolling wave of ecstasy through me. My thighs squeezed him fiercely as I came apart beneath him again and again and again.

He caught my lower lip between his teeth, chewing and sucking before forcing his tongue into my mouth. With a breathy groan, he fell to ruin, his hips crashing into mine so fervently that we shifted up the sand and I felt his cum spill inside me, his cock so rigid and so deep within me that I felt as if we were one being. Pleasure dripped from his lustful gaze as he held me in place, finding a release that made every one of his muscles tense.

His lips fell to mine and sand, salt and sea was all I could taste. When he leaned back, he brushed the sand from my forehead with a bark of laughter.

"You're covered," he said, pulling out of me and tugging up his pants.

I felt like I'd fallen to ruin on the ground beneath him, unable to move as I watched him slide a hand into his boxers and reorganise himself.

"Let's go wash." He pointed to the sea and I shook my head.

"I can't move."

He grinned devilishly, leaning down and scooping me into his arms before striding out into the water. Spray speckled my skin and I dipped my toes in as he waded further out then laid me down to float atop the calm waves. I sank under and rubbed the sand from my skin before rising at his side, completely entranced by him.

"You're so, so beautiful, Montana," he said, running a hand over the damp strands of hair that clung to my shoulders. "And not just because of how you look. It's your soul. I've never met anyone so full of life."

Emotion swelled inside me and my heart whispered sweet promises of forever to me.

We will always be together. Always.

I moved into his arms and he held me close, kissing me sweetly and sending a flood of love into my body as if it had come directly from his heart.

I bathed in the moment of calm, knowing once we continued our journey tomorrow, reality would hit home again. Who knew what we would have to face once we reached the holy mountain? More trials could await us, but tonight I'd enjoy my time with Erik. It was one of the few peaceful days we'd been offered, but it wasn't entirely without the shadow of Valentina looming over us.

"I used to dream of places like this," I said, gazing up the beach to the line of trees that flanked it, rustling in a gentle breeze. "Our Realm was all concrete, the only green I ever saw was beyond the fences."

Erik frowned and I laid my hand over his heart, glancing up at the man who had once been my captor.

"Whatever happens after we find the mountain, we can live wherever you want. The beach, the mountains, the city. Whatever it is, I'll give it to you," he promised.

I gave him a knowing look. "You have a responsibility to rule the empire, Prince Erik."

"If we become human again, there'll be no empire to lead," he said, his brows pinching together. "At least...I assume not."

"The country will still need guidance," I said thoughtfully. "But I can't imagine what the world will look like without vampires in it. Will the humans accept them even if all the vampires return to their mortal forms?"

"My experience of the world is that people only find a way to get along if they have a united cause. They'll need a reason to live side by side. They'll need hope, a promise of a better world."

"And who will give them that if you relinquish your throne?" I pressed.

Erik sighed, looking up at the cloudless sky above and I followed his gaze to the sight of the sprawling heavens. "Perhaps you'll do it," he suggested lightly and I prodded him in the ribs.

"Don't be ridiculous," I laughed.

"I'm not." He looked down at me. "You and your sister are the only ones who've closed the bridge between mortals and vampires. Maybe the two of you should lead us in the future."

"Ha. Ha," I said dryly.

He captured my chin. "Of course, I'll happily advise you on how to run a country, princess."

"Well you *are* good at bossing people around."

"Mhmm," he hummed, pressing his lips to mine once more.

I let go of the strange suggestion he'd made, knowing there was no point in any such discussion until we actually broke the curse. Right now, all I wanted was him, the ocean and a single peaceful night to commit to memory and carry with me when our time here was up.

CALLIE

CHAPTER TWENTY FIVE

I laughed as my sister raced away down the beach with Erik and I headed to my tent to get changed.

As the night was drawing in, the temperature was dropping but the huge fire Julius had built was more than enough to keep the worst of the cold at bay.

I rummaged through my things in search of a sweater but gave up as I spotted one of Magnar's on top of his pack. I grinned as I tugged it on and the thick, blue wool dropped down to skim my thighs. For some reason I got a real kick out of stealing his clothes and I grinned like a naughty kid as I rolled back the sleeves to release my hands from the overlarge material.

I left my legs bare, sticking with my shorts and enjoying the feeling of the sand between my toes. I located a hair tie next and headed back across the sand towards the fire once more.

Before I could get more than a few steps, Julius poked his head out of his tent and he frowned as he spotted me. "I have a bone to pick with you," he said, prodding my bare foot with his finger.

"Really?" I asked, raising an eyebrow as I looked down at him and started twisting my hair into a braid over my shoulder.

"Yes. You've made my brother too happy."

"Too happy?" I asked with a smirk.

He nodded darkly. "My life wasn't missing a damn thing. Me and Magnar were just fine, plenty of battles to fight, ale to drink, a different woman every night-" I raised an eyebrow at that remark and he coughed awkwardly, glancing back at the fire as if he expected Magnar to have overheard him. "*Anyway* the point is, that then *you* come along and now he's got this constant look on his face like...like you're literally the best fucking thing."

"Am I taking his attention away from you?" I teased.

"No. Not that. You've taken *my* contentedness."

"Are you sure that's a word?" I frowned.

"It is. And I was. I was perfectly content. *Before* you made me see that maybe I'm not," he accused.

"You've lost me," I admitted.

"Pfft." Julius waved me off and I laughed as I stretched my arms above my head, arching my back to stretch it out too.

"Well, when you're done being cryptic, I can smell dinner." I turned from him and headed towards the fire with my stomach rumbling.

I dropped down beside Clarice as I arrived and she looked to me with a smile. Fabian and Chickoa were sitting to our right talking in low voices and she almost seemed happy in his company.

"Hungry?" Clarice asked as the smell of the food Magnar was making washed over us.

He'd found ingredients growing wild close to the beach and I was excited to see what he cooked. He'd been mixing all kinds of herbs and roots with the tinned food we'd brought from the mall.

I looked across the fire at him and he smiled at me in greeting. He'd left his shirt off and the flames cast flickering shadows over his bronze skin and tattoos.

"Very," I agreed as I eyed his bare chest.

"You're as bad as your sister and Erik," Clarice said with a laugh.

"I don't know what you mean," I replied innocently as I turned back to look at her.

Julius arrived and dropped down to my left, his eyes set on the fire as he started twirling a large white seashell between his fingers.

"Just in time," Magnar announced as he moved towards us with two steaming bowls of food.

I accepted mine with a wide smile as the smell set my mouth watering.

I devoured a heaped spoonful of the stew and groaned despite the fact that it burnt my tongue.

"This. Is. Everything," I sighed, closing my eyes.

Though the dehydrated food we'd taken from the camping store was definitely an improvement on the junk food we'd had to survive on before that, it couldn't compare to a properly cooked meal. And Magnar was a damn good cook.

Fabian got up and walked away without a word and I watched him go with a faint frown.

"This is why I'm glad you parasites don't eat," Julius said as he shovelled the food into his mouth. "So that there's more for me."

Clarice snorted a laugh and her eyes stayed fixed on Julius while he ate.

"By the gods, I wish I could remember what that was like," she murmured.

"With a bit of luck you can find out again soon," I said.

"I want that more than anything in the world," she replied softly.

Magnar nudged his brother aside and sat down beside me, pulling my feet into his lap. I shivered a little at the contact with his cool skin but it wasn't unpleasant.

"No," he grumbled as he reached for my hair and tugged the hair tie out of the end of it. I rolled my eyes as I continued to eat while he pulled my hair out of the braid again, leaving it loose down my back and trailing his fingers through it.

Clarice watched us with amusement in her gaze and I noticed Chickoa smiling at us from the corner of my eye.

"Have you been stealing my clothes again?" Magnar teased as he released my hair and his fingers trailed across my ankle instead.

"I think you like it," I replied with a smirk. I lifted another spoonful of food to my mouth but somehow managed to miss and the red sauce splattered down the front of his sweater.

Julius barked a laugh at me and I grinned sheepishly as I scooped it back off with my finger and put it in my mouth.

"On the bright side, you don't get cold so you don't really *need* a sweater," I pointed out.

"Well in that case, feel free to steal all of my clothes then," Magnar said shaking his head.

"I will," I agreed.

"They look better on you anyway," he murmured, his eyes skimming over my bare legs. "So I guess I'll just have to go without."

"Pity," I replied.

Fabian reappeared with two large bottles in hand. I looked at the amber liquid curiously and he grinned as he noticed everyone's attention on it.

"I figured if this could be one of my last nights as an immortal then I should make use of my body's ability to heal from the effects of this," he said as he unscrewed the top from the first bottle and took a swig.

"Where did you get that from?" Clarice asked incredulously.

"I took them from the mall and I've been waiting for the right time to drink myself into oblivion alone. But I decided to share instead."

He passed one to Chickoa and she gave him half a smile before taking a drink herself.

I finished with my meal as Magnar took a sip from the bottle and he passed it to me next.

I sniffed it, wrinkling my nose as the scent burned the back of my throat. "What is that?" I asked in disgust, not feeling remotely tempted to drink it.

"Whiskey," Fabian replied. "You tried some in my dream once."

"Oh yeah," I said as Magnar shifted uncomfortably. "It was gross." I tipped a mouthful of the liquid into my mouth and shuddered as it passed down my throat. "It's gross in real life too."

I passed the bottle to Julius and he chuckled at my obvious disgust.

Heat simmered in the pit of my stomach as the drink found a home there and I smiled a little as the warmth of the alcohol tingled beneath my skin.

Magnar took my empty bowl from me and headed away with it.

"Well trained, isn't he?" Fabian teased.

"A real man looks after those he cares about," Julius replied darkly, daring Fabian to contradict him. "Perhaps if you'd done that a thousand years ago, the woman you loved wouldn't hate you now."

Fabian scowled at him and Chickoa inspected her nails, clearly agreeing with Julius.

Clarice was eyeing Julius like she wanted to say something but she kept her mouth shut.

"Well this is cosy," I said, tugging the bottle from Julius's hand and taking a long drink of the disgusting liquid.

Magnar reappeared and he tossed a large greenish fruit to Julius before passing a second one to me. He sat down beside me again and handed me a knife from his belt so that I could cut into it.

"What is it?" I asked.

Fabian sighed dramatically before Magnar could answer and I raised an eyebrow at him, wondering what had him on edge.

"It's a mango," Fabian said. "Which no doubt you've never seen before. So you can add it to the endless list of fuck-ups you attribute to me and point out what a piece of shit I am. Yet again."

I narrowed my eyes at Fabian, deciding not to respond to that as I cut into the fruit.

"You know, you probably wouldn't feel so touchy about everything you'd denied her if you just apologised for it," Chickoa murmured.

"I don't think Callie is interested in my apologies at this point," Fabian replied.

"You could give it a whirl," I muttered.

Fabian's gaze fixed on me as he opened the second bottle of whiskey. He tipped the contents into his mouth and didn't stop drinking until it was half empty.

"I'm sorry," he blurted as he pulled the bottle away from his lips. "Sorry that I fucked up the Realms so that you never saw the sea or the grass or a fucking mango before. Sorry that I kidnapped you and married you and wanted you when you didn't want me. Sorry that I didn't fight against the bond the gods put on us and tried to make you love me. Sorry for all of the screwed up shit I'm responsible for directly and indirectly to you, your family, humanity and my own siblings... Miles and Warren..."

I shifted uncomfortably and no one said anything as he lifted the bottle to his lips again.

"But most of all," Fabian continued, his gaze turning to Chickoa. "I'm sorry that I was ever stupid and selfish enough to believe that you wanted to love me for eternity. I never should have turned you. I should have just loved you for as long as you were supposed to have and accepted the inevitability of your death."

He tossed the empty bottle into the fire then stood and shot away into the trees.

My lips parted in surprise and Clarice began to rise to follow him.

"No," Chickoa said as she got to her feet instead. "I'll go. I think it's time Fabian and I had a long talk."

I watched as she darted into the trees after Fabian and I bit my lip awkwardly. I lifted the mango to my mouth and chewed on it for several seconds. The sickly flavour washed over my tastebuds and I stopped chewing as the urge to spit it out seized me.

I fought against it for several seconds but I really couldn't force myself to swallow it. I spat the fruit into my hand and Julius laughed loudly.

"After all that drama, you don't even like it." Magnar barked a laugh as he took the rest of the fruit from my hand and passed it to his brother. I tossed the half chewed piece into the fire and frowned.

"Sorry."

"You're apologising because you don't like the taste of something?" Magnar asked in amusement.

"Well you went to the effort of finding it for me-"

"That was no effort, there's a tree full of them over there."

"I've never really been able to turn my nose up at food and it feels kinda ungrateful when I know what starvation feels like-"

Magnar frowned as he drew me closer to him. "I will never see you go without again," he growled. "So if you want to spit out a mango then just spit it out. I'll find you an apple or an orange or a coconut if you want it instead. You'll never go hungry while you're with me."

My chest tightened at his words and I leaned in to press a kiss to his lips, grazing my fingers along his jaw as I did so. My family and I had made the most of our situation in the Realm but we'd always been helpless, wishing for the world to be better and surviving against the odds. But when Magnar promised to look after me, I knew he'd do it. I was safe with him in a way I'd never dreamed of being. He'd always love and protect me and I'd do the same for him too.

"Do you two never get tired of each other?" Clarice asked and her tone wasn't mocking, only inquisitive.

Julius released a low laugh. "You should hear them when they argue. The two of them are as stubborn as each other - I've never known my brother to lose an argument before he met this one. But he's met his match in her."

Magnar chuckled, taking the bottle of whiskey from his brother and raising it to his lips.

"Well what's love without passion?" he asked as he offered the bottle to me but I shook my head in refusal and he passed it to Clarice instead.

"You think arguing is a good thing?" Clarice mocked as she finished her drink then passed it to Julius again. She brushed her fingers against his and he hesitated a moment before drawing away.

"It can be," Magnar said. "Or are you going to deny the way your blood rises when you bait my brother?"

Julius straightened his spine at the remark and Clarice shook her head in fierce denial.

"I don't enjoy arguing with him," she replied. "He's an arrogant, jumped-up-"

"The two of you should stop dancing around each other," Magnar said, ignoring her. "Life's too short."

Julius frowned at Magnar as if he had no idea what to say. "You can't seriously be encouraging me to..."

"To what?" Magnar caught my waist and pulled me into his lap. "Be happy? Little brother, I died when I killed Idun. I shouldn't be here now but I stayed for this woman in my arms. The cost of remaining with her means I have to feed from her. Do you really think I would judge *you* poorly for loving a vampire after all of that?"

Julius's gaze slid to Clarice and she fell unnaturally still.

"Loving her?" he asked and I could tell he'd meant it to come out dismissively but his voice was weirdly strained instead.

"Give it up, Brother. It's written all over your face." Magnar's grip tightened on my waist and I leaned against his chest as I tried not to smile.

Julius's frown deepened. "So you don't even care that I..."

Magnar shook his head and Julius looked at Clarice again, releasing a heavy breath.

"Fuck it then." He upended the bottle of whiskey into his mouth and tossed it into the fire with a loud smash.

Julius pushed himself to his feet and crossed the space in front of us in three long strides.

"What are you doing?" Clarice gasped as she gazed up at him.

"Offering you the world apparently. If you want it?" He held his hand out to her and her lips parted as she stared up at him.

The moment hung between them endlessly and I shifted in Magnar's arms, worried she was about to turn him down.

"I want it," Clarice breathed, placing her hand in his.

Julius yanked her to her feet and caught her mouth with his as she coiled her arms around him.

Magnar released a deep laugh and I grinned as he tightened his grip on me.

Clarice moaned with desire and Julius hoisted her into his arms as she wrapped her legs around his waist. His hands shifted beneath her shirt, pushing the material up at the back and I couldn't help but laugh as he started to carry her back towards the tents.

I turned to Magnar as we were left alone by the fire and I reached up to cup his face in my hand, grazing my thumb through the stubble I found there.

"You're a good brother," I said as I watched the flickering flames reflected in his golden eyes.

"I have my moments," he agreed with a smile. "Though we may end up regretting that happening."

"Why?" I asked.

"Because now we're going to have to listen to what they're getting up to for the rest of the night."

Clarice cried out in pleasure from the tents behind us and I couldn't help but laugh as I leaned against Magnar's chest.

"Well maybe we just need to distract ourselves from it. Besides, you still haven't fed yet." I twisted to face him, pressing a kiss to his mouth and I could feel him smiling against my lips.

"That sounds like a good idea to me," Magnar agreed.

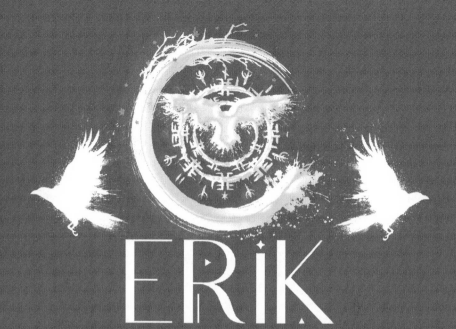

ERIK

CHAPTER TWENTY SIX

I hummed to myself as I woke early and scaled a palm tree at the edge of the beach. I ripped a few coconuts from the top, tossing them down into the sand. Hooking my legs around the narrow trunk, I slid to the ground and scooped up my hoard.

"Are you singing?" Clarice called to me, stepping out of Julius's tent and sashaying towards the embers of the fire. She was definitely wearing his t-shirt.

I fell silent. "No, I was humming."

"Humming is a form of singing," she accused and I shook my head.

"That is wildly incorrect." I dropped down to sit before the fire, giving her a bemused look. "Did you just walk out of Julius's tent like it was completely normal?"

Clarice bit into her lower lip, her eyes igniting with so much passion and love that my brows lifted.

"Yes," she whispered, tugging at the hem of Julius's shirt.

My lips hooked up at the corner and as I opened my mouth, she cut over me.

"Don't you dare say I told you so." She pointed accusingly.

"I wasn't going to." My smile widened. "I was going to say I'm thrilled for you. He makes you happy, does he not?"

She nodded eagerly. "So happy." She half moaned with some memory and I pursed my lips.

"I don't need the details," I added.

She sighed dramatically. "A thousand years with no sister to talk to, Erik. Only brothers. You always listened to me before."

"True, but this is different. Back then, you were just complaining about how no man could satisfy you. But the look in your eyes says you're going to tell me something else. And I'm not sure I'm prepared to hear it."

She crawled closer across the sand with a mischievous grin. "Come on... you're one of the few people in the world I get to share my secrets with." She snatched my hand and I tilted my head to one side.

"You can talk to Montana and Callie, you know," I pointed out.

"Alright," she huffed and fell quiet. She glanced back towards the tents, her feet digging into the sand as she fiddled with her hair.

I sighed, knowing she was dying to say something. "Go on then," I encouraged.

She lurched into my arms and pressed her hands down on my shoulders. "He's *everything*, Erik. By the gods – *argh* - what he did to me-" She moaned again and I fought my instincts as I tried not to grimace.

"You know he can probably hear you right now," I pointed out with a bark of laughter.

"I can!" Julius called from his tent. "Please keep going."

Clarice laughed and I dragged her into my arms, squeezing her tight. "It's good to see you like this."

"I never thought I'd accept them, Erik," she whispered, a line forming between her brows. "How did we get here?"

Montana and Callie exited their tents almost simultaneously and we both looked up, my sister and I sharing a glance that said the answer lay in them. The twins had come crashing into our lives and altered the entire face of this world, and I couldn't be more grateful for the disruption.

They moved toward us, both yawning in sync with the other. Sometimes, they seemed so similar. They were weirdly tuned into each other, like two halves of one being.

They hurried over and sat either side of me as Clarice dropped back into the sand.

"Morning." I leaned in to kiss Montana and she smiled sleepily.

I cracked one of the coconuts against my knee and it broke in half. Callie eyed it curiously and I passed her half of the fruit.

She frowned deeply as she took it. "What the fuck is that? It looks like a hairy-"

"Ballsack?" Julius offered as he stepped out of his tent.

Callie and Montana burst into laughter and I passed my wife the other half of it.

Clarice jumped up and eyed him as if she was unsure if he was going to approach her. He closed the distance between them in half a second, snaring her waist and dragging her into a kiss that was bordering on pornographic.

When they were done with their ungodly display, they dropped down side by side and their hands remained in one another's. "You didn't finish your sentence," Julius teased her. "What exactly is it I do to you?"

Montana watched them with a smile, sharing a look with Callie that said they were fully on board with Julius and Clarice's newfound relationship.

Clarice brushed her fingers down Julius's face with a taunting grin. "You make me come twelve times in one night apparently."

"*Clarice,*" I hissed, my brow furrowing. I did not want to hear about what Julius had done to my sister.

Julius smirked, glancing at the horizon where the sun was just cresting. "We have time to make it thirteen."

Clarice gave him a hungry look but shook her head at him, rolling her eyes like she didn't care to return to his bed, which was clearly bullshit.

"What is this?" Callie changed the subject as she gazed down at the fruit in her hand.

"I think dad told us about those once," Montana said. "It's a cockonut."

"Close. It's a coconut," I said with a chuckle.

"That's what I said," she insisted, stubborn little thing that she was.

'You definitely said *cock*onut," Julius said with a matter-of-fact nod.

"Anyway, it's a fruit. You can drink the milk."

"Fruit milk..." Montana wrinkled her nose and I nudged her. "Shouldn't we keep this for Callie and Julius?"

"There's plenty for everyone," I said. "Try it."

She took a swig and Callie mimicked her. Their eyes lit up at the same time and I grinned in satisfaction.

"I want!" Julius lunged toward us, kicking up sand over our knees. He took his sword from his hip, swinging it down in a fierce arc and slashing another one of the coconuts in half.

"You're spilling it." I snatched up the two pieces before any more was lost to the sand and handed him one.

He drank deeply and I sipped from my own, the sugary taste floating across my tongue.

Magnar appeared from his tent as Clarice moved to pick up the other coconut, breaking it open on her knee.

"Ah...I remember these." Magnar took a half as Clarice offered it. "We ate many when we first came upon this land."

I eyed him intently, thinking back on those days. "It can't have been far from here."

Magnar nodded, his jaw tightening. "Remember the first time we found one?" he asked Julius.

Julius laughed, nodding enthusiastically as he rounded on the group to tell the story. "We made camp on the beach and Aelfric slept under a palm tree. A coconut came right down on his head in the night and he had a welt on his brow for days."

Magnar laughed then looked out across the sea. "I miss him...all of them."

"I'm sure they had a wonderful life," Julius said, his eyes growing dark as his gaze swung to me. "So long as none of you got your teeth into them."

"We avoided the slayers for a hundred years after Valentina brought news of your deaths," I said in a low tone. "No more of your friends died at our hands."

"That's something at least," Magnar grumbled.

"Where are Fabian and Chickoa?" I glanced around the camp, wanting to change the subject.

"They haven't come back since they went to talk last night," Clarice said.

"They seem to be getting along better," Montana said with a smile.

My eyebrows raised at her tone, and I hoped Fabian had found a resolution with Chickoa. It had only taken him a thousand years.

I finished the remains of my coconut, rising to my feet and starting to pack up our gear. The clouds were out today so at least we wouldn't have to carry anyone to the holy mountain. From the ring's assessment, I'd estimated we were thirty miles or so from its location now. I remembered these lands well. The swamps were our next challenge, but we'd come this far, and so long as we continued to avoid Valentina, we should be fit to make it within the day.

I was sad to be leaving the beach behind, a part of me wanting to remain here and bask in its beauty a while longer. But we had a task to do. And it was time we completed it.

Four hours was all it took to reach the swamps. The heat in the air was thick and wafting, a dampness clinging to our skin as we forged a path onward. Julius and Callie were the ones who had to weather out the discomfort of it. If we did break the curse, I knew we were all going to have to face these trials on our way home too. But I would have taken any heat, any sweat and blister or bruise just to feel human again. To have my heart beat solidly in my chest, promising me growth and change with every thump. I wanted to age, strange as that was. But I'd lived as this same being for so many years and it was unnatural. I yearned for mortal flesh that tanned and burned and bled human blood.

With every stride we took, that longing in me grew more fierce. It was close now. Closer than it had ever been. To think I could ever have found the answer to the prophecy another way was delusional. It was always meant to be this way. Montana and Callie were supposed to be in our lives. And maybe the slayer brothers were too. I was bound to those two men; our fates had been entwined our entire lives and I was glad we finally walked the same path. No longer enemies, but friends. I was starting to think I'd never want them to leave when this was over too.

None of us had discussed what we'd do if we truly broke the curse. Would we part ways? And if so, I didn't think Montana and Callie would choose to separate from each other for the sake of Magnar and me.

I gazed at the back of Magnar's head as we charted a path through the swamp, vines hanging everywhere and dipping into the water we waded through. The persistent call of cicadas filled the air and it reminded me of the time I'd lived in a village south of here. The one we'd named ourselves after.

Bel Vedere.

I moved to Magnar's side and he nodded as he noted my arrival. The rest of the group had fallen behind but I was grateful for a moment alone with him, feeling it was time to voice my thoughts on our futures.

"I've been wondering...when this is done, what will you do? Where will you go?"

Magnar grunted, not looking at me as he used one of his swords to cut a path through the vines hanging over the murky water. "Wherever Callie goes."

I rested my hand on his back and he stilled, turning to me. I gave him a hesitant smile. "I just want you to know, you have a home owed to you. From me. Anywhere you want. It's done."

He eyed me curiously then placed a hand on my shoulder, nodding in affirmation.

"I suppose we'll not see so much of each other after this," I said vaguely, wondering if he was going to contradict me, and kind of hoping he would.

He chuckled deeply, squeezing my arm. "Who knows, Belvedere. Maybe we'll be neighbours." He started striding away and I followed after him with a grin.

"You'll be my brother-in-law if you marry Callie," I said with a taunt to my voice.

He glanced back over his shoulder, his eyebrows lifting. "I never thought of that...we'll be family."

"Yes," I agreed. "And if Julius marries my sister, you will be her brother-in-law too."

Magnar released a laugh. "Damn, how am I to avoid it?"

"Do you wish to?" I asked.

He remained quiet in thought and I wondered if my jibing had gone too far. Maybe the slayer could never bear to join my family.

"Perhaps I'm starting to see you as a brother already, so it won't be much different," Magnar mused at last and I released a breath of laughter, unable to believe how far we'd come from pledging to kill one another.

"I'm not sure I'll mind that at all," I said, the amusement falling from my tone.

Magnar stilled, turning back to me with his brows pulled sharply together. "Me neither, brother."

The day slid by and I took every final moment of our journey to enjoy Montana's company. With each step we took now, instead of hope, doubt was blossoming inside me. What if this was all some big joke of the gods' creation? Or what if we found the mountain and instead of the answers to our prayers, we only found more riddles and prophecies to drive us mad?

We'd reached drier land at last, moving through a forest so thick that the sun couldn't penetrate it, even if it had been out. But the sun had started to set and we hadn't stopped. We were too close. A mile or less now. There was no going back, no more nights under the stars, no more delaying the inevitable. The mountain was waiting for us and it was time we faced it.

Montana walked at my side, my hand around hers as we traversed the path that seemed to guide our feet, as if we were fated to walk it. And perhaps we were.

"I haven't said I love you today," I murmured, gripping her fingers tighter.

"That's true," she said with a teasing smile. "You'd better say it then."

I brushed away the hair from her ear, leaning in so my mouth was right against it. "I love you."

She released a slow breath as if my words caused a physical reaction in her.

"I love you too," she said, her expression serious as she turned to me.

I sensed a tension growing between us and I tapped her on the nose to break it. No point dwelling on the impossible pressure of our situation. I just wanted to soak in her smile, her laugh, all the light in her.

"I don't want to see a single frown on your face today," I ordered and she laughed softly, her shoulder knocking into mine.

Callie glanced back at us from where she was walking with Magnar and I sensed they were having a similar conversation to ours. All the words that needed to be said...just in case.

"We're going to call our first child Miles," Montana announced and my heart ached at her words.

"What if it's a girl?" I asked.

"I quite like Warren for a girl," she mused.

"Well I certainly like the sentiment." I dropped my arm over her shoulders, placing a kiss to her temple.

The group suddenly stopped up ahead and I realised why as Montana and I pushed through a wall of power hanging in the air around us. My mouth parted as I gazed at the sight before us, the strange bubble we'd passed into revealing it to us: the holy mountain. Rising high into the sky above the forest where birds circled and clouds clung to its peak, motionless.

"We made it!" Julius whooped, pulling Clarice into a fierce hug.

Montana jogged forward and crashed into Callie, the two of them hugging and jumping into the air at the same time.

Fabian pumped his fist above his head, turning back to catch my eye with a wide grin. "We found it, brother, after all these years."

"I thought you liked being immortal," I called to him with a note of teasing to my tone.

"I think I've changed my mind," he laughed, turning and dragging Chickoa into his arms.

She tilted her chin up and their mouths suddenly met. Everyone fell still, staring at them in surprise as she clung to him, scraping her nails down his neck as if they didn't have an audience. He groaned, grabbing her waist and I grinned at their display, so glad my brother had finally regained the love he'd lost all those years ago.

I watched as Magnar and Julius embraced fiercely then Magnar turned to me.

"Erik." He beckoned me over and I moved to his side with trepidation and anticipation stirring inside me over what we were about to face.

"Yes?" I asked and he answered by dragging me into the tightest embrace of my life.

I was pretty sure one of my shoulders popped out of its socket, but the second he released me, I found I was alright. I patted his face affectionately. "Always knew you had a soft spot for me, Magnar."

"Ah yes, when I was trying to rip your head off every time I encountered you over the years, all I really wanted was a kiss."

"And you got a few in the end, didn't you?" I smirked.

He thumped my chest and I stumbled back a step, but he was grinning from ear to ear.

"Right then, assholes," Julius said to the group with a hungry glint in his gaze. "Who's ready to break this gods-forsaken curse?"

CALLIE

CHAPTER TWENTY SEVEN

The mountain towered overhead like an inescapable beacon, calling me on. My blood was alive with the magic of this place. The weight of the power in the air pressed down on my back, drawing me to it, calling me.

Montana held my hand and we led the way towards it in silence.

A deep rhythm started up all around us like the beating of a drum which rolled from the heart of the mountain across all that surrounded it. The deep *ba-bam, ba-bam, ba-bam* sang to me in a way I was powerless to resist and my heartbeat fell into the rhythm it created. Our fate was calling us on and it was impatient for us to face it.

The long grass before our feet parted in an unnatural breeze but instead of blowing in one direction, it split straight down the middle, carving a path into existence which hadn't been there before. Even the trees bowed to it, their thick trunks leaning left and right as the pulse thrummed through the air.

Montana gasped. "My heart's beating," she breathed in astonishment, her hand pressed to her chest.

Neither of us stopped walking but I turned to look at her in amazement. Her features were still that of a vampire but her eyes were wide with the thumping of her heart.

As we reached the edge of the trees, we paused to look up at the holy mountain. Helgafell towered above us impossibly high. Its sides were sheer and covered in emerald green foliage which fell away to grey rock. I could see snow glimmering on its highest slopes just before it disappeared into the clouds which hung around its peak.

Birds of every size and colour swooped across the open plain before us, from brightest green to shimmering gold, pink, blue and yellow. Their cries were lilting and musical, combining to create a sorrowful lament which wound together with the beating of the mountain's heart by perfect, unnatural design.

I could feel the others following at our backs but this place hadn't appeared for them. It was meant for us. Twins of sun and moon.

Everything in our lives had drawn us here. Now that I stood beneath the mountain, I could feel it in my soul.

This was where our journey ended. This was what it had all been for.

Time to pay the debt. The voice rumbled through the fabric of the world and stirred my blood with the force of its power.

We stepped out onto the plain and the grass fluttered in a breeze I couldn't feel, tossing side to side, shimmering silver then gold and back again.

Ba-bam, ba-bam, ba-bam. That heartbeat was my heartbeat. Montana's. One and the same. We were bound together as one soul. Alive and dead. Before and after.

To our right the sun hung low in the sky, a burning orb of power which threw brilliant golden light across my flesh and sung with the warmth of every day that had ever passed.

To our left, beyond Montana, the moon had risen, low and fat, a shimmering ball of silver in a dark, star-filled sky. The light it cast swept out, highlighting my sister's pale skin in a cool breeze which carried the depths of every night in the memory of the world.

Where our hands met, the two celestial beings collided, but instead of a struggle for power, the light found a natural equilibrium and an echoing sense of balance prevailed.

We crossed the plain and that heartbeat grew louder, stronger. We were in its grasp and I didn't think we could have turned back even if we'd wished to. But we didn't want to. This was our destiny. The end of our path.

As we reached the middle of the plain, the wind picked up and we paused as it swirled around us.

I felt the kiss of the sun and the brush of the moon on my skin, in my hair, weaving through the blood in my veins and the air in my lungs.

When the wind dropped away, I gazed at my sister in surprise. She was wearing a dress which seemed to have been carved out of moonlight itself. It spilled over the curves of her body and pooled at her feet in the deepest shade of silver. Her arms were bare and the pale, near-transparency of her skin glimmered faintly. Her hair seemed even darker than before, tumbling down her back in silky waves and her lips were deepest red as if they were stained by the colour of the blood which sustained her immortal body.

Her lips parted as she took in the change in my appearance too. My dress was weaved from sunlight, though it was the twin of hers in all other ways. I could feel the warmth of it as it coiled about my flesh and twisted to the ground.

As I looked at our joined hands, I noticed the perfection of my skin with a hint of surprise; every cut and bite had been smoothed away as if they had never existed at all. And the warmth of my blood shone through it as if sunlight lived beneath my flesh.

My palm started to itch where it was clasped in my sister's hand and I released her to look at it as the partnership rune which bound me to Fabian was stripped away. Montana held her left hand before her eyes, watching as the mark which tied her to Erik faded too.

Fabian groaned behind me and I turned my head to look at our friends. It was harder to do than it should have been, but eventually my gaze found his. Fabian's eyes rounded with a deep pain for a moment but as the rune finally faded, his shoulders sagged and it seemed like a weight was lifted from him.

His eyes left mine and he turned to Chickoa instead, offering her the hand which had marked him as mine. She took it and I almost smiled but the mountain's heartbeat was growing stronger, more demanding and it didn't want me wasting any more time.

Montana took my hand again and we headed on.

At the foot of the mountain, a huge cave stood waiting for us, yawning wide like a mouth hoping to swallow us whole.

I couldn't tell what was within the pressing darkness that filled it but I knew that was where we were going.

Ba-bam, ba-bam, ba-bam. On we walked and my eyes stayed fixed on that cave. Nothing else existed but that. Nothing else mattered but what was within it.

The ring on my finger was burning, aching, pleading to be reunited with whatever lay in wait.

A harsh cry sounded somewhere behind us but I didn't turn.

People were shouting, screaming, fighting. It didn't matter. Destiny called us and we walked towards it on bare feet.

A small piece of me was aware of leaving something behind but it was what awaited me that truly mattered.

Montana's grip on my fingers was firm and unyielding and we walked together to the end of the world.

Ba-bam, ba-bam, ba-bam. We stopped as we reached the mouth of the cave. Darkness stretched so thickly within it that I couldn't see a thing beyond the next step we had to take.

Ba-bam, ba-bam, ba-bam- the beating of the drums ceased and the stillness it left behind stole the air from my lungs.

I looked at my sister and a faint smile lifted her red lips. This was it.

I almost stepped forward but something called me back and I could feel Montana hesitating too.

I turned my head, pressing my will against our destiny for one last look at the man I loved. He couldn't follow me here. Once we stepped inside I knew none of them could pursue us.

Montana pressed against the compulsion to continue too and we both looked over our shoulders at the men we loved one last time.

I sucked in a sharp breath as my gaze fell on the scene behind us.

Valentina had arrived with an army of Biters to try and stop us from breaking the curse.

The rest of our group had fallen into battle to defend us from her so that we could go on. Erik was tearing the plain apart with his power over the earth and the air writhed with an unnatural storm in Valentina's control.

My eyes found Magnar amongst the mayhem, his swords raised high as he carved a path between the Biters who sought to halt our destiny with his immeasurable strength.

My heart seized as I looked at him and for the briefest moment, his gaze caught mine. Pain filled my chest as my love for him overwhelmed me and I ached to turn and run back into his arms. But I couldn't. It was too late. Our fate called to us and there was no other way on but this.

A tear slid from my eye as I turned away from him and we stepped into the eternal darkness of the cave.

The mountain swallowed us and we delved deeper and deeper into it as the world fell away behind us.

My sister's hand was tight around mine and I clung to her as the pain of leaving Magnar behind filled me. We had come here for a reason and I wouldn't turn back from it now. But with each step we took, I couldn't help but feel like I'd just said goodbye.

MONTANA

CHAPTER TWENTY EIGHT

Callie and I headed through the dark tunnel, the power of this place so oppressive I could feel it in my lungs like the heaviest air in the universe. We moved side by side into the blackness, walking ever on through the passage which held nothing ahead of us and nothing behind. Our feet were guided by the persistent tug in the air and nothing else.

My mind flitted to Erik and for half a second, I longed to turn back again, sure he was in danger. But the power drilled into my body once more and I was a captive to it. Lost, confounded and aching for something I couldn't quite grasp.

Light grew from our dresses, the brightness tangling into an intense glow that lit the way forward.

An enormous golden door appeared ahead of us, seeming suspended in the darkness. A swirling mass of runes was inlaid in the metal, pulsating with the aura of the gods. My heart thundered at the sight and my gut clenched at the intense power which rolled off of it in waves.

Callie drifted closer to the door, sliding the ring from her finger and the runes moved as if drawn to it magnetically. She reached out, in a trance as she placed it against the door.

A heavy thunk filled my ears and the runes dissolved with a sound like falling rain. The door slowly swung open and my heart beat and beat and beat.

A groaning gust of air washed over us, thick and hot, and I sensed it was the breath of a god. And their relief at our approach was clear. Silently, we stepped into the impenetrable darkness that awaited us beyond the door. With a clanging noise that filled me with dread, the door fell shut behind us.

All at once, my heart ceased to beat and the light of our dresses faded away, leaving us in the impervious blackness.

I reached for Callie's hand; she was the only solid thing in this forsaken place and I needed to reassure myself that she was still there. The warmth of her skin tingled against my fingers and I gripped her tighter as the sound of our breathing filled the space.

"Erik," I groaned, turning back to face the golden door, but I could no longer see it as the darkness pressed in. He was in trouble and I knew the only way to stop it was by ending this curse. We had to finish what we'd come here to do. There was no going back and I sensed my sister knew that too.

"Come on," she whispered. "Let's get on with it."

We started running and the ground met my feet, though I couldn't see the way forward. I reached out with my free hand to try and find a wall to guide us on, but there was nothing there. We never faltered, just kept sprinting, hunting for our salvation.

We were trapped in this infernal tunnel, speeding through what felt like a nothingness between two worlds. And the further we moved, the more certain I was that we were leaving the mortal world behind and stepping into something far greater.

Nightmare was vibrating frantically at my hip. I reached for its hilt, drawing on its aura to give me another ounce of strength as our feet pounded against the solid ground.

In a holy mountain the earth will heal, then the dead shall live and the curse will keel.

My blade sang the line of the prophecy over and over in mind until it resounded like the ringing of a gong.

"So close, we're so damn close, Callie," I called to her, tightening my hold on her hand.

The biters were outside. Our friends were fighting for their lives. The men we loved were powerful, they could hold them off. But not forever.

We could make it. We had to make it.

"Let's finish this," Callie said through her teeth and a renewed spurt of energy guided my limbs.

No more blood. I'd never have to drink it again. Erik and I would be free to start our life together. Our hearts would beat, our love would grow and grow and the gods could watch until we were laid to rest and they forgot all about us.

A light grew up ahead and I dragged Callie on with every ounce of strength I had.

"Not far," I urged, and she nodded eagerly.

We sprinted into a room, arriving at the top of a huge stone staircase which led down into a cavernous chamber. Ornate torches burned with golden fire in sconces on every wall, illuminating the cave. Words couldn't begin to describe the beauty that lay before me. My eyes swam with the sight of so much treasure.

A huge mound of glittering gold coins lay at the base of the steps, so high it was almost as tall as the stairs itself. Beyond the coins was a long stone table with an array of golden weapons laying upon it. A huge mirror stood behind that, oval and as tall as a man. The frame was silver and glittered like moonlight. Above us, a fireball flamed in a giant sphere, rotating like a hungry eye as it watched us.

Callie's breathing grew shallow and I sensed her anticipation of what we were about to do. I held on tighter, needing her strength as much as I needed my own as we started down the stairs.

We arrived before the table and I absorbed the sight of the weapons before us. An enormous hammer, a cross-shaped amulet, a curved horn, a dagger, a huge sword and a bow with a quiver of arrows. Each of them sat in a slot in the stone, carved perfectly to fit them. At the far end of the stone table was a small, circular hole and I knew exactly what would fit into it.

Callie slipped the ring from her finger, releasing my hand as she moved toward the hole. She held my eye for a moment and my breath caught as she slid it in.

A thunk sounded through the space surrounding us like the world had somehow shifted. My heart squeezed with anticipation, hope, fear.

Is this it? Is the curse about to break?

A heavy rumbling filled the air and some of the gold coins cascaded from the top of the pile.

I trembled, looking to Callie, then to my hands. I pressed a palm to my chest above my unmoving heart, expecting to feel it stir as life was returned to my body. But there was nothing. No beat, no pulse. I was still a vampire. But why?

A deep, thundering laugh filled the air. It held so much joy that I could feel it running through my blood, driving the same emotion into my veins and curving my mouth up into a smile.

The mirror behind the table rippled and our reflection shimmered and changed, revealing Andvari instead. He wore a fine black robe, a stark contrast to his usual tattered brown rags. His face was perfect and terrifying, his eyes turning to a sparkling gold as bright as the treasure in the cave.

He pressed his hand to the pane of glass, stepping through it as easily as if it were liquid. The god stood before us in all his magnificent glory, his power emanating from him in waves. The mirth he was emitting left my body and fear found me instead, driving into my heart like nails.

"So you have returned it," he sighed as his gaze fell on the ring and a strong wind pulled back our hair. "A thousand years is an awfully long time to wait. But I have been patient...and at last I have it back." He reached toward the hole, taking the ring and pushing it onto his finger. "My love...Andvaranaut, did you miss me?" he purred to it. He caressed the ring and murmured to it in a language I didn't know. When he was done, his eyes lit with some knowledge. "I have seen all who ever kept my dear ring from me. Erik Larsen's mother was a fool. She gifted the ring to a village to make peace between them and kept the truth of what she'd done from her worthless husband. The woman who led that tribe became the first slayer of Idun's creation, then all those in her clan were gifted too. My ring has passed hand to hand, generation to generation until it fell to the likes of you."

I shared a look with Callie, my mouth parting with that knowledge. That we were direct descendants of the first ever slayer. That our mother had held that same powerful blood in her veins. And this ring had miraculously remained within our family for a thousand years, only to fall into Callie's hands as a treasured gift from our father.

"We did what you asked," Callie said, turning to Andvari once more as she pushed away that incredible knowledge and faced our final task. "Now break the curse."

I nodded eagerly, stepping forward with longing.

Andvari's face twisted as if in confusion. "But my dears, you haven't paid the debt." He placed the ring back in the recess where it belonged, eyeing us intently.

I shook my head furiously. "The ring is the debt." I pointed at it and he moved toward me, stepping through the stone table as if it were made of nothing, before brushing his fingers over my cheek. His touch was icily cold and I felt it like a deadly kiss stinging my skin.

"No, it is not," he said, his eyes swinging between us as if awaiting something else.

"What is it then? What more do you want?" Callie demanded, her posture tensing with fury.

"A riddle, perhaps, to help you work it out?" Andvari offered, then went on before we agreed. "What is endless, cold and dark? What creeps up and seizes hearts? What are wounds that cut too deep, a mortal in the clutches of eternal sleep...what is it, my loves, a hangman comes to reap?"

A word came to my lips, my body racked with fear as I prepared to give him the answer he craved, the answer that sealed our fates and stole everything – *everything*- from us.

"Death."

MAGNAR

CHAPTER TWENTY NINE

As the girl I loved and her twin were consumed by the mountain, an echoing gong sounded across the plain around us. It was like an announcement for the gods and I felt the air swarming with unseen power as countless deities swept closer to watch us.

This moment was important enough for all of them to be present. I heard the heavy footfalls of the giants, the cry of a war horn and the laughter of Loki the trickster. I stared up at the skies in wonder for a moment before turning my eyes from the heavens. The gods may have been watching this exchange but this was a battle for men.

I bellowed a challenge as the Biters swarmed towards the six of us and I raised my swords above my head as I dove into the fray.

My brother and Clarice stood ready to hold back the left flank while Fabian and Chickoa stood against the right.

Erik and I drove into the centre of the line.

The ground writhed beneath us as Erik wielded his powers over the Earth.

Valentina stood in the middle of her followers, dragging a storm from the heavens at her bidding.

I charged and the ground shifted beneath me as Erik built a staircase out of rocks at my feet. I sped up it as the jagged earth carved through every Biter it hit, tearing them apart and dragging their remains into the foundations of the structure. I raced up and up, spearing between the middle of Valentina's army on a platform they couldn't reach.

At the top of the stairs, I dove from them, my swords held above my head as I roared a challenge and threw myself towards Valentina, promising her death with every fibre of my being.

She looked up as I plummeted towards her, her eyes widening in horror as she took in my immortal form and the cataclysmic power Erik wielded.

Valentina raised her arms and a battering gale slammed into me, throwing me off course before I could impale her upon my blades.

I smashed into the midst of her army, tumbling over and over, crashing through flesh and bone before I skidded to a halt surrounded by my enemies.

I swung my blades before I even made it to my feet again, carving through the legs of any vampires unlucky enough to be that close to me.

The Biters leapt at me, recovering fast from the initial shock of my landing. I was swarmed by a mass of bodies, pressing me to the earth, biting, punching, kicking, stabbing.

But my flesh was like steel and the injuries they caused me healed almost as soon as they were created. I managed to flip myself over beneath the press of their bodies and force myself to my feet with all of my enhanced strength.

Vampires were tossed away from me, slamming into each other and falling back as I swung Venom through their ranks, casting them to ash in droves.

Tempest bayed for its chance at blood in my left hand and I spun, granting its wish as bright red fluid coated both it and me.

The vampires started backing away from me, raising guns as they tried to take aim between their comrades.

I shot forward as the gunfire rattled out, my vampire abilities combining with my strength and allowing me to carve right through the heart of their army like a battering ram. A handful of bullets found my flesh but I ignored the searing pain as I began to heal. The only wound that could stop me would be one to my heart and I didn't intend to stop for anything less.

I held my blades at my sides as I ran, causing death and injury on a colossal scale without even needing to take aim.

The ground rattled beneath my feet as I closed in on Erik again and I cried out to him, trying to locate him within the crowd.

"Magnar!" he bellowed in reply and I searched for him in the mayhem.

Hammering rain fell from the sky as Valentina built her storm and lightning struck the ground before me as I turned towards the sound of Erik's voice.

The Biters scattered at her command and I spotted her across the plain, smiling wickedly as the heavens split above my head.

I cried out, charging straight for her at an impossible speed as her lightning slammed into the ground again and again. She missed me time after time and I felt the heat of the strikes crashing into the soil at my back as she underestimated my speed.

Her lips fell open as I made it within a few feet of her, springing forward with Tempest poised to cleave her body apart.

Lightning slammed into me before I could land the hit and I crashed backwards into the earth with fire ripping my veins apart. I dropped my blades as electricity shot through the metal, burning the flesh from my palms.

Valentina shrieked with glee as she advanced on me and lightning forked from the sky again. Three, four, five bolts slammed into my body as she raised her hands to the heavens and my spine arced beneath her onslaught. Even the intensity of my ability to heal struggled to counter the ferocity of her attacks.

The sky split open above me once more as lightning raced directly for my heart but before it could strike me, a shelf of earth exploded from the ground beside me, curving over me and absorbing the blow, burying me in the safety of the soil.

Dirt covered me, cloying, pressing, suffocating, but my undead body didn't need to breathe.

Valentina screamed in terror beyond the mound of earth which contained me and a savage smile pulled at my face.

I lay still for several seconds as my body healed the extensive damage done by the lightning and my limbs flooded with strength once more.

I started clawing at the earth, digging, dragging, raking it aside as I pulled myself out of the grave which had saved me.

Light spilled through the soil as I reached the surface and I wrenched my body towards it like a corpse rising from the ground.

Valentina was desperately battling Erik's gifts ahead of me, a savage wind pummelling against the rocks and gravel he drove at her.

Her gaze turned to me for a moment and horror filled her eyes at the sight of her betrothed ascending from the dirt, filthy with blood, gore and soil.

I bared my teeth at her as I charged again, snatching my blades from the ground as I went.

Erik saw me coming and a ferocious grin lit his face as we moved to face her together. This woman had chained us to her will, mind, body and soul. But she was about to find out why you shouldn't keep monsters as pets.

ERiK

CHAPTER THIRTY

Power was leaking from my body from every bone, every fibre, every sinew. The thirst was growing, demanding I pay it attention as I weakened under the use of my immense gifts. But I wouldn't bow to it, I wouldn't buckle to it before this was done.

Magnar cut through the Biters as they closed ranks in front of Valentina. Shoulder to shoulder, fangs bared, faces contorted and snarling.

Nothing but determination filled me. This battle would be my last and I would bathe in the glory of its victory alongside my family.

A yell of fury cut the air apart as Clarice ripped through our enemies' bodies with nails and teeth alone. Fabian and Chickoa worked as a unit in my periphery, tearing through the masses like demons sent straight from the pits of hell. Valentina had come to this fight prepared, but she'd underestimated the force of our combined strength.

They were baying for our deaths and nothing else, while we fought with the yearning, screaming hunger of a thousand years under the gods' rule. We were done losing to anyone and no matter how few of us there were. We. Would. Win.

I wielded my gifts to take hold of the forest at Valentina's back as she conjured another storm. The clouds rumbled with her rage and lightning flashed menacingly in the rippling darkness above. The roots of the trees tore from the ground under my will, shooting toward her and catching her legs before she could bring another lightning strike down on our heads.

She yelped in fright as she hit the ground and I battled to hold her down, the tangle of roots gripping her limbs.

Magnar slashed and ripped through the onslaught of Biters, cutting a path toward her. I stepped forward with a roar of might, the ground shuddering ferociously beneath my feet. A ripple of energy passed across the land as the goddess's gifts lent more power to my body. I curled my hands into fists, drawing blood on my palms as my nails sliced my flesh open. The vines around Valentina grew tighter, tighter, tighter.

Four biters slammed into me at once and I dug my heels into the earth as I absorbed the blow. I smashed my fists into their faces. Teeth broke, blood spewed. The ground tore apart around me and a chasm slashed the earth open at my feet in a ring, creating a platform at the heart of it where only I could stand. My assailants fell to their deaths, tumbling into the belly of the earth with wails of horror.

I fell to one knee, gritting my teeth while I willed my body to hold out as I tried to regain control of Valentina. The biters hauled her out of the net I'd created and she fell against them, stumbling back with the promise of retreat in her eyes.

"Magnar!" I yelled to him as he launched a male vampire into a tree and impaled him on a broken branch.

He turned to me with blood pouring down his brow, but it wasn't his.

"She's going to run!" I bellowed, pointing to Valentina as she struggled to heal from her injuries. The sky lightened, her powers ebbing away.

Magnar nodded stiffly, swinging his swords as red and gold flashed on the blades.

I shuddered as my throat burned and a haze drifted into my mind. The bloodlust fell on me like a ravenous beast and I willed it away with all my heart.

Not now!

Magnar fought with all his strength, but the sheer numbers held him back, giving Valentina a chance to flee into the forest.

"No!" I roared my fury as she darted between the boughs.

I ground my teeth, trying to rise but finding myself immobilised by the pain that racked my body. My senses shifted to something purely animal, the hunger growing in me and begging to be sated.

A waft of the most delicious scent in the world drifted under my nose and my muscles seized up as I fought off the urge to seek it out. Because there was only one person left that it could belong to. And I would not hurt Julius. I refused to drink ever again.

The blood drew closer and a heavy grunt sounded as the platform I knelt on trembled with the impact of someone's feet.

His scent slammed into me all at once and I looked up to find Julius there, his brow dripping sweat and his face flecked with the blood of our enemies.

"No – get back!" I begged, lurching away, but he fell to his knees before me, lifting his wrist under my nose.

"One last drink, Erik. End this," he begged.

My eyes locked with his and I knew what he was sacrificing, how much he was willing to give to win this fight.

"NOW!" he commanded and I dug my fangs into his wrist, feasting on his blood.

I took mouthful after mouthful, far too much, enough to flood energy into my veins. Julius hissed through his teeth, placing a hand on my back.

"Take all you need," he growled. "Take it and finish this!"

I swallowed again and again, the sweetness intoxicating me, setting my body on fire like pure sunlight was pounding through my blood.

I yanked my fangs free, rising to my feet with all the strength of the gods tearing through my limbs. Julius sagged to the ground, clearly woozy. Clarice ran toward us, diving onto the platform and snatching hold of his hand.

"Go!" she hissed at me and I didn't hesitate, knowing I had to make use of the incredible offering Julius had given me.

I ran forward, diving off of the platform and hitting the ground on the other side. I caught a Biter by the throat, forcing jagged rocks up from the dirt beneath us and slamming him onto them. He turned to ash as the sharp stones ripped through his body and I ran on, speeding toward the masses Magnar was fighting alone.

I sprinted into battle at his side, slamming my fists through chests and crushing hearts between my hands. Blood coated us and the sky grew dark once more as Valentina gathered another storm as she sped away from the fight. The clouds swirled above us in an ominous coil and with every passing second I knew she was getting further away. Abandoning this fight and throwing her force into the cosmos to try and finish us off as she left.

Lightning poured from the sky, the electricity in the air making every hair on my body stand on end. I killed another biter with my bare hands, gathering the dirt around our feet, weaving it around Magnar and me as I tried to protect us from what was about to come. The lightning flooded the ground around us, taking out biters so they exploded to dust, creating a fog of death.

I brought huge vines up from the ground, shooting them into the air so they absorbed the lightning. They charred under the force of the electrical current running through them, falling to ash. The scent of burning flesh, bone and foliage snared my senses.

I spotted Fabian on the ground, crawling backwards as he nursed a searing wound on his arm.

The biters closed in again, their faces dark and twisted. Our deaths sparkled in their eyes as more and more of them surrounded us. An endless army. And no matter how strong we were, I feared how long we could hold out against so many.

CALLIE

CHAPTER THIRTY ONE

Montana shifted closer to me, her arm brushing against mine as we stood in the face of the god who wanted our lives.

"Yes," Andvari purred with glee. "Death should pay for life. Don't you agree?"

"There must be something else," I protested as my heartbeat thundered in my ears. "Something else you want in place of our lives?"

I refused to accept what he was saying. That we'd come all this way, sacrificed so much, defeated all that was stacked against us just to find the cost of salvation was so high.

"Nothing holds value equal to the souls of sun and moon," he purred. "It is a high price for the lives of many a foul creature, I will admit. But if you want the curse broken then that is the price."

His voice held no room for negotiation, no option to offer anything less. He had his sights set on our souls and I knew nothing else would ever be enough to clear this debt.

"No," I breathed, taking a step back. My life waited for me beyond this mountain, the man I loved, everything I'd ever wanted was just beyond the walls of this infernal cave. How could I abandon all of that when we'd fought so hard to claim it for our own? We'd barely had a taste of freedom and never even sampled safety. Was this really all we got to take from life?

Montana's eyes slipped to mine, a tear tracking down her face and her gaze filled with a desperate kind of acceptance.

"Not her," I snarled, pointing at my sister. "She's already died once for this curse. I won't let her do it again."

"Undead is not quite dead," Andvari commented. "Though her heart has ceased to beat, her soul remains right where it always was."

"If it's a soul you want then have mine," I snarled.

"No!" Montana cried, catching my arm as I took a step towards the god. "I'm already dead, Callie. I'm on borrowed time as it is. He can have me and you can still-"

"As touching and noble as all this talk of sacrificing yourselves to save the other is, that isn't the price I require. I do not wish for half a payment; your souls are linked to each other's. You are two halves of the same whole and the price of ending this curse is the complete set. Sun *and* Moon."

"No deal," I growled, pushing Montana back a step. I refused to let him have her. She was too good to die like that. She was the kind one, the forgiving, honest, sacrificing one. And she'd given too much to this already. I wasn't going to let her die in this hole beneath the ground for the sake of some curse which was never our responsibility to begin with.

"You may be interested to know your time is running short if you wish to save your friends," Andvari murmured.

The huge mirror behind him rippled like it was made of water and suddenly I was looking at Magnar as he was slammed into the mud by the fury of Valentina's storm. Lightning struck him again and again and his cries of pain cleaved my heart in two.

Erik appeared a moment later, hurling lumps of earth through the air with the full force of his gifts but a swarm of Biters fired on him with rifles and he was knocked from his feet, blood flying.

A choked sob escaped Montana's lips and she pressed a hand to her mouth to stifle it.

Clarice, Julius, Fabian and Chickoa fought valiantly side by side at the entrance to the cave but the numbers were vastly against them and it was only a matter of time before their ranks would break and they would be overwhelmed.

"How about a sweetener?" Andvari asked as the vision faded and the mirror returned to pale glass, though nothing was reflected back to us in it.

"What?" I breathed, a lump forming in my throat as I scrambled to think of any way out of this that didn't end with my sister's death.

"I will give each of your immortal friends one extra minute in the clutches of the curse. That way, when all those who stand against them find themselves human once more, they will have the time to cut through them before their own transformation occurs. It would be a shame for them to return to humanity just in time to die at the hands of an enraged army after all."

Andvari smiled wickedly and it felt as though an icy hand was gripping my heart.

I looked at my sister with tears welling in my eyes. How could I agree to him taking her soul? But if I didn't then what? Even if we could leave this cave we'd be killed by the army waiting for us outside. At least this way we could save the people we loved. And if I had to die for anything then I knew in my heart it would be that.

"We'll be together?" Montana asked. "Wherever you take us?"

"Yes," Andvari purred eagerly. "Your souls are useless apart. I will keep you together for all of eternity, though you may wish in the end that I hadn't."

My lower lip started trembling at his words. He wanted our souls for some foul reason of his own design and I couldn't begin to imagine what it might be. But despite the fear coursing through me, I knew that we had no choice. I would give my life for Magnar. For Erik, the man my sister loved. For humanity and the chance for the world to heal again.

Montana took my other hand and as I looked into her eyes, my tears came flooding past the last of my defences.

I would make this sacrifice ten times over if I could spare her from the same fate.

"Then we are agreed?" Andvari asked eagerly. He swept closer, his breath washing over my skin as my pulse thundered in my ears, desperate to beat as many times as possible before it had to stop.

I didn't look at the cruel god, refusing to allow his face to be the last thing I saw in this unforgiving world.

I kept my eyes on my sister instead, clinging onto her hands like they were all that kept me rooted to this spot.

"Yes," we breathed as one and Andvari reached out to place a hand upon our shoulders.

Montana's eyes widened with wonder as the vampire curse was stripped from her and her features returned to their beautiful human imperfection. Her cheeks flushed with colour as her heart started beating and mine slammed against my ribs almost painfully too.

Her return to life only lasted half a second before I felt the chill of Andvari's grip on my shoulder slipping beneath my flesh.

I gasped, taking my final breath as his fist closed around something deep within me and the tightness of his grip seemed likely to suffocate everything that made me who I was.

I reached for Montana in a way that was anything but physical as he plucked our souls from our bodies and the flesh which had once housed us tumbled to the floor of the cave.

Darkness prevailed, filled with pain and loss and longing but somewhere amongst it I found her, crying out to be united with me one final time.

My soul clung to hers with a desperate, aching need and for one last moment, I fell into her embrace before the arms of death stole even that from us.

And we were no more.

ERIK

CHAPTER THIRTY TWO

"We have to get to Valentina!" I shouted to Magnar as he ripped off limbs with his bare hands. A mound of broken vampire bodies mingled with the dust, forming a ring around us.

Several more sprang onto the pile to intercept us and I split the earth open again, taking the living and the dead with it.

Magnar stumbled back from the ledge as the great fissure left us with a handful of our enemies.

We slashed through the final Biters blocking our path to Valentina and Magnar leapt to my side as we sprinted into the forest.

Trunks whipped past me, a veil of green. I was moving so fast the world was nothing but a speeding blur in my periphery. Magnar matched my pace, our boots ripping up the mud beneath our feet and spewing it out behind us.

A biter ran to intercept us and was dashed to pieces as he met the full force of our bodies colliding with him like a truck.

A blade stuck out of my arm and I yanked it free with a hiss of pain, throwing it forward with the speed of a bullet as I spotted Valentina's entourage up ahead.

The male it hit turned to ash and Valentina glanced over her shoulder with terror in her gaze. She raised her hands and the heavens crackled expectantly.

Lightning sped toward us, so blindingly white it was as if she was bringing the entire sky down on our heads.

She planted her feet, screaming fiercely, the sound raking against my eardrums. The lightning forked down from every direction and I shifted the earth, trying to bring it up to shelter us.

A boom sounded behind us in the mountain and a ripple of impossibly strong power ripped every tree around us from its roots.

Magnar and I hit the ground, carving a great crater in the earth as we skidded forward under the immensity of the shockwave. The storm flashed and died above us and every ounce of light in the world seemed to falter with it.

Silence reigned as I clawed my way over the mound of earth before me and Magnar moved at my side; two warriors united in our single cause. We crested the dirt and my gaze fell on Valentina and the surviving group of biters beside her.

She gasped in horror, slamming a hand to her chest. A beat reached my ears, then more and more of them, clamouring in the chests of our enemies.

Valentina's cheeks flushed with colour and she shook her head, fear spewing from her eyes as she looked toward us.

They were human. All of them.

I glanced at Magnar, reaching for my own heart as he did the same. Nothing came in response.

His lip peeled back and he rose to his feet as the world seemed to shudder around his gallant form.

I rose beside him, my thoughts abandoning me. All I knew was that our enemies were human, weak, wholly vulnerable. And we were not.

Magnar and I charged forward, ripping the biters apart as they tried to scatter in vain. Blood and bone broke under my hands and no ash came. They fell apart, their humans forms shattered beyond repair.

Valentina remained standing, backing up step by step. She knew she couldn't run. Defeat flared in her gaze and terror clutched her beautiful features.

"No – please!" she begged, falling to her knees and clasping her hands together as she gazed up at us in a desperate prayer.

Magnar strode forward at my side and I bared my fangs, the fury at what this woman had done to us thickening the atmosphere.

I caught her by the throat, a hunger for revenge singing in my veins.

"We have the right to bite," I snarled, heaving her into the air.

Her screams bled into every space inside me as I dug my fangs into her neck and ripped into her flesh with no desire for her blood. Death was what I wanted, painful and enduring.

She slapped and kicked and thrashed, but her mortal body held nothing of the power she needed to defeat me.

I shoved her to the ground again, spitting her blood out. Magnar raised one of his swords over his head.

"For my mother!" he roared, slashing it down through the air in a deadly arc.

Valentina's shrieks were cut off as he beheaded her, his blade slamming into the ground with such magnitude that the earth was carved apart.

Her blood mixed with the soil as her ruined body lay at our feet.

The mountain boomed again and another wave of power flooded the land, this time like a rush of wind, forcing us to our knees side by side as the air battered us. Magnar rested a hand on my shoulder and I laid one on his, gritting my teeth as the gods' took hold of our bodies. Their strength dripped through me, wave after wave and my immortal flesh changed under the onslaught. My blood grew hot, near boiling then simmered, simmered, simmered to a deeply human warmth.

The quiet ache in my throat faded to nothing and I felt my fangs retracting and smoothing out.

I gasped as my heart thumped, then again and again, jolted to life as electricity charged my veins and drove blood through it for the first time in over a thousand years.

My body weakened and my muscles tightened against the strange tide that rolled through me. The wind died and quiet rang in my ears.

I rose to my feet and my legs trembled beneath me. I sucked in a long breath of air, my lungs expanding, my chest rising. My heart quickened in response as I dragged in another deep breath.

I was alive. Human. A monster no more.

Magnar stayed on his knees and I eyed the flush of colour in his cheeks, mortality shining from his skin.

I shut my eyes and relished the fluttering beat of my heart beneath my palm as everything I'd ever wanted came to fruition. The prophecy had come to pass. We'd paid our debt. And no divine power or immortal existence could ever compare to the human body I was returned to.

I was me again; a man who'd been living in a shell, frozen in time, captured by a curse and was now, impossibly, free.

MAGNAR

CHAPTER THIRTY THREE

I sagged forward on my knees as the curse of immortality was ripped from my body and my heart stirred within my chest. I released my hold on my blade, pressing my palms to the floor as I doubled over, and every human sensation came flooding back to me.

My lungs inhaled deeply and exhaled again automatically. Not because I felt like doing it. But because I *needed* to.

My heart thumped solidly in my chest. And again.

A deep laugh fell from my lips as it kept going, falling into the familiar rhythm I'd missed so much while I was a monster.

My shirt was torn open across my chest and my gaze caught on the flesh above my heart. My laughter grew as I spotted the clean skin there where the tattoo binding me to Valentina used to reside.

A cool wind gusted around us and goosebumps raised along my skin. I ran my tongue over my teeth and no longer found the sharpened canines of a beast waiting to puncture flesh.

I looked up and found Erik beside me, his face lit with the widest smile I'd ever seen as he held a hand to his own chest, feeling his heartbeat for the first time in over a thousand years. I wondered what the hell it would feel like to have waited so long for it; the few weeks I'd spent cursed had already made me forget some of this feeling. To him it would be barely more than the distant memory of a dream and to feel it again after so long must have been more than a little baffling.

I pushed myself to my feet and gazed about at the battlefield, squinting as I adjusted to the change in my eyesight. The fine details of the world were lost to me again but I found I didn't miss them. I could still see the glow of the setting sun and the glimmer of the first stars meeting in the unnatural sky above and both were as beautiful as they needed to be.

"They did it," Erik said in astonishment. "They actually fucking did it!"

I stared in disbelief at the difference in his features as a human man looked back at me. His skin was flush with life though it was aching for the touch of the sun and his smile was completely altered now that his mouth was lacking fangs.

"Brother!" Julius bellowed in excitement and I looked around just in time for him to barrel into me and knock us both back into the dirt.

I laughed as I clung to him fiercely, delighting in the warmth of my own skin as his didn't burn against me for the first time in weeks. He placed a wet kiss on my forehead and I shoved him off, tussling him to the ground and gaining my feet again.

I lifted my swords from the dirt and was surprised at how heavy they felt in my grip. I still had the gifts of the slayers but I'd clearly grown used to the immense strength that the curse had leant me during my time under its spell.

Erik was clinging to his siblings and Clarice was crying tears of relief and sorrow for the brother who never got to feel this freedom.

I turned back in the direction of the cave and strolled towards it, sheathing my blades on my back as I went.

"Callie?" I called eagerly, wondering why she hadn't returned yet.

The curse was broken and our life was waiting for us. I intended to take her in my arms and march her straight up the aisle just as soon as we got back to some semblance of civilisation.

I crossed the battlefield at a quick pace, wiping the worst of the blood and dirt from my face with the back of my arm as I went.

Erik bellowed Montana's name with as much longing as I felt to be reunited with her sister and ran to catch up with me.

I turned as he approached and his foot caught on a rifle left abandoned on the battlefield. I caught his arm before he could face-plant onto the ground and a deep laugh left my throat as his lips parted in surprise.

"By the gods, I don't think I've had to concentrate this much on walking in...well I guess in nearly thirteen hundred years!" He laughed loudly and slapped my back by way of thanks for me saving him from falling.

I couldn't stop smiling as I approached the cave, expecting Callie and Montana to step out at any moment.

"Callie?" I called again, wondering why she still hadn't appeared. Surely they'd be as desperate as we were to get on with our lives now?

"Rebel?" Erik yelled and his voice echoed back from the dark space beneath the mountain.

There was no reply and I frowned, moving to cross the threshold of the cave but a deep power resonated through the air and I found myself unable to step over it.

Erik tried too and the smile fell from my face as he was also denied access to the mountain of the gods.

"Where are they?" Clarice asked as the others drew closer behind us.

I gritted my teeth and tried to force entry to the cave again but the air was like a writhing, living thing and it wouldn't let me pass.

A thunderclap sounded in the heavens and the noise of it was so loud that I flinched as the mountain shook in reply. I turned to see what had caused it and the sky parted above us, letting through the brightest rays of light which came from neither the sun nor the moon.

Odin leapt from the crevice in the sky and landed with an earth-rattling boom in the centre of the battlefield.

I pulled my swords from my back as I turned to face the ethereal being. The last time I'd come face to face with a deity I'd killed her and earned my own death in return. I didn't intend to let my guard down against one of the gods again.

"So," Odin rumbled as he surveyed us through his one icily blue eye. "It is done."

I glanced at my brother and he shifted his weight so that he stood between Clarice and the king of gods.

"Where are the twins?" Erik demanded and Odin's gaze swivelled to him.

"They have paid the debt," he said darkly. "You should be glad of what they've done for you."

"I am," Erik breathed. "But where-"

"How does mortality suit you?" the god asked. "The world is set to rights once again. Was it worth the price?"

"Let us into the mountain," I snarled, taking a step towards him as my gut twisted at his words.

"Opening the door between realms is no simple thing," Odin growled. "What would you offer me in return?"

"Haven't we paid our price in blood with this war?" Fabian demanded. "Surely the death surrounding us is enough to sate you?"

Odin eyed the battlefield as if he was seeing it for the first time.

"If you enter Helgafell you may not like what you find," the god warned as he dropped to one knee and pressed his hand into the blood which stained the battlefield.

"Let us in," I demanded as my heart pounded with concern for the woman I loved. She should have come back to us by now and this deity knew more about her fate than he was letting on.

"As you wish," Odin sighed and a wild breeze whipped around us, sending dirt and blood flying through the air. A heavy pressure washed over me and when the power of it faded and I opened my eyes, the last rays of sunlight illuminated the entrance to the cave.

Odin stepped back into the wind and we were left alone before the entrance to the mountain between planes.

I exchanged a glance with Erik and his brow was furrowed with concern as he moved toward the entrance.

With a deep breath I stepped inside, keeping my swords ready as I went. This place reeked of death and the promise of the beyond. We were about to cross into the realm of the gods themselves and I was afraid of what we might find there.

ERIK

CHAPTER THIRTY FOUR

We moved through the dark passage at a furious pace, the only sound around us the clamour of our footfalls. I started running, sprinting, desperate to find Montana. To have her in my arms, see the life in her eyes and feel her heart beat against mine.

Everything I'd ever wanted hung in these final moments between now and reuniting with her. As soon as she was at my side, I'd take her far from here and never look back. We'd start our life together. A real life. One where we'd grow older, make a family, be happy.

But none of that was possible until I had her back.

My heart beat with panic for the first time in so many hundreds of years. I struggled to get used to all of the new sensations coursing through me. The cold licked my skin and rose the hairs across my arms. The blood of the battle had soaked my clothes and was drying against my flesh, the sticky film plastering my shirt to my chest.

My breathing grew ragged as we charged on and I heard everyone panting around me in a similar fashion, our mortal bodies racked by the limitations of humanity. But none of that mattered; if anything, I treasured the way my muscles laboured and my heart hammered. I was a true man and with this body I would find my wife and never let go of her.

A golden light grew up ahead and I spotted the source as a huge door came into view. The structure was shimmering and smooth, lit with the power of the gods. We slowed to a halt before it, searching for a handle. There had to be a way forward. Montana was on the other side of this door. She had to be.

I moved forward, taking hold of the edge of the metal and yanking with all my strength. Magnar moved to help me but our combined efforts were futile. My nails broke and I stumbled back at the bite of pain that seized my hands.

"Fuck," I hissed, glaring at the door before throwing a sharp kick to it. My knee jolted uncomfortably and I gritted my teeth, gazing back at the others.

"What do we do?" Clarice asked anxiously, staring at the huge structure.

"Odin!" Magnar roared. "You swore we'd get through! Is this some joke to taunt us?"

A rumbling noise sounded as the cave trembled with the intensity of Odin's power falling over us. The door clunked heavily and swung open, leading to another black tunnel beyond.

I sighed my relief, darting through the doorway with Magnar tearing along ahead of me. We quickened our pace until we were flat out sprinting. My lungs laboured and my skin grew slick with sweat. Heat invaded my veins and I relished every inch of it as it poured through me like liquid fire.

We tore into a cavern which stretched out ahead of us. I stalled as Magnar came to a halt and we stared across the incredible mound of treasure that lay at the heart of it.

My gaze raked down it to the base of the stairs. And there, at the very point my eyes landed, my world came apart.

Montana lay at Callie's side, the two of them lifeless and so still it sent a wave of terror through me which I wasn't nearly strong enough to face.

"*No.*" I refused the situation, willing it out of existence. But it wouldn't leave, it stared back at me and dared me to face it.

I half tumbled down the stairs as I ran to her: my light, my universe, my everything.

I crashed to my knees and reached for Montana's pulse. No beat fluttered beneath my fingertips. Her eyes were shut as if she slept and I started to hope, beg, plead that she was still in her vampire form. That this was not her mortal body in my arms in the clutches of true death.

I pulled her against my chest, her limbs limp like a doll's. Her head lolled and her hair tumbled out beneath her like a waterfall of ink.

Magnar bellowed so loud the walls shook. But I wouldn't believe it. I wouldn't accept it.

"Wake up," I demanded, shaking her then pressing my ear to her chest. *Beat, dammit, beat!*

"Erik..." Clarice said tentatively but I refused to acknowledge her.

"This is not the end," I snarled at Montana. "We made a promise to each other and I need you to fulfil it, rebel. Just open your eyes." I shook her again and the pain found me, burrowing deep, trying to drill the acceptance of it into my newly beating heart.

"No!" I laid her on the ground and threw my fist into the stone beside her head. My knuckles flared with agony, but I didn't care. Nothing mattered except her coming back to me. Her laughter, her kisses, her smile. They were all so out of reach. Losing her was akin to extinguishing every ounce of hope to grace the world.

"You don't get to leave," I insisted, cupping her cheek as tears seared my eyes and threatened to unravel me. "They can't take you from me."

I rested my forehead to hers as grief threatened to devour me. And once it bit down, it would never let go. I tried to reject it but it burrowed deeper with sharp teeth. Every inch of my body hurt and I despised it.

What good was a mortal body without her to share it with? She owned it anyway. How could she not be here to claim it?

"I lost you once, I won't lose you again," I growled, the emotion in my voice cracking and breaking every word.

"This is the debt," Fabian breathed in realisation, and I winced at his words because if they were true, it meant she'd done this for us. She'd paid this price willingly and that was an even more horrifying thought than the gods simply taking it.

"Not for me," I breathed as I clutched her tighter, her skin cold and unforgiving against my hands, not offering any of the electricity her touch had always charged in me. Because she wasn't here. She wasn't in this body anymore. I was left with a shell and an empty heart that would pine for her eternally. "Not for this man who owes you everything and you owe nothing," I insisted as if I could somehow undo the decision she'd made.

This mortal body was worthless without her. I'd sought to break the curse without true cause until I'd met her. But I'd finally had something to live for and she had been it. The sole desire of my being, the reason for my existence. Now she was gone. And that made me into nothing but a broken being in a cursed body once more.

I shook my head as the pounding agony in my veins turned to rage, hatred. A magnetic desire for revenge pulled and tugged at my soul and told me to find the one responsible for this.

Andvari.

I'd hunt him down and rip him from every world, every dark shadow he tried to hide in. And when it was done, I'd cast this body to ruin and join my lover in the afterlife. I'd set my soul free and seek her out in the depths of the gods' halls and stay with her for all eternity.

I pressed my mouth to Montana's icy lips with the most desperate and earnest vow I could make.

Andvari's death is written.

Mine is too.

I pledge the final hours of my humanity to avenge you, my love.

MAGNAR

CHAPTER THIRTY FIVE

I stayed crumpled on the floor with the body of the woman I'd waited a thousand years to love cold in my arms and the weight of her death crushing my soul.

I couldn't breathe. Couldn't think or feel anything beyond this pain which was devouring every inch of me.

This can't be real.

I took Callie's hand in mine and pressed it to my cheek, her fingers unresponsive against my flesh. I placed a kiss on her palm, her wrist, her lips which were so, so cold against mine.

Her weight hung loose in my grasp, her head lolling back as soon as I released my grip on her.

This pain was more than I could hold. It felt like the weight of a thousand souls were bearing down on mine, determined to reduce me to soot and ash and I didn't much care if they did.

I wanted nothing from a life without her in it. There could be no joy, no satisfaction in a world where she didn't exist.

I didn't cry. I couldn't. Where the chasm of pain had ripped through me, there was nothing left which was strong enough to feel grief.

I was hollow. Empty. Undone by the absence of her.

What had it all been for if this was the cost of it? How could the curse have required such a sacrifice? The gods could hold no sense of justice if they could steal such innocent souls in payment for the freedom of humanity.

What had Callie and Montana ever done to be selected for such a role? They were good, kind, brave and loyal. And their reward for such qualities was death?

Julius laid a hand on my shoulder, his grip firm but his hand trembling as he tried to comfort me in some small way.

Clarice was crying, the sound of her muffled sobs echoing off of the stone walls of the towering cave.

"Damn the gods," Fabian swore behind me and the sound of something heavy hitting the ground resounded off of the walls. "They deserve the foulest of deaths for all they've done!"

A glimmering golden coin rolled across the floor towards me, striking my boot before starting a tailspin. The noise of the coin circling faster and faster drew all of my attention. It was the only sound in the world. The only thing that existed outside of this pain. The coin drew closer and closer to the end of its torment, the sound it made against the stone piercing the silence before it finally fell to the ground with a dull click.

I pushed myself to my feet, lifting Callie's lifeless body in my arms as I moved away from my brother.

Erik was laying over Montana's body, whispering things to her which she was far from being able to hear.

A stone altar lay to the right of the cavernous space, its top laid out with a shrine devoted to Andvari. I swept everything from it; the candles, offerings, books and glimmering flowers. Each item held immeasurable value and yet none of them worth a thing.

I laid Callie down, brushing my fingers through her golden hair one last time

Her face was peaceful in death. No teasing smile pulled at her full lips. Her blue eyes were closed for the final time, never to dance with joy and light again.

The fissure her absence carved in my heart was bloody and raw and I knew nothing in this world would ever fill it again.

"You were everything I ever wanted," I breathed as I trailed my fingertips along the cold lines of her face. "And you were too good for me. Too good for this to be your end."

I cupped her face in my hand and tilted her chin so that I could kiss her but not even a glimmer of the girl I loved lay within the cold confines of her flesh.

Tears slipped from my eyes onto her cheeks and I pulled back as I blinked them away. If I gave in to this tide of grief now then I knew that I'd never finish what I had to do.

I stepped away from her, leaving my heart in her care as I turned toward the table which lay beneath the shimmering mirror on the other side of the room.

"Brother?" Julius asked in confusion as I strode across the space and my chest filled with the solid strength of my final purpose.

I built a wall of ice around my heart, my pain turning to rage at the injustice done to the girl who'd blazed with the fierceness of the sun and her twin who'd glimmered with the power of the moon.

I paused before the table, looking down at the items which were laid into the stone as if it had been carved from the earth to hold only them.

I could feel the brush of power coming from those items. They were no normal weapons.

I reached for Callie's ring first, the reason she'd come to this infernal place to begin with. As I pulled it from the recess, a wave of power washed over me. Andvari knew someone was claiming his treasure but he would be powerless to find us here now.

I ground my teeth as I pushed the ring onto my finger and wielded its energy to hide this place from him as I turned my attention to the other items before me.

There were seven in all, including the ring. And I could tell these were no ordinary items. Each piece held the runes of the gods carved into the gold which decorated them. Each sung with a deep well of power which called to me even before I'd touched them.

There was a curling horn, a bow, a sword, a dagger, an amulet and a huge war hammer inlaid with runes of power and destruction. They called to me with the promise of eternal power and an unstoppable dominion, but that wasn't why I wanted them.

I felt someone approaching and looked around as Erik moved to stand by my side. He'd laid Montana on the altar beside Callie, the two of them united in death as they'd always been in life.

My gaze met his and I could feel his anger as deeply as my own.

"I'm going to kill him," I said and I didn't need to say who I meant. Andvari's death was the only thing that held any meaning to either of us now.

"I'm coming with you," he replied.

I nodded once then reached out to take the hammer.

My fingers curled around the thick handle and power flowed through my muscles as I hefted it into my grasp. It was heavier than anything I'd ever held, the weight of it so much more than just physical. But the power of my love for the woman who lay dead on the far side of the room leant me what strength I required to wield it.

"Is that Thor's hammer?" Clarice gasped and I could tell she didn't think I should be wielding such a thing.

My eyes slid past her and I didn't respond as I stepped up onto the platform beyond the stone dais and headed for the rear wall of the cave.

"This place lies between the realm of the gods and the realm of men," I growled as I lifted the immense hammer into my arms.

"Magnar," Julius began, hurrying towards me. "You can't-"

I swung the hammer with all of my strength, slamming it into the wall with a resounding crash.

The mountain groaned and wailed above us and I snarled as I swung the hammer again. And again.

Julius pulled Clarice into his arms and started backing away from me as the wall resisted my efforts to cleave it apart. But the gods had gifted me my strength and the power to wield their weapons and now they were about to find out just what that meant.

I roared with effort as I swung the hammer at the wall again and a huge shudder raced through the ground at my feet as a crack split the rock apart.

I snarled as I heaved the hammer back for one final strike and my muscles began to tremble with the effort of wielding such a weapon. But I refused to stop. I wouldn't back down from this fight. Andvari would pay for what he'd taken from me and Callie's life would be avenged.

I bellowed my rage, my grief, my pain into that blow and the hammer collided with such force that the wall split apart. Rocks cascaded around my feet and a roughly hewn doorway appeared before me.

I dropped the hammer beside me, no longer able to bear the weight of it.

The space beyond the doorway shimmered with green and blue light like the surface of some deep pool. I knew crossing that threshold would take so much more from me than the movement of my flesh but whatever price I had to pay would be worth it. Andvari's life would end at my blade or I would die in the attempt of taking it.

I turned back to the room filled with treasure which held no value to me. My eyes trailed over my brother with regret.

I closed the distance between us and he released his hold on Clarice as his eyes met mine.

"I'm coming with you," he said fiercely but I shook my head.

"You are the one thing I cannot bear to leave behind," I told him as I caught his face between my hands. "But you still have a life to lead and I will not draw you into death with me."

I could see the refusal simmering in his eyes and I pressed my forehead to his. My heart slammed against my ribs painfully as I prepared to part ways with him. But he had found something which was truly worth living for. And I would never take such a thing from him.

"I would follow you to the end of the Earth," Julius snarled, his hands gripping my wrists as I held him.

"And you have, Little Brother," I replied. "But now my path leads me beyond the Earth and into the realm of gods. It is no place for those with a reason left to live."

Julius shook his head and I pulled back so that I could look him in his eyes which were glimmering with emotion.

"*Love her,*" I snarled. "Live for her and die with her when your time has come. And I will wait for you in the golden hall with a tankard of ale and our friends at my side."

Julius glanced at Clarice as she clung to Erik, having much the same argument as we were. I could see the pain of this decision hanging on my brother but I wasn't giving him the choice. His path had granted him everything a man could wish for and I would sooner cut my own heart out than let him abandon it for me. I took the ring from my finger and pressed it into his hand.

"Protect her from them," I snarled. "And know that I love you more fiercely than I could ever put into words."

"I can't let you go-" he breathed, his fingers curling around the ring as he refused to accept what had to happen.

"I will see you again," I growled. "But not in this life."

Julius opened his mouth to protest and I pulled him into my arms, crushing him in a final embrace which ended our argument.

"I love you, Magnar," he choked as his hand fisted in the back of my shirt and his tears fell against my neck.

"Then live for me," I replied, kissing his cheek before pulling away from him.

Clarice fell into his arms as Erik released her and he turned to embrace Fabian one final time. Chickoa sobbed as he stepped back towards her but I looked away from the horror in her eyes.

I moved to the table laden with the treasure of the gods and placed the horn over my shoulder, followed by the bow.

I passed Erik the sword as he approached me and he took it with a nod before claiming the dagger and the amulet as well.

"Come then, enemy of mine," I said darkly as I held his eye.

"Let us show the gods what we're capable of when we're united," he replied.

We turned towards the fissure I'd carved into the side of the mountain and I took a final breath, glancing back at my brother and the woman he loved one last time, before stepping into the void.

ERIK

CHAPTER THIRTY SIX

Magnar and I moved into the sheen of rippling blue and green light that I was sure would lead us to the land of the dead. I threw a lingering glance back at my family, knowing it would be the last time I saw them until they one day joined me in death.

We stepped into the waiting clutches of the rift between worlds and it took us in its hold, sweeping us away from every Earth-dwelling thing we'd ever known.

My body was dragged through a vortex of swirling light. I couldn't breathe, couldn't think, couldn't feel. I was nothing but atoms as my physical being tore apart into a billion tiny fragments. I felt Magnar's presence as the foundations of our flesh scattered through a strange wind, dragging us toward our decided fate.

The pieces of myself re-joined and my feet hit soft ground. Magnar stood beside me, raising the bow he'd taken from the gods' trove. My mouth parted as I spied the strange black robes he was dressed in. A red cloak hung from golden crests on his shoulders, falling down his back and making him resemble a king. I glanced down at myself, finding the same clothes on my body.

"What is this?" Magnar breathed, plucking at the cape that hung from his shoulders.

"Who knows," I murmured, eyeing the landscape ahead of us with a dark scowl.

We stood on the edge of a black river which disappeared into a thick mist before us. The fog pressed in on all sides as if it were all that existed above the bubbling water. A silver chain stretched out into the mist, attached to a huge metal bolt on the riverbank.

I stepped forward and the wind seemed to shift around me as if it were thicker than the air on Earth. The heat was oppressive and the smell of sulphur rose in my nostrils. As I gazed at the river more closely, I realised it wasn't mist but steam rising up from its surface.

Something in my bones told me we needed to cross it but as I stepped forward and placed my boot on the stream, the water hissed and the scalding heat of it made me pull back. My boot was fine, but somehow my skin was scorched within it and I grunted in pain.

I turned to Magnar who frowned heavily, his brows drawn low. "How do we cross it?"

In answer, a rattling noise filled the air and the chain started juddering as something moved our way.

I sucked in a breath as a Viking longboat appeared, its hull a deathly black and the prow curved up into a tall head in the shape of a dragon. Wooden shields were attached to the outer edges, the sigils representing the tribes of old. There were no oars rowing it; it was pulled to shore by a figure in a hooded cloak as he used the chain to drag the boat to the edge of the river.

I gazed upon the strange apparition, lifting my chin as he moved to the side of the boat and surveyed us. I couldn't see anything within the impenetrable darkness of his hood and a chill fled down my spine as his fearsome presence slid over me.

"We need to cross," Magnar said gruffly.

"It is the dead who pass to the other side, I cannot take you on this ride," a dry, rattling voice emitted from the hood and a cloud of vapour filled the air with his rancid breath.

"We will," I growled as anger stormed through my body. "Give us passage across or we'll kill you and take your boat."

The wraith angled his head towards the treasures we held and a rasping chuckle followed. "Never have I seen such weapons in the hands of mortals, why do you seek to travel through the final portals?"

"We have something to do," I said, despising his rhymes. He didn't fear us, but I'd make him fear me if he believed he wasn't going to help.

"You know what these weapons are capable of," Magnar snarled, stepping forward in an aggressive stance. "Take us and keep your life."

The hooded wraith regarded us, flexing his bony fingers. "You seek something I cannot give, and it makes no difference if I live."

"There must be something we can offer?" I demanded and another cloud of vapour filled the air as the wraith sighed. He lifted his hands and curled his fingers, a strange power emitting from them. The amulet I'd taken from the gods' treasure floated up from where it hung on a chain around my neck. It moved over my head and dangled in the space between us, slowly circling.

"Eternal years the souls have come, speaking of the Earth they lived upon. I yearn for all their knowledge to be mine, I look upon their faces and truly pine. But this amulet of the god Mimir, could teach me everything I long to hear. The whispers of a thousand souls, the knowledge of the world untold. Would you give it to this being on his lonely pond, who wonders at the mysteries of the world beyond?"

"Here." I snatched it from the air and tossed it to him. An imprint seemed to be left on my palm and I sucked in a breath as a vision of the world filled my mind. Mere seconds passed but it was as if I'd witnessed the beginnings of time, the Earth created under the great power of the gods. Volcanoes spewing, oceans forming, the first glimmer of life stirring in the ether.

I released a choked noise as the powerful sensation ebbed from my body. Magnar eyed me with a frown, then looked back at the wraith. "A deal is made, take us across."

The wraith fingered the amulet hungrily, then stowed it in his robes, starting to laugh. "Oh, I have seen what you have been," he said excitedly. "Children of moon and blood and sun, united in their cause as one."

I reached for the edge of the boat, hauling myself into it and Magnar sprang up after me, landing at my side.

"Stop with the poems," I growled, taking a seat and Magnar dropped down beside me.

The wraith fell silent and took hold of the chain, yanking it hard and towing the boat out into the river.

The water lapped and bubbled around us as the steam swallowed us up, heating my skin. I forced the red cloak from my shoulders and Magnar did the same, grunting his anger at the item.

My heart hurt so much, the only thing keeping me grounded was our bid for revenge. Andvari had to die. I couldn't let him live after he'd taken my entire life from me. My love.

Montana was lost and with every tug of the chain, we drew closer to the land her soul was housed in with her sister's. Two startling bright lights which would never stop burning, even in the home of the dead. And mine would burn beside hers soon...

We reached the other side and the steam parted, revealing a desolate land beyond. A dark plain of nothingness, but at the heart of it was a staircase of gold, glimmering as if it were wrought from sunlight itself.

"The hall of Valhalla awaits, I wish you well upon your fates," the wraith said and we leapt from the boat, heading across the dusty ground.

We started running, tearing over the land toward the towering stairway that reached into a thick mass of swirling white clouds above.

My foot hit the first step and a gong resounded like bells ringing in the sky. Magnar and I sped up them side by side, climbing, climbing, climbing.

We ascended into the clouds and all I could see was a blur of bright light. It moved around us, parting to reveal a huge wooden door.

Magnar strode forward, gripping the bronze handle and yanking it open.

A cacophony of noise filled my ears. Laughter, chatter, raucous cheers. We ran into the room, prepared to fight if Andvari were close. But no gods awaited us, only souls. A cavernous golden room of them, stretching on forever. The sprawling hall was filled with rows of tables and an endless flow of ale ran from a waterfall above us into an enormous iron fountain. The men and women scooped it into silver tankards, sitting at tables, laughing merrily as they drank. I could tell they were souls by the strange, near-transparency of their bodies.

"The Hall of the Fallen," Magnar breathed in awe and I nodded as we hurried forward, knowing we needed to find a way out. Another door, a gate – *something*.

"Erik?" a voice caught my ear and I turned sharply. Shock spilled through me and stole every other emotion away for a single moment. It was the voice of a man I knew so well. A man who had been my brother for over a thousand years. A Belvedere.

"Miles?" I gasped, spotting him rising from a table with Warren at his side. The two of them looked younger than I remembered, dressed in fine robes, the same as those Magnar and I wore.

I shook my head, unable to believe the impossible sight before me. They ran forward and I noticed more differences in them. Their bodies weren't quite solid but somewhere in between. But their eyes were brighter and filled with more warmth than I'd ever seen in their earthly forms.

Miles crashed into me and I felt the real presence of him with pain ripping at my insides.

"*Brother.*" I clung to him more fiercely, holding him tight, never wanting to let go again.

"You're dead?" he asked, stepping back, his azure eyes falling down me. He frowned as if seeing the differences in our physiques. "No...you're not."

I nodded, an ache growing in me that hurt too much to focus on. "I'm here for Andvari," I snarled, latching onto the single reason I still existed.

"Have a drink with us!" Warren begged, turning to scoop a pint of ale into a tankard.

I shook my head, a lump growing and growing in my throat. "Montana and Callie," I choked out. "They're dead."

Miles's mouth parted in horror and I gazed around the hall, suddenly struck by the hope that they could be here.

Miles clapped a hand to my shoulder. "How is this possible?"

I started explaining what had happened, noticing Magnar had slipped away into the crowd. I kept stealing glances around the place, praying my wife's dark eyes would meet mine across the room.

But they never did.

"They're not here," Warren said eventually, tilting his head with a sad expression. "There are many lands from here on out. If Andvari has them, he will have taken them to his own domain."

"Where is that?" I begged, my heart cracking.

"Across the battlefield. Beyond that, I don't know," Warren said gravely. "But Erik...if Andvari took them, they're already lost. We've learned in this place what he does with the souls that are pledged to him."

"What?" I demanded through my teeth, the heat rising in my veins.

"He devours them," Miles replied, his face pale and his eyes apologetic.

I didn't need to hear any more as tears threatened to overwhelm me. I'd known she was gone, but at least if she'd been here amongst friends she might have been happy. But this was too much to bear.

I pulled my brother into another tight embrace, prepared to do whatever I could to finish Andvari and rid the world of his plague. "Goodbye, Miles."

"That sounds like forever," he growled, pushing me back so he could look into my eyes. "If you die here, you'll come back to the Hall of the Fallen. You'll be with us."

I gritted my jaw, staring back at him. "No. When Andvari is gone, I will be too. I cannot remain in any form, here or otherwise. Not without her."

Miles shook his head fiercely. "No Erik. You have to live. How can you say such things?"

"Because I don't want mortality without her, I don't want *any* life," I growled and Miles's gaze glowed with pain.

"I love you," he breathed. "Please don't do this."

I sighed, knowing I couldn't convince him to accept this. But he would have to. "I'm dead already, my heart just hasn't realised it yet."

MAGNAR

CHAPTER THIRTY SEVEN

My eyes scoured the vast hall while Erik was reunited with his brother and a fierce longing gripped me as I turned away from him.

I started walking, weaving between the revelling warriors as my heart pounded with hope for who I might find in this place of legend.

I crossed through an arching doorway and the sound of drums drew me on.

A deep pressure filled the air and it felt as though a hand had taken mine, drawing me further between the press of bodies.

I passed through another door and found myself in a part of the hall without a roof so that gleaming sunlight shone down over those who gathered there.

"Magnar!" Elissa screamed, launching herself into my arms before I could turn towards the sound of her voice.

I pushed her back, staring at her face in wonder as she laughed with joy. She looked just as I remembered her and for a moment I worried that meant she'd died young but as I looked at the sea of faces around me I realised everyone here was youthful and full of energy. It was as if the hall chose to house them in their strongest forms so that they were the best warriors they could possibly be for the rest of time.

"We've waited too long for you dear brother!" Aelfric bellowed, slamming into us too and an incredulous laugh fell from my lips as I was reunited with my dearest friends.

"I thought I'd never see you again," I gasped, the memory of my grief for them rising like an angry beast in my heart.

"How could you have such little faith?" Elissa teased as she stepped back. "Wait until you see how tall little Magnar grew."

Aelfric slapped an arm around my shoulders and I gripped him fiercely as we followed his wife through the crowd towards a group of warriors who bore resemblances to the two of them.

A man rose from the centre of the group and he smiled broadly as he recognised me.

"I often wondered if I'd just dreamed up how damn big you were," he said as he looked me over.

"This can't be little Magnar?" I breathed in disbelief. He was nearly as tall as me and he had his father's muscular build. The last time I'd seen him he'd been a small child.

"You know they never stopped calling me that," he said with a laugh. "Even when I was older than you had been before you slept, the whole clan still called me little Magnar. I could never live up to the legend I was named after."

"That's why he grew so tall," a girl added. "In hopes that he would outgrow his little nickname." She looked so similar to little Magnar that I was sure she must have been his sibling.

"How many babes did you have in the end?" I asked my friends eagerly, lapping up this chance to find out what had become of those I'd had to leave behind when I slept.

"Thirteen," Elissa replied ruefully.

"She's a damn saint," Aelfric added proudly.

"And they gave us forty seven grandchildren between them," she added.

I smiled widely, wanting to hear about each of them as the fractured remnants of my heart swelled with happiness at the knowledge that they'd led full lives. It had been my dearest wish for them.

"Are you going to leave me waiting much longer, my boy?" a deep voice called from behind me and I stilled as recognition washed over me.

I held my breath, afraid to turn while desperate to see him in equal measures.

I spun around slowly and the warriors surrounding us moved away so that a wide space was left between me and my father.

He was just as I remembered, although a little younger. His skin was warm with the echoes of life, his long hair braided with beads marked with runes. A smile hid beneath his beard and his golden eyes sparked with joy at the sight of me before him.

So many nights I'd spent lying awake, doubting what I'd done to him. Especially since my own transformation had taken place and I'd been forced to wonder if he might have been able to survive beyond the curse. But as I looked at him I knew I'd done the right thing by him. There was no accusation in his eyes. No judgement or regret. Just a shimmering pool of love and joy at our reunion.

I gave up all effort at holding back and ran to meet him, colliding with him with such force as to knock a lesser man from his feet.

My father laughed as he wrapped his arms around me, slapping my back with a fearsome joy as I shook in his arms, overwhelmed with the emotion of seeing him again.

Another set of arms wound their way around us and I laughed as I recognised my mother's embrace. She was here. With him. Just as I knew she'd longed to be from the moment of his death.

"It was worth the price of my life just to see the two of you again," I murmured as I bathed in the love of my family.

My father pushed me back so that he could look at me more closely and I was surprised to realise I was a little taller than him now.

"You're not dead yet, boy," he said fiercely.

"And your fight isn't done," my mother agreed. "We've been watching you, we saw what Andvari did. You have to claim vengeance for your love."

"Is she here?" I asked suddenly, desperately wondering if Callie was close. She'd given her life for humanity and if that wasn't a warrior's death then I didn't know what was, so I was certain she had earned her place in the hall.

"No," Mother replied sadly. "Andvari took their souls for his own purposes. He devoured them. They are lost to all planes of existence."

The pain of that fact ripped into me like a fresh wound. The god had done more than just kill them; he'd destroyed them entirely. There was no hope of me ever reuniting with the woman who'd set my heart alight and I refused to face an eternity in this hall without her.

"Where is he?" I snarled. I would kill that demon among the gods and take from him everything he'd stolen from me and more. And when it was done, I would cast my soul into the unending fire. I wouldn't exist in any form without her by my side.

"Beyond the eternal war," Mother sighed, reaching up to brush her fingers along my face.

"Further even than that, my boy. If you want to kill that monster it may take more than you can give," Father added.

"I will give it all. Every fibre of my soul in the name of her," I replied fiercely. Nothing mattered to me now but exacting revenge upon the creature who had taken my love from me. And there was nothing I wouldn't sacrifice to see his end at my hand.

"Then you should go now," Mother said sadly. "This is no place for the living, the longer you are here the more it will take from you."

She brushed her hand over mine and for a moment my skin seemed near transparent. I curled my fingers into a fist and the colour returned to my flesh but her warning was clear.

I eyed the people I loved with a pang of regret before turning and heading away from them. I didn't say goodbye and neither did they. We would meet again when my time came or I would follow Callie into the jaws of the god who had claimed her soul. Either way, the dead didn't need farewells.

Erik met me before I could search for him and I nodded to him as he turned towards the far end of the hall.

We passed between warriors of every ilk. Enemies drinking alongside old friends. Valhalla was a place for joy and revelry and we didn't belong within its golden walls with our broken hearts and fractured souls.

It seemed as if we walked forever but eventually we came upon a door at the farthest reach of the great hall. It was small and dark and hidden within a shadowy corner where none of the warriors seemed to look. They were happy where they were and this exit meant nothing to them but it called to us with the promise of vengeance.

Erik led the way through it and we found ourselves upon a hilltop which overlooked an immense battle raging across the flat plains below.

The sea of warriors stretched away endlessly in every direction and I stared at them in wonder as the clamour of clashing steel set the air alight with noise.

The sky above them was deepest red as if it reflected back the blood which stained the ground below.

As I watched, warriors were cut down, falling in battle as their blood poured from their bodies only to flow back in so that they could rise again and fight on. It was never ending. They died and were remade. Time and again. Always rising to re-join the fight, never slowing, never ceasing. It was a battle which would rage for all of time and I could see no way for us to pass it by without having to join the fray.

"How do you like our chances there?" Erik asked stoically and I frowned.

"I do not see a way that we could cross that sea with our lives intact," I murmured in reply. My death did not concern me anymore but I wasn't sure if I would be able to complete this task if I was without my flesh.

A faint pressure was growing on my back and I frowned as the weight of it grew and grew. I reached over my shoulder and drew the war horn that I'd taken from Andvari's treasure into my grasp.

Erik eyed me with interest as I brushed my fingers over the runes which were carved into the golden instrument. The essence of the horn washed through me and the runes spoke inside my head.

"This is the Gjallarhorn," I murmured and Erik's eyebrows rose in recognition. "Andvari must have stolen it from the god Heimdall. It will call every warrior in that hall to our aid."

"You would rouse every warrior in Valhalla into battle before Ragnarök?" Erik asked.

"If the gods can use mortal souls to build their army then a mortal should be free to call on their aid in return," I growled, lifting the horn to my lips.

I blew on it and the most triumphant cry rang from the golden instrument. The hill trembled with the power of it. The air around us seemed to vibrate as the trumpeting call carried on and on.

A great roar came from the hall behind us and I turned just as the doors were thrown open.

Every warrior in Valhalla charged towards us in an endless line of men and women holding weapons high and bellowing a battle cry.

They parted around us like a tide divided by a great rock and I stared on as they rushed by. I caught sight of my clansmen, my parents, Warren and Miles. Even my old war horse, Baltian, sped past with Aelfric and Elissa screaming for blood upon his back.

My heart lightened at the sight of so many great warriors clamouring to aid us against the evil of Andvari.

As the warriors slammed into the battle, they carved a great path into place along its centre.

I set the horn down at the top of the hill and we started running for the gap between the fighting warriors.

The sound and stench of battle overwhelmed me as we were engulfed in the midst of the unending war and we charged between the ranks with a conflict of our own in mind.

Each step we took was bringing us closer to Andvari. And I could scent his death on the wind.

ERIK

CHAPTER THIRTY EIGHT

The cry of battle died away behind us as we approached a wall that stretched into the distance across the plain of land. No end was in sight and I sensed we wouldn't find one even if we searched for years. It was so high it rose into the clouds and disappeared into eternity. It was as black as night, smooth as glass and there was no way we could climb it.

I pressed my palm to the surface, a deep frown gripping my features as I faced this impossible roadblock.

"How do we get past it?" Magnar snarled, pacing up and down as he hunted for a way through.

There was no gate, no tunnel, no possible way forward. I sank down to a crouch, eyeing the dirt and sifting it into my hand.

"Fuck," I snarled, tossing the dirt away and bracing myself on the wall instead. I rested my forehead to it as I begged for what I wanted. What I needed more than anything.

Nothing happened.

Magnar released a deafening roar as he slammed his sword against the stone. A boom sounded in response, but the wall didn't shift, not a crack, not a dent.

Magnar struck it again and again, but it made no difference.

He dropped the sword to the ground then lunged upwards, trying to find a handhold in the wall. He soon gave up, dropping to the floor beside me as we contemplated our predicament.

"What do we do?" he begged as he took his sword up and sheathed it on his back.

I shook my head, having no answer to offer.

A trickling noise caught my ear and I tilted my head up, spying a line of blood rolling down the wall in a steady stream. I backed up, gazing up at the huge wall as a phrase was painted across it in my native tongue.

Ingen dødelig skal passere.

"No mortal shall pass," I translated and Magnar's eyes grew dark with some decision.

"Then it's time we shed these bodies," he growled.

My heart thundered in response to his words as if its final beat was imminent. And it was. Nothing could stop us getting our revenge, even death.

I took the golden dagger from my hip and Magnar moved closer. I flipped it in my hand and held the hilt out to him and he took it as I unsheathed the gods' sword at my hip.

Dainsleif, it purred in my mind and my heart stalled as I recognised the name. This was the sword of Odin, a blade which couldn't be sheathed until it ended a life. But that seemed fitting now, as it was exactly what I was going to offer it.

"You always did want to kill me," I said with a heavy sigh.

"Though now it pains me to do so, brother." Magnar rested a hand on my shoulder and I drew closer to him. Suddenly the two of us embraced because we knew this was the end. That we might not come back from this. That it was a gamble that might lead us to our revenge or to an eternity in hell.

If we made it beyond this final hurdle, then the time of our vengeance was close. And when it was done and we cast whatever remained of our souls into eternal darkness, I knew that if any piece of me still existed it would search for Montana's life force in vain. Hopelessly lost and forever without its mate.

Magnar pressed the tip of the gods' dagger to my back and I inhaled, resting my forehead to his. I gritted my teeth and he gave me a sorrowful look.

"Together," I said, lifting Odin's sword and resting it against his back where I'd momentarily drive it through to his heart.

"See you on the other side," he growled and drove the dagger under my ribs.

I forced my hand against the sword as pain ripped through my body. I snarled through my teeth, driving the blade towards Magnar's heart as he shuddered with the agony of it.

His dagger drove home and my heart was forced to an abrupt end, pierced and outraged by me taking away its newfound life so soon.

My lasting breath was filled with the taste of blood and I crashed to the ground, feeling Magnar falling with me as the two us took each other's lives in a way we could never have imagined.

I woke to an existence that was anything but natural. My body felt as light as air as I dragged myself to my knees, finding the wall now behind me and a huge cavern surrounding us.

Magnar stood and I eyed the form his soul had taken. The weight of our trials had eased from his eyes and a shimmer of light seemed to hang around him. I moved to his side, reaching for my heart but there was nothing left to beat. This body felt full of light, swimming inside me like water. It wasn't bad, but it was sobering, knowing darkness was all the future held for us now.

The dagger was gone, but Magnar still had his own swords and the bow. Odin's sword had remained with me too as if it had some destiny yet to fulfil.

We moved through the cave, our footsteps silent as we traversed the dark place which was weighed with the presence of a deity. I felt as though I was floating, like I could move with nothing more than a thought.

A snarl caught my ear up ahead and I tensed, raising Dainsleif before me. If it wanted more death, I would gladly give it to the blade.

A tremor rocked the ground and I eyed Magnar warily as we braced for whatever was coming our way.

Heavy footfalls sounded one after the other, making the earth quake beneath my feet.

This was no god...

I clutched the sword tighter, my body humming, telling me a strange spirit was nearing us.

A guttural snarl sounded and a beast burst out of the pitch black at the end of the cave. A wolf, ten times the size of a mortal creature. A row of jagged spines ran down its back and its skin was bare and smooth. Its face was a picture of horror, a hundred huge teeth bared in an elongated jaw. It had a single red eye that honed in on us as it sped our way on swift legs.

With nothing but pure rage, I lunged forward to meet it as it leapt into the air, rolling beneath its huge paws and slashing its hind leg. The sword shuddered in my hand, the blade unable to penetrate its skin.

I cursed, frustration coursing through me.

Magnar slashed at its throat with the force of his two swords, but a metallic clang rang out and no blood was spilled.

We were already dead and I didn't know what this beast was capable of doing to us, but the look in its single eye as it swung to face us again told me it could do *something*.

It sprang into the air and I swung my blade for its belly this time, roaring as I forced all of my strength into the blow. My arms jerked backwards as the strike didn't cut into flesh and I slammed to the ground as its back legs trampled me.

Magnar caught my arm, dragging me upright and sprinting away from the wolf in the direction it had come from. If we couldn't kill it, we had to outpace it, but that hope was short-lived as it dove through the air above us and landed on all four paws. It turned sharply, stalking back and forth, whipping its spiny tail from side to side.

Its eye swivelled left and right between us and Magnar took the bow from his shoulder with a feral growl.

Tension rippled through my gut as he took aim, loosing one of five arrows he had in his quiver.

The beast snapped it out of the air, crushing it with his teeth.

I waved my arms so its attention was directed on me, then turned and fled, hearing it pounding after me. I ran away as fast as I could but the beast's jaw locked around my arm and I cried out in pain as it tossed me up into the air. I fell down on its back and the spines sliced into my ethereal body, spilling liquid light from my wounds. I might have been dead, but the pain was as real as it had been in my mortal form.

I gasped, pushing myself upright and taking hold of its neck. I squeezed with all my might and the wolf yelped, jerking its head wildly to throw me off.

"Hold it still!" Magnar bellowed as an arrow whistled past my ear.

"What do you think I'm trying to do?!" I yelled in response.

The wolf charged forward, shaking wildly so I lost my grip and flew into a stone wall. I hit the ground, pain blossoming through me. The wounds started to knit back together and I gazed at my body in astonishment at the strange power my soul form held.

Magnar loosed two more arrows, their tips ricocheting off of the wolf's face.

"The eye!" I insisted, racing to help him.

"I know!" Magnar shouted, retreating as he tried to aim once more.

He had one final shot and he had to make it count.

"Hey fucker!" I bellowed, waving my arms in front of the beast.

It came upon me like a storm and I held firm, not moving an inch as it lunged down and its teeth clamped around me. I stabbed the inside of its mouth as the wolf tried to swallow.

Panic reared through me.

Blood poured from its wounds as my sword cut into the meat of its gums.

The wolf's tongue drew me backwards and I dug my heels into the red flesh around me to stop it trying to swallow. I drove my sword upwards but it clanged against the roof of its mouth.

Fear consumed me.

Teeth sliced into my arm, my leg.

I'm going to fucking die – again!

A violent tremor rocked through the body of the wolf and I fell out of its mouth covered in slobber and blood. Blinding agony hit me but the strange light leaking from my injuries started healing over.

I pushed myself away from the creature's lolling tongue, spotting an arrow embedded deep within its eye and drew in a shuddering breath. Magnar helped me upright, surveying me with concern.

"Fucking hell," he breathed, watching the way the golden light pouring from my body slid back into me and my skin stitched together.

"Yeah," I said, nodding. "That about sums it up." I clapped his shoulder and he discarded the bow on the ground, shaking his head.

We headed deeper into the dark cave and the drool and blood on my body slowly vanished to nothing, and my dark robes reformed where they'd been torn away.

I lifted the sword higher in my grip, a resounding power growing in the air around me as we closed in on the deity we hunted. Dainsleif burned in my hands, demanding I offer it the death it craved.

Vengeance is calling your name, Andvari.

MAGNAR

CHAPTER THIRTY NINE

Erik stayed close to me as we travelled further into the cloying darkness. It was more than just the absence of light. It was the presence of something bleak and foreboding.

We were nearing the end of our hunt. I could feel it in the vibrations of the air, like a breath on the back of my neck.

But instead of feeling triumph at the fact that we had finally cornered our prey, the deepest sense of apprehension filled me. Like we were hunting a rattlesnake but were about to come face to face with a mountain lion instead.

I rolled my shoulders back as I carried on regardless. We had given everything in the name of taking this revenge. And if in the end that wasn't enough and my soul ended up as a feast for the creature who had devoured the girl I loved, then so be it. I would sooner waste away in the darkness where she had found her end than linger on in the light, destined to walk alone for all of time.

My foot collided with something and I stumbled as Erik caught my elbow to steady me.

A faint silver light appeared above us and I tilted my head as it brightened bit by bit until a shining black staircase was revealed before us.

I glanced at Erik and took heart from the determination I found in his gaze. We had been set apart for so many years, destined to be enemies for all of time. And yet chance had delivered our hearts to women who shared the same blood. And though they had been worthy of men far greater than two wretches like us, they had given us their hearts and lost their lives because of it.

Somehow this man beside me had become my kin instead of my enemy and I was proud to be facing my fate at his side.

We started up the stairs and the light began to grow. I could feel the air simmering with unease as each step we took drew us closer and closer to the god we sought.

Whether he'd known we were hunting him from the moment we stole his treasure or whether our arrival in this place had been the first he knew of it, I wasn't sure. But he could feel us approaching now.

I could hear it in the echo of our footfalls, taste it on the breeze that slipped into my lungs. Andvari was close. And he was ready for us.

We emerged at the top of the staircase in a huge, circular chamber lined with countless mirrors.

I drew my swords as I stepped forward on silent feet and Erik raised the blade he'd stolen too.

We edged on, watching the shadows between the silvery mirrors for any sign of the deity, but all was still.

On the far side of the room a huge mirror drew my attention, its frame built from dry branches which were engulfed in unnatural flames which didn't destroy it.

I glanced at the mirror closest to me and was surprised to find I cast no reflection. I looked down at my body to be sure it was still there and my confusion at the mirrors grew.

Erik stilled beside me and I moved to stand with my back to his as the air grew thick with pressure.

Blood red eyes appeared in the mirror directly before me and I inhaled sharply at the sight of them.

Movement to my right caught my attention and a gilded mirror resting on the floor revealed a smiling mouth lined with razor sharp fangs.

Erik snarled beneath his breath and I glanced over my shoulder to see a grasping hand reaching for him from yet another mirror. The flesh which covered it was grey and rotting and the fingernails were caked with blood. As its fingertips brushed the glass, they passed through and the taloned nails grew longer, reaching, clawing-

Erik lunged forward and slammed his blade through the arm but it turned to smoke under the strike and reappeared in a mirror closer to me instead.

The fingertips skimmed the inside of the glass as I watched it but the hand stayed beneath the surface of the mirror before fading away.

The silence was thick with promise as we waited for the next glimpse of the god we'd come here to end and he kept us suspended in the torment before his arrival.

"Show yourself, coward," I snarled, growing tired of his games. We had come here for a purpose and I intended to see it done.

Haunting laughter rang out from within the mirrors and the glass vibrated as fire sprung to life in each reflection, eyes staring out at us from every angle within the flames.

My anger grew wilder and I cried out in rage, slamming my boot into a heavy mirror before me, the frame of which was made of finest slate.

The mirror rocked back, leaning so far that it almost crashed to the stone floor before Andvari's magic caught it and it rotated upright once more as if it were on hinges.

"Well now, Erik Larsen," a thick voice purred from everywhere at once. "It seems you've brought me a savage soul to feast on."

"If it's a feast you want then why not come and get it?" I urged, my eyes flicking from one mirror to the next.

As I tried to anticipate his tricks, the flames died away, leaving the reflections blank again.

Eerie laughter rang out from everywhere at once and Erik growled, drawing my attention to the mirrors on his side of the room.

A slender mirror with a frame of iron flashed with power and suddenly the god's pale face appeared within the pane.

Andvari stepped from the glass in a long, black robe with a huge cowl pulled close about his head. Beneath the shadow of the hood, his eyes dragged over us and a trembling power built in the fabric of the dark chamber.

He stood up straight and was taller than even I could claim to be. He held his arms wide as if he'd gladly take the blow we were so desperate to deliver and I had to fight against the urge to break forward and attack him.

This foul creature had stolen all that I had ever asked of this unfair world and I gripped my swords tighter as I waited for my chance to return the favour.

Whatever followed now would still amount to the same thing; one way or another, the end of my path was close. I breathed in the scent of violence as it carried to me on a wind which should never have existed in the first place.

Andvari turned his neck and it kept going and going, far beyond the realm of what should had been possible.

I moved to stand beside Erik as we faced this creature together. The end of our hunt was here and it was time we faced our destiny.

ERIK

CHAPTER FORTY

"Your death awaits you on the edge of this blade." I lifted Dainsleif and Andvari eyed it with a flicker of discomfort.

"That sword cannot be sheathed again until you make a kill," he hissed, his eyes slipping to Magnar. "It is powerful enough to wipe even a soul from existence. Let us see who it is you end up truly killing."

He raised a hand and I shifted in fear as he tried to press his will into mine. He snarled, pushing harder and I felt his powers trying to snare me, but they couldn't get a grip. A light broke out around Magnar and I in a shimmer of gold that circled us.

"*Odin,*" Andvari growled. "Well if the king of gods has turned against me in favour of two worthless souls, he will soon learn that I am not to be trifled with." He stepped backwards into the glass until his reflection faded and he reappeared in another mirror across the hall.

His form had changed; he was younger, his eyes cat-like and yellow. He stepped from the glass with a twisted smile that raised the hairs on the back of my neck.

I set my jaw, my gaze trained on him.

"You took my wife," I spat, lifting my sword.

"And how delicious she was," he cackled and I started running, fuelled by pure rage.

Magnar sprang to action on my left, charging forward with a battle cry.

More reflections appeared, ten of them in total, slipping out of the glass and surrounding us. Andvari was different in every one. Young, old, some with serrated teeth, others so achingly beautiful they made my stomach churn. I collided with the one with yellow eyes, swinging Dainsleif in a deadly arc. Andvari moved in a blur of motion, circling behind me and slamming a kick into my spine. I smashed into the mirror and great shards of glass fell around me.

I turned, slashing the blade through the air with all the skills of my youth fuelling my movements. I'd once been a warrior, and it was poetic that it would end the way it had started. With me running at the god, sword drawn in defiance. But I'd not saved my family that day. And I hadn't saved Montana in the end either. All was lost, fallen to ruin, but I would have his heart and justice would be mine for those he'd taken from me.

"Just as weak as always, Erik Larsen," the yellow-eyed Andvari taunted me as I spotted Magnar clashing with several of the god's forms behind him.

I ran at him again, raising the sword above my head. He threw a punch to my gut, but I swept the blade down through the air and severed his hand from his wrist. The god wailed, stumbling backwards in surprise. I kept coming like a turbulent storm. I rammed the sword through his exposed belly, releasing a hiss through my teeth.

His yellow eyes met mine in shock.

"I am not Erik Larsen anymore," I growled then dragged the blade upwards to sever him in half. Bright green embers burned where there should have been blood and the figure was cast to ash in a flashfire of jade. His eyes were all that remained, staring up at me from amongst the ash.

Another of his forms collided with me and I hit the ground, rolling to avoid a harsh kick. This one I knew well. The one with sharp teeth, his eyes as dark as the pits of hell.

He'd mocked me often when I'd called upon his reflection in a pool of water in a forest, a long, long time ago.

"I am a god!" he cried, leaning down to grab my robes in his fists. I brought up the sword, but he stamped on my wrist to hold me in place. His strength was immense, but nothing compared to my fury. I would not be held.

"And you will die as Idun died!" I bellowed, rearing up and throwing a punch to his jaw.

He bit down on my knuckles and pain flared, followed by a sucking sensation which drew the light inside me to the very edges of my skin. I yanked my hand back in disgust and Andvari laughed raucously, landing another kick to my side. I flew across the space, smashing more mirrors and landing in a pile of glass.

Pain flared across my torn flesh and light spilled from the wounds in a torrent. Several of the forms fell on it, kneeling on the ground and lapping at my life force. I groaned as some part of myself was lost to their mouths. Pieces of my past melted away, memories, friends. I shook my head, clinging on to the single memory that mattered. Rebel was dead. And Andvari was responsible.

As my wounds healed, I darted to my feet to end every last one of the apparitions.

"I'll devour you both as I devoured the twins of sun and moon. The light of your souls will fuel my body, lift me higher in the ranks of gods. And you shall cease to exist, just as they did," the Andvari laughed and every form in the space started laughing too.

Pain clawed at my insides, tearing at what was left of my fractured heart. Montana was gone. Her light had been devoured by this accursed creature and everything she was had been snuffed out of the universe.

Magnar cut down one of the beautiful illusions of the god and emerald fire flared in its place.

"No," snarled the beast who I'd been fighting and I set my sights on him, wondering if he was the true god or if all of them were somehow part of the deity.

Dainsleif hungered for death in my hands and I would gladly give it what it wanted. I crashed into the one with serrated teeth, but found myself hitting a mirror instead. I gasped as glass cut into my cheek, turning to find only my reflection cast back at me. But it wasn't truly me. It was him. The way he'd often come to me. My face not quite mine, my eyes endlessly dark.

Everything in the room faded away until it was just me and him. Nothing else existed.

I side-stepped to the left and he side-stepped right. My perfect equal in every way. But I had revenge in my heart and a god's sword in my hands. I would win. And I would never again have my image seized by this creature of hell.

"I gave you a gift," Andvari purred in my own voice.

"You gave me a curse," I threw back at him, matching every step he took as we circled one another.

"You had more than a thousand years on Earth, more than any man has ever seen. The debt was always going to be high," he hissed.

"I paid my debt over and over," I spat. "And you took the one thing from me you knew I'd never want to live without. How heartless can you be?"

He held his chest as if an actual heart beat in there. I hoped it did, because I was going to cut it out. "You always knew there was a debt to pay. Your parents wronged me, then you deceived me by hiding under the protection of *my* ring. You must learn the consequences of your actions," he said with a low laugh.

I made my first move, but a glittering sword appeared in his hand at the same moment and he parried my blow. The clash of metal rang out and I swung at him again, left, right, centre. He knew my moves. He was mimicking me somehow, and I knew I had to change tact if I was going to beat him.

I backed up again, falling into the slow rhythm as we circled once more.

"I didn't make the prophecy," Andvari whispered. "Odin designed it. So perhaps it is he you should truly blame..."

"You were the one who took them," I said in a deadly tone. "So you will be the one to pay the price." I slashed at him again but he parried once more, matching me blow for blow as neither of us landed a hit.

He backed up this time, tilting his head and spreading a sickly sweet smile across his face. *My* face.

I needed to find the weakness in him. And I realised with a jolt that perhaps it was my own weakness that he would have in this form. My strength as a warrior had always been in my skill with the blade. But if anyone got behind me, I failed.

I stopped moving and Andvari halted too.

I moved my gaze beyond his head and twisted my expression into excitement. "Magnar!" I cried, though he wasn't there. Andvari turned and I shot forward, whipping Dainsleif through the air.

Andvari lurched aside as he realised his mistake, but I was faster, taking his head from his shoulders with a fierce strike of my blade. Flames burst to life and the form that had haunted me the most fell apart at my feet.

The room shuddered and Magnar was revealed to me once more. Andvari had him by the throat and was sucking the air as a golden light floated from the slayer's mouth into the god's.

Anger consumed me and charged my muscles with bloodlust. I threw Dainsleif with all my might and it carved through the side of the form holding my friend.

Magnar hit the ground and I reached him in a heartbeat, dragging him up to stand. He blinked heavily then raised his swords once more. I took up Dainsleif with a desperate hunger in my heart.

Six forms remained.

And we would kill them all.

MAGNAR

CHAPTER FORTY ONE

I blinked heavily as I adjusted to the huge chunks of my past which had been ripped away from me. Lumps of my childhood had been reduced to black holes, pieces of the very things that made me, *me* were just...gone. Consumed by this creature before me and left as nothing in his wake.

I stood beside Erik as the six Andvaris circled us like a pack of wolves. Venom burned for vengeance in my right hand while Tempest hissed curses in my left.

They leapt at us as one and I raised my blades with a cry of rage as the power of the deity's forms collided with me, sending me crashing back into Erik.

I rolled as I hit the floor, tumbling beneath their legs and scrambling forward as bony fingers clutched at my limbs. Their touch burned, searing away the essence of my skin, devouring my flesh.

I kicked at them, rolling again to try and free myself.

An impossibly tall Andvari slammed into me, pinning me to the ground as his toothless mouth pressed close to my face, sucking in a breath of air with enough force to pull my hair towards his lips.

Golden light was dragged from me again and I could feel the beast hunting for the parts of me that loved Callie.

"No," I snarled as an image of her in my arms began to slip from my mind. "Not her." This foul creation could take every miserable piece of my soul but I would never let him take her from me. My memories of her were all I had left and I would sacrifice everything to keep them with me until the very end.

I roared a challenge, driving my forehead into the bridge of his nose and black ichor spewed from the wound as he reared back. I head-butted him again, snapping bone and caving in the left side of his face.

The Andvari tried to rise off of me, releasing my arms as he struggled to back up but I followed him with the rage of my fractured heart.

I slammed my fist into his face then swung Tempest between us, spilling his guts so that emerald fire burst from the wound.

The Andvari started screaming, the pitch of it so high that some of the smaller mirrors in the room shattered, glass tumbling to the cavern floor all around us.

I pressed my advantage, springing to my feet as I swung Venom for his over-long neck. The form lunged backwards, raising an arm which met the sharp edge of my blade and was severed. More emerald fire blazed from the wound and I slammed my foot into his chest, sending him flying back into the towering mirror with a frame made of burning branches.

He hit the glass but instead of it breaking, he fell into the reflection, shrieking in panic as he was sucked inside.

The Andvari started slamming his fists against the glass and a dark smile lit my face as I realised he was trapped.

Another form collided with me before I could advance on the trapped fragment of Andvari's body and I was thrown back.

I crashed into a row of mirrors to the left of the room and glass shredded my skin as it shattered all around me. I hit the ground amongst the sharp fragments and grasping hands reached for me from every unbroken mirror.

Erik was bellowing in pain on the other side of the cavern as two of the Andvaris tried to pull his arms in different directions and rip him apart.

I lunged for them, losing my hold on Tempest as one of the hands snatched it away. I charged across the cavern, yelling my rage as golden light poured from Erik's soul and into the gaping mouths of the forms as they began to devour him.

I collided with the closest one, slamming my shoulder into the curve of his hunched back and driving Venom straight through his chest.

He shrieked in pain as I forced the blade up, poisonous blood coating my hands as I threw all of my strength into finishing this beast.

Erik fell on the Andvari which still clung to his other arm as it dug its teeth into his flesh. It was shorter than Erik's midriff but thick with muscle and it clung to him fiercely. The Andvari's teeth clamped deeply into Erik's skin while golden light poured into his mouth and he moaned in pleasure as he began to drain my friend's soul.

Erik cried out, stabbing and stabbing at it but his blows glanced off of its skin like it was made of metal and only scratches bleeding dark ichor were left on its flesh from his attacks.

I ran to his aid, slamming into the beastly creature and forcing it from Erik's arm.

Erik bellowed with rage, kicking out at the short form and knocking it across the room towards the flaming mirror.

I raced after it as it tumbled across the stone floor, slamming my shoulder into it again as it began to rise and sending it flying into the glass.

I fell to my knees from the collision and looked up as the Andvari shrieked in panic.

As he fell through the pane of glass, he merged with the one already trapped there, their features combining into a more gruesome version of the two forms. He took on the stumpy body of one and the sickly pale skin of the other and he wailed as he drove his fists against the inside of the mirror, but he couldn't break out.

My eye met Erik's across the room and a snarl pulled at his lip as the three remaining forms moved between us. Venom hungered for more of the god's blood in my grip and I pushed myself to my feet as I prepared to grant its wish.

ERIK

CHAPTER FORTY TWO

Two of Andvari's forms came at me at once, one with boils lining his flesh and another with a twisted foot. I aimed for the weaker one, swinging Dainsleif towards his crippled leg. I missed the shot as the two of them leapt forward together, digging their nails into my flesh and biting into me.

I cried out as they started sucking the light from my soul, the strength going out of my body as I buckled to my knees. I threw elbows and tried to get my sword up to meet them but they held me down with a ferocious strength.

My mind became fuzzy and my thoughts were lost as quickly as they came. More of me was taken, memories of my childhood, my mother, my years in solitude, the battles with the slayers. I ground my teeth, bracing myself against the ground as I tried to recall why I was even here.

A vision flitted into my mind with a dark-haired girl, her skin as pale as the moon who owned every wretched piece of my heart.

"I'll find you," I told her as Andvari's teeth sank deeper into my body. "And I'll stay with you forever."

A yell called to me from afar and a golden sword slammed into the bodies of the two Andvaris.

I hit the ground and the haze of light they'd stolen from me slipped out of the burning remains of their bodies and came back to me.

I sucked in a breath as Magnar dragged me to my feet and I blinked away the fog in my mind. Magnar grinned wildly, angling me to face the final Andvari in the room. The god's skin was covered in coarse black hair and his face was set into a furious grimace.

We ran at him again but he stepped back into a mirror, his laughter ringing out as he sprinted through the panes. I threw the hilt of my sword into each one, breaking them so that he'd have nowhere left to run. Following him, hunting, stalking. I smashed more and more as his laughter rang out and Magnar joined me, shattering glass everywhere until only a few mirrors remained.

Andvari rushed out of one of them, darting forward with a menacing gleam in his eyes. He moved like the wind, a short blade appearing in his grip as he darted past Magnar and slashed open his side.

Magnar clasped the wound with a hiss and I turned to try and catch sight of the beast who'd cut him.

A blur of movement in my periphery warned me of his approach and I lunged forward, driving my sword through the air. I slashed a deep wound across his cheek and he yelled in anger, ducking low and slicing along the back of my thigh.

I kicked out with my uninjured leg, knocking him to the ground and he skidded backwards. Golden light dripped from his blade and he licked it off with a hungry smile.

"The gods will bow to me when this is done. I will have two more strong souls in my body. The twins of sun and moon were already so powerful but with how long each of you have lived, I will be all the more invincible," Andvari laughed, running at us again.

Magnar snatched up the sword he'd dropped and swung both of his blades in his grip. He charged Andvari down and I darted forward so that we could intercept the final form together.

Andvari ducked and darted, faster than lightning as he moved about us, avoiding the deadly swings of our blades. Anger flooded me, heating every inch of my body as I released a bellow of fury, driving my sword toward the blur of movement in the corner of my eye. A blade grazed my back, the same moment my sword struck its target.

"No!" Andvari wailed, hitting the floor and scrabbling backwards as black blood leaked from the gaping wound on his stomach.

Magnar ran forward to help as I drove Dainsleif down into Andvari's chest. Magnar skewered him too for good measure and I released a breath through my teeth as emerald fire burst to life at our feet.

I gazed across the remaining mirrors in the room, waiting for him to appear once more. But he didn't come.

The black ash left by his fallen bodies started to shift, moving in an ethereal wind that carried it all towards one another, swirling in a vortex before us. We raised our swords and the floating ashes moved backwards as we advanced. We drove it toward the flaming mirror where the short, sickly pale form struggled to get out. As the ash slid through the pane, it tangled around Andvari and his final form appeared, holding features from each of the fallen mirages.

A naked, short, male squatted before us with yellow eyes, serrated teeth and a gnarled face. His body was coated in thick hair, one foot was twisted and boils lined his flesh.

Something in my blood told me this was his true form. Ugly as sin.

"No!" he wailed. "What have you done!?" He dropped down to all fours, clawing at his face.

I hounded closer, my heart swelling at the sight of him reduced to this wasted creature before me.

He held one clawed hand up to try and keep us back. "Get away!" he snarled. "I am not this. This is not me!"

"This is exactly who you are," I growled.

He lurched away but there was nowhere to go. He was trapped inside the glass and couldn't break out.

"No!" he begged again, clawing at his eyes as if it would be better to gouge them out than to see himself this way.

Magnar and I shared a nod, a silent decision passing between us as we grabbed one of the final mirrors and angled it to face him.

I wanted to see him squirm and beg and fall apart under the sight of his own reflection. I wanted to strip away any ounce of hope he had left. Because he was done. *I* was ending him. The man he'd tormented for over a thousand years. Who he'd forced to do unspeakable things. Who he'd taken everything from. And now he was going to fall at my feet.

His eyes opened and he shrieked in horror as he gazed at himself.

"Erik Larsen!" he begged, shuddering as he squinted through his eyelids to look at me, his face contorting in a pathetic effort to find mercy in me.

We moved the mirror closer until he was forced to gaze upon only himself. He groaned, trying to pull the dark hair from his head, scratching at his cheeks, his neck.

Magnar and I threw the mirror we were holding to the ground and I strode toward Andvari with a snarl. "I am not your pawn, I am not a slave to your curse and my name is not Erik Larsen. I am Erik Belvedere, Andvari. And I am your death."

He screamed as his hands scraped uselessly against the glass. He had nowhere to go, his connection to the other mirrors was broken. And we'd stripped away every one of his forms until this was all that remained.

Magnar ran forward, taking hold of the edge of the burning mirror and I grabbed the other side of it. Andvari screamed and screamed, pounding his fists against the glass as he begged to be released.

We forced the mirror to the ground with a fierce push, yelling our victory. Andvari's cries rang around the room, so loud the noise tore and bit at my ears. The pane hit the floor and the glass was dashed to pieces with the sound of a thunderclap.

Magnar and I were thrown to the stone floor as a powerful blast ripped through the air. Every memory, every ounce of my soul was returned to me in a swathe of amber light. I sucked in a breath as I held onto all the precious moments he'd stolen from me.

The glass scattered in every direction and black blood poured from within it. Teeth and bone and fingers skittered amongst the devastation, Andvari's true form obliterated along with the mirror.

Andvari's screams echoed away and silence fell, the only noise the tinkling of the shards as they scattered across the room. The power in the space lifted, departing from this domain as if it had never been. Andvari was dead. Our revenge was dealt. Our sole purpose of living had come to an end.

Silence reigned eternally.

I turned to Magnar, his chin held high as he gazed upon the remains of the god who'd thought he could win. But our love for the twins had prevailed. And in this final act we'd done them justice.

Though it didn't soothe any of the grief flooding my body.

I pushed myself to my knees as it overwhelmed me. I'd known this wouldn't be enough. But it was something. It meant the beast who'd taken my rebel from me was no longer a plague on the world. That he'd never hurt anyone as he had hurt me or my family again.

Magnar placed a hand on my shoulder, dropping down before me, his knees crunching against the glass. He cupped the back of my neck and pressed his forehead to mine. "It's done," he sighed.

"Yes," I breathed, knowing what came next, but holding onto this brief moment with Magnar a moment longer before we departed from this world. Neither of us could remain here without the twins. And if only eternal darkness awaited me when I destroyed my immortal soul, then I knew that was far better than existing in a world where Montana didn't.

"I am humbled to have truly known you, Brother," Magnar said, the weight of his final words tearing through me. He handed me one of his swords and my brows raised at the incredible gesture.

"I'm glad my last fight was at your side," I said firmly. "There is no greater honour than that."

"That is true. My final hour has been spent well in your company." His eyes dropped to his blades between us. "It is a fine death to die by these swords."

"Then let us go," I said, the last ounces of my resolve fading away and a strange peace washing through me as I rested the hilt of the sword on the ground, angling it toward my heart.

"These blades are capable of killing gods," Magnar growled as he did the same. "They hold the power to end us."

I nodded firmly, the tip of the blade biting into my skin. "Go well, dear friend."

MAGNAR

CHAPTER FORTY THREE

The cold stone pressed against my knees as I bowed my head and let out a heavy sigh.

A pit of despair was opening up before me as I held Venom to my heart, preparing to end all that I was.

We had finished Andvari and gotten revenge for the deaths of the women we loved but in the end it hadn't done anything to lessen the pain of their loss.

"I do not wish to exist in any form now," I murmured. "I will cast my soul into the eternal flame and let it be burned out of this world forever more."

I took a moment to think of my friends from before my sleep and after it. Of my mother and father and my brother and the love we'd all shared. I clung to every good memory I could find of them, wrapping them around my heart in a final farewell before turning my mind to Callie.

Her life had been so short. So savage and unfair. She'd barely even begun to live when fate had demanded her death.

I thought of the way she'd mocked me and teased me, laughed with me and loved me. Of her eyes which were as blue as a summer sky and her lips which set my skin alight with a desire for everything she was. And of her long, golden hair which seemed to shine with the light of the sun even in the darkest of nights.

Any amount of pain was worth the price of a moment in her arms. And if there had been any place for her in any level of existence then I would have gladly followed her there. But her fate was so much worse than that. To have been wiped from the world as if she'd never been there in the first place was the greatest crime imaginable. The world would grieve for all eternity that such a soul had been lost for all time.

What had happened to her wasn't right. To have been consumed by a beast so foul as the god who had cursed the Earth...

I gripped my blade more tightly, pressing its tip to my heart as I leaned my weight forward, preparing to throw myself down upon it.

I wondered if it would hurt? If destroying my soul was akin to ending my time in my flesh? Or if I'd just simmer away, fading from memory into nothing but an unfulfilled dream.

I took a deep breath, my last in any sense of the word and I felt Venom cutting into my flesh.

A deep warmth brushed against my cheeks and a golden aura shone through the thin skin of my eyelids, reaching out to me despite the fact that I wanted nothing more from this world.

I hesitated for the briefest second, wondering if the gods had been kind enough to grant me one last moment in the sun with the girl I loved. Even if it wasn't real, I'd take it. The thought of her gaze locked with mine, her lips on my lips, her breath on my cheek...

I opened my eyes and I frowned at the sight which reached me.

The blazing frame of Andvari's last mirror was laying on the dark floor, burning brightly as flames consumed the final echoes of his power.

My mouth fell open as a golden figure spilled from the smoke which rose from the blaze, thickening into the form of a man who stumbled forward in confusion.

The soul's eyes found mine and he reached out, his fingers brushing my skin in thanks before he headed on, aiming for the stairwell which would take him from this place.

"Erik," I breathed as my friend gritted his teeth, about to plunge Tempest into his heart. "Something strange is happening."

I didn't want to voice the guess which was forming in my mind. But as I watched, another soul clawed her way from the smoke pouring from the frame.

"Thank you," she breathed before hurrying away and my heart pounded with the most desperate of pleas.

"You don't think-" Erik began and I could tell he was just as afraid to hope as I was.

If we were witnessing the release of the souls that Andvari had devoured then maybe, just maybe...

Erik pulled the blade away from his heart. Just an inch. But the small gap held a thousand hopes in the space between heartbeats.

I loosened my hold on Venom too, feeling a bead of sweat slide along my skin beneath the black robes I wore in this realm.

We watched in silence as soul after soul rose from the smoke and slowly but surely the flames burned low.

When there was barely more than a simmering ember left and no more beings rose from the ashes, my stomach dropped.

I dipped my head, hating myself for hoping and bringing this pain on myself for a second time.

I ached for a resolution to this nightmare which didn't end in a death so final as that which had been dealt to my love. But Callie was gone. Lost in every sense of the word and I had to accept it even though my heart refused to do so with every desperate beat it took. It didn't matter that I was dead already. It only mattered that she was gone. My true love. My destiny. My end.

I reached for my sword again, ready to finish this suffering once and for all, when a strange light rose from the ashes of the frame as the final ember extinguished.

It was at once silver and golden, light and dark, night and day.

It rose from the depths of the soot which had once been Andvari and twisted itself into a shape.

My breath caught in my throat as a woman appeared before us. She was both familiar and unknown. A friend and a stranger. I knew her with every inch of my heart and yet I was sure I'd never met her before.

She was clad in a gown which flickered in a wind I couldn't feel and it seemed to be crafted from the light of the stars. Golden and silver and everything in between.

Her eyes fell on me and Erik as we knelt before her and a strangled noise left the throat of my friend.

"Is it you?" he breathed and I frowned because it wasn't her but it was at the same time.

She stepped forward and her lips were the ones I hungered for but her eyes were alight for Erik.

I shook my head in confusion, like I was looking at a riddle I couldn't understand.

"I love you," she breathed, reaching for me while looking at Erik. She stilled like she could feel that that wasn't right and her brown eyes swung to me. Eyes I knew but didn't love.

"Callie always said they were two halves of one whole," I murmured as I looked at this creature who was mine and wasn't all at once.

My blood heated with the realisation of who she was. The joining of two souls who had shared everything, starting with a womb. Their lives were linked, tied together in ways which defied all logic and yet was always so true to the essence of who they were. And in death they'd clung to each other, refusing to part ways when Andvari had stolen them from the lives they should have had.

I raised my arm to meet the hand she still held extended to me, unsure what this transformation meant but knowing I had to find out. If this was Callie. In even the slightest way. Then I had to know. I had to be sure.

Her fingers brushed mine and I was transported through every moment I'd ever spent in her company.

I saw myself through her eyes, fierce, determined, strong. She was watching me when she should have been sleeping. Loving me when I drove her to rage. Fighting for me when my mind had been stolen and aching for me when I wasn't by her side.

With a deep breath which carved the air in two, Callie tumbled into my arms, the soul fracturing in half to release her and leaving Montana gasping for breath before Erik.

My heart stopped beating. The world stopped spinning. The sun stopped blazing. None of it mattered but the woman in my arms.

She was trembling, her eyes brimming with fear and confusion as her nails dug into my arms and she looked at me like I was the answer to every question she'd ever asked.

"Magnar?" she whispered and my name on her lips was my undoing like always.

"It's you," I breathed, needing to confirm it out loud to convince myself that it was true.

My world filled with light as I held her again and my chest seized almost painfully as my love for her overwhelmed me.

A thousand thoughts filled my mind at once but none of them mattered as I fisted my hand in her dress and dragged her against me with a passion which was so fierce I was sure it was going to burn us to dust.

She melted against me, her arms wrapping around my neck as she pressed her body to mine and the world fell away from us.

We may have been in the darkest pits of the underworld but none of it mattered. Only the scent of her skin, and the touch of her lips, the caress of her body and the utter beauty of the fact that she was *here* mattered to me now.

I'd wanted to burn when I knew she was lost but now I was burning with her as we were reunited. And if the fire of our love was enough to consume us then so be it. This moment was all I had begged for and all that I needed. If the flames took me now then I would leave this place happy for one final moment. But selfishly I wanted more. And as I gripped her tightly, feeling every inch of her here in this moment with me, I swore to myself that this wasn't it.

The gods had never wanted us to be together and we'd shown them what we thought of their plans.

So if they'd decided that our time was up then I refused to accept it. Everything with them was a negotiation and I refused to take no for an answer.

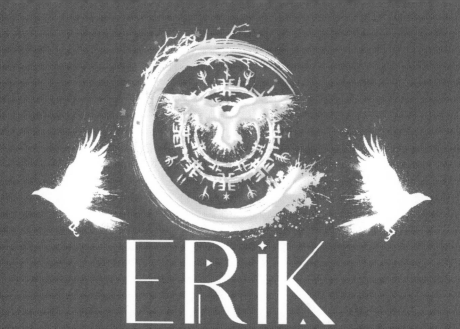

ERIK

CHAPTER FORTY FOUR

My fate had been balancing on the edge of a blade, all the light in the world had extinguished and now, impossibly, the love of my life was handed to me once more. The scales of fate had tipped in my favour, and I could hardly dare to believe it was true.

I drank in every inch of her pearly skin, her dark eyes like two liquid pools of bronze, her crimson lips and the tumble of her hair which was as black as midnight.

"Rebel?" I asked because I was still suspended in disbelief. That fate couldn't possibly offer me this now, not after everything. And yet here she was: my reason to live. And *fuck* I wanted to live. I wanted to breathe and grow and share everything I had to offer with this beautiful being. But we were still just two souls in the deepest realms of the afterlife.

She nodded, reaching for me and I lifted a trembling palm to meet hers in the space parting us. I wanted to grab her, bury my nose in her hair, drink in the cherished scent of her, but I was still afraid. Afraid that this was some mirage to drive me mad, afraid the gods had their claws in me once more, afraid that if I blinked she'd vanish and I'd never lay my eyes on her again.

Our palms pressed together and I released a shuddering breath.

She's here. She's real. She's not going away.

Where our skin touched, our life forces flowed between us in the same way the rune of partnership had allowed. The fear in me was washed away by a flood of relief, so powerful it swept through every corner of my body. I sighed, the aching grief in my heart finally parting, chased away by all of the love that rolled between us.

She released a whimper of pain, excitement and hope, then threw herself at me, winding her limbs around me in the tightest embrace.

I crushed her against my body and every fibre of my being met her like our nerve endings were joining, our souls truly united.

Her mouth found mine and I groaned with absolute bliss over a kiss I'd never thought I'd have again. Her lips were as warm as sunlight, her skin as soft as cotton.

She's here and I love her so powerfully my body's going to break apart.

"You saved us," she breathed as she pulled away, brushing her thumbs over my cheeks as she held me.

My heart beat and beat and beat and I almost felt as human as I had before I'd shed my mortal skin.

"You saved *me*," I whispered. "Everything I am is because of you. I exist because of you. And you didn't just save me, you and your sister saved the entire world by making the greatest sacrifice."

Tears slid from her eyes and pure light glimmered within them. I kissed them away, shaking my head because I didn't want her to cry ever again. This woman deserved so much more than an eternity in the afterlife. Her time on Earth had been cut too short. She'd passed on long before it was fair and she'd barely seen a glimmer of what life could have offered her.

"I'm sorry," I sighed, resting my forehead to hers. "I wish I could give you more than this. I wish it didn't have to be this way."

She wound her fingers around the back of my neck as another tear slid from her eye. "Don't be sorry," she begged. "We have each other now, that's all that matters."

I nodded but a weight hung over me. We were surrounded by this dark world and I didn't know where in the afterlife we'd be able to reside. How could this be where the child of the moon ended up? She was the most divine, merciful, compassionate woman I'd ever met. The gods knew that. And yet they were still allowing this. I hated them for that more than I'd ever hated them for anything.

"You deserve more than this," I growled, clutching her to me.

She brushed her fingers into my hair. "Oh Erik," she sighed. "So do you. Don't you see what you've done? You and Magnar have changed everything. You faced death itself and won. You destroyed the creature who cursed the entire Earth. And you've saved Callie and me from an unspeakable fate."

"Did he hurt you?" I choked, cupping her cheek. "When he took you, did he…"

"No," she whispered. "There was no pain. Only the pain of knowing I'd never see you again." She took a slow breath. "It kills me that you gave up the human body you spent a thousand years waiting for." More tears fell from her eyes and I willed them away with all my heart.

"I thought I was waiting for that, rebel, but I wasn't. I was waiting for you. I was waiting for a love so fierce it thwarted even death. There's no boundary, no realm on Earth or otherwise that I wouldn't cross to find you. And if there's a life after this, I'll find you there, and again and again." I took her hand, pressing my lips to her knuckles and she inhaled deeply before her mouth met mine once more.

"But I still wish I could give you more than this," I said heavily as I drew away.

"We have each other," she said earnestly. "And that's more than we ever could have had if you hadn't killed Andvari."

Montana was right; this was more than I ever could have dreamed for just moments ago. Perhaps that could be enough. Any place in life or death was a sweet gift so long as I was in her company.

I kissed her again to take away the sting in my heart, to know how deeply wronged she'd been. That the full wrath of the prophecy had fallen on her and her sister's heads. That they'd had to make a sacrifice too big.

It wasn't fair, or good, or just. It just was. And there was nothing I could do to make it right.

CALLIE

CHAPTER FORTY FIVE

I clung to Magnar like he was all that was holding me together. His strong arms engulfed me and I trembled as I buried my face against his chest.

I'd been lost to the darkness. Existing without feeling or thinking or truly being at all.

His hands were in my hair and running down my back and his touch was firm, demanding and possessive. He wasn't going to let me go ever again and I was never going to leave.

"I can't believe you're really here," he murmured and I pulled back just enough to look into his eyes.

They were filled with a deep pit of longing and I could feel the pain I'd left him in when Andvari had taken my soul.

"How did you find us?" I breathed, trailing my fingers along the side of his face.

A frown pulled at my brow as I noticed the translucent sheen to his skin, the way he seemed to be here right before me and yet not at all.

"No!" My lips parted in horror as I realised what that meant. My warrior, the man who had faced a thousand foes, fought against the most powerful creatures ever to have existed and killed a goddess, was dead.

I pulled back but he held me tightly, refusing to let me withdraw so much as an inch.

"I would die a million deaths for a moment with you," he growled.

I shook my head, denying that what I could see with my own eyes was true.

Before I could voice any more protests, he pressed his lips to mine and every argument I'd been forming shattered to sand which was blown away as my heart raced with the love I felt for him.

Electricity poured across my skin as his mouth moved against mine and I wound my arms around his neck. It felt like the essence of our souls were merging with one another in that kiss.

Of course he'd come for me. Just as I would have come for him. I had claimed this man for my own and *nothing*, not even death, would tear us apart.

He gripped my waist and I arched against him as I pressed my tongue into his mouth and held his face between my hands. His hold on me tightened and I could feel his aching desire to keep me close forever more.

"What now?" Montana's voice came from behind me and I withdrew from Magnar, though I couldn't bring myself to look away from him.

The love burning in his gaze filled me up and lit every inch of me with a sense of safety. While I was with him, I was home. He would keep me from harm and love me with as much intensity as I would love him.

"We can return to Valhalla," Erik suggested. "And live on in the great hall."

"That's not living," I replied quietly, finally tearing my gaze from the man I loved as I turned to look at them.

"We aren't alive anymore," Montana said softly but I shook my head.

"We didn't do all of this just to pay for it with our deaths," I growled. "The gods owe us our lives. And what greater payment could we offer Odin for them than the death of a god?"

"You think he might agree to that?" Montana gasped.

"Only one way to find out," Magnar said fiercely.

Erik nodded keenly and moved towards the pile of ash and bone which marked the place where Andvari had met his end. "Odin!" he cried, his desperation clear.

The black stone walls of the chamber trembled as a deep power drew near and Magnar pulled me against him, raising Venom an inch as if he half expected us to come under attack.

The rear wall of the chamber rumbled angrily and a terrible screeching sound split the air. Erik moved to protect Montana and the four of us drew together as my sister reached for my hand.

The wall ripped apart with an echoing boom and Odin stepped out of the devastation to stand before us.

I craned my neck to look up at the king of gods and his lone eye raked over the chamber and all that Erik and Magnar had achieved in their battle against Andvari before he finally let his attention still on the four of us.

"So, you have crossed into the realm of the gods and murdered one of my own within the walls of my domain?" he asked fiercely and his anger set the broken glass which lined the ground rattling.

"It wasn't murder," Magnar snarled. "It was justice."

Odin's eye fell on him and I could feel the power of his gaze pressing against Magnar as he fought to stand beneath it. His muscles bulged with the effort of remaining on his feet and his jaw clenched in pain as Odin tried to force him to his knees.

"Stop it!" I demanded, moving between them and forcing Odin's attention onto me instead. "I won't let you hurt him."

Odin surveyed me for a long moment as Magnar tried to force me back but I refused to give an inch. He'd come through death to find me and I wouldn't see him bow to one of the deities who had caused us so much pain.

"You still burn with all the passion of the sun," Odin mused. "Even after your time in darkness."

I glared at him, unsure how to respond to that and his eye swivelled towards Montana.

"And you still shine with the steady faith of the moon," Odin added.

Magnar forced me back to his side and my anger started to quell into fear. This god was the only hope we had left and I had no way of knowing whether he would help us.

"Idun and Andvari were ever fond of testing my patience," Odin murmured.

"You wanted this," Erik accused. "Didn't you? You wanted them dead!"

"I could not have turned against my own without inciting a war among the gods," Odin rumbled in denial.

"Then it sounds as if we saved you a lot of trouble," Magnar growled.

345

Odin sighed and the force of his power washed over us like a rush of water. Only my hold on Magnar kept me on my feet. The god stooped to pick up a sword from the floor by his feet and for a moment I almost thought he was going to smile.

"Dainsleif... I had my suspicions about Andvari's involvement in your disappearance," he murmured thoughtfully.

I exchanged a glance with Montana as I tried to figure out what the god was thinking. His gaze swept over us one final time.

"I accept this sacrifice before me," Odin growled. "And I look forward to seeing you all at Ragnarok."

A blue light built around us and I gasped as the air was sucked from the room. The light grew and grew and Montana's fingers tightened around mine until I felt sure they were the only thing keeping me in place.

My body began to tremble and a deep heat flooded me, building in the pit of my stomach until it consumed every inch of my flesh. Just as I was sure I could take no more of it, Odin's voice sounded in my ear.

Live well twins of Sun and Moon. Your sacrifices won't have been for naught.

I took a shuddering breath as the heat spilled away from me and I tried to make sense of my surroundings.

I was on my back, laying on hard stone with my sister's fingers still entwined with my own.

My heart pounded with fervour in my chest and a smile tugged at my lips as I heard someone inhale sharply.

"By the gods! You're back?" Julius cried in surprise and Clarice shrieked excitedly.

My eyes fluttered open and I turned my head as I found myself in the chamber which held Andvari's treasure once more. But Julius and the others weren't looking at me. Their attention was on a deep fissure in the rock on the far side of the room which Magnar and Erik had just stepped through.

Montana shifted beside me and I turned to look at her with a wide smile on my lips as Julius and the others pounced on Magnar and Erik.

"We're alive," Montana breathed, grinning at me from ear to ear.

A laugh fell from my lips and Julius swore as he turned towards us next.

I pushed myself upright on the stone altar as the others all rushed at us and I couldn't help but laugh again at the looks on their faces.

"How?" Fabian breathed in disbelief.

"That is a very long story, Brother," Erik replied, his eyes fixed on Montana with so much love that it made my heart swell with happiness for her.

"Then we have to hear it," Clarice insisted.

"You will," Erik replied. "We'll tell you on the way."

"Where are we going?" Julius asked. His arm was firmly around Magnar's shoulders and it didn't seem as though he had any intention of letting him go any time soon.

"We have an empire to rebuild," Erik replied. "And a lot of humans to set free."

My heart raced with excitement at his words. This was it. It was finally over. Everything we'd ever dreamed of in the Realm had finally come to pass. There was no more curse, no more vampires and finally every one of the humans were going to be set free.

I pushed myself up, dropping from the altar and moving to Magnar's side once again, feeling the warmth of his human flesh with a rush of happiness.

There were still some things to be done before the world would be set to rights entirely.

But it was finally time for us to begin our lives together. And I wasn't going to waste a second of it.

MONTANA

CHAPTER FORTY SIX

Weeks and weeks passed as we headed back to New York. Our human bodies were slower; we needed more rest than the slayers, but we had all the time in the world now.

As we closed in on the city, an ounce of trepidation filled my heart at what we'd find there. But when we arrived, the newly turned humans weren't in disarray. In fact, it looked as though a party had been going on here since the moment the curse had been broken. The final biters had either died in the battle at the holy mountain or had quietly fallen into the shadows of society where I hoped they'd never hurt anyone again.

As the eight of us marched up the road toward the castle walls under the light of the midday sun, eyes fell on us from those drinking or dancing in the streets. Cheers rose up as they screamed their joy at the return of their rulers.

Erik gripped my hand as we walked in our silent procession, the eight of us marching in a row, united eternally by what we'd endured.

I wondered whether the people would ever know what had caused their return to humanity. But so many smiling faces was enough for me. I didn't want to be celebrated for the sacrifice my sister and I had made. I wanted to find a place in this world where we could live a normal life, one we'd dreamed about since we were children.

The days fell away as Erik and the other Belvederes busied themselves with reorganising the empire. Announcements were made to open the Realms and soon Callie, Erik, Magnar, Julius and Clarice and I were on a train to the west where the first of the Realms would be opened. Our Realm. Our old home, the only one we'd ever known and even now I didn't know where we would find another. But somehow, with Erik by my side, I knew we would.

Fabian had remained in New York with Chickoa to ensure the city was kept in order. The Belvederes were working toward a future I was so excited about I could barely contain it. They were going to build schools, hospitals, houses, farms. Everything we'd ever dreamed about growing up in Realm G.

The country had changed before my eyes in the past weeks. The mortal world was shaping up to be the finest it had ever been. And I prayed the humans in the Realms would find a way to one day forgive the vampires, but I didn't think it would be so simple.

As we arrived outside Realm G, I gazed through the layers of fencing that led into the town I knew so well. Except now it looked rebuilt. Renovations were taking place everywhere and the people inside were jovially taking part in the construction work.

A couple of guards opened the iron gates for us and I took Callie's hand as we led the way inside. Two sisters, returned to where it had all started, walking through the gates as free women. We'd changed so much and yet in the face of the familiar streets and buildings, I knew this part of us would never truly leave our hearts.

Eyes fell on us and those who knew us seemed confused by the sight. Perhaps they'd thought we were dead after we'd escaped all those months ago. And I imagined it was a strange sight indeed to see us in the company of two Belvederes.

Erik and Clarice moved ahead of us and Erik called out to everyone within earshot. "Your Realm is no longer a prison. This town is yours and the gates will never be closed again. Food will be sent here until the surrounding lands are farmed and you can support yourselves. The New Empire welcomes you to remain under our rule, but you will have no obligation to do anything but enjoy your free lives now."

Clarice took over, gazing around at everyone with a hopeful smile. "If you wish to work, there will be many positions available to be filled. To rebuild this world, we must band together. And in repayment for what we've taken from you, every family in every Realm will be given compensation for the blood you and your families have provided throughout your lives."

Several guards who'd accompanied us from the city set to work tearing down the gates and fences. The people of the Realm broke into cheers, rushing forward to help as they broke down the walls which had confined them for their entire lives.

I turned to embrace Callie, my heart singing at the sight of seeing our people freed at long last.

"I wish Dad was here," I whispered and Callie nodded against my shoulder.

"I'm sure he's watching," she breathed. "Now we know about the afterlife, I'm more certain than ever that he can see us."

I blinked back tears, drawing away from her as Magnar slid an arm around her shoulders.

Erik approached and I bit down on my lip as a secret grew on my lips. One I'd been hiding until I was sure it was true. And he'd been so busy lately with work, we'd hardly spoken of anything else but how the new world was going to look. He longed for my input and listened to every word I spoke of the way I wished the world to be. I didn't know if my musings were really good enough to be put into practice, but he seemed to think so. And he'd soon announced Callie and I as ambassadors for the Realms. In the coming days, we'd listen to the people and try to bridge the gap between the once-vampires and the mortals. In time, I hoped it would work. But right now, there was only one thing on my mind.

I took Erik's hand, overjoyed by this incredible day and sure now was the moment I wanted to voice what was circling in my mind. I drew him deeper into the Realm, passing down streets I knew as well as my own pulse. I located my old apartment block, marvelling at how the structure had changed. Newly painted, the broken windows fixed, even a new door in place of the one that had always swollen shut in the rain.

My eyes pooled with tears as I gazed up at it, wishing it could have been this way when I'd grown up here.

"Do you want to go inside?" Erik asked, pushing a lock of my hair behind my ear.

I shook my head, turning to him and taking his hands. "My past lives in there," I whispered. "And I'm ready for my future now. *Our* future."

He smirked, leaning in for a kiss, but I pressed a hand to his chest to hold him back.

"Are you ready for the future Erik?" I asked, a teasing smile on my lips.

"Yes," he growled, hounding forward so my back pressed to the wall. His fingers skated down my hips and butterflies danced in my stomach. Weeks of sickness and the small swell in my belly had confirmed this truth to me just days ago. I took his hand, placing it on my stomach, anticipation rolling through me at his reaction.

"Are you sure?" I breathed. "Because your future is ready for you."

His eyes widened as he realised what I meant and his gaze fell to my stomach with a look of awe.

"You mean...?" he asked, hope shining from his expression and I nodded as tears of joy slid down my cheeks.

He kissed me and all the happiness in the universe seemed to meet at the place our lips joined. He tugged me against him, wrapping his arms around me. I soaked in the feeling of his embrace: the safest place in the world.

We didn't have a home yet, but I knew we'd find one. Somewhere our child would grow up and live a free life, where Erik and I would spend countless hours in each other's company, and where every day would be lived to its fullest. Months and years stretched out ahead of us, ready to offer us all we ever could have dreamed of. And I bathed in that dream, clinging to it with my heart beaming and my body trembling.

I'm ready to live.

CALLIE

CHAPTER FORTY SEVEN

The sun shone down fiercely and a cool breeze blew along the beach as I stepped out onto the sand.

Montana smiled brightly in encouragement as I paused for a moment, taking in a deep breath. She was wearing a flowing lavender gown which complimented her colouring and skimmed over the swell of her stomach where my niece or nephew lay waiting to meet me. Her dark eyes danced with excitement as she looked to me.

"I suppose I shouldn't keep him waiting," I murmured as my heart pattered in my chest and I clenched my fists to stop my hands from shaking.

"I think he'd wait all day and all night if he had to," Montana replied with a smirk. "So if you need a few minutes-"

"No," I said quickly. "I was just thinking about Mom and Dad and wishing... it doesn't matter." I shook my head and took another step but Montana moved into my path and threw her arms around me.

"They might have been a little intimidated by him at first," she said ruefully. "But any man who would chase you into death would most certainly have won them around in the end."

I released a nervous laugh as I nodded. She was right. Of course she was right. But they should have been here for this moment and it felt right to think of them before I went through with this.

I looked up at the blue sky with a smile. Maybe they *were* here anyway. After all we'd learned of the gods and the afterlife it wasn't hard to imagine them looking down on us now. Being a part of this even if we couldn't see them. I gripped the chain at my neck for a moment and a single tear tracked down my cheek.

Montana inhaled sharply as she quickly brushed it away. "Clarice will lose her mind if you ruin her masterpiece," she chided and I couldn't help but grin.

Clarice had insisted on putting me through the whole rigmarole of hair and makeup styling yet again. My hair was loose at my insistence, though Clarice had made sure her people had curled it and gotten them to weave white flowers through the golden strands. Not that I could claim to mind that really. If she wanted to help me look my best then I wasn't going to complain about it. Not this time.

"Are you ready then?" Montana urged and I gave her a bright smile as I took her hand and we started walking.

The white dress I wore was simple, much to Clarice's disgust. It hung without straps, hugging my figure and trailing behind my bare feet as I moved further down the beach. I'd refused the veil six times before she'd begrudgingly accepted my choice in the matter and I was glad as the breeze blew again, twisting through my hair.

Butterflies danced in my stomach as I chewed on my lip and the reality of this moment sank in.

It had taken so much for us to get here, but impossibly, I was walking towards a fate I'd chosen for myself at last.

As I crested a dune, the sea was revealed before me, a never ending ocean of deepest blue, spreading away to the horizon. The sound of the waves lapping against the shore filled the air and I could taste the faintest hint of salt on my lips.

Standing before the water were the people I cared most about in this world. Erik, Fabian, Clarice and Chickoa stood together, looking up at me as I approached. And behind them Magnar and Julius stood, looking out to sea with their backs to me.

Montana squeezed my fingers as I paused one last time.

I took another step and the sound of a string quartet reached me from somewhere hidden within the dunes to our right.

I frowned at Clarice with a hint of irritation and a bit more amusement. I'd made it clear that I didn't want to lay eyes on anyone other than the eight of us today and she'd found a way around it to get the music she'd so desired - I couldn't *see* the musicians at all. But I could definitely hear them.

Montana laughed as she glanced at my face and I rolled my eyes as she tugged me into motion again.

I looked up and found Magnar facing me across the sand.

My breath caught in my throat as I looked at him and I stilled again as my pulse thundered in my ears.

This was it. The moment we'd both dreamed of and hardly dared hope would ever happen.

His golden eyes burned fiercely as he looked up at me and my mouth grew dry as I felt a blush growing in my cheeks.

Montana urged me on and my feet started moving, driving me towards my destiny.

The closer we got to him, the faster my heart beat and I could see the same desperation for us to do this in the tension of his posture.

He was wearing a pair of pale grey trousers with a white shirt which he'd left open at the neck. Julius was dressed the same but I noticed that Erik and Fabian both wore grey waistcoats and ties to match the trousers and I guessed that Clarice was probably pretty annoyed at the slayers for simplifying their outfits right about now.

Julius smiled broadly as we reached them but my eyes were fixed on his brother.

Montana passed my hand to Magnar and he smiled at me as he accepted it. Electricity danced across my skin at the feeling of his palm against mine. I hadn't seen him for a week which had been another of Clarice's ideas; Julius and Erik had gotten him drunk and put him on a plane to this hidden island in the South Pacific while he was too inebriated to object. By the time I'd found out about it they were already gone but I was actually kind of pleased now.

A week was a long time to miss the feeling of his skin against mine and I could already see the desire pooling in his eyes as his gaze slid over me. Clarice had assured me that her idea had been in aid of making our wedding

357

night as memorable as possible and I bit my lip as I realised she was probably right about that. Magnar was looking at me like he'd never seen me before and even the small contact we held between our hands was enough to send heat flooding through my veins.

Julius stepped back so that he was between us and the sea. Magnar had insisted that he didn't care which way he married me just so long as he did it but I'd wanted it to be done in the way of his people. He'd lost so much when he'd left them behind and now that the curse was lifted, we knew for certain that the three of us were the last slayers who would ever live. Though our children would have our blood, none of them would take their vows.

And it seemed right to me that the last Earl of the slayers should have the last slayer wedding ever to take place.

Julius smirked at the two of us as Montana moved to stand with Erik and the others. He took my hand from Magnar's, lifting it and placing it over his heart. I could feel it beating solidly beneath my palm and I smiled up at the man I loved as excitement gripped me. Julius lifted Magnar's hand next, placing it on my chest too. My heart rate picked up as his calloused hand pressed against my skin.

"Those gathered here will bear witness to the union of your souls. Speak the words and let your lives be tied together from now until the end of time. This union will bind you for all eternity and lead to the birth of blessed children. Do you understand the oath you are making?" Julius asked.

"Yes," Magnar replied firmly.

"I do," I added.

"Magnar of the Clan of War, do you claim this woman?"

"I claim Callie Ford of the Clan of Dreams for my wife. My heart is hers. My life is hers. I will love her for all of time, father her children and fight for her until my dying breath...and beyond then too," he added with a smirk. "We are one."

The fierceness of his words washed over me and I was filled with the deepest sense of love for this man before me. I didn't need to marry him to know he was mine but I wanted to. I wanted to tie myself to him in every way possible, to carve his name into my heart and make sure there could never be any doubt about where we belonged.

"Callie of the Clan of Dreams, do you claim this man?" Julius asked me.

I knew the words because Julius had taught me them but nerves swirled in my stomach as I opened my mouth to speak them. Magnar smiled encouragingly and I pushed aside my hesitation so that I could say the things I felt in my heart.

"I claim Magnar Elioson of the Clan of War to be my husband. My heart is his. My life is his. I will love him for all of time, be the mother of his children and fight for him until my dying breath." I held Magnar's eye as I prepared to speak the last line which would tie our lives together forever.

"We are one."

I knew that at this point the goddess's power should have bound our souls together but with Idun dead no deity appeared to seal our vow. But I didn't care. I didn't want a goddess or anyone else to tie me to this man before me. I was totally capable of doing so myself.

We had all the power we needed in the love we shared and nothing in this world or beyond it was more meaningful than that.

Julius handed Magnar a ring and I smiled at him as he took my hand from his heart and slid it onto my finger. I lifted an eyebrow in surprise as I recognised my mother's wedding ring and Julius shrugged.

"The gods didn't ask for it back again and it belongs in your family," he said with a wink. "Besides, I didn't think you'd mind being invisible to them again."

I smirked at him as I felt the ring's power nudging against my mind and Magnar brushed his thumb across it, drawing my gaze back to his.

"Let the power of your love guide you and the strength of your bond unite you," Julius said. "Seal this declaration with a kiss and go forth as man and wife."

Magnar caught my waist and dragged me against him with a groan of longing and I laughed as he pressed his lips to mine.

Our friends started clapping and cheering and Clarice and Montana threw handfuls of white petals over us.

I stood on my tiptoes, wrapping my arms around Magnar's neck and smiling through the kiss which sent shivers running right to the base of my spine.

No one could take this moment from us. I was his and he was mine. We had tied ourselves together in every way we could and I refused to relinquish another moment in his arms for the rest of my life.

We had done everything the gods had required of us to break the curse and save humanity from the vampires and now the world had been born anew, filled with hope and promises of better days to come.

There was only one thing left for us to do. And I intended to do it as well as I possibly could. Our life was waiting for us. And I couldn't wait to start it.

MONTANA

CHAPTER FORTY EIGHT

"**M**iles Belvedere stop punching your cousin this instant!" I shouted, pointing at him as he raised his fist to hit Bjorn again. Callie's little boy was as fair as my sister with Magnar's strong build and golden eyes. He was just as involved in their fight as Miles was. And although the two of them were enjoying themselves I still wasn't happy about them mimicking their fathers. Magnar and Erik had been sparring out in the yard again this morning and now our two eldest sons were copying them. As usual.

Miles dropped his hands, but his eyes glowed with rebellion. He was the image of his father, dark hair and chiselled features, but his eyes were completely mine. And that expression was one I knew well. It was *my* expression. My defiant, pissed off, it's-not-fair expression which I'd used on his father a thousand times.

"Go inside and stay with your sister," I urged Miles, pointing up to the line of houses on the hill. Mine and Erik's on the left, Clarice and Julius's in the middle and Magnar and Callie's on the right. Erik had claimed the huge plot of land in the east of New York and had the houses built as a surprise while we'd remained in his home in Westchester. That had been four years ago. And with my two kids and Callie's two sets of twins, it was the most perfect place to raise them.

Clarice exited her house as Miles sprinted up the hill and crashed into her legs, clinging to her. "Aunt Clarice!"

She gasped, reaching down to embrace him over the huge swell of her stomach.

I jogged up the hill towards them, leaving Bjorn playing on the lawn with his little sister Astrid who had been watching their brawl excitedly. As I moved to grab Miles so Clarice could catch her breath, my son darted into our house with a mischievous laugh that brought a smile to my lips.

"It's a blessing, I won't say otherwise. But by the gods, my back is killing me," Clarice groaned as Julius exited the house behind her.

He slid his arm around her shoulders, placing a kiss to her temple. "Just a few more weeks, baby."

"Monty, have you seen Bjorn?" Callie jogged out of her house, carrying little Ivar in her arms. He had long dark locks which Magnar refused to let Callie cut, and I suspected he was going to be the image of his father when he grew up.

"He's down the hill, he's been sparring with Miles again," I said, unable to fight a laugh.

She shook her head, her eyes glittering with mirth. "Why doesn't that surprise me?" She placed Ivar in Julius's arms then ran down the hill to fetch Bjorn.

A crash sounded in my house and I ran away, darting inside to find Miles and his sister, Warren, gazing at each other excitedly.

"What's going on?" I asked.

"Daddy and Uncle Magnar are fighting *inside*," Warren said with a wide grin, her ebony curls tumbling around her shoulders as she giggled.

I darted into the kitchen, finding the two of them wrestling on the kitchen table. The back door was wide open and a line of devastation led up to where they were sparring.

"The kids are watching," I sang, planting myself in front of them as Magnar choked my husband on the table.

"I yield," Erik spluttered and Magnar released him with a triumphant laugh.

Magnar stood upright, glancing at the mess they'd made with a guilty look. "Sorry Montana."

I broke a laugh. "Have us over for dinner tonight and make it up to me."

Magnar beamed. "Done."

Erik sat up on the edge of the table, his chest bare and his skin marred with scratches.

Warren and Miles darted after Magnar as he headed out of the back door, the kids tugging at his jeans. "Tell us about the slayer's vow again. I'm going to take it when I'm old enough!" Miles called.

"There's no vow to take," Magnar started, lifting Warren into his arms as they walked into the garden.

"Why does my son want to be a slayer?" Erik asked, pursing his lips as I wet a cloth in the sink and moved forward to tend his wounds.

"Because he's a rebel," I said with a grin as I started wiping away the line of blood running down his chest.

"Like you." He tilted up my chin and my heart stuttered as I gazed at his face, love pounding through my body. He leaned down, brushing his mouth over mine, gently biting down on my lower lip.

"I miss your fangs," I teased and he released a rumbling laugh.

"I can bite you just fine without them." He tilted my head, scraping his teeth over my throat and desire pooled in my belly.

"The kids," I breathed as his bites turned to kisses, trailing to my ear and sending a ripple of energy through to my core.

"Magnar has them," he growled, brushing his lips over the shell of my ear. "And while he's keeping them busy, I suggest we try making a few more kids."

"A few more?" I laughed, running my hands down the hard planes of his chest.

"Yes, a whole army," he breathed, dropping to the floor and snaring me in his arms. He walked me backwards so we hit the kitchen counter and a teacup dropped onto the tiles, smashing amongst the rest of the broken objects he and Magnar had shattered.

"We don't need an army, there's nothing to fight anymore," I said against his mouth, our breaths growing heavy as his hand slid up the back of my shirt. His skin was fire against mine and I relished the way our bodies combined in this human way. It was even better than it had been as a vampire. Hot flesh, the burn in my muscles and the breathlessness that made my head spin was far better than eternal energy. It meant every time we united, it had to come to an end. And we always wrung every drop of pleasure out of each other for as long as our mortal bodies could last.

I hooked a leg around his hip as he ground shamelessly against me. I was half aware of the open door and the blinds pulled up over the window. But I was lost in the moment, captivated by his skin on mine, his wandering hands.

"I love you," he growled into my mouth and I swallowed his words, feeling them running through my blood like liquid fire.

"I love you back," I gasped. "Fuck it, have your army."

He laughed and I fell into the hands of the man who loved me flesh and soul. We were always trying to reach toward that aching closeness we'd found in the afterlife where our bodies were stripped away and we were nothing but pure light. And when his body claimed mine, we found it once more.

We ate out on the terrace at the back of Magnar and Callie's home, drinking wine and delighting in the incredible food placed before us. The summer sun still heated our backs as it sank low on the horizon beyond the hill.

Our kids played out on the lawn and Clarice watched them eagerly, circling her hand on her swollen belly. Fabian and Chickoa had joined us with their newborn. She slept in Fabian's arms while he gazed upon her restful features. I'd never seen such peace in him since the two of them had married. It was hard to remember him ever looking at Callie the way he looked at Chickoa nowadays.

I sat between Erik and my sister, sipping on my wine as peace washed through me in waves. The Empire was shaping up and we'd taken a well-deserved break for once. The humans of the Realms had made an alliance with the newly-mortal vampires and though there was still progress to make, they were cooperating enough to keep everyone content.

Callie's daughter Freya strolled hand in hand with Warren down the grass, talking animatedly. Freya was as fair-haired as Warren was dark and of all our children they resembled Callie and I the most. They seemed drawn to

366

each other too, like two peas in a pod. Callie watched them with a bemused expression then turned to me.

"Should we tell them it's bedtime?" she asked with a smirk.

"Let them stay up," Erik said, waving a hand. "They'll sleep in later tomorrow."

"I like the sound of that." Magnar reached across the table to refill Callie's glass with a mischievous glint in his gaze.

"Magnar and I never had a bedtime and it never did us any harm," Julius pitched in, holding his glass out to his brother for more wine.

"On second thoughts, maybe we should send them to bed," Erik teased and Julius chuckled.

"Wanna go for a walk?" I asked Callie and she nodded keenly as we stood from our chairs and headed down the lawn past our children.

The night air blew around us and her hand slid effortlessly into mine.

"It's hard to believe this life is really ours," Callie said and I nodded in agreement, my heart aching at what we'd almost lost at the holy mountain.

"I'm not a fan of the gods, but I do have a soft spot for Odin for giving us one more chance at life," I said.

We reached the edge of the lawn where a sparkling stream stretched out before us beneath the light of the moon. It flowed all the way to the sea where the waves lapped the shore and gulls cried their final lament before they headed down to roost.

"It's strange...I feel like we were always meant to end up here," Callie said quietly and I squeezed her fingers.

"I think our fate was always ours to choose somehow. Even though the gods pushed and pulled us one way or the other. We wanted to end up here, so we did."

We gazed out at the view as time seemed to slow. Forever awaited us beyond this world. But before then, we would drink every drop of life that we could. We'd bask in the sun, gaze at the moon, and brand every perfect moment into our souls. So when we left our mortal bodies behind for the final time, we would have a million memories to carry with us. And we couldn't really ask for more than that.

"I'm glad we're here," Callie said, turning to me and her blue eyes glittered with tears of joy.

"We'll always be together. It's just the way it is." I pulled her into my arms and the two halves of us fell together.

The sun and the moon.

Light and dark in perfect balance.

Two sisters bound forever in an endless dusk and dawn.

AUTHOR NOTE

And so we come to the end of the very first series Caroline and I wrote together. The end of Callie and Montana's journey really was the beginning of ours in many ways and seeing it come to a close is a sweet kind of relief.

I hope you found a place in your hearts for our twins of sun and moon. I hope that you are prepared for the apocalypse and have now added an 'in case of Vampire dominion' note to your endless list of survival plans – it's not just me who has one of those, right? – and I hope that you continue to delve into the hearts and minds of our hard fated characters for many more books to come.

Thank you so much for joining us on this journey, for reading our books and embracing our chaos with us. Everything we do is for the love of these worlds and the pleasure of inviting you into them.

So let us journey on into many more kingdoms and curses together through pages wet with tears and gripped tight in laughter, through breathless romance and terrifying tyrants.

If you enjoyed the twins' story and want more romantasy with dark hearted vampires and brooding men, then you might enjoy our #1 Wall Street Journal and Amazon bestselling series Zodiac Academy. Check it out on Amazon and enjoy the wild ride.

Love,

Susanne and Caroline XOXO

WANT MORE?

To find out more, grab yourself some freebies and to join our reader group, scan the QR code below.

Made in the USA
Coppell, TX
24 May 2024

32727928R00217